A Year Without Underwear

A Year Without Underwear

Exploring the World on a Bicycle

Ralph Monfort

iUniverse, Inc.
New York Lincoln Shanghai

A Year Without Underwear
Exploring the World on a Bicycle

iUniverse books may be ordered through booksellers or by contacting:

iUniverse
2021 Pine Lake Road, Suite 100
Lincoln, NE 68512
www.iuniverse.com
1-800-Authors (1-800-288-4677)

ISBN-13: 978-0-595-40754-5 (pbk)
ISBN-13: 978-0-595-85119-5 (ebk)
ISBN-10: 0-595-40754-4 (pbk)
ISBN-10: 0-595-85119-3 (ebk)

Printed in the United States of America

For my parents

"…and he sailed off through night and day, and in and out of weeks and almost over a year to where the Wild Things are." Maurice Sendak

Contents

Acknowledgements

I want to thank my sister Kam Martin for her help in editing this book and for her encouragement along the tedious path of self-publishing. I also owe a big thank-you to Tim Kneeland, without whose imagination, energy, perseverance, and courage, the Odyssey 2003 trip would never have happened and this book would not have been written.

Introduction

Bike riding is not my passion. Yes, I have had a bicycle and have ridden it with some regularity my whole adult life. I commuted by bicycle to work at several of my duty stations when I was in the Air Force, and a Saturday ride was part of my workout agenda for many years. However, I had never gotten obsessive the way a lot of people get. In all those years, forty miles was the longest ride I had ever done. I didn't and still don't know the differences among the various bikes out there and don't care much about all the accessories. I don't like bike clothes in general and only bought a couple of pairs of those god-awful, Lycra bike shorts for this trip. I don't think I've ever worn one of those colorful bike jerseys; I've never liked the feel of them. So why in the world did I sign up to do a yearlong, worldwide bike trip? Good question.

In the fall of 2001, I retired from the U.S. Air Force at age fifty after a twenty-seven-year career in space operations bemused at the length of my career when my goal was to stay only as long as I was still having fun. In determining my next move, I considered that with my Air Force pension and my low-maintenance lifestyle coupled with a savings portfolio enhanced by more bull than bear years, I could afford to do some of the things I had always wanted to do—which included travel. The summer before I retired, my friend, Cheryl, had gotten the "bike tour" bug. So we rode across Iowa that summer with 9,998 other people on RAGBRAI, the granddaddy of all intrastate bike rides, and the next year we rode across North Carolina. Then, in late January 2002, Cheryl was surfing the Worldwide Web and came across a bike tour called Odyssey 2003 that planned to visit forty-one countries over the course of a full year. She said I should check it out. I did and was attracted to an itinerary that spanned the globe with biking on six continents. I called Tim Kneeland of Tim Kneeland & Associates (TK&A), the trip's sponsor, with a few questions and, within a couple of weeks, had made up my mind to go. The big draw for me was the number of different locations; it was like a global sampler. The fact that it was a bike trip was almost incidental. Hadn't I had kept myself fit all these years for just such a contingency? The sixty-one mile per day average was more than I might have liked but not more than I could do, so I was in. Since the price increased the later you signed up, I sent my check to TK&A before the end of February 2002. Even so, I was the last of only four world tour riders to sign up. In addition, Tim also offered the trip in twelve stages for those with either limited time or funds, so we were to have many people join us throughout the year to ride certain segments of the trip.

I had ten months to prepare. Of course the first concern was to ensure I was bike-fit so that I could enjoy the trip, and it wouldn't become a "slog." I increased my rides with the New Mexico Touring Society, our local Albuquerque bike club, and during that summer I did three weeklong bike rides in Indiana, Maine, and Nova Scotia. I also rode an easy century just to make sure I could do one since there were a few days throughout the trip that hit the hundred-mile mark. All in all, I rode about six thousand miles in 2002 including thirteen hundred miles on my new Odyssey 2003 bike that I had picked up in Burbank, California, in early November (all the other miles were on an old mountain bike fitted with "slicks," i.e., smooth, not knobby, tires). The Odyssey bike was custom-made for TK&A by an Italian firm called Torelli. TK&A had decided to include it in the cost of the trip of the four world riders so that their chore of maintaining the bikes would be eased.

Knowing we would have a limited time in the places we would be visiting, I wanted to maximize my touring time, so I read the latest versions of the *Lonely Planet Guides* for each of the countries we were to visit. I hit the history, customs, and basic info sections (i.e., currency, phones, mail, e-mail, etc.), and I then delved into the attractions for each of the cities through which we would ride with special emphasis on our planned layover days. It helped that TK&A had provided us with a detailed day-by-day itinerary in our info packet. I then summarized the salient points on the computer and printed a copy for quick reference on the trip. Because I'm an avid reader, I also made a list of books (mostly novels) for my trip. My main criterion was that each book should add to my enjoyment of the places I was to visit (i.e., they should take place in or be about those countries visited). Then I had to find paperback versions that were travel-friendly. I also took my booklist with me so I could search bookstores when in country. My booklist with comments is included in appendix C.

Naturally there were many mundane tasks to complete: getting the shots recommended by the CDC, getting medications to take with me (e.g., malaria pills), putting all my stuff into a storage shed and my car into a storage lot, making sure my few bills were being automatically paid by my bank, making an inventory of things to take with me on the trip and then slashing it unmercifully, and so on. My passport was current, and TK&A took care of the few visas needed for traveling so I was set there. Finally everything was taken care of, and I was ready to go.

This book is based on a series of e-mail reports I sent to family and friends while on the road describing my experiences on the Odyssey 2003 World Bicycle Trip. To keep the narrative sounding as fresh as possible, I decided to modify the reports only for clarification or correction. The two exceptions to this rule are the accounts from New Zealand and Australia, our first two destinations. Because I had previously spent considerable time in both countries (I had lived in Australia for two years while in the Air Force), and because I wasn't too sure what my online readership's interests would be, my two initial e-mail reports were much abbreviated from my later accounts of travels in uncharted territories. For the sake of consistency in this book, I have referred to my journal to fill in details for these first two reports.

Because I was often at the mercy of internet availability and tight time constraints, I couldn't always end the reports at natural transition points like leaving one country to enter another. Therefore the titles of some reports don't cleanly reflect the content within them; for instance the title of report number twelve leads you to believe you will be reading about Ireland, but it is some pages into the report before we actually board the ferry to Dublin. I have also included information that I learned either after the report had been sent or, in some cases, after the trip was over. I think it is information the reader will appreciate. These additions are set off in brackets, < >, to alert the reader. American readers might be put off by my use of kilometers when talking about biking mileage. I stayed with kilometers since that is what TK&A provided us throughout the trip on our daily route guides (DRG's). For non-biking estimates of distances, I usually use English units. Finally, we were traveling during the build-up for and the early stages of the U.S. invasion of Iraq. I did not edit out the few political comments I included in my initial reports home because they add context to our travels.

Oh yes, the title. While whittling my list of things to take, I paid much attention to clothing. Obviously, on a world bike tour, you must be prepared for any weather contingency, therefore bike clothing formed a large part of my wardrobe. For street clothes, the bare minimum, not only in amount but also in weight and in maintenance, was my goal—I wanted utilitarian clothing that would serve multiple purposes and, when washed, would dry quickly. This ruled out denim jeans and cotton T-shirts, two items of clothing that, along with my sandals, have become my post-retirement uniform. But I also decided that I would take only a few pairs of cotton briefs and would instead use nylon running shorts that can be rinsed out and dried in a couple of hours as a sane replacement in most instances. In fact, these shorts did the trick so well that I didn't wear my cotton briefs even once on the trip. Therefore, I quite literally had "a year without underwear."

Report #1: Greetings from the Antipodes

Good day relatives and friends,

My "round the world" bike trip began on January 1, 2003, in Los Angeles when the riders and staff congregated at the Sheraton Hotel near LAX. We stayed at the Sheraton for two nights so we could bike our one day on the North American continent and get ready for the flight to New Zealand. Cheryl and I had driven from Albuquerque in two easy days with my bike and two bags of "stuff" for the year. It was at the Sheraton where I first met my fellow travelers. We make a diverse group. Andy is a forty-six-year-old accountant for a big hotel in Pottsville, Pennsylvania. Kirby (he jettisoned "Dan" shortly after the younger folks began calling him "Kirby") is a fifty-nine-year-old chemical analyst from Boston, Massachusetts. Stacia is a twenty-four-year-old recent Pepperdine grad who majored in sports medicine while working her way through college on a soccer scholarship. She's sort of a combination female jock and (self-described) princess from Westlake Village northwest of Los Angeles. This past summer she was an au pair for a family in Spain and then worked as a personal trainer at a local gym until the trip started. Andy and Kirby have previously taken multiple bike trips both in and out of country. Andy has ridden across the United States on one of TK&A's previous trips so he knows Tim Kneeland and some of his staff well. Kirby has taken numerous bike trips including two to the African nations of Togo and Benin and so he has interesting stories to tell. Stacia is a newcomer to bike touring, but she has been training for this trip and, with her athletic background and youth, should have no problems.

Since the number one question I get from friends and strangers about my trip is, "How can you afford time from your job to take a yearlong trip?" I will provide the answer for the four riders. For me, it's easy—I'm retired and not working. Andy was able to get a leave of absence from his accounting job. He didn't even have to ask his boss who, upon hearing about the trip, asked if Andy would like his job held for him! Pretty savvy boss I'd say. Kirby had to quit his job in order to take the year off. He requested a leave of absence, but his boss wouldn't bite. His lovely wife, Barbara, will continue her job throughout the year though. <Interestingly, Kirby checked from time to time on the trip to see if his previous job had been filled, but it still showed vacant as we flew home at the end. However, neither Kirby nor Andy is keen about returning to the same job, and both are considering career changes.> Stacia had known about the trip since she graduated from Pepperdine and so purposely did not take a long-term job.

Two staffers will be with us for the duration of the trip. Dennis, the trip leader, is a fifty-six-year-old mechanic/jack-of-all-trades from Washington State near the Canadian border. He and his wife have an even more minimalist lifestyle than I do. Tim, our mechanic, is a twenty-four-year-old recent UC-Santa Barbara history grad who lives in Livermore, California. Tim quickly became "young Tim" whenever Tim Kneeland was around. Dennis and young Tim are also taking their bikes on the trip and plan to alternate riding every other day while the other provides SAG support as long as all other needs are met. SAG is a biking acronym that, according to one source, stands for "Support And Gear" (i.e., they drive the support van). This is a great deal for them, mixing business and pleasure. <As it happened, Dennis left the trip after Viet Nam for family reasons, and Tim left after Thailand for health reasons. Other staffers filled in for the remainder of the trip as described in the appropriate reports.> To round out the group heading to New Zealand, Tim K. joined us for the first couple of weeks to ensure everything started out okay, and then he flew to Hong Kong to firm up the Southeast Asia part of the trip.

TK&A paired Kirby and me in one room and Andy with Stacia in a second room for this initial stay in L.A. with the proviso that this combination was not set, and we could change at any time. <As it turned out, whenever our accommodations were two to a room, Kirby and I roomed together throughout the trip with few exceptions. We were as compatible as two strangers are likely to be.>

After unpacking and settling in we drove across town for our first Odyssey meal together at a fancy Chinese restaurant in L.A.'s Chinatown. I drove to and from the restaurant with young Tim, the mechanic. I discovered he had focused on western water usage in getting his degree so between that, movies (he's a buff), and Bush's imperialistic martial tendencies we had much to talk about. We had a helluva time keeping up with Tim K. who was driving the big van with everyone else. As we careened down the L.A. highway system we agreed that Tim K. must have learned his driving skills from watching *Bullitt* and *The French Connection* movies. At the restaurant a good time was had by all. Sitting next to Dennis and his wife I had a chance to hear about their experiences on the Odyssey 2000 trip for which both had been staff members. Odyssey 2000 was TK&A's first attempt at a yearlong, worldwide trip, but this one had almost 250 riders and a staff of thirty to forty personnel—what a difference from our trip! At the short group meeting after the meal, we learned Kirby has brought his bagpipes which he is learning to play. Hmmm, this could either be a good thing or a bad thing; only time will tell.

The next day was our first Odyssey 2003 bike ride. Together with a passel of local Odyssey 2000 alumni we rode from the hotel to the beach and then along a beautiful bike path through the colorful Venice Beach community to Santa Monica. From there we headed into the hills up Mulholland Drive (didn't see David Lynch) and past the huge Hollywood sign to Bobbi's house; Bobbi is Tim's partner, and her house serves as TK&A headquarters. We took mandatory group pictures along the way including one in front of the Hollywood sign. The day was an auspicious start for our trip, as beautifully clear as I have ever seen Los Angeles. The views from the hilltop ride were spectacular! At Bobbi's we had a scrumptious barbecue meal compliments of Bobbi and her crew. The Odyssey 2000 group, maybe six to eight people, were enthusiastic to the point of avidity and had many experiences and stories to share. For them, the ride had been the proverbial "trip of a lifetime," and they were ready to do it again.

On January 3, since our overnight flight to New Zealand wasn't until late evening, Kirby, Cheryl, and I took the opportunity to visit the Los Angeles Zoo while Dennis and young Tim boxed our bikes for the flight. Then we returned to Bobbi's for a hearty lasagna meal and celebratory cake before heading to the airport. The whole day felt surreal knowing the next year was to be a global game of hopscotch starting in just a few hours.

Night flights are disorienting to me especially since I don't sleep well sitting upright. During RAGBRAI, my first bike tour across the state of Iowa in the summer of 2000, I had learned to appreciate ear plugs, so I had a pair of them in my carry-on bag along with black eye shades but neither helped much. There's also the matter of crossing the International Date Line and losing a day but, when you're just starting a yearlong vacation where time is all but irrelevant, that didn't faze me much. Besides, I had flown to New Zealand twice before, both times sitting backwards in the hull of a military cargo plane with just one small porthole on each side of the craft and an extremely variable temperature situation, so who was I to complain?

We arrived with the sun in Auckland which is situated at the top end of the northernmost of the two main islands that constitute New Zealand or, as the native Maori call it, *Aotearoa* (land of the long white cloud). We gathered our bikes and bags and waited while Dennis, Tim K., and young Tim negotiated our SAG rental van. Getting through Kiwi customs was about what I had expected. Since both New Zealand and Australia are separated by lots of water from other large landmasses, they are extremely careful about letting in exotic plant and animal matter. I had to open both bags so they could examine my boots and camping equipment to ensure I didn't import any contaminated U.S. soil.

With boxed bikes and an extra person (i.e., Tim K.), we had to make three trips to the hotel. Stacia, Andy, and I were in the first transfer and passed the time waiting for the others to arrive by wandering through the beautiful rose garden just across the street from our hotel and then down to a pretty lagoon. An older man was swimming across the lagoon with his dog leading the way. When he arrived back on our side, he told us the lagoon is tidal and nearly empties twice each day into a bay at the far end. This was enough to convince me I needed a dip, so I returned to the hotel to see if our luggage had arrived. It had and so after helping move the bags to their respective rooms, I changed to my gym shorts, grabbed my mask and snorkel, and was off for my first swim of the trip. The cool water felt great after such a long trip stuffed like so much offal in a flying sausage.

After a short nap I wandered down to the lively wharf area where the others had gone for lunch. There was much bustle with crowds gawking at some of the America's Cup sailboats at anchor, strange looking craft. That evening for supper I had tender New Zealand lamb in a wonderful mint sauce with veggies and a squid salad. The squid was sautéed and not at all tough as most squid I've tried.

The next day was a recovery day, and I spent the morning exploring the city museum. I most enjoyed the exhibit explaining the Maori wars with the top attraction a full-sized replica of a Maori canoe that holds about fifty people. The exhibit reminded me of a fact I learned from an Australian TV program while living there in the late 70s: of those lands colonized by the British or Europeans, the Maori are the only indigenous people in the world never subjugated through war. After several bloody battles over many years, the English finally gained the upper hand through "the treaty process" (a euphemism those with knowledge of our own country's negotiations with the American Indian tribes will understand). After the museum I braved a few sprinkles to walk to the top of volcanic Mt. Eden for a splendid panorama of the city. From here I could see the other two volcanic hills around which, with Mt. Eden, Auckland is built.

Back at the hotel, the weather had cleared so I put on my gym shorts and walked down to the lagoon to see if there was enough water for a swim. It was here I had one of those "dumb" adventures that result when expectations conflict with the reality of the situation and one responds with bad judgment. The tide was out but, as it had receded into the bay, it sealed a considerable amount of water in the lagoon against the far shore that looked plenty deep for swimming. Hankering for a swim, I took off my sandals and began wading across the mud flat. Well, the further I went, the deeper I sank into the mud. I changed tack and tried to walk around the outside of the mud flat to get to the far shore which was much closer to the water. This didn't work either as I was soon amuck almost to my knees. I finally realized I would not be swimming this day since I would not be able to get close to the water through this mud flat. All I could do was slop to the nearest firm ground and then clamber around the steep shoreline back to where the showers were located hoping no one would see the silly situation I was in. To ensure I didn't forget the lapse of judgment too soon, I had incurred a gouge in my right foot when I stepped on a shell or other detritus imbedded in the mudflat. Luckily I didn't pick up an infection that would've impacted my riding, but I did walk gingerly for several days.

Before plunging into a description of my New Zealand riding adventure, here is a short summary of our route to give you a basic idea of where we've been if you look at a map. From Auckland at the top of the North Island we rode south to Wellington at the bottom. We then took the ferry to Picton at the top of the South Island and biked along the west coast to Haast and then cut across to Queenstown about three-fourths of the way to the southern coast. After a couple layover days we then rode in the van to Christchurch to fly to Tasmania for the second stage of the trip on February 2.

Our first two days of riding in New Zealand following the coast toward the southeast were challenging (110 and 137 kilometers) with stiff winds, a few decent climbs, and a little rain on both days. The second night we camped at the base of Mount Maunganui, a good-sized hill on a slender spit of land jutting into the Bay of Plenty on the northern coast. From our campsite we could walk to either a crashing oceanfront beach or a placid bay beach with not more than an eighth of a mile separating them across the neck of the peninsula. The whole length of this promontory couldn't have been more than a half mile total with our campground nestled in a copse of trees against the mount about halfway down. This site sure had a sense of location! The next morning I rose early and walked to the top of Mount Maunganui in a light rain. On the way up I had good views of the ocean crashing against the shore but, at the top, a pea soup fog cut visibility to nothing. I was surprised that, although it had rained steadily all night, the mud trail, though wet, was neither slippery nor mucky. It must be very dense clay.

That day we had a relatively short (87.7-kilometer) ride due south to Rotorua, the geothermal capital of New Zealand. Because this day was maybe the worst weather for riding during the entire trip <it was>, I'll include my journal entry from that evening:

Tough day. We had breakfasted right on the ocean and could watch the sea spray whip down the street in nearly gale force winds. Naturally our route headed right into it. For the first few kilometers we made slow progress. Sometime in that period my bike computer stopped registering the wheel count so I lost the odometer, speed, etc. and had only the clock function remaining. Subsequent attempts to fix it throughout the day failed…bummer! I'll fiddle with it some more. <Sometime later in the trip I finally realized that the contacts won't make if they get too wet, like in a heavy rain. I tried a little oil on the contacts and also tied a plastic bag over the readout whenever it rained heavily. This did the trick.>

Along with the wind, it rained almost the whole day, anywhere from a sprinkle to a deluge. We were soaked almost from the start. At times the wind drove the rain into our faces like it was hail. Not very pleasant.

Somewhat less than halfway we stopped for lunch in a heavy rain. I had not planned to stop but figured the rain might slacken. I didn't get any food, but Tim K. kindly bought us all hot chocolate (with two refills). It definitely hit the spot.

All the time we were in the roadside café it poured. In fact we stayed longer than planned because no one wanted to go out in it. When it finally abated, we did go out and actually got a short way down the road before we were soaked again. The only thing to do at that point was to keep going. Stacia and I rode together most of the way.

I was glad to get to camp. Tim had traded our camp spot for a four-person cabin…much appreciated (I think he was feeling guilty because of the lousy weather). Right now our room is festooned with wet stuff. Pretty much all our camping and riding gear got soaked last night and today.

That evening we enjoyed one of the thermal pools for which the region is famous. However, we didn't get to see some of the other geothermal wonders (similar to Yellowstone) that I had visited on my last trip here about ten years ago.

The following day was much more pleasant, the rolling hills made even more gentle by the tailwind we had most of the day. The route to Taupo was rural with pasturelands and pine tree farms in straight, clean rows. Purportedly, Taupo, in the middle of the North Island, has the largest trout in the world. The trout are not native but are introduced, and they really like it here! The funny thing in Taupo is that you cannot buy a trout meal in the restaurants; you must catch your own trout in order to eat one! Our layover day here was relaxed especially since the rest of the gang stayed out at one of the local watering holes until around two o'clock in the morning our first night. Also, Taupo is a lazy resort town with not much doing during the off-season. I spent the morning hiking to Huka Falls on the Waikato River. The river flows out of Lake Taupo down a gorge that narrows near the falls to produce a turbulent set of rapids. The water is crystal clear, and I could easily see sunlight dancing on the bottom when it wasn't too deep. After maybe a hundred yards of these rapids the river spills over a thirty-foot redoubt, not terribly high but with an impressive amount of water roiling over it. On my return, I stopped to take a dip in the hot springs that flow into the river near the beginning of the falls trail mainly to soak the soreness out of my shoulder (more on this later). Several families and couples were enjoying the rough-edged pools of various temperatures depending on their distance into the river…a pleasant place to while away an hour or an afternoon. On my hike I had done some birding and saw several interesting species that I later identified from a field guide in the museum when I got to Wellington: Australasian harrier, white-faced heron, goldfinch (not the species we have in America—this one had a bright red cap), a song thrush whose shape and behavior reminded me of our American robin, and what was probably a North Island fantail.

From Taupo we rode four moderate days to Wellington, New Zealand's capital city, via Otaki Beach on the southwest coast. The ride from Taupo had nicely varied scenery beginning with a long stretch following the shoreline of beautiful Lake Taupo and eventually climbing to a New Zealand style desert region with distant views of volcanic mountains still draped with a surprising amount of snow. The second day was even more striking with many hilly vistas and rushing streams. The landscape seems raw with only a veneer of cultivation. The temporary users haven't done much to smooth things out. We talked to a bloke at breakky (not sure of the conventional spelling, but I saw this on a "Bed and Breakky" sign) that morning who runs a thousand milk cows. He said the only crops we'd see in this region are those grown for feed. The great majority of land is pasture which is probably why the landscape looks so rough. The meal that night is worth a few words. The lady, who is temporarily managing the campground, laid out a feast of lamb with mint sauce (not that feeble mint jelly served in the States but a viable condiment in its own right), tender roast beef, perfectly cooked chicken, delicious roast potatoes (among the best I've ever eaten), pumpkin, sweet potatoes, succotash and, for dessert, pineapple upside down cake with both cream and ice cream. Simply scrumptious, the best meal yet (could this just be the rider's appetite speaking?). As usual I overate. I need to cut back on my food intake <By the way, this never happened!>.

My pre-trip reading had alerted me to a beautiful drive from our Otaki Beach campground through Otaki Gorge, and it didn't take much coercing to get Tim K. to drive us in the support van up the long, narrow, unpaved, winding road with heart-stopping drop-offs at regular intervals. Now Tim is not a timid driver, as mentioned above, and I'll admit I had a fleeting thought that a miscue on this road could put an early and permanent end to this trip. But the views were worth the trepidation of the drive. I later discovered this area had been the setting for Hobbiton in the *Lord of the Rings* (*LOTR*) movies.

The ride to Wellington was another of Kirby's *best ride of the trip so far!* rides <which he announced regularly throughout the trip right up until the last day>. No one could argue this one with him as Tim K. had routed us away from the main road along the coast. We turned east to climb over the coastal range and then cruised through a deeply forested region on a less traveled road taking us through the town of Lower Hutt before spilling us back out into the open just before entering Wellington. To say that the Lower Hutt area was used as the setting for the Elfin Kingdom in the *LOTR* movies is sufficient description for anyone who has seen the movies. It felt magical. The climb over the coastal mountains was a push, but the sweeping downhill run seemed to last forever. However, it was more than a bit brisk, and I stopped part way down to pull on the windbreaker I had removed before the climb. Still I wasn't sure I could trust my cold-stiff fingers as I navigated the perpetually damp road surface. I was reminded of the roads through the dark, damp redwood forests I regularly biked just off the central California coast and wouldn't have been surprised to see one of California's fat, baby-shit-yellow banana slugs crossing the road.

Coming into Wellington was another matter, lots of traffic, lots of turns, and lots of one-way streets. Trying to read your route guide while examining the street signs while trying to maintain appropriate speed with heavy vehicular traffic in a city with which you are unfamiliar is…well, a bit unnerving. Knowing this was but the first of many such rides in some of the busiest cities around the world really didn't make the matter any easier since we already had plenty of things to think about. Suffice to say we all made it safely to our inner-city, high-rise, dorm-style accommodations. How Tim K. finds these interesting places to stay is a mystery. This one seemed to have been something else in a previous life but has been converted into dorms for foreign students attending some type of educational program in New Zealand. Since it was the summer holiday not many students were hanging around. One of the highlights of the trip so far is our chance meetings with interesting people along the way. The head cook and manager of the small cafeteria in our dorm was a man from China whose family immigrated to New Zealand in the 1860s gold rush…but they came from the San Francisco area not China! I wonder how far back he can trace his family tree—and what a wonderful story it would make.

I had a great layover day in Wellington. Besides picking up handlebar extensions for my bike and hitting a few book stores, I spent most of my time (maybe seven hours) in the recently opened (1998) Te Papa Museum. I first hit a special exhibit on the making of the *LOTR* movies that was absolutely terrific. Wellington is the first stop on a worldwide tour of this exhibit. Don't miss it when it comes to your neighborhood if you are either interested in Tolkien's masterpiece or modern filmmaking with all its incredible new special effects. The audio tour allows you to listen to interviews with many of the actors, craftsmen, and movie makers telling how they put the films together. Te Papa's permanent exhibitions were also very good. While I wasn't as impressed with the Maori exhibit as I was with the one in Auckland, the Te Papa did have a good exhibit on immigration told through many firsthand accounts. I was also able to find a bird identification book to look up my sight-ings to date. Finally, before leaving the museum, I checked my e-mails for the first time on the trip, something I need to do regularly since it's the only sure method of communicating with friends and family stateside.

After eight days of riding I suspect I should provide a bit of a riding sum-mary for New Zealand. We ride on the left side of the road which took maybe half a day to get used to and maybe a week to get *really* used to. The roads here are much rougher than in the United States. They use larger stones in a chip-seal and don't roll the roads after laying the bitumen so, when fresh, they are rough on a bike. Because of this, after the first four days of riding, I had aggra-vated my left shoulder rotator cuff. My arm was extremely sore for several days and almost useless except, strangely enough, to grip the bike handles. It proved to be particularly painful when I did the "forbidden things" like raise my arm over my head or put my arm behind my back or turn over in bed. Luckily, Cheryl had insisted I bring a regular pharmacopoeia with me, and I took anti-inflammatory pills and shifted my handgrip regularly so that the soreness cleared up almost completely by the time I got to Wellington. I'm now starting to exercise the muscles in that shoulder to strengthen them. Also, I got handlebar extensions in Wellington that give me the option of a com-pletely different grip. Everything together has healed me. I got plenty of good advice from Stacia and young Tim who are both well-versed in the treatment of sports injuries.

For the most part, there is much less traffic here than in the States except in the urban areas where it can be dicey. It's never fun to have the large tour buses and double semi rigs blasting past you on the narrow roads, but we cer-tainly get some of that. The tour buses are especially unnerving as they are silent until they whoosh past you unnervingly close. We've gotten much more rain than I'm used to (in Albuquerque I can choose not to ride in the rain), but again it comes with the territory. Mostly we've had gentle rains or sprinkles that have, at times, been a welcome cool-down, but as described above, we also rode most of one day in a virtual deluge. The New Zealand summer has been cooler than I expected which has usually made it more pleasant for riding.

And now on to the South Island.…After our layover day in Wellington we biked to its extensive harbor (past a large anti-Bush, anti-war poster) and took the ferry across Cook's Strait to Picton on the northeast coast of the South Island. The weather improved as we sailed south, from the overcast gray of Wellington to the big, puffy clouds scattered across Picton's bright blue sky.

Our spirits rose accordingly. The 124-kilometer ride to Nelson was glorious. From Picton we climbed to a ridge overlooking the large harbor and then followed the north coast with its many secluded bays of beautiful light aquamarine water for the first twenty to twenty-five kilometers. Cutting across the neck of a large peninsula we stopped for lunch at the "green mussel capital of the world" for a bowl of good mussel chowder. (It was better than my first experience with New Zealand mussels years ago when, on the second night of a backpacking trip on Stewart Island, the small island off the southern coast of the South Island, a friend and I gathered a couple handfuls of mussels and boiled them till they opened. They were tasty and tender, but we had nothing with which to enhance their flavor.) The rest of the ride to Nelson was pleasant with a couple of good climbs and long downhill runs. On the second hill, a double trailer log truck passed me just as we crested the top, and I was able to keep up with it for at least half the downhill run which is always satisfying and fun. Of course, an aggressive rider on a racing bike would have passed the truck and beaten it to the bottom, but that goes in someone else's story.

From Nelson we rode two days to the west coast town of Westport through terrain that reminded me of a Rocky Mountain river valley. The first day was hot, and the alternately calm and turbulent Owens River flowing beside us looked inviting. Our camp that night was on the outskirts of a small, rural town with tame deer in an adjacent fenced area. At dusk that evening I spotted my first live hedgehog after seeing so many dead ones along the road. It was crossing a road, and we nudged it to the side as a car came past. It rolled into a ball until it felt safe and then bolted for the brush. We've seen a surprising number of roadkill animals for a country that had only two indigenous mammals, both bats, when the Europeans arrived. All the other mammals (or their ancestors) currently in New Zealand were brought here from elsewhere. I suspect I've seen at least a hundred flattened hedgehogs and about as many opossums (the attractive Australian kind, not the beauty-challenged U.S. variety). That night we watched a full moon rise between a cleft of mountain just before it disappeared into a large cloud for the remainder of the night. Thanks to my sister Elizabeth's gift of a 2003 moon cycle card, I plan to track the moon on this trip when it isn't obscured by cloud cover.

I took it easier on the rides for the next three days to Franz Josef Glacier down the spectacular west coast. Although I had driven the same route in reverse about ten years ago, you get a more personal feel for it when you're on a bicycle. The large lumps of earth dotted all along the coast have obviously been calved off the mainland by the erosive forces of sea and wind over thousands of years. They are large enough to be completely vegetated, like mini-islands tantalizingly close offshore. I suspect that generations of young imaginations, even to ancient Maori times, have populated them with strange beasts and even stranger spirits. Even I felt these youthful stirrings though I am well into middle age.

Punakaiki, our first stop, had the Pancake Rocks (eroded spires of rock straight out of a Dr. Seuss book looking for all the world like a tall stack of flapjacks), an ocean blowhole, and a surprisingly extensive cave to explore, so after a little lunch (I had three scoops), a shower, and setting up camp, young Tim and I set out to explore. I was surprised to find the cave still active with nice examples of ribbon stalactites. You can roam at will (so unlike a similar site in America would be). Tim and I clambered back to the far reaches of the cave where we turned out our lights to experience pitch darkness. After a half-hour of good discussion, we heard other visitors approaching and sat silently to give them a thrill when they finally discovered us in their flashlight beams. The cave had a few glowworms though these were high on the ceiling and showed up only as small pinpricks of light. These glowworms are the larvae of certain species of flies. They dangle themselves from self-generated strings of mucus and use biophosphorescence in the darkened cave to attract flying food which gets stuck in the mucus. After supper I walked the beach and watched the sun set into the ocean. A misty haze over the heavily vegetated hills that slope sharply to the sea gave a wistful, melancholy, even romantic feel to the evening as I headed back to camp.

The first half of the following day was biking at its best, rolling hills with sheer cliffs or dense jungle on the left and a white-crested ocean on the right. Each new climb and turn provided a different spectacle including a few native birds, the flightless, moorhen-like weka, the colorful, nearly-flightless pukeko, and the tui, a largish black bird with a single white feather, like a bit of down stuck to its chest. That night we stayed in an old pub in the historic gold-mining town of Ross. I'm not sure if it was something I ate, but early the next morning I had three dreams in a row in which I was going to my favorite New Mexican lunch place for their Wednesday special shredded beef burrito smothered in green chile. Each time I was with a different person. In none of them did I get to the point of actually eating anything. I count them unrequited dreams...and on a Wednesday no less!

The ride to Franz Josef Glacier, our next layover location, was wet. I guess it might be expected since much of the way was through rain forest. We were happy to be inside for the next couple of nights; I'm beginning to get used to the soft mattresses we are finding in New Zealand. Our layover day was overcast and rainy. In the morning I took a couple short hikes into the rain forest, and in the afternoon we all did a half-day glacier hike. It was the first time I had worn crampons, but I quickly learned to trust them as the guide took us up and down steep piles of ice. My legs were sore from the exertion. It rained a good part of the time we were on the glacier, and I was soaked through, long before we were done, despite the Gortex jacket provided. My hands were so stiff with the cold by the end I could barely untie the crampons. The glacier itself was massive, but dirtier and without the really deep blueness of the Alaskan glaciers I've seen. However, these glaciers are the only ones in the world that flow right down to rain forest. Just as we were leaving the glacier we got a good look at the world's only mountain parrot (the kea for you crossword puzzle lovers), a nuisance almost as clever as Yogi and his friends in Jellystone. There are signs everywhere warning you not to leave anything lying around or else it will be pilfered or torn to shreds by the keas.

The ride to Fox Glacier the next day was short (only twenty-eight kilometers) but beautiful as we wound through rain forest with wispy clouds threaded through the hills. Although heavily overcast, it did not rain for which we were grateful. For supper we ate at a nice restaurant outside of town on Lake Matheson heralded for its spectacular reflective view of Mt. Cook and Mt. Tasman. Alas, the cloud cover was complete, and we seemed to be socked in for the duration. However, later in that long summer twilight (we were at about the same latitude as Boston but south), while I was reading in the common area of our hotel, young Tim came to tell me the sky was clearing. Incongruous though it sounded, he was right, so we jumped into the van and drove to a point where we could see the truly magnificent Mt. Cook with its ermine-white cloak still catching the rays of the sun now vanished to our eyes over the western horizon.

The next morning, to my surprise, the sky was still clear, and we got another great view of Mt. Cook on the way to breakfast. The ride to Haast was long (120 kilometers) but relatively flat with a few rolling hills and a couple of groaners. Haast is a small, almost nonexistent town, and our hotel was in the middle of nowhere. However, they had a functioning hot tub which several of us quickly put to use relaxing our muscles in preparation for the climb over Haast Pass on the morrow starting the three-day ride to Queenstown.

Haast Pass was not worth worrying about as it turned out. The way to the pass was due east and gently uphill along a wide river valley. At about fifty kilometers we had a steep three-kilometer climb followed by rolling hills to the pass, a piece of cake, and we had pretty mountain vistas and waterfalls all along the way. Then it was a nice, mostly downhill ride to Makarora, an even smaller dot on the map than Haast, nothing more than a tourist center with café, store, and petrol station. It sprinkled that night, but we had no rain for the ride to Wanaka, just a delightful tailwind for much of the route. I arrived before lunch and laid out my camping kit to dry. As soon as everyone was in and ready, we drove to town. While the others had lunch, I visited the library to research questions that had arisen in discussion. Afterwards we visited Puzzling World, the site of the world's first large outdoor maze, which we duly attempted. In addition, they had a series of puzzle rooms with optical illusions and many hands-on puzzles to test your wit, will, stamina, and patience.

For our last ride in New Zealand, Tim K. routed us the back way to Queensland over the Crown Range road. It was quite a climb to the top of the range, the toughest climb of the trip so far, as we wound our way through hills that rose steeply on both sides of the road. I was surprised the grade remained as reasonable as it did, given the vertiginous slopes on both sides, but I was sucking air when I reached the support van at the top nonetheless. The view at the top was magnificent as we scanned a broad valley with mountains in the distance and Queenstown within sight, though it looked farther than the kilometers we had remaining in the ride. I hadn't counted on the precipitous descent that took us to the bottom of the range in short order. I was riding the brakes all the way down and, with the cold, wet day, my hands quickly became numb which was worrisome; I regretted not grabbing my mittens from the van at the top. But I survived to tell the tale after riding the remaining twenty kilometers of rolling hills to Queenstown with only a bit of bothersome traffic. On reflection, I wouldn't want to do that ride in the reverse direction.

Our first night in Queenstown, TK&A treated us to a gondola ride up to the mountain restaurant, the best view in town bar none. Seeing all of Queenstown lying in front of me, I could tell it has sure grown since I was last here. According to one guidebook, it is the fastest growing town in all of Australasia. Since we were among the first people seated, we were given a table with a spectacular view of the city. Just less spectacular was the generous buffet with two seafood tables containing whole New Zealand salmon, mussels, scallops, oysters, and other delicacies; two soup and bread stations; a cheese and cracker station with three types of local cheeses; two main stations with roast beef and lamb, a venison ragout, baked chicken and fish with several vegetable dishes; and a dessert station with a wide variety of dainties including our favorite, pavlova. Needless to say for those who know me well, I stuffed myself, but I slowed the pace considerably from my normal excursions into gluttony. Getting there early turned out to be a good idea for, as the restaurant filled, the serving tables became more crowded and a mild sense of desperation seemed to emanate from the newcomers, a sort of "so much to eat and so little time" feeling we were smugly able to treat with disdain as we sampled our third and fourth desserts. This was the first time in New Zealand where it was obvious we were at a tourist destination. The meal was a resounding success, and I rode the gondola back down with Dennis. We watched the first *LOTR* movie, piped into our room from the hotel's video player, and I turned in around midnight, a content and happy man.

We had two layover days in Queenstown. On the first, I just lazed around arranging notes for this e-mail before walking to town to type in my notes at an Internet café and to check out the town post office, library, book shops, and grocery situation. On the second, I found a nice trail up a heavily forested ravine that wound its way up the mountain with a nice stream and a couple of small waterfalls cascading down it. The stream had once powered a gold mining operation but now was used as a secondary water supply for the town. On the way back, as I passed through a residential area, I caught a glimpse of the shy bellbird drinking nectar from a backyard feeder. That evening we went to a Maori feast or *hangi*, and it was a big hit. The guys participated in a Maori posture dance or *haka* complete with thigh and chest slapping while sticking out our tongues and making big eyes. This dance mimics the posturing that ancient Maoris performed from shore when hostile or unknown sailors approached their island. With all the face and body paint and tattoos, it would have been an intimidating sight. On an interesting cultural note, besides our small group, there were a few other westerners, but the largest contingent was Asian, Japanese I think. When the Maori emcee called for men to participate in the *haka*, only the western men were enticed to come up for the participative fun/humiliation; not even one of the Asian men gave it a try. However, a few of the Asian women were game to try the women's version of the dance with Stacia.

The next day we drove in the support van from Queenstown to Christchurch for another layover day before flying to Hobart, Tasmania. On the long drive north we got a great view of Mt. Cook, the highest peak in the Southern Alps, across a cool blue lake. It was an awesome sight! Unfortunately, Dennis had to wrestle the high-profile van the entire way as the northwest wind was extremely strong and unrelenting. All I could think of was that I was glad I was not riding my bike.

On our layover day in Christchurch I visited the museum (so-so) and saw a new New Zealand movie called *Whale Rider* that depicts modern Maori life interwoven with their mythology, a great picture I can highly recommend to anyone interested in other cultures. I also roamed the library and hit several book stores. That evening we had a barbecue at the home of Kirby's wife's cousins (whom Kirby had never met). They are expats who have claimed Kiwi citizenship after living in New Zealand the past twenty-plus years. He taught physics at the university in Christchurch. Now retired, they live "the life of Riley" in a nice country home atop a hill overlooking beautiful farmland. They grow a few olives since some form of crop is required by the government for homes built on fertile land (an interesting concept when you consider what has happened in California to arguably the best agricultural land in the United States). We received unique perspectives from them and thoroughly enjoyed their company and hospitality (ummm, more pavlova!)

I'll now add some summary comments before ending this report. I'm glad I made the effort to ride lots of miles last year to get my legs in shape for this trip. So far I have not had any problems with my legs or the miles. In summary, we have ridden on nineteen days in New Zealand for a total of 1,921 kilometers or 1,191 miles.

My non-exercise pre-trip preparations have also worked well. The notes I made from all the travel books I read last year have helped me make good use of my time here, and the books about each country I brought have been fascinating. I've also been able to use the libraries to look up information we've had questions about, like what birds we're seeing.

Although I've mentioned some meals above, I'll give a short summary of our experience with New Zealand cuisine. We've been eating hearty meals since we're exercising so much. In most places the quantity has been plenty and the quality has been surprisingly good though I'm eating much more meat than I usually do. As you would expect, the lamb has been good, and their mint sauces are better than any I've had in the States. We've seen lots of deer farms and have had quite a bit of good venison. Of course, we've had pavlova for dessert several times, which I think is the national dessert; it's a lighter meringue than the Monfort family recipe makes. Also, I've had lots of baked squash and sweet potatoes which are often mixed, and jacketed (i.e., baked) and roast potatoes that have all been good comfort food. We generally get dessert with our evening meal so my sweet tooth has been satisfied, though

Rick, my Wednesday shredded beef burrito lunch partner, will be surprised that I haven't had any sweetened iced tea in a month. The best meals have been those cooked by the camp hosts at a few of the places we've stopped.

The accommodations have been good. We've camped only seven times and have been in cabins, motels, dorms, etc. the other times. We enjoy the camping but appreciate in-door accommodations too. So far, no complaints at all.

I'm not taking as many pictures as I had planned because I realized I will have the chance to obtain digital pictures from the Odyssey Web site and Kirby's personal Web site. So, in the end I should have a much better collection of pictures.

Hope this did not sound too rushed. I tried to put order into my notes before I started typing. I've been keeping a journal, and I scanned it for the highlights to put in this e-mail. My plan is to send one of these out about every trip stage, which is about once a month. They will probably evolve as I find my stride. Hope you enjoyed it and have a little bit better appreciation for what I've gotten myself into. I also hope that everything is going well with you and yours.

Take care,

Ralph

Report #2: Greetings from Oz

February 24, 2003

G'day blokes and sheilas,

This is the second installment of my great bicycle trip covering the Australia or Oz stage. I don't know where the Aussies' new advertisement strategy came from (i.e., this "Oz" bit), but I have a few guesses: 1) It might be a play on how they pronounce Australia as *Oz-trail-ya*; or 2) It might be a reference to their convict past a la the pay-for-TV serial, *Oz*, about prison life, or 3) Based on the vast fields of commercial poppies I saw growing in the river bottoms of northern Tasmania, it might refer to the scene in the Wizard of You-Know-Where when Dorothy and mammal friends succumb to the poppies. But, enough of this etymological drollery—you're interested in my trip, mate!

The travel to Hobart, the capital of Tasmania (one of Australia's six states and the only one that's an island), took the whole day. I happened to flip on the TV before we left the hotel in Christchurch and learned of the Columbia Space Shuttle disaster. It was strange watching two friends from my NASA days giving the main interviews. I felt for them because I know they were deeply grieving their friends killed on the flight. We had a long wait at the airport and then another delay in Melbourne while we went through Australian customs before flying to Hobart. This was a piece of cake since we were arriving from New Zealand. We saw a beautiful red sunset sky (sailor's delight) as we crossed the Bass Strait to Tasmania. Upon arrival we gathered our bags and boxes while young Tim and Dennis rented our support van. We then stuffed it to the gills for the twenty minute ride to the hotel. I was so jammed into a back seat and completely covered with baggage that I could scarcely move—glad I didn't have an itch.

Our layover day in Hobart went quickly. I stopped at the state library, picked up an Australian historical novel at a bookstore, and spent a couple of hours in the city museum and art gallery. Each museum seems to have its own specialty areas. This one had a great beetle collection arranged by color to dazzling effect. It also had a decent history section and interesting natural history exhibits including film footage of the last known Tasmanian tiger, a predatory marsupial. When I was here in 1980, an expedition was underway to the forbidding southwest coast of the island looking for any sign of the tiger, but it failed as have all others since.

That evening we met our first stage riders, Stephanie and Allen, who were joining the ride for Tasmania. They had both ridden on Odyssey 2000 making it all the way to Australia (with just Southeast Asia to go) at which point Allen decided he liked Oz and just stayed put. Stephanie wanted to see Asia and completed the tour. She then rejoined Allen in Australia, and they have lived there ever since! They are still U.S. citizens but, as of now, they plan to stay in Australia. They gave us good insight into the Odyssey 2000 trip. As our trip progressed, they were amazed at the differences between their 2000 trip and this one. With only four riders we can have meals as houseguests or in restaurants. This luxury was all but impossible with 240-plus riders and thirty-plus staffers on Odyssey 2000. They were also surprised to arrive in camp to find their tent already up (put up by the riders who arrive first) and to have Tim, our mechanic, come to their tent to see if they needed help with anything (waiting in line to see a mechanic on the 2000 trip was evidently a torturous affair). All in all, the Odyssey 2000 ride sounded much more impersonal than ours is. The four Odyssey 2003 world riders let them know we appreciated their pathfinding in 2000 which gave TK&A many ideas on how to make this such a great trip.

The first Oz ride to Bothwell was pleasant with good hills but very warm. Just outside Hobart the scene was quintessential Aussie bush with a vast expanse of hills covered sparsely with the majestic gum (or eucalyptus)—its distinctive white bark and dusty green leaves not quite covering the limbs—and, of course, that menthol smell. We also passed several gum forests much denser than I remember seeing anywhere else in Australia. They have a feel unlike any other forest I've experienced, certainly not dark and thick but with a mystery all their own. I watched a couple of sulfur-crested cockatoos clowning in the gums, hanging upside down and squawking raucously. Seeing these premier pet shop birds in the wild seems incongruous, but Australia has cockatiels, galahs, zebra finches, and so many other such popular "pet" birds flying wild that eventually you get used to it.

Our first meal on the road was a barbecue at the home of the owner of the bakery in this remote village. T-bones, sausages, deer patties, salads, rolls, and dessert, all good tucker, but the best part of the evening was the superb conversation. The matriarch was delightful, straightforward and levelheaded, with five daughters and two sons all grown. Her husband was a bit provincial but interesting for it. He thoroughly detests Tasmanian devils which he shoots on sight. They are evidently hell on chickens and other small livestock. Late that night I got my first good look at the Southern Cross (or Crux) when I ventured from my tent on an urgent mission. We never did get a good explanation for why the Aussie flag displays five stars in this constellation while the New Zealand flag displays only four. The explanations I did get sounded like "down under" versions of an urban legend.

The next morning I chanced upon a real Tasmanian devil, four in fact, all very dead, along with a wombat, a wallaby, rabbits, and assorted other small varmints. We saw lots and lots of roadkill, so much in fact that a few days hence I started taking pictures of different species for a "Roadkill Animals of the World" section in my memory book. <Unfortunately, this idea died when I got to Southeast Asia where we saw no, and I mean no, wild animal roadkill...but I'm getting ahead of my story.> Also that day we found ourselves behind a cattle drive and had to wind our way among wary cows, calves, and steers, not unlike I've done in the American west from time to time.

When I arrived in camp, I put on my swimming togs and jumped into the adjacent fast-flowing river. I found out later the flow was controlled by the hydroelectric folks upriver which could explain the unexpectedly cold water. I turned numb quickly, but the flow was so strong I just had to play in it. I put on my mask and snorkel and dove to the bottom where the current swept me downstream so fast I felt like an underwater superman. Young Tim and I took turns until we were both a pretty shade of blue. The hot day warmed us up fast though. A local mentioned he had seen a platypus in this same river just a few nights before, but I had no such luck. Again, we had a local barbecue with a small steak, a nice lamb chop, chook meat (Oz for chicken), salads, apple pie with hot custard, and a truffle. Good fare, but I'm not used to so much meat in my diet. A kookaburra sang us to sleep that night and roused us in the morning. Although it was in the campground and I scanned the trees with my binos, I never saw it. Its stark laugh always reminds me of the old jungle movies I watched as a kid which regularly used the kookaburra's call to depict the "wildness" of a place, even though it was usually misplaced in Africa.

For the second day in a row we had a long, wonderful downhill with great views without commensurate uphill climbs. None of us can figure out what gives, but of course we're not complaining. When you're biking Oz you don't look a gift kangaroo in the pouch. That afternoon in Scottsdale, I walked to an Eco-Center on the edge of town, but I agreed with young Tim that the exhibits and placards reeked of propaganda for the timber industry. Nevertheless, the building-within-a-building structure was interesting with small trees between the two sets of walls and lots of automatically controlled louvers. Supposedly, it is 20 percent cheaper to heat and cool than conventional methods. We stayed the night in an old pub that provided decent accommodations.

After riding north through the middle of the island from Hobart the last three days, we were now headed to the east coast and then a three-day ride back to Hobart thus completing a big loop. The ride to our coastal layover day in St. Helens was not long, but it was tough with two ridges to cross. Near the top of the first ridge, Stacia spotted an echidna (also called a spiny anteater), one of only two monotremes (mammals that lay eggs) in the world; the other is the more commonly known duck-billed platypus. I tried to turn it over so we could see its face, but echidnas are persistent and strong with heavy claws to grip the forest floor. When I finally flipped it over, it tried to hide its face behind its claws. We got just a glimpse of the cute, pink face before this shy creature turned over and dug in again. Although it has superficial resemblance to the hedgehog which is a placental mammal, the echidna is biologically far removed—a good example of parallel evolution (i.e., animals developing similar structures to fill the same niche in different parts of the world).

Our layover day in St. Helens coincided with their annual abalone cook-off. I could only imagine my mother swooning from all the imaginative recipes. I went through the line twice and sampled maybe ten different dishes all containing some variation of her favorite seafood. I also took advantage of our location to take a swim in the clear, cold water of the Tasman Sea. I was somewhat disappointed that I didn't see much sea life, but I had better luck with birds and added over a dozen to my list including two types of honeyeaters: the yellow-throated and the New Holland.

The next day we began closing the loop to Hobart down the beautiful east coast. The day was brilliant and the course moderate with spectacular ocean views interspersed with pretty forest rides and no wind or rain, about as perfect as biking can be. I took a longish hike after my ride to do a bit of birding and found some delicious blackberries, ripe and as big as my thumb, to keep the hungries at bay until supper. I swam a mile off a jetty and got cold-soaked as expected, but walking back to camp and a hot shower cleared that up. After supper we took a night tour to see Fairy (or Little) Penguins. These diminutive seabirds spend two to three days in the ocean gorging on fish before returning to feed their young. Their nests are located in holes in the ground well up from waterline. What amazed me more than seeing penguins walking past just a foot away was the fact that they wouldn't be here at all except for two surfer dudes who witnessed a similar phenomenon some years ago. They bought up the nearby land and brought the penguins back from the brink of extinction against fierce opposition from the local anti-environmentalists who are common in Tasmania it seems. The dudes have had little help from the government and have only just begun to bring around some of the townspeople who realize they are making a pretty good living on ecotourism. Nevertheless, trying to pass leash laws for dogs and cats and other regulations to protect the penguins continues to be difficult. One of the interesting facts from the tour is that the winters for the last ten years have been so mild, the penguins have been nesting year-round.

It was another three days to Hobart with nice oceanfront biking and scenic inland routes. On the second day we observed the Aussie penchant for interesting names when we rode up Bust-me-gall hill and Break-me-neck hill before topping Black Charles Summit and swooping down the other side on the way to Seven-mile Beach. Our route into Hobart diverted us onto back roads, which we appreciated, with lots of twists and turns. Crossing the bay bridge into Hobart was a bit hairy though because, although the bike path was separated from the traffic flow, it was narrow with bridge parts sometimes jutting into it, and we had a strong, gusty crosswind to keep us off balance. Regardless, we all made it to our hotel for our last night in Tasmania where we boxed our bikes and had a farewell supper with Stephanie and Allen.

While in Tassie I finished the book known as the first great Australian novel, *The Recollections of Geoffry Hamlyn* by Henry Kingsley, that I had found in a secondhand shop when I first arrived in Hobart. I enjoyed it immensely. Written around 1859, it depicts the lives and exploits of several families moving from England to the Australian bush of New South Wales.

I should mention that the Tasmania of this trip did not look like the Tasmania I remember from a visit in 1980. On that visit we drove in a big loop around the whole island, and I remember being most impressed with the northwest part of the island which is mountainous and forested with pine—very dark and mysterious. Somewhere I read that Tolkien used Tasmania as his model for Middle Earth when he wrote *The Lord of the Rings* trilogy; it must have been the northwest area he was remembering. I should also probably mention that this beautiful island was the scene of one of the worst genocidal pogroms in history, as thorough and horrible as the world has ever seen. The local "final solution" to the Tasmanian aboriginal "problem" was to form a cordon of armed men across the island who then marched together to sweep up and virtually eliminate the entire aboriginal population. One woman, a housemaid for a white settler, was spared.

From Hobart, we flew to Sydney for a couple of R & R days, leaving our boxed bikes locked in a hotel storage room. I did some of the Sydney *tourista* stuff like visiting the Opera House, the bridge, the Rocks, and Darling Harbor. I also spent almost six hours in the museum and, of course, visited their library to do some research. I sure do love libraries and will miss them in all the non-English speaking places we'll visit in the following months. We had a weather shock getting to Sydney where it was much warmer and much more humid than Tassie, but that was nothing next to Townsville where it was very, very warm, and very, very humid. We were in for a different kind of riding!

Because of the heat and humidity in the tropical northeast coast of Queensland, finding ways to keep cool became more important. The day I arrived in Townsville, I checked out the swimming situation. It was not too good as February is still box jellyfish season along this coast which means you don't get into the water unless you find a "stinger secure area" netted to keep the little beasties out. I did find a couple of secure areas which were double netted with tighter mesh to keep out an even smaller species of jellyfish that has started showing up (some think the reason is global warming). I did take a dip both days we were there, but the water was warm, murky, and somewhat turbulent—okay to play in but not much fun for swimming any distance. Nevertheless, it did cool me down somewhat.

On our layover day, I visited the new Tropical Queensland Museum with its wonderful exhibit on the *HMS Pandora*, the ship that was sent from England to find and bring back the *HMS Bounty* mutineers (yes, you remember *Mutiny on the Bounty* with Douglas Fairbanks or Clark Gable or Mel Gibson, depending on how old you are). After finding fourteen of the mutineers, the *Pandora* was heading back to England when it got too close to the Great Barrier Reef in rough weather and sunk not far from here. It is possibly the most studied wreck in history, and the museum has the whole story nicely laid out. I spent quite some time there and even manned a crew to fire an authentic six-pound cannon (fake cannonball)…and I have the pictures to prove it. The museum also had a hands-on science area that was fun and a tropical Queensland exhibit worth more time than I had to spend. The night before heading north I spotted just a glimpse of the freshly risen full moon before it ducked beneath a cloud.

From Townsville we cycled up the coast for three days before heading inland and up onto the Atherton tablelands where it was a wee bit cooler and less humid. All four days we got rain, but don't get the impression this was a bad thing. No, this was a good thing. As hot as it was, we were already wet from sweat so the rain was welcomed as a cooling agent. Also, and most importantly, rain means no sun on your back. Regardless, though, it was damned hot! I almost became addicted to Lemon Squash, a popular soft drink here because, after a ride, I would buy the largest cold bottle I could find to help rehydrate myself. Any hotel room with a ceiling fan and/or air conditioning on this leg rated extra stars.

The first three days were flat coastal riding with a quick look at a museum for the sugar cane industry as the sole diversion, but on the fourth we turned west and climbed to the Atherton plateau. The first forty-kilometer climb to Crawford's Lookout was gradual and pleasant. Here Dennis and Tim had parked the van to hike to the lookout through a dense rainforest. I did part of the hike enjoying the dense green weave of the forest. From there, though, the going got steeper. At one point we hit a five-kilometer stretch that was a real strain. A sign warned motorists about the steepness…and it was no joke! It helped that we lost some of the heat and humidity as we gained elevation. Finally, we crested the plateau to confront a seemingly endless series of rolling hills as we crossed the plateau to our hotel. By the time we arrived I was sure tired of hills, but the views had been grand and the wind had even felt a bit cool as we neared our destination. That evening we took the van to an ancient curtain fig tree, truly impressive, and stopped at a platypus viewing area but were blanked again. One of the best things about Australia to this point had to be the big country pubs in which we spent several nights along the way. These wonderful old structures, each with its own distinctive character, were inhabited by a variety of interesting denizens that defined Queensland "bush."

The next morning we enjoyed a beautiful riding day with no rain. It was cooler starting out with gentle rolling hills until we reached the edge of the tablelands at which point we coasted down a wonderful six-kilometer decline with gently winding curves, the most pleasant and fun downhill run of our trip so far. Unfortunately, as we descended, we again picked up the muggy atmosphere of the coast as well as the more heavily trafficked roads on our way to a rest day in Port Douglas.

For our layover day, the four riders and young Tim took a day cruise to the outer Great Barrier Reef. Since I had taken a three-day SCUBA trip to the reef with son Joe just two years previously, I decided to snorkel, especially since the three locations we visited were relatively shallow. The day was beautiful, the water clear and the reef as incredible as ever. I paired with young Tim who had never snorkeled in such a place before, and it was fun watching his amazement in discovery. Our favorite sighting was a white-tipped reef shark. What a great way to spend a layover day!

Our final Australia ride to Cairns (pronounced *cans* for no reason I can see) was pretty and fast. Most of the way we alternated between hugging the coast with its pristine, but empty, beaches and riding through rainforest that stretched down to the water. We had the wind to our backs and were skimming along at over thirty kilometers per hour part of the time. The next day we were all very busy since we would fly to Hong Kong on the following morning. I spent it buying a couple extra tires and a chain for my bike since their availability in China was unknown, going to the library (my last visit for some time), posting a card, hitting the ATM, and calling home...and I still had time for two movies.

Before leaving Oz, however, there are a few things I need to mention. One is the *splendifferous* life you see along this tropical coast (yeah, yeah, I know *spendifferous* is not a word, but it's still the best fit for the thought). As noted above, we had rain several times while riding which was much appreciated by us, but it was also appreciated by the myriad frogs along the highways that deafened us with their din whenever we passed a swampy area. Similarly, the cicadas here sing in unison which, from a distance, sounds like heavy machinery. Several times, I looked for the earthmovers in barren stretches of coastal forest only to realize it was the insects. Heard up close, those same cicadas can addle your thinking. Twice we had raucous birds in trees just outside our hotel rooms (once it was parrots, and once it was a bird called the metallic starling that nests in great communal clumps). They squawk and squabble until well after dark and are at it again first thing in the morning. And then, there are the huge schools of tiny and medium fish on the reef, and then there's the coral reef itself—just incredible. I sure love life in its excesses! Queensland boasts two UNESCO World Heritage Sites adjacent to each other: the Great Barrier Reef and the rainforest in northern Queensland. Son Joe told me it's the only such dual site in the world.

Of lesser note, but interesting nonetheless, we got to see more cane toads, mostly in the form of roadkill, than we had wanted. This introduced immigrant could be a testament to man's arrogance. After thorough research, the toad was brought into this region specifically to help rid the farmers of the cane beetle that was devastating their harvest. Unfortunately, this particular cane beetle spends its time high up on the cane while the large, lumpish cane toad is grounded by its own mass. So the toad found other food and became a problem in its own right. The poison it secretes for defense has also killed many wild and domestic predators. Unfortunately, the toad manifestly likes it here based on its population explosion and range expansion. Sounds an awful lot like the problem of the rat and the mongoose in Hawaii doesn't it?

I haven't mentioned much about food on our mainland Oz stage, but I had lots of great seafood, primarily barramundi, the Aussie's premier fish. Well, that's it for this installment. I'm not sure when I'll get to the next one. China and Vietnam comprise the next stage and Thailand and Malaysia, the one after that. We'll see what kind of e-mail connection I can find. Until then, I hope all is well with you and yours, and I'll keep you posted.

Your world correspondent,

Ralph

Report #3: Greetings from SE Asia

March 5, 2003

Ni hao ("hello" in Mandarin) to family and friends from China,

Yes, I know I said I was going to send just one e-mail after each stage, but this summary was getting so long I thought I'd better close it out and send it. I guess I'll play it by ear as to when the next one goes out. Right now we are having a layover day in Yangshuo (*yawn sean*) after riding three days on mainland China. We have seven more riding days and two more layover days before we head to Viet Nam.

The flight from Australia with a 5 a.m. wake-up, a two-hour layover in Brisbane, and a three-movie flight to Hong Kong made for a long day. I had a brief sense of euphoria getting on the plane in Brisbane, an intense emotional feeling a friend calls the "shiver dance," realizing I was stepping into the unknown. And Hong Kong did not disappoint. We were there for only three nights and two days, but I was constantly on the go and got to see quite a bit. First let me orient you (no pun intended): Hong Kong consists of Hong Kong Island, Kowloon Peninsula, the New Territories, and about 260 other islands. China ceded Hong Kong Island to the Brits after the Opium Wars and gave them the Kowloon Peninsula sometime later. Then they leased the New Territories to the Brits for ninety-nine years in 1898. The New Territories is a large chunk of land north of Kowloon up to the Shenzhen River which is the demarcation line between Hong Kong and China. The area near the river is patrolled as a no-man's-land since the border is still closed. As you might know, the lease on the New Territories was up in 1997 with China reclaiming the territories, but prior to that time China negotiated with the Brits to return

27

the ceded lands as well. Therefore, in 1997, all of Hong Kong was handed over to China. According to the deal, China was not to make any drastic changes for fifty years…at which time all bets are off. That's how things stand now; the official euphemism is "one country, two systems"…at least for the time being.

We landed at Hong Kong's international airport which is on a good-sized island entirely reclaimed from the bay. In fact, a good portion of Hong Kong, particularly in Kowloon, is reclaimed land. A highly simplified explanation is that they knock mountains down and put the fill into the bay. Our nighttime bus ride to our hotel on Kowloon made our eyes big. Hong Kong is much larger than I expected and, boy, is it vertical! Most buildings are skyscrapers it seems. About half the people in the city live in tall high-rise apartments with about 450 square feet per family, if I remember the figure correctly. There are several big bridges that span the bay between the peninsula and the various islands, three underwater tunnels from Kowloon to Hong Kong Island, and multiple tunnels through the mountain range running the length of Hong Kong Island and also through the range that separates Kowloon from the New Territories. Many of the streets feel like tunnels since the buildings are so tall on all sides. The crowded streets themselves have the same closeness as do Chinatown streets in any of a dozen cities in the United States. They are jam-packed with shops of all sorts. Hong Kong certainly ranks with the other major cities of vision and industry throughout the ages. It is indeed impressive how they use all available space.

Our hotel in Kowloon was called the BP International House. We later found out the "BP" stands for Baden-Powell who was the founder of the Boy Scout program. Two floors of this impressive hotel house the international headquarters for Boy Scouts in Hong Kong. The Boy Scout fleur-de-lis design in the lobby first tipped us off. Unfortunately, I only discovered as we were checking out that the Boy Scouts maintain an exhibit area on one of the floors. It was at the hotel where we met our new stage rider, Carol, a whippet-thin woman about my age who seems to have traveled widely. She will ride with us in China and from Nanning will fly to Beijing for further solo touring.

While sitting in the lobby of the hotel waiting for dinner that first afternoon in Hong Kong, we were approached by a group of young men in formal business attire. It turned out they were part of a wedding party for a ceremony to take place later that day. The bridegroom handed us a wedding card that already had several signatures with good wishes on it. We added our greetings and signed it while his cameraman captured the moment. Then the bridegroom gave us each a wedding cookie. It seemed a very nice custom. The young men were sure having a great time.

Since we had two free days here, the riders took two half-day morning tours, one to see the sights on Hong Kong Island and one to tour Kowloon and the New Territories. We had informative guides for both, and I learned bunches of new facts most of which have already dribbled out my ears I'm afraid, but the feeling of learning new stuff stays with me still and, hey, isn't that the important thing?

On the Hong Kong Island tour we drove to Victoria Peak, the highest point on the island, where we got a great view of the busy commercial section of Hong Kong Island, the waterfront area of Kowloon, the New Territories beyond, and, off in the distance, China—what a skyline this city has! We visited the Aberdeen fishing village where fisher-families still live on sampans in the tradition of their ancestors who were members of one of the four clans that settled this area. We also experienced the claustrophobic Stanley Market at the far southeast corner of the island. Actually, instead of shopping, I walked through the market to the bay and then strolled around the shore to find a small temple (complete with burning incense to ensure safe passage for seafarers) that was tucked away on a wooded point a mile from the market.

On the backside of the island, the guide pointed out a large, modern high-rise building set against the mountain, but what was unusual was the large square hole in the middle of the building. The guide explained that the hole was designed into the building in accordance with *feng shui* or "wind water," a Chinese term for harmony with nature. She told us the large building would have cut off the view of the bay from the mountain which is shaped like a dragon at rest. The hole allows the mountain-dragon an escape route. On the Victoria Harbor side of the island was another example of this concept. A building in the shape of a large white column had been built without consideration of *feng shui*. Unfortunately, the building reminded people of a large white candle which is a symbol for death in China. The owner consulted a geomancer who recommended putting a pool on the roof allowing the water to extinguish the flame of the candle, and this was done. Interestingly, the book I brought about Hong Kong called *Kowloon Tong* by Paul Theroux discusses how the two partners of a textile factory take great care to situate the factory in consonance with *feng shui*. <This was my first experience with the concept, but, when I returned home, I found *feng shui* was all the rage in certain architectural circles in the United States>

On the Kowloon/New Territories tour we stopped at a traditional Buddhist Temple, visited the seven-hundred-year-old walled village of Kam Tin, which is now mostly occupied by very old but very spry residents, and drove to a vantage point at Lok Ma Chau overlooking the Shenzhen River into China. An elderly lady was selling postcards of the view from this same vantage point taken twenty years ago, and the difference was shocking. Twenty years ago there was nothing but fields on either side of the river. Now, the modern city of Shenzhen with its many skyscrapers looms large on the Chinese side. In earlier times, we were told, the Chinese erected the façades of buildings to make the folks from British Hong Kong think business was booming in Shenzhen. Today, the job loss the United States is experiencing also happens here. Since the labor is much cheaper in China than in Hong Kong, the Chinese built factories and a city just across the river; many of the "Made in Hong Kong" manufactured articles are now made there. A modern highway and fast train have been built to accommodate the traffic between the Shenzhen factories and Hong Kong, the busiest port in the world.

Our last stop on the tour was at the wishing tree where, for a small fee (HK$5 which is about US$0.60), we bought a prayer sheet on a string attached to an orange. The idea is to write a single wish on the prayer sheet, roll it up with string, and then, using the orange as a projectile, throw the whole thing as high into the tree as you can until it gets caught in the branches and unscrolls. If you're successful in this operation, then, sometime over the next year, Buddha will smile upon you and grant your wish. Of course, near the end of both tours our guide took us to a jewelry factory where we were held captive…er…I mean got to see how jewelry is made with a visit afterwards to the showroom where each visitor had two sales assistants to help with any purchases.

In the afternoons and evenings on both layover days, I did a lot of walking around. I visited the night market that invades a chunk of street space over several blocks after the main stores have closed. People set up booths and sell just about anything you might imagine until about 11 p.m. I suspect they all have day jobs as well, which must make for very long days. I counted over forty-five fortune readers in a row along what must have been Necromancer Alley, and maybe fifteen to twenty of them had customers. This and a lengthy discussion by one of our guides about lucky numbers made me realize how much superstition plays in the lives of the people here.

I also visited the flower and bird markets, a couple of blocks with nothing but flowers and then a couple with caged birds of all kinds. The bird market interested me most as many of the birds were wild birds caught and caged for sale. I noticed that the caged birds attracted a wide range of free birds that hovered around and perched on the cages. The men at the bird market, especially the older men, used the birds as a meditative focus. I have read that it is popular to buy these caged birds and to then free them in a sort of absolution or life-affirming act. Near the bird market are streets with shops selling live fish, turtles, cats, dogs, rodents, etc., streets with nothing but women's goods, streets for electronic goods, and so on. For any commodity you might desire, you can find a street with shops pandering to your needs. What a different concept from the American mall or the department store where one store houses a wide variety of goods for one-stop shopping.

I did make it to the Museum of History on my second afternoon for a too short visit. They had a special exhibit of the terra cotta soldiers from the Qin and Han Dynasties that were uncovered not many years ago (you might remember the article in *National Geographic* magazine). Although this exhibit contained only about twenty of these full-size statues, nearly 8,000, a veritable army, have been uncovered. The museum also had a great standing exhibit on the history of Hong Kong. It doesn't exactly make you want to cheer for colonialism.

As I have mentioned, our hotel in Hong Kong was top notch, and this was reflected in the fantastic seafood buffet we enjoyed on our last two evenings there. It served great sushi along with a wide variety of other dishes, many I had not tried before. Only the desserts, although interesting to look at, were ultimately unfulfilling, but then you scarcely needed dessert. The hotel also offered a couple of free Internet consoles which we appreciated as it obviated the need to find an Internet café. All in all we had a great time in Hong Kong.

From Hong Kong, we were ferried upriver through Guangdong Province to Zhao Qing on an overcast and hazy morning where we met Andy Pan who was to be our Chinese guide/interpreter for the rest of this stage along with our driver, Juan. As I understand the rules, a Chinese driver is required when renting a vehicle in China. Andy speaks pretty good English, certainly enough to work all the arrangements with Dennis and young Tim but not so good that we could have extended conversations with him about Chinese culture, history, and such. Juan speaks no English at all. Both are friendly, and Andy presented us with small gifts as is the custom. After some wrangling, Andy Pan found space on a bus for gear that didn't fit in our rental van. Then we were off to Wuzhou (*woo jo*) where our biking was to begin through Guangxi Province. Our hotel at Wuzhou was much larger than I expected (our room was on the fourteenth floor) and as nice as any in which we've stayed with the exception of Hong Kong. We will not camp again until we hit Europe. Tim K. had told us at the beginning of the trip that he could find no camping facilities in Southeast Asia.

That afternoon as we were walking around Wuzhou before supper, we were approached in a crowded market by a Chinese man on a bike with his three-year-old daughter perched on the back. He introduced himself in English as Mr. Su and invited us to talk over a cup of tea. In the ensuing conversation, we learned that Mr. Su teaches young Chinese adults three evenings a week in all phases of conversational English. He invited us to his classroom that evening to chat with his students since they don't get much chance to practice. So after supper, Kirby and I walked to the class. All we had for directions was Mr. Su's card in Chinese with the address circled. We asked directions of seven different people before a shopgirl finally took pity on us and walked us up a dark alley to the "school" which was located on the second floor of a building that looked otherwise closed. We would never have found it on our own.

At Mr. Su's suggestion, Kirby and I each joined a small group of students and just chatted with them for a couple of hours. My group consisted of six young women, and their enthusiasm was contagious. They obviously enjoyed practicing their English, but they were also curious about who we were, what we were doing, where we were from, and different aspects of American life. Stacia had been reluctant to come because Mr. Su had told us the students would be curious about our opinions on the Iraq situation, but this topic never came up in my group. A most delightful evening spent!

At 10 p.m. the class got booted out of the room. The students escorted us back to our hotel pumping us for more information the whole way. When we got there, we took them to the storage area and showed them our bikes. I don't know what time the party finally broke up. A couple of them took our e-mail addresses, and I began getting e-mails from them in their broken English almost immediately. <I was still corresponding with two of the young women a year later.>

The next day we cycled to Xindu (*zin do*) which was one of the most eye-opening days of the whole trip for me, so I thought the best thing I could do was to share with you my rather long journal entry for that day just as I wrote it. Where further explanation is needed in this entry I have used brackets, [ ]. Each entry in my journal starts with the same format as the one below: the date, day of the week, time, place, number of kilometers ridden preceded by a "B" for bike, the time it took to ride the distance, and the average/maximum kilometers per hour for the ride. These last four figures come from my bike computer. Where you see numbers in parentheses like (2:23), it means I took a picture of the scene, the twenty-third picture on my second role of film. Yeah, I know it's somewhat anal, but on a trip this long I'd forget the pictures' context otherwise. So here it goes…

2 Mar 03, Sunday 2:20 p.m. Xindu, China, B100, 4+08, 24.1/57.1

Kirby's and my room last night overlooked the large river the town and main highway abut (2:23). The government, after much pleading by the three-hundred thousand villagers, has constructed a dike of concrete along the length of the river to keep it from flooding the village. Amy, one of the young women in Mr. Su's class, said that before this year the village became flooded four times each year for four to seven days. The water reached to the second floor of the buildings in the main market area so that people had to travel by boat. She said Wuzhou's once proud status as a major business center, because of its location on the river, has been eroded by the new highway and the flooding. The dike will be finished in a year. Mr. Su said the villagers have never been privy to the plan and don't know if the large dike will have a foot/bicycle path with greenery (his preference) or a road built on the dike for cars. He said many very old Banyan trees were cut down for the project.

Anyway, because of the project, the air is continuously full of dust. A water truck makes periodic runs down the highway to dampen the dust. The dust combined with all the smoke and fumes makes the air hard to breathe and perpetually misty. After we returned from the class, we pulled the window closed part way and pulled the drapes to filter the air for the night. I was getting congested and was hacking, but this solution helped a lot.

We got a good night's sleep and got up early to a big Chinese breakfast. No more muesuli and toast for awhile it seems. We had chicken and rice soup, tofu sandwiched around a meat paste with a sauce, fried rice, a large soggy wonton, a large doughy pastry with a meat filling, mini-sized plain omelets (I skipped them), apple and pear chunks in a mayonnaise sauce, and a few other dishes all served family style. Last night we finished most of the many bowls of food, but this morning we left a lot of food—you just don't want that much heavy food before riding.

Getting out of Wuzhou was chaotic. The morning traffic of bicycles, tricycles with shelters, motor scooters, motorcycles, three-wheeled motor-cycles called tuk-tuks, a few cars, more trucks with three and four wheels, buses, three-wheeled truck-lets, van-lets, something called a grasshopper which is a three-wheeled truck with its engine and front wheel sticking out three feet in front, and lots and lots of people on foot with only general traffic guidelines keeps a foreign rider on his toes. We four began together but each had to make our own way out of the city center. The further out you got the more orderly it seemed. The many villages we passed through today weren't as bad because we were always on the main highway, but the motor vehicles still blew their horns as they zoomed past to warn and scatter the pedestrians and bicyclists. Horns are integral to driving here, much welcomed by the bicyclist for the warning you get.

Within Wuzhou and for the first 12 km outside of it, the road was largely broken and cracked though the surface itself was a smoother pavement than in New Zealand or Oz. However, when we turned onto a new major highway (two lanes), the surface was wonderfully smooth with wide lanes and very nice shoulders. This dream road was our route for most of the rest of the day. It was as good as, if not better than, similar roads in the States. [We later learned that for Odyssey 2000, this road was under construction and the riders rode through mud!] The white lines on the side and middle of the road were not painted but were a mosaic of broken pieces of porcelain hand-pressed into place!

The sky was overcast the whole day. Only once did the sun try to come through, but it didn't quite make it. All the vistas were shrouded in haze that seemed a mixture of smoke, dust, and atmospheric moisture. We often came upon small, tended fires, and most buildings and trees were covered in a patina of dust. Many buildings we passed today were made of a handsome red brick. We also saw bricks being transported and stored. It seems to be one of the region's industries. For the most part though, it is a largely agrarian area. We passed field after field being prepared for the upcoming rice planting. Some fields were still dry stubble, but many had been flooded, and the farmers were running motorized rototillers through ankle deep mud while others used large-bladed hoes. The workhorse of Asia, the water buffalo, was also much used—a beast more reflective of centuries-evolved domestication I can't imagine. The animals are powerful, yet docile, sometimes controlled by the youngest of children. I felt as if I were witnessing scenes as old as China.

Although the living conditions were obviously far below the average American town, I saw no abject poverty. People were largely afoot; the personal conveyance is the bicycle or motor scooter. Although we saw a few personal or family cars, by far most of the motor vehicles were commercial trucks, buses, and vans.

Much more than in New Zealand or Oz, being on bicycle brought us closer to the people. I often called out *Ni Hao* (pronounced *knee ha*, "hello" in Mandarin Chinese), but more often people, mostly kids and young adults, called a cheery "hello" or, once or twice, "hi" to us as we passed. The greetings were enthusiastic and friendly. I suspect I greeted well over a hundred people today compared to maybe a handful on a comparable day in the United States, New Zealand, or Oz. Never has it been brought home to me so clearly how isolating the car really is!

The landscape so far has been varied. We traveled through and past lots of green hills and can see large hills or maybe small mountains in the distance. Instead of bulldozing everything into a straight and level line for their roads (though there was some evidence of cutting through hills), the road we took sometimes followed a river course, or up and down gentle inclines. We had no major climbs today at all. I was somewhat surprised at how much wooded land could be seen off in the distance and, although I'd been told I wouldn't see any birds, I did hear birds singing from time to time. To be sure, I didn't see any roadkill at all which, compared to a similar ride in Tassie, was like a minor miracle, but I'm reluctant to speculate yet on the reasons. Maybe I'll pulse Andy Pan, our Chinese guide [I did later and Andy noted pollution, deforestation, and villagers with guns as the reason. The Chinese government has recently banned individual possession of guns, and the birds are starting to come back.] On a couple occasions I saw groups of steep sloped hills, called limestone karsts, jutting from the plain. Especially with the haze, they gave the landscape a mysterious, very foreign feel...like a scene from the *Lord of the Rings* or other fantasy.

I must learn to stop and snap (photos, that is). Besides the aforementioned karsts, I saw a large pot-bellied pig posing on the roadside and a couple of water buffalo with calves.

Our hotel room (fourth floor) in Xindu overlooks the main street with all the attendant traffic noise and incessant honking (2:26). There are good-sized hills off in the distance to the east.

Morning. I forgot to mention the amenities. The hotel in which we stayed in Wuzhou was as nice as any we've seen with everything you would expect from a hotel including a toothbrush and a phone beside the toilet. They had a note in Chinese and English stating that if you took anything for a souvenir to pay for it, and on the backside it listed the price for everything in the room including the furniture.

The hotel last night had a very hard bed (which was nice), and a TV, but it was the bathroom that was different. It had a "squat toilet" which is a hole in the floor surrounded by a horse-collar-shaped piece of porcelain over which, as the name implies, you squat. The sink's drain is connected to a hose that runs the water to the floor pointed in the general direction of the toilet hole. The shower is a handheld hose with shower nozzle next to the sink with no separate drain or curtain. The water hits the floor and drains to the toilet. To get hot water you turn on a propane tank, which lights a flame under the hot water pipe to give inline heating. The hotel did supply a toothbrush, toothpaste, a small roll of TP, a thermos of hot water for tea, and two packets each of tear-open "Bath Liquid" and "Beautiful Shampoo." The squat toilet is the norm in China and, I think, most of

Southeast Asia. Of course, the hotels catering to westerners have the porcelain gods to which we're accustomed.

And with the end of this entry, that'll be it for now.

Ralph

Report #4: Greetings from China

March 14, 2003

Ni hao again from China,

On the road from Xindu, where I left you last time, to Zhongshan (*zone sean*), I witnessed two traffic accidents just after they happened and one accident about to happen. One guy driving a short van had run off the road, over an embankment, and into a rice field. I had to dodge all the field hands running across the road to see it. The driver was climbing out of his window as I rode past. The second accident was an overturned truck in the middle of the road. An ambulance was already there when I rode by with one guy stretched out alongside the road and a woman sitting beside him with what appeared to be injuries. The accident in the making was a guy lying under his truck which had stalled across two-thirds of his lane with the guy's legs sticking out into the other third. So I thought this might be a good time to talk a bit more about the traffic here.

As I mentioned in my first China summary, there is an almost infinite variety of vehicles on the road each going at slightly different speeds. Therefore, you have people constantly passing one another all along the route. When there is heavy traffic you often see what I call the fish cartoon analogy. You've seen the picture with the little fish about to be swallowed by a larger fish which, in turn, is about to be swallowed by a still larger fish, which is about...but you get the idea. In China, I've seen instances where a slow bicycle is being passed by a faster bicycle that is being passed simultaneously by a tuk-tuk that is being passed by a truck with a car behind honking to pass the truck. All this is happening while another vehicle is coming fast in the opposite direction adding its horn to the din. It sounds and looks chaotic, but it works. I think we Odyssey riders have added a disruption to this seemingly random order because, although we're on a bicycle, we travel through traffic at least as fast as a tuk-tuk and sometimes even pass trucks, grasshoppers, etc. I've seen and heard expressions of surprise many times as I've zoomed by.

When you enter a larger town or city, there are usually wide bicycle lanes separated from the rest of the traffic by a substantial barrier of some kind. This slows us down because we are continuously weaving in and around all the bike and pedestrian traffic, but it does provide a measure of safety from automotive traffic you generally don't have in most U.S. cities. There are not many stoplights in the places we've been, and most of those have countdown clocks so you can see when the light will change (great idea!). There are more round-abouts than lights, but the rules for Chinese roundabouts are different from those in New Zealand or Oz. In China, you get through the roundabout any way you can which, in most cases, means cutting in front of the roundabout. It's really every person for him/herself. As far as I could tell, intersections have no signs or rules and, as a result, everyone attacks the intersection as if they have the right of way. Regardless of your means of transport, you need to be careful around these intersections.

That evening in Zhongshan we met a couple of Canadian women who are teaching English in China for a year at a private school. They were elated to run into English speakers and so we chatted with them quite awhile. They told us the kids they teach (first and second graders for one, third and fourth graders for the other) went to school from 8 a.m. to 8 p.m. with several long-ish breaks in-between. They were amazed at what the children were expected to learn. One of the women also told me she visited a Chinese friend going to a university in Guilin (*gway lin*). The students must board at the university with eight girls to a room in two sets of bunk beds. Each girl is assigned one desk drawer and one clothes closet. There is no heating or cooling so they sleep in their coats in winter. With no running water, they must carry buckets of water to their room for sponge showers, and they do their own laundry—by hand, of course. Geez, I don't remember college being this rough!

That evening while I was walking around town, the temperature dropped twenty degrees in the space of a few minutes. It reminded me of a Texas norther. For the next several days it stayed between cool and cold, a damp, penetrating, San Francisco cold. It was during this cold spell that dressing for dinner meant putting on everything you brought with you. So our ride the next morning to Yangshuo (*yawn saw*), our first layover town in China, was a bit chilly, and I was cold-soaked when I arrived. The scenery along the way, however, was remarkable. We had seen the occasional limestone karst earlier in our riding, but, on this day, we rode into an army of them. Over the centuries, erosion has worn away what must have been an immense layer of limestone until just the harder lumps remained. Weather has continued working on these lumps, randomly sculpting each one differently, leaving fantastical shapes strewn across the landscape. The city of Yangshuo is built in and around these karsts making it a premier tourist attraction in this region.

Yangshuo is the hometown of Andy Pan, our Chinese interpreter. Andy's partner, among other ventures, runs an English class for high school girls from the island of Hainan which is due south of here. So that evening we were again invited to visit an English class. This time all five riders went. Again, the teacher split us up among the class, and the girls practiced their English on us by asking questions. My group also tried to teach me a little Chinese and had great fun at my limited success. These girls were younger than and not as accomplished as the young women on the previous occasion, so it was much more difficult to make a connection with them. I could sense their burning desire to ask the kinds of questions the girls in the previous class had, but neither they nor I had the language skills to converse on a deeper level. Too bad.

I mentioned Andy Pan's partner. He is quite the entrepreneur. Besides running the English classes, he has a tour business and an Internet café all in one building. There are many signs of the entrepreneurial spirit in China. But, of course, the leash has been loosened before with the result that people bold enough to take advantage of the new freedoms run the risk of getting cut off at the knees if the government cracks down again (remember the Cultural Revolution and Tien-An-Men Square). Let's hope it doesn't happen again or Andy Pan and his partner might end up casualties of what I will call "cultural evolution."

On our layover day, Andy Pan had set up a half-day tuk-tuk tour around the countryside. We were bundled two to a tuk-tuk, the tight fit welcome as it was a cold, dank day, and the open-air tuk-tuk had only a cloth window on one side to keep the breeze out. We stopped at several of the more photogenic spots to view the odd-shaped karsts including Moon Hill with a half-moon shaped divot that has fallen away to create a nice arch. At one point along a river, we saw a woman beating her laundry against a smooth rock. Watching her I felt uncomfortable with the incongruity of the two completely different worlds in which she and I live.

That evening, Andy Pan invited us to his family home where his mother and father were to prepare us supper. On the way to the village, Andy wanted to show us the house he is building in Yangshuo where he, his future wife (not yet identified), and his parents will live. It is a nice four-story building to the exact dimension and specification that he is allotted by the government. Because house builders don't get much land, they just build more stories. This makes for a lot of climbing but does provide nice views. The interior stairs are all marble (as are many of the sidewalks wherever we go—marble is cut in this district and is used everywhere) and the rooms are quite large. The toilet is a squat variety as is the norm here. Overall, I was impressed. He will have an awesome view of the karsts. What a switch from his childhood home.

Andy Pan's childhood home was very open and very cold. I did not see a means to heat it. The dining area was separated from the kitchen area and the other buildings. Everything was minimal. The kitchen was very basic with a dirt floor. The doors were kept open so the dogs roamed in and out. We sat huddled around an ingenious coal stove embedded into the dining table. The coal is pressed into columnar canisters with a symmetrical pattern of holes through the entire length to get the maximum amount of heat. The coal canister is then slid into a hole in the table of exactly the right size and lit to provide a steady, hot surface at the top. Over this stove his father placed a large bowl of soup. As we scooped out the contents, his mother or father would dump more ingredients into the broth that continued boiling right on the table. The meal was good (one of the dishes had whole chicken feet in it which is common in many cultures). Andy's parents were friendly but knew no English and acted more like servants than hosts. They did not eat with us which I found a bit uncomfortable. After this visit I felt that Andy's parents are going to have a real shock when they move to his new house.

While there, I needed to use the toilet and was led to the pig barn where a couple of porkers were shouldering each other for slop. I looked around and saw a *real* squat toilet. No porcelain horse collar on this number, just a four-inch slot between a couple of cement bricks on the floor of the shed (anyway, I sure hope that was the toilet). Since I mentioned the squat toilet again, I should tell you that Andy Pan told us we would discover many of the western style toilets in China are a bit wobbly or broken. He said it's because many Chinese don't know how to use them so they stand on the lid and squat from there. Reminds me of Crocodile Dundee trying to figure out the bidet in a ritzy New York City hotel.

The next day's ride to Guilin (*gway lin*) was short and cold, but Guilin's a big city, and our hotel had all the amenities, including a bath, so I indulged myself with a hot soak. It was heaven...well, maybe a bit small for heaven. Because we're being fed so well at breakfast and supper, I usually just go to a bakery and select a delectable or two for a snack after our day's ride, but this day I cruised the market district and stopped at a noodle hut for lunch. For two Chinese yuan (about a quarter) they plopped a goodly amount of dry noodles in boiling water, added my choice of meat (chicken in this case), and handed me my soup within two minutes. Then I was able to select my choice of condiments from about a dozen, most of which I didn't recognize. I did identify the hot peppers though and spiced my soup with about six of what looked like the most interesting. It was delicious. Also on my wanderings among the crowded streets, I came upon a couple of street hawkers using microphones to broadcast their spiels while dramatically demonstrating their wares. One was selling an aluminum pot holder to put over your stove burner to somehow concentrate the heat, and the other had a tool to cut glass; both drew large crowds.

At Guilin we all decided to use our layover day to tour the city's parks on bicycle. This was one of my most enjoyable riding days. We didn't do many miles and did those at a leisurely pace stopping often, but it was a beautiful day (for a change) in a pretty place. We went to the Seven Star Park and toured the Seven Star Cave which is massive but looks like it's been plundered often through the years, so most of the cave structures have been damaged or destroyed. We strolled through the zoo in the park, which was most unpleasant with a small collection of sad looking animals. They even had a large, old tiger on which people sat to get their pictures taken! We were accosted by a troop of monkeys who live in the park—the only relatively wild animals I've seen in China except for a few rats. Later, I rode to Fubo Shan Park (or Wave-subduing Hill) which provides a wonderful aerial view of the city, and I strolled through Pearl-Returning Cave which led to One Thousand Buddhas Cave where many stone Buddhas have either been carved into the cave or cemented onto the walls. It was an enjoyable day.

The two evenings I spent wandering the streets in Guilin I was again struck by the dramatic change night brings. At night the cities are brightly lit with people coursing through the streets in numbers almost as great as during the day. All the shops stay open until late but, when they close, the night markets seem to sprout on the streets in certain districts like mushrooms after a rain. Every night has a festive air as the business buildings, bridges, parks, and monuments are all outlined in multicolored lights often with designs like bursting fireworks or pinwheels outlining their façades. The street vendors are out in force, and piped music hangs in the air wherever you walk in the main business district. Another sensory delight is the smell of freshly baked sweet potatoes that seem to be a favorite snack here. In Hong Kong, I think it is the lack of real living space in their apartments that drives people to the streets...I wonder if it's the same situation here. Both evenings in Guilin I found myself walking around a lake near a fancy hotel with a manmade waterfall adjacent to it, both lit up to a pleasing effect. This was also the first place on my trip I encountered pimps on the street. I was approached at least a half dozen times, within sight of my hotel, by men asking if I was interested in sex or a "foot massage."

The next day we hit our first real climbs in China on the way to another layover day in Longsheng (*long sang*), but we also had great views of terraced farmland and tea fields. The following day Andy Pan and Huan drove us to Longji Titain or the Dragon's Backbone rice terraces. This is on someone's "wonders of the world" list according to a couple of tour books and is well worth seeing. We were there in the fallow season, just before planting time. Nevertheless, the terraced fields in the mountains are a sight to behold; they lay out before you as far as you can see. The people who first cultivated these mountain slopes hundred of years ago did so to avoid the warlike people below. They just moved to a place no one else wanted. Sounds like the ancient people at Mesa Verde in the southwest corner of Colorado, doesn't it?

Twice while in Longsheng a young girl approached me on the street to ask if she could practice her English. It seems gutsy to me for a young girl to approach a foreigner, but I've gotten the impression their teachers told them to do it as a homework assignment. One told me as much saying that her teacher does not speak English well. Both times, we just strolled down the street talking in rather broken English. I'm impressed with their success. Both young girls said they had taken English for several years but had only started conversational English in the last six months. I know I didn't have that much success with my German language studies.

From Longsheng we had a five-day ride to Nanning, our last stopping point in China. The first day's ride to Rong'an (*yo awn*) was our longest at 141 kilometers but was the nicest ride we had in China. The weather was pleas-antly cool as we biked along a pretty river with great vistas. I actually saw and heard several birds on this ride which certainly raised my spirits. Andy Pan tried Dennis' bike for about thirty kilometers, in street clothes no less. The next day to Liu Zhou (*lee jo*) was not pleasant. It drizzled the whole day, and we were drenched most of the ride despite rain jackets and pants. The clouds were so low all day and my glasses so spotted with rain that I didn't get much appreciation for the scenery though I did hear birds which was nice. The last twenty kilometers we were on a substandard road that, with the rain, was beaten into a quagmire by all the traffic and left us caked with road grime. When we arrived at the hotel, one of the attendants hosed us and our bikes off before we went inside. With the little off-route excursions I've done in some of the towns, I've come to view the roads of China like the little girl of nursery rhyme, "When they are good, they are very, very good, and when they are bad, they are horrid!"

The next day to Heshan (*her son*) it rained continuously for the first half of the ride and then on and off for the last half. On the way I stopped at one of the little stone shed-like structures that serve as public toilets. Of course, the only time I made use of one of them, our support van drove by. All I could think to do was just wave at them since my head and shoulders were clearly visible above the top of the wall. Later I caught grief from them since I had evidently chosen the female cubicle. I hadn't realized they were even marked. With all these cold, rainy days, we learned to appreciate the thermos of hot water and tea bags that inevitably grace the hotel rooms in China. The thermos is the most efficient I have ever seen. The water is still near boiling in the morning!

The final two days of riding to Binyang (*bin yawn*) and Nanning (*nan ning*) were uneventful with mist and a few sprinkles. At a hotel in Binyang we had a long wait for hot water after our ride. A solar heating system doesn't work without sun, which we hadn't seen in days, so they had to turn on their backup system. Into Nanning we had a tailwind that boosted us over the gentle rises without having to downshift, a biker's dream. I did have one of my few scares of the trip, however. I hit an unexpected bump doing about thirty kilometers per hour down a hill. My hands were on my handlebar extensions and wet with the rain so that the bump caused my left hand to slip off the grip. I began to wobble, but I was able to get my grip back just as I hit the dirt shoulder. I was going too fast for the dirt but was able to slip my hands down to my brakes and slow down just enough to swerve back onto the pavement. It could have been bad.

Somewhere in these last days of riding I finally noticed just how well-dressed most of the people are that you see along the roads. It is not unusual to see a man in the equivalent of a three-piece suit (sans necktie) plowing a rice field or driving a water buffalo down the road! This reminds me that I've seen few neckties, an indication of the antiquity and concomitant wisdom of the Chinese culture.

While staying in the five-star Mingyuan Xindu Hotel in Nanning, we had a surreal experience. Everywhere we looked there were Caucasian couples pushing, carrying, burping, and otherwise parenting Chinese toddlers. It seems the hotel is some sort of Mecca for groups from abroad coming to adopt Chinese babies (I didn't see any little boys, just girls). We saw a group from Switzerland and one from Canada, but there might have been others. The dining room in the evening was like a kindergarten. It made me wonder how Americans would react if there was a large contingent of Asian couples in a big hotel in, say, Omaha, pushing around blond-haired, blue-eyed toddlers ready to take them to China the next day.

Having the amenities of a five-star hotel was a nice change. I used the weight room, swam a mile in the double-length—but very cold—pool, and even weighed myself for the first time on the trip. We've all lost weight if the scale can be believed. That afternoon I went looking for an Internet café and saw my first and only cat in China. I don't know if they all get eaten or just aren't popular. Speaking of which, I have seen dogs hanging from meat hooks in several markets. Andy Pan told us that the dogs of the breed we've been seeing all along our route are raised specifically for food. This explains why I've never been able to coax one to come to me for a scratch behind the ears. Even the ones at Andy's parents' house, that I had assumed to be pets, gave us a wide berth.

The dichotomy between the old and the new in China today was most starkly driven home to me when seeking out a place to prepare these reports. I would walk to the town's area of commerce and pass stall after stall of beautiful produce and meat in a crowded, completely open-air market with a timeless feel. I would then turn a corner, down a back alley, to find fifty young people in a darkened, noisy, smoky shell of a building playing computer games on row after row of computers. I haven't seen any of the kids on the Internet yet, but this is where we go to access the Internet. Fortunately, as I type this, I'm next to the open garage door so the deafening game noise is only blowing out my right ear. Internet access is surprisingly cheap. Our hotel in Hong Kong provided it free. In Yongshua, I bought a bowl of soup in a café and was able to use their Internet for free. Otherwise I've been paying one Chinese yuan or the U.S. equivalent of twelve and a half cents an hour! The big problems are getting the Hotmail site to work (sometimes the connection is so slow you just leave and come back later) and, of course, you hope there's somebody in the place that can change your screen from Chinese characters to the

English alphabet. Stacia sent one message out to her e-mail address list in Chinese by mistake.

Toward the end of this stage, we started to tire of Chinese food for every meal, although we always had a nice variety as Andy Pan selected all our menus, and we could make suggestions. We usually had eight to ten courses for supper and about a half dozen for breakfast. Our meals, especially our breakfasts, were prepared specifically for us by our own cook so that our food came out one dish at a time as they were prepared, often with the rice last. It made for interesting eating. The food was somewhat bland and not at all like what you find in an average Chinese restaurant in America. I did discover one interesting fruit, though, called dragon eyes with the shape and feel of real eyeballs and a big seed in the middle of the translucent flesh. I got all I wanted of these as the others didn't care much for them. (By the way, I have three very loud young girls leaning over my cubicle commenting in Chinese on my every move. In addition, the young man playing a computer game next to me has been watching my screen almost as much as his. You get used to being an oddity with people staring at you all the time. Often the youngsters just break into laughter...don't know why. Andy Pan hasn't been able to or won't tell us.)

Okay, here's more bike stuff for those interested in bike stuff 'cause, after all, this is a bike trip. I've not had a flat tire on the trip yet!!!! Yes, for someone who had flats a couple of dozen times in the month of December 2002 while gearing up for this trip in Albuquerque, I know this sounds almost impossible (duh, no goatheads!). I've had a slow leak in my rear tire that I pump up every third or fourth day but no flats. Our mechanic put on a new chain at three thousand miles just after getting to China (I had about one thousand miles on the chain before the Odyssey trip started). About 250 miles after that Tim found a kink in my rear derailleur cable and changed it out. And that's it for repairs. Tim checks the bikes regularly and ensures the drive train is working well and is clean and oiled. Overall, my bike has been running great. I am in Nanning, and it is our last night in China. Tomorrow we take a bus to the Viet Nam border, carry our gear about a quarter mile across "no-man's-land," and then take another bus to Hanoi. So, I am closing this report and will send it on to you.

I hope you are enjoying these. The next one will probably come toward the end of the Viet Nam stage.

Take care,

Ralph

Report #5: Good Morning Viet Nam!

March 20, 2003

Greetings from Viet Nam,

Our trip from Nanning to Hanoi was a bit of an odyssey in and of itself. We drove by van about five hours from Nanning to the China–Viet Nam border where we said our good-byes to Andy Pan and Juan. We then spent an hour to get out of China, acceding to at least five passport checks. Having completed the vigorous out-processing from China, we began lugging all our gear across "no-man's-land." It took us several trips across the quarter-mile expanse before we touched Vietnamese soil. This all seemed like overkill until I realized that it was not long ago that China and Viet Nam had border conflicts in this region. In fact, our guide-for-the-day, who was getting us to Hanoi, told us this was the site of several historic Chinese invasions. In one memorable conflict, the Vietnamese electrified the river to keep the Chinese out! After ensuring all our gear got loaded onto the bus, we then clambered aboard for the two-hour trip to the outskirts of Hanoi where we waited another hour before the bus could enter Hanoi. It seems that many major Vietnamese cities have restrictions on when large vehicles are permitted to enter the city. On that Saturday, no large vehicles could enter the city before 6:30 p.m.—pretty nifty traffic management for a city. Can't you just hear the screams if you tried that in the States? Finally, we arrived at the Ministry of Defense (MOD) Guesthouse that was to be our home for our two nights in Hanoi.

The bus ride to Hanoi gave me a chance to observe the traffic, and I noticed immediately that the rules here seem to be as chaotic as in China with one added nuance: since our bus was one of the fastest vehicles on the road, it straddled the center line almost the entire trip. It was always preparing to pass, passing, or pulling in from passing another vehicle. I noticed other big, fast vehicles doing the same thing.

Before the trip Tim Kneeland had described that traveling from China to Viet Nam is like landing in Oz from Kansas—suddenly everything is in color. I didn't notice a contrast that sharp, but I will say that Viet Nam is greener, more modern and certainly cleaner than what I saw of China. The greener part could be partly attributed to the simple fact that we are further into spring here, and the rice crop is standing between six and eight inches high. In China, the rice was just being planted. With regard to the cleaner part, it's not just that there's less garbage everywhere, you get the impression that everything, including the environment, is cleaner. For instance, I began seeing lots of geckos from the time we arrived at the MOD Guesthouse in Hanoi. We also had a loud, very active mating scene in the overgrown fountain among the local *Rani* genus (frogs, that is). I loved all that croaking! And it was a different croak than I've ever heard before. But my point is that reptiles and especially amphibians, like geckos and frogs, are bellwether animals signaling the presence or absence of pollutants—having them around is a good indication of a healthy environment.

On our first evening in Hanoi, we took a walk around the neighborhood of our hotel to get the lay of the land. The first thing that jumped out at us was the enormous number of motorbikes. We weren't in a particularly busy part of town but, when the stoplight turned red, easily a hundred motorbikes would queue up in a thick pack waiting for the green. The roar and organized chaos each green light released was like the starting flag at the Indy 500 or, maybe, the opening of Pandora's Box. This scene was repeated over and over for the entire time we were out exploring.

I made another important discovery that night: they have ice cream here!!! We found an ice cream shop that was hopping on a Saturday night. The choices were few, but the cones and stick ice creams were just flying off the shelf. The clientele was mostly couples and families with some of the kids in their pj's. It had the feel of a time-honored town tradition, a Vietnamese Norman Rockwell scene. The ice cream served was only so-so, more like ice milk, but it sure was better than no ice cream.

While in Hanoi, we found a tourist agency and hired a guide for a full-day tour. Our first stop was Ho Chi Minh's mausoleum where we joined a long line of people who were there to pay respects to a major national hero. Ho was a remarkable man who unified his country and showed them how to win independence (I had just bought a biography of him). The many guards ensured respect and were quick to scold anyone with hands in their pockets, behind their backs, or otherwise engaged in rude behavior. I was impressed! Equally impressive was the Ho Chi Minh Museum adjacent to the mausoleum. The memory of Uncle Ho, as he is widely known, is treated with much love and respect. I did not feel the museum was filled with anti-American propaganda. Rather, the "American War," as they call it here, was treated sparingly. In many ways it was the opposite of how we would sensationalize the same information in America. I could have spent the rest of the day there. Outside the museum I explored the One Pillar Pagoda situated on the same grounds. It was old and interesting and one of the big tourist attractions, but I wasn't much impressed. I suspect it has much to do with my ignorance of their traditions and the pillar's significance.

However, the next stops at the Literature Temple and Quoc Tu Gian were worth more time than we were able to spend there. The Literature Temple became the first university of Viet Nam in 1070. The curriculum was based on the teachings of Confucius who has his own temple, ranked by his four major students, in one of the several courtyards. This surprised me because Confucius is, of course, Chinese, and China and Viet Nam have been enemies for centuries. Education has always been important in Viet Nam, but one of the early emperors was so strong on education that he, himself, gave the final exam to the doctoral students whose names were then etched onto stelae (stone blocks) which ride atop giant stone turtles that signify longevity. Both the Literature Temple and Uncle Ho's museum had much information translated into English, which was great for us. We also visited a cultural museum which treated Viet Nam's fifty-plus ethnic groups in some depth. Although most of the placards were again provided in English, so much new information was presented on a subject of which I was previously ignorant that it was a bit overwhelming, and I'm afraid not much of it stuck. The city's history museum unfortunately had no English translations, so it became for me just a collection of interesting things with no relevance beyond what I could deduce. We also visited several more temples, but by then we were toured out for the day.

The next day I swam in the hotel pool, lounged, and read until the start of Hanoi's famous water puppet show. The troop has traveled internationally bringing their mastery of this uniquely Vietnamese traditional art form to a wide audience. The theater was packed, proving that the art still resonates strongly with the locals. Our ticket price included a cassette tape of the music played during the performance and a program with English translation describing the set pieces. It was good fun. I could only imagine the strength of the puppeteers' arms and backs as they must manipulate some rather large puppets across water from behind a façade.

Shortly after we returned to the Guesthouse, we took a van to the train station and boarded an overnight train to Hue (*whey*). We had two nice staterooms if that's not too grand a word for four-berth compartments each stuffed with three good-sized adults and lots of luggage. Nevertheless, we had a sound sleep on the way to Hue. Upon arrival, we received a forceful lesson on how the Vietnamese make their trains run on time as we barely got all our gear off the train before it started moving again. I was shuttling our gear from our compartment to the platform and was literally shoved off the train by a very agitated porter on my last trip just as the train pulled out!

Here we met Tom, our Vietnamese interpreter/tour guide for the remainder of our stay in Viet Nam along with his cousin Bao and our driver Kwai. With these additions to our group, we now had more staff than riders! Boy, did we expect good service. As it turned out, we couldn't have gotten a better guide. Tom was a student in Saigon (now Ho Chi Minh City) at the end of the Viet Nam War and is now married and teaches English in addition to providing a tour service. He was willing to talk and answer questions about anything which added immeasurably to our understanding of what we were experiencing in Viet Nam. Evidently, the major changes in our Viet Nam itinerary from the Odyssey 2000 trip were based on Tom's recommendations to Tim K. <In looking back over the trip, I chose Viet Nam as my favorite stage, and it was Tom's outstanding stewardship that tipped the balance.>

One of the first things I did in Hue was to get my hair cut and most of my beard lopped off; Kirby got a haircut at the same time. The female barbers did a good job but had some consternation on how to tackle my beard, first with scissors and then with an electric shaver. This was definitely not a standard tonsorial task for them. After being shorn, everyone remarked I looked much younger, but my main concern was the heat as we continue moving south with summer coming on.

After supper in Hue that first night, Tom had arranged a dragon boat ride on the Perfume River. The six Americans were in a boat with six local folk musicians who played for a couple of hours while we cruised on the river. My favorites were a song where a man is identifying the ten things he likes about his lover—the repeated chorus was very nice. By the end, we could all have chimed in. The other I liked was a back and forth song between one of the gals and one of the guys. It depicts a village tradition in which a young man goes to the village, where his lady love lives, to be quizzed. His answers don't necessarily have to be accurate (such as the answer to the question, "How many feathers does that flying dove have?"), but they must be rapid-fire and clever. His success in winning the girl may depend on his performance. Sometimes the young people working in the fields will practice their questions and answers as a kind of flirting. Anyway, it was obvious that the song we heard was ad-libbed. At first the self-possessed young woman seemed to have the edge, but soon the older, more experienced man evidently provided some telling answers because the young woman became flustered. It was wonderful to watch them even if we could not understand the language. At the end of the evening we lit a candle, affixed it to a piece of paper, and set it upon the calm Perfume River to float away, each carrying a separate wish. It was a lovely evening.

The next day Tom hired a guide to take us to the mausoleums of the fourth and twelfth emperors of the Nguyen Dynasty (Emperor Tu Duc, 1848–1883 and Emperor Khai Diah, 1916–1925). This was the last dynasty in Viet Nam with thirteen emperors reigning from 1802–1945. The architecture of Tu Duc's tomb was traditional Vietnamese, and it was obvious things don't hold up well in this climate as it looked much older than it is. This is the Dynasty that lost Viet Nam to the French who began exerting their influence by forcing several of the next emperors into abdication and exile when they would not comply with the French colonial dictates. The architects of Khai Diah's tomb had obviously been influenced by the French as it had a more European feel. Most of the materials came from Europe, with France footing the bill, which says something about the insidious insertion of colonialism in all aspects of the host people's lives.

We also visited an old pagoda (the equivalent of a monk's monastery) and the Imperial City, Viet Nam's capital in Hue during the Nguyen Dynasty. The thirteen emperors mentioned above ruled from this three-walled city. Our soft-spoken young female guide told us that much of the city was destroyed by American high-altitude bombing during the 1970s. It was only the second time she had mentioned the "American War" during the tour. The Imperial City has since been declared a cultural World Heritage Site and has gotten some money from UNESCO. The renovation accomplished so far is extensive, even though it is being done almost exclusively without heavy machinery. I hope they are able to continue the work because the city is truly impressive.

I mentioned that our guide talked obliquely of the war twice. The first time was when, from the top of the twelfth emperor's tomb, she pointed across the hills to a large standing Buddha on an adjacent hillside. She quietly told us it was erected near a village that had been completely destroyed by American bombing during the war. The Buddha was erected to help guide the souls of the dead to the emperor's tomb. Since arriving in country, everything I had read and heard about our recent involvement in Viet Nam had been much understated and played down. The History Museum didn't even cover that period of their history, and even Ho's Museum downplayed that part of his life to an almost unbelievable degree. Tom told us that most people in Viet Nam accept what has happened in the past and concentrate on the present and future; I got the impression it is something of a cultural attribute.

With the time we spent in two of Viet Nam's major cities, I began paying attention to road signs again. I had learned to zone them out in China as I rode through the countryside or wandered through towns since their symbology is so foreign to me. The Vietnamese language, on the other hand, uses our alphabet (albeit without the *f*, *w*, *j*, or *z*), so I can sound out the words and get them to stick in my mind. Of course, they also have six different tones so that, depending on the accent, words take on entirely different meanings which can be tricky and even embarrassing. Everyone here, though, was forgiving and encouraged us to give it a try. Their language is also completely monosyllabic (i.e., all their words have only one syllable), which is why I've spelled Viet Nam as two words in these reports (yes, "Viet" is only one syllable the way they pronounce it).

After five days in Viet Nam, we finally got back on our bikes and rode from Hue to Hoi An right down Highway 1. The road was every bit as good as the best Chinese roads which, if you remember, I said were terrific. It was smooth, well-made, and had wide shoulders for the bikers. Only once did I run into any impediment in the bike lane. This was a crop of copra, or dried cocoanut meat, drying along the shoulder. Tom told us we would see all kinds of crops drying in the bike lane/shoulder since it is a convenient flat, warm place for the farmers, but we were there in early spring so not much was coming ripe.

I should say something about the traffic we have encountered so far. There are many fewer "weird" vehicles in Viet Nam than in China. I only saw a few grasshopper and tuk-tuk type vehicles, and those were being used for farm work in the countryside. There are many more scooters, mopeds, and motorcycles, mostly more powerful than in China, and proportionately fewer bicycles. In Hanoi and Hue, hoards of tricycles with what looked like wheelchairs attached to the front for taxi service flooded the streets. At Hue's Imperial City, we were inundated by an armada of fifty to sixty of the beasts, each with an oversized westerner wedged into it on some type of tour (I've heard two veteran travelers say that, if you see an overweight person in France, chances are it is an American. I wonder if that holds true here.). And yes, horns are still an essential part of driving here but, again, they were regularly used to warn other vehicles and pedestrians and, in general, we appreciated them. Unfortunately, some of the trucks are equipped with especially loud and piercing air horns that are more than a bit annoying when blasted at close range.

People here are as friendly, or maybe even a little friendlier, than in China, if that's possible. I had bunches of people call out "hello" to me on that first ride, and it was not just the kids. I got to the point where I would initiate a "hello" to adults as well as kids and, when I could see their reactions, they almost always broke into big grins and replied in kind. I felt very comfortable here. Throughout our time in Viet Nam I noticed that the children inevitably repeated their "hello" after I said "hello" to them, and their inflection and tone on their second try were dead perfect to my "hello." This behavior was so consistent that there must be a reason for it. I guess it makes sense that they would learn their own language through immediate repetition since their language has the six different tones to change the meanings of their various words. I also noted that more folks speak better English here than in China. The only downside to this is that the hawkers are more persistent and take the "let's be friends" approach making it harder to say, "No!"

That first day's ride was an indicator of things to come, hot and humid! The route was relatively flat with a good climb in the middle that provided nice views. I sure could have used a cold drink along the way and even went out of my way by a couple of kilometers looking for something cold, but I was shut out until I got to our hotel in Hoi An.

Before I close out this report, I have a couple of other "gee whiz" subjects to discuss and the first one is food! The Vietnamese food is spicier which, for me, means better than the Chinese food. *Pho* (pronounced "ff"), a noodle soup that is the national dish, along with a baguette (a French influence) with butter (the word for butter in Vietnamese is the same as French because, before the French, there was no butter here) and jam quickly became my normal breakfast. Also, I tried some very good new-to-me fruits. Sabolie was my favorite, but I also liked mangosteens quite a bit and dragon fruit to a lesser extent.

Don't ask me to try to describe the tastes and textures of these fruit. Their oranges were green on the outside (I've been told we often dye ours orange in the States to make them sell better). They also had great watermelon and pineapple. Viet Nam also had *real* coffee for those in the group who care for such things (not me). This again is the French influence.

Cooks in both China and Viet Nam know how to fix squid and duck much better than we do stateside. I had my best squid and duck ever on this trip! However, Viet Nam seems to have much less variety in things like bottled drinks and cookies than China, and this surprised me. China had small supermarkets where you could find a good variety of the aforementioned items along with many others. I didn't find such stores in Viet Nam. The street vendors had Fanta Orange, Coke, sometimes Pepsi, 7-Up, and a few others, but I didn't find any noncarbonated drinks in those first days and no cold drinks.

I was in heaven in Hoi An when I found several small bookstores with a limited but interesting collection of English language books! I bought a couple. I looked hard for, but didn't find, a paperback copy of Robert McNamara's *In Retrospect*, his account of the Kennedy/Johnson administration's bungling of our Viet Nam policy (paraphrased from his own words, I swear). While the shops had lots of used books, they also stocked new paperback books on the racks. These are inevitably bound in shrink-wrap plastic and, based on the quality of the workmanship, are obviously rip-offs. A wise shopper ensured all the pages were there, especially for the larger books. Kirby discovered that a tour book he bought was missing pages from the last section.

The official Vietnamese currency, the dong, was a little hard to get used to. It runs about 15,400 dong to one U.S. dollar so making the conversion in your head on every transaction is tedious—good thing I was a math major. Some example prices at a street vendor: D3,000 for a scoop of ice cream or *kem* (about twenty cents), D2,000 for a bowl of *pho*, and the Internet where I typed this report was D6,000 an hour, but I've also found an Internet at D3,000 and it can run you twenty or thirty times that much to use the Internet at a hotel catering to westerners. Tom told us to let him make any purchases for us because the merchants charge visitors higher prices. The entry fees for the temples, museums, and other attractions are more expensive for foreigners than for the locals (which I don't mind—they do this in New Mexico). However, the phone situation here is out of control. I made a call that cost around two dollars per minute so I'll stick to the Internet until we move on to Thailand.

That's all for now. Take care and be safe. If you haven't already, maybe you should write or call the White House or your Congress people and let them know what you think about our recent incursions into Iraq. Maybe it's time we started taking America back from our politicians.

Ralph

Report #6: Good-bye Viet Nam

April 1, 2003

Greetings from Patong Beach on Phuket Island, Thailand,

With this e-mail I will close out my comments on our Viet Nam stage. I left you in Hoi An last time. We had a layover day there, and Tom, our guide, planned an all-day outing (at TK&A's expense no less!). The tour Tom arranged for us was the best yet. We spent most of our time at an ancient Champa site called My Son. The Champa were an "Indian-ized" people who had adopted the Hindu religion and used Sanskrit for their sacred writing, much of which still covers many of the surfaces of the buildings. The Champa rule lasted from the late second century to about the fifteenth century when the Vietnamese eventually absorbed them. The site consisted of a series of old towers each of which was constructed for a different purpose. For instance, the Champa might erect a new tower to honor a leader or to commemorate a victory. The site is an UNESCO World Heritage Site with money promised for restoration. American bombing during the war destroyed much of the site. We saw workers laying out what looked like a giant jigsaw puzzle as they pieced together a damaged tower adjacent to a couple of large bomb craters from a B-52 raid that had destroyed it.

The towers look ancient because the environment is hard on them. The original towers were made of bamboo, but these burned down in the seventh century and were rebuilt with brick. The Champa had an ingenious scheme to create a solid foundation. They built the tower with bricks that had only been partially fired. Then they stacked wood inside and outside the tower and fired the whole thing at once thus melding the bricks together. The site was filled with phallic symbols. One was an altar with a rounded stone column rising out of a stone bowl supposedly representing the male and female or yin and yang.

The Cham priest would pour the purest spring water over the male symbol where it would then be captured in the bowl. This consecrated water was then stored in one of the towers. The Cham civilization is still poorly understood; many foreign and Vietnamese archeologists are currently working to unlock its mysteries.

Leaving Hoi An we rode for twelve hours to Tom's hometown of Nha Trang (*na traing*) in a van made for Vietnamese-sized people. The road was under construction (hence the van ride) and very rough. We were all glad to get there. The next day was yet another layover day and again TK&A treated us to an all-day, three-island tour with Tom as our guide. We went to a small, but nice, aquarium and hand-fed dried fish to the red snapper and sea turtles enclosed in a small pond. Then we boated to a tiny island surrounded by a small, live coral reef where we snorkeled to our hearts' content—a real treat; the water was a perfect temperature for long-term immersion. For lunch, we then stopped at a fishing island where we selected the live lobster, fish, or cuttlefish (a relative of the squid) from the holding nets to be cooked-to-order. It was expensive though; even after Tom knocked the price down, I paid D270,000 (about US$13.50) for a piece of fish—exorbitant by Vietnamese standards! That same day before supper, I had my first ever mineral mud bath and full body massage by a professional masseuse. The young woman used her hands, wrists, knees, and feet in an artful combination. She walked up and down my back and legs, popped my neck and fingers, and generally did a thorough job for forty-five minutes, and all this for something less than US$7.50 including a generous tip!

Supper was at Tom's home that night, which gave us a glimpse into family life in Viet Nam. Tom's house is among many that line one of the main streets of Nha Trang. The front room is open to the street (like the front wall had been removed) and, while we ate at a table within fifteen feet of the wide "front door," the family sold cigarettes to passersby from a small stall beside the door. Most houses on that main street have one of these little stalls, all selling about the same things. Although I had seen these stalls wherever we went, it was the first time I realized they are actually the front rooms of residences. I guess it's a way to earn extra dong on the side since both Tom and his wife have decent jobs. Maybe it was just a way to keep Tom's parents busy. The entrepreneurial spirit is fiercely strong in Viet Nam. Oh yes, I must mention a couple of superb dishes served by Tom's wife amidst a generally delicious meal. The first was a banana soup that was to die for—warm, sweet, with just the right flavor of pureed banana. Though it might sound a bit much for your taste, we all loved it; I might be able to make some believers if I can ever find a comparable recipe (I put this on my "to do" list for when I return home). The second was a cuttlefish appetizer that Tom's wife kept coming fresh out of the oven during the entire meal. We all became instant addicts!

From Nha Trang we had a relatively flat ride to Phan Rang (*fan rang*) with a tailwind no less. There we stayed in quaint, hobbit-like huts on a beautiful beach. The huts were shaped and painted like huge tree trunks hollowed out for apartments though they seemed to be made of something like plaster of paris. Despite the somewhat bizarre accommodations, the beach was great, and I spent several sweet hours either in the surf or reading under a thatched awning with a strong sea breeze in my face. Dawn was a particularly beautiful time here as the locals and regional guests alike were all at the beach doing a variety of exercises (jogging, Tai Chi, stretching, and swimming) while the sun came up. The local folks know the best time of the day for exercising in this heat.

While most of our riding in Viet Nam was relatively flat, the ride from Phan Rang to the mountain town of Da Lat (*da lot*) was anything but flat. The 125-kilometer ride had a five thousand foot elevation gain in the last third of the ride. Unfortunately, it was the only day so far on the trip that I just didn't feel like riding—all I could think about was the lovely sea breeze on the beach in Phan Rang! It was hot and humid, and I stopped often to buy a cool drink and to soak my head and shirt with water. I actually perked up when we hit the first climb. The steady grind coupled with a pleasant change in scenery from what we had seen so far seemed to give me energy. However, the last ten-kilometer climb into Da Lat was steep and unrelenting. By the time I stopped in front of our beautiful hotel my legs were rubbery. I was about as tired as I've been after a ride—ever. Of course, it probably didn't help that I swam a mile in the surf at the beach before jumping on the bike that morning…but then, how could one resist?

We stayed two nights in Da Lat, which is Viet Nam's honeymoon capital, with its reputed "eternal spring" weather and, indeed, the weather was much cooler than on the coast. During the war, the North and South, under common, but probably tacit, agreement did not damage the city. Evidently both the Viet Cong and South Vietnamese muckety-mucks had villas here. This is fortunate because the city is indeed beautifully situated atop a mountain with great vistas complemented by great weather.

Again for our layover day here, Tom hired a guide who took us for a day tour. We visited one of the last Vietnamese emperor's palaces. I enjoyed the discretion our young female guide used to explain the emperor's many dalliances and how he maneuvered them around his wife and family. The "crazy house" was next on our itinerary. This series of mostly interconnected hotel rooms built like an ancient forest gone wild was designed by the late President's daughter who is an architect. Each room has an animal theme (e.g., tiger, kangaroo, ant, or an eagle that has the head of a hornbill!) built into the fireplace. I don't think there's a square corner in the place, and the beds are built to fit into whatever space there is available which makes for some very irregularly shaped beds. It's a hit with honeymooning couples and reminded me of similar theme hotels in the States. This whimsical hotel is a work-in-progress as the architect continues adding more and more unusual touches.

One of the other memorable stops was the "mystery table." This is just a small, ordinary table with a round top that fits via a dowel onto the stand. When two or more people put their hands on it and say "left" or "right," the table will begin turning in that direction. If you say "faster," it goes faster, "slower" and it goes slower, "stop" and it stops. It has been studied by scientists and seems to work regardless of language. We read several of the many testimonials of previous visitors (the ones in English that is). So, we had to try it. Tom helped us get it going, and then we couldn't believe the wild ride it gave us. I'm not going to say any more, but I don't have a clue how it works. It was exceedingly strange. The family who owns it only discovered the table's mysterious properties maybe fifteen years ago. They allow people to drop in and try it without charge which makes me think it's not a scam. Anyway, enough said about things I don't understand. Our other stops on the tour were a wonderful Vietnamese garden in full bloom, an eight-year-old pagoda built with donations from Vietnamese-Americans and a gondola ride to the top of the mountain for great views.

From Da Lat it was back to the hobbit huts at Phan Rang and the beautiful beach for another night. Coming down the mountain was a lot more fun than going up, and I used the brakes more than the pedals for the first forty kilometers or so. Needless to say, we had a much better average speed that day than our ride to Da Lat! The waters of the South China Sea felt just as wonderful as they had two days before.

Our last two days riding in Viet Nam to Phan Thiet (*fan thee ut*) and then to the outskirts of Ho Chi Minh City (i.e., old Saigon) were long and hot, about 177 miles over the two days. Though mostly flat with good shoulders, the rides in Viet Nam took their toll because of the heat, so I thought I'd describe some of my survival techniques. Because of the heat, I needed cool drinks which, as I said in my last report, were not easy to find, especially when riding through the smaller towns and villages. Sometimes I would stop when I saw one of the clear glass commercial refrigerators (like Coca Cola) displaying their wares. However, these cases were usually not even plugged in and, sometimes, the proprietors had no place in which to plug it. Even when the shopkeepers did have drinks on ice or in a working refrigerator, they first wanted to sell me a drink over ice (local water and ice were on our "no no" list for Southeast Asia). Since most of these rural folk didn't speak English and I don't speak Vietnamese, I resorted to sign language and gesticulations to get my point across. When the shops did have cold drinks, they were often of new and interesting varieties. One of my favorites was Winter Melon Tea, which is just what its name implies and has a nice nutty taste. I also tried a couple of power drinks: Red Bull which is available in the States and tastes like melted lime Jell-O and #1 which Kirby said is straight sucrose, like medicine going down. Since I don't go in for sports drinks much in the States, these were both new to me. I tried a drink called Birdsnest which, according to Tom, actually contains a small part of a bird's nest in it (similar to the eponymous ingredient in bird's nest soup that is made from the spittle of a certain species of swallow). This drink was extremely sweet and had small bits of what felt like tapioca in it and was actually quite good. Then I tried Green Grass Jelly Drink that was also very sweet and was filled with about a hundred BB-sized pieces of what felt like Jell-O that melted in your mouth as you drank it—pretty weird but good. Tom told me this is an herbal drink made in Da Lat.

In addition to the cold drinks, I had to train myself to drink more water, something which I had never done well when hiking or biking in the past. But with the heat here and the kilometers we were doing, I felt I better stay hydrated. I knew it wouldn't work if I just drank when I felt thirsty, so I started taking a few sips from my water bottle every ten kilometers or so, and that seemed to work for me. Also, to keep cool, I would ask the shopkeepers from whom I purchased my cold drinks if I could douse myself with their hoses. They always agreed, and everyone enjoyed watching me soak my head and shirt. Once, just before the last climb to Da Lat, I passed a young farmer irrigating his field and caught his eye. I walked to the edge of the field, and he watered me down. Several times I also balled up my shirt and soaked it in the ice water our SAG van kept to keep our water cold. The cooling effect of biking in a wet shirt with the wind blowing through it worked well for quite a few kilometers until the shirt dried.

The hazards of the road in Viet Nam were not great. We were on Highway 1 most of the trip, and it made for great riding, smooth with a wide bike shoulder and just a few rough spots. You still had to keep your eyes open for the unexpected, like several vehicles all passing one another at the same time—at one point I came close to bailing completely off the road when one such configuration came barreling down the road at me. You also had to watch for unusual things in the road like a farmer driving water buffalo across it or, once, workers with a two-inch pipe lying across the road like a big speed bump. And then there are the armadas of kids going to and from school on their bikes at all speeds, conversing a mile-a-minute, with not much attention to the task at hand. But overall, like in China, the drivers are used to and mindful of bicycle traffic.

However, Tom and Tim K. did not feel comfortable having us ride into the heart of Ho Chi Minh City (HCMC) when they were writing our route guides, so we stopped at the outskirts and were shuttled the last seventy kilometers to our hotel. Ho Chi Minh City is about eight million souls (that would be sixteen million soles give or take) and every other one of them is on a motorbike! It must be seen to be believed! As a pedestrian, you quickly learn to just wade in and watch the "waters" part as you cross. If you waited for an opening, you would be appreciably older before you got to the other side. When learning this technique, it's probably best to keep your eyes averted from the oncoming traffic since it is a bit unnerving. I wonder that there aren't more accidents, but people just know how to make it work. I think a big part of it is that people don't demand the right of way as we do in the States. The drivers, motorbikers, and pedestrians all make way so that everybody can get to where they want to go with a minimum of hassle. As I've written before, it looks absolutely chaotic, but it undeniably works.

I haven't mentioned much about food in this report yet, but I must describe our first evening meal in HCMC. While still in China I had told Stacia about the great Vietnamese spring rolls that are stuffed with veggies but are not deep-fried since she is not a fan of anything fried. Well, it turns out they are not as common in Viet Nam as they are in Vietnamese restaurants in the States and that spring rolls in Viet Nam are fried by definition. It wasn't until we were in HCMC that Tom found a restaurant that serves the fresh kind, but the wait was worth it! We "rolled our own" from a stack of rice wrappers with several types of green leaves (including fresh mint), a type of mild sausage, and a crunchy deep-fried stick of some sort of meat. Then you dipped it into a divine sauce that I mixed with a surfeit of equally divine chili paste.

They just kept bringing more and more and more of the ingredients, and I seriously overate. I paid for it that night and the next morning but, if ever food was worth gastrointestinal discomfort, then that was the time.

We had a layover day here as well and again Tom took us on a tour. On our way to the Co Chi district not far outside HCMC, we visited a small amusement park where the big attraction was three hundred performing ducks (though they also had rice wine making demonstrations, native dancing and singing, and other local arts and crafts). A guy with a long stick would herd the ducks up onto a large slide from which they would glide down into a pond. I must say I was somewhat underwhelmed, but the locals thought it was great fun. Our real destination this day, however, was the Co Chi tunnel system about seventy kilometers outside Saigon. The Co Chi district is honeycombed with tunnels built by the local anti-American people who were fighting for the liberation of Viet Nam during the American War. The tunnels were multilayered spanning over two hundred kilometers. We were able to travel through several tunnels that had been made wider, higher and smoother so that large tourist-types like us could duckwalk or crawl through them. In one of the tunnels I felt a bat fluttering between my back and the ceiling as it tried to escape. The earth is clay and perfectly suited to the purpose. We had minimal lighting which made us appreciate what it must have been like when all the lights were turned out during an attack. It would have been severely claustrophobic. There were more bombs and defoliant dropped here than in any comparable area during the war but, though some tunnels were damaged or destroyed, the complex remained a major thorn in the side of the American and South Vietnamese forces right up until the end. The tunnel entrances were hidden, booby-trapped, and just too dangerous to mess with except by repeatedly bombing the hell out of them.

After lunch, we visited the War Remnants Museum in HCMC. Although we didn't get through all of it because of time limitations, we saw enough to make me retract my previous comments about the Vietnamese downplaying the war in their museums. This was a shockingly frank exhibit with stark pictures of wounded, dead, and tortured souls, including those directly exposed to napalm or Agent Orange, and children born with deformities caused by their parents' exposure. The museum had a couple of fetuses in large bottles that would rival any sideshow exhibit. The short English-translated captions also hit the mark. Although much of it sounded like propaganda, I had previously seen many of the pictures and read much of the information in the States and so knew it to be true. It just felt like it had a sharper edge when viewed in the country where the atrocities were perpetrated. In fact, the museum was previously called *The French and American Atrocities Museum* and was only changed, Tom thought, in 1986, probably to attract more western tourists. It was hard to look at and even harder to think about. Just outside the museum, I was able to snag a cheap copy of McNamara's book about the war from a hawker. <I finished McNamara's *In Retrospect* before I left Southeast Asia. The ten-page last chapter with his lessons from Viet Nam should be mandatory reading for anyone working in international relations within the United States. The Bush administration violated most of these lessons in Iraq while I was on this leg of the trip. Won't we ever learn?>

Tom's teenage daughter and a friend joined us on the HCMC tour and for supper the first night. They both attend school in HCMC. I got a chance to talk with the friend for awhile and was impressed with her English which she had learned from Tom in his other job as English teacher. Both girls, though a bit homesick for Nha Trang, seemed to be enjoying life in the big city.

Our last night in Viet Nam, Dennis, our trip leader, dropped a bomb. It seems that he had to fly home on family business, so we were going to have just one staffer and a Thai driver for the Thailand segment. Young Tim was to shoulder the whole burden of making the trip arrangements; of course, the four riders determined we would help him out as much as we could.

Before I sign off from Viet Nam, here are a few tidbits that I didn't fit in elsewhere: 1) Tom gave us milky fruit (that's its name) one day. It was sweet and a little gummy with big seeds in a core kind of like an apple. The weird thing is that the juice acts almost like glue and coats your fingers, lips, or anything else with a second-skin-like coating that takes some rubbing to get off. 2) There are more varieties of dogs in Viet Nam than the ubiquitous one I kept seeing in China, and many of the dogs look much more like real pets. 3) Just as we were leaving Viet Nam we saw a poster that said the phone rate was going to drop 30 percent! Guess we were here a bit too soon. 4) The girls and women in Viet Nam dress very modestly. The school kids wear school uniforms, which for the high school girls is the traditional white long-sleeved dress that is very comely. I don't know how they keep them so clean and white, but they really are lovely. Tim met a young western girl who had been spat upon and strongly abused verbally by older women on two occasions in Hanoi because she was wearing low-cut jeans and a short blouse that showed her midriff. I find I have little sympathy for people who, when visiting other countries, are completely ignorant of the local culture or choose to ignore it.

While in China and Viet Nam I wore long pants in deference to their modest customs when not on my bicycle or swimming.

Well, that was pretty much Viet Nam. The next day on March 31, 2003, we flew from HCMC to Bangkok and then to Phuket Island, Thailand. The flight attendants provided facemasks to avoid the SARS (Severe Acute Respiratory Syndrome) virus that seems to be following us around (Hong Kong, China, Viet Nam, and now Thailand). Kirby and I wore them for both flight segments.

Everyone take care,

Ralph

Report #7: Ralph and the Kingdom of Siam

April 10, 2003

Hello from Hat Yai, Thailand,

From Ho Chi Minh City we flew first to Bangkok and then straight down the Gulf of Thailand, across the snaky neck of the Malay Peninsula, and over a small gulf of the Andaman Sea to Phuket Island. We had magnificent views of huge rock karsts rising out of the gulf, just like in the James Bond movie for which they were filmed. These karsts reminded me of those we saw in China, but they are even more startling to see jutting out of the water. We were to get closer looks at them later on this stage of the trip. That evening, after the three-hour van ride from Phuket Island's airport to the resort town of Patong Beach, I just had time for a dip in our five-star hotel's impressive pool before heading out for our first Thai meal which was extremely flavorful with a wonderful curry soup. I was sure looking forward to almost two full weeks of Thai cuisine!

In the morning we got another jolt from Odyssey management. We had heard several days earlier that Tim Kneeland was considering a decision to bring us all home from Thailand because of the SARS virus in Singapore plus a Muslim population in Malaysia upset by the Iraq War and possibly hostile to Americans. In fact, I had sent Tim an e-mail the evening before telling him my input was to stick to the plan, that the dangers of continuing the trip were not more than the dangers of flying to the States and then back to Europe. Well, he had a tough decision to make, and Tim decided to fly us home when we get to southern Thailand before riding into Malaysia. The new plan is to spend the twelve days scheduled for Malaysia at home and then fly to Prague to catch up with the normal itinerary at the end of April. I was a bit bummed since I had been keen to ride down the Malay Peninsula to Singapore. We would have been following a route similar to the one that the Japanese Army bicycled during World War II. They caught the British, who were guarding their interests at the tip of the peninsula but who expected a sea attack, completely by surprise.

We stayed two days at the Patong Beach community on Phuket Island—I was not impressed. More forcefully, it was the nadir of our trip so far, an area of the worst tourist excesses. I suspect it is one of the hot spots for the well-known Thai sex vacation. Everywhere I looked western men of all shapes, sizes, and ages had slim, young (sometimes very young) Thai women draped on their arms or on the back of their motorbikes. It was so prevalent, it became cliché. In addition, our beautiful hotel was surrounded by an extremely active gay community with many businesses advertising gay massage, gay bar, gay karaoke, and gay whatever. Also, transsexuals have become so common here that the Thais have coined a new word for them, *katoey* or "lady man." After walking to the beach on the first day, I didn't bother to go back. Especially after all the rural places we've been, I felt like I was in a tourist slum. I'm no prude, and I don't much care how other folks live their lives (after all some of my best friends are Catholic), but I also believe in a certain amount of discretion and found the in-your-face excesses evident here somewhat disconcerting.

Our first direct indication of how Mr. Bush's war is being received abroad happened at Patong Beach. Andy was listening to the lounge singers until late, as he is wont to do when given the chance, when one of the young women addressed the audience to find out where people were from. Now Andy is very, very proud of his Pottsvale, Pennsylvania, home, and he volunteered this fact. Right in the middle of the next song, the singer stopped, looked right at Andy, and said, "We make love in this country, not war" and "We don't kill babies." Of course, Andy was nonplussed.

From the west coast of Phuket Island we bussed to the east coast and ferried across a deep bay to an island called Koh Phi Phi Don known locally as "Pee Pee Island" (*ko* or sometimes *koh* means "island" in Thai). Before boarding the ferry, we said good-bye to Mr. Rose, our Thai driver, who drove to Krabi (*gra bee*) with our bikes and most of our gear (we each took just a knapsack) to meet us three days later. Koh Phi Phi Don is a resort island, and it was a paradise. We stayed there two days in small bungalows just off the beach on a gorgeous natural harbor with a sheer karst wall forming the western side of the bowl. While I waited for our room to be cleaned, a young girl, maybe five or six years old, who was with the woman cleaning the room, ran to the locals' housing area just behind our bungalows and came back a few minutes later with her grandfather. He came up and took my arm indicating I should get my camera and come with him. When we reached his house, I could see a monkey tethered in a tree just outside their hut. The older man called a younger man, maybe the girl's father, who climbed the tree to retrieve the monkey. He tied the monkey to another tree and then used a hose to fill a tub of water. After that he began squirting the monkey with the hose. The monkey avoided the water as much as he could but was soon soaked. At that point he ran to the bucket of water and dunked himself in it, fully immersing himself. It was an odd sight. I didn't get the impression the monkey was enjoying itself. The young girl seemed a bit afraid of the monkey.

On our layover day on Koh Phi Phi Don, Kirby and I took an all-day boat ride to five snorkeling locations around this and other local islands. The coral was not bad and the number of fish was impressive. It was a great way to beat the heat of the island which was stifling. At one place I followed a small school of colorful parrot fish as they dined on the coral. I could hear them nipping off pieces of it. The karst islands we were snorkeling around are amazing, worth the price of the day-trip themselves. Erosion is obviously their major shaping factor with their sheer walls, many caves, and places where huge slabs have sloughed off into the water creating small islands of their own with interesting water passages between them. I enjoyed swimming through these passages. One, in particular, was very narrow. I swam its length underwater and was greeted by huge sea fans and other reef growth, much like diving a coral wall and way cool!

I discovered even better snorkeling against the western scarp of our own island. I found the coral reef there by accident the afternoon I arrived when I swam over to get a closer look at the wall. Evidently nobody tells the tourists about it because both times I swam to it (the second time the morning we left) I had the place to myself. It was the best location I've snorkeled outside the Great Barrier Reef. I went once at high tide and then again at low tide when I could more easily get to the lower reef. It was great fun. It was there I saw the biggest puffer fish I've ever seen along with colorful clams that closed in jerks as I swam by, beautiful multicolored angelfish, gelatinous masses of fish eggs the size of those really big grapes, and schools of small fish numbering in the thousands. One huge school of tiny fish was clustered around a short-armed staghorn coral, like a thick cloud. When I would blink, the whole scene seemed to shift like an optical illusion. I had a hard time judging depth perception while I watched them. Another school of two- to three-inch fish would swim right at me whenever I was in their neighborhood and then follow behind me a few feet while I swam by. I stopped once to see what they would do and got a nip on my back for my curiosity. After that I continued moving whenever they were around. I kept thinking about the compys in the book *Jurassic Park*—remember those tiny carnivorous dinosaurs that hunted in packs and killed the park's creator at the end of the book?

Well, we had to leave paradise sometime and straddle our bikes again, so we took the ferry to Krabi Town on the mainland. The cab from the ferry terminal to the hotel was the first real car I had ridden in since I left Los Angeles. Of course, with the four world riders crammed into the back seat of a small sedan, I can't say I enjoyed the ride. We stayed a night in a five-star hotel that had been taken over by a film crew remaking *Around The World in 80 Days* starring Jackie Chan (didn't see him though). The hotel grounds were very nice with an artificial lagoon and two large karsts just off our balcony.

After a good night's sleep, we began biking in Thailand, and it was back to the left side of the road again. We headed south and crossed two ferries to get to Koh Lanta Yai for another layover day. The riding was hot, hot, hot, but Mr. Rose and Tim kept us well supplied with cold water along the route. I wonder how many gallons per day I was drinking during this stage? We did have a couple of bad moments on this ride. Southern Thailand is heavily Muslim, and Koh Lanta Yai is 95% Muslim. Whether this has anything to do with the following incidents, I don't know. Young Tim and Mr. Rose stopped for coffee on the way down the island. In response to questions, Mr. Rose told the men sitting in the café that Tim and the riders were from America. Tim told me later that, although he couldn't understand any of the language, he got some of the darkest looks he's ever gotten. That same day, Stacia got groped by a motorbike rider who rode up close to her and just grabbed. Understandably, she was a bit shaken. We'll never know the reason for his action, but many of the women we passed were obviously Muslim by their conservative dress. Stacia, in her sleeveless shirt and shorty bike shorts, certainly stood out. She might have gotten caught in the mindset that such clothing meant she was a loose woman. Of course, he could have been just a run-of-the-mill cad. Luckily, this was the worst of it on this stage.

While on Koh Lanta Yai, Andy and I took an elephant trek. It seems the elephants are mostly out of work in Thailand but have been retained to do these treks (we were told an out-of-work elephant is not a happy elephant).

We rode the elephant into the rain forest for half an hour and then hiked another forty-five minutes or so to Tiger Cave. Our guide had a flashlight, and we crawled through the cave for an hour or more while he spotlighted various formations and a couple of sleeping bats. Our guide spoke broken English, but we could communicate well enough. Shortly after entering the cave, he started calling me "papa" and wanted me to go ahead of Andy whenever we crawled into some new place. I'm not sure if it was an age thing or what. At one point, he shined his light into a dark hole and said something like "No Osama there" and laughed. Because of our communication gap, Andy and I weren't sure if he was making fun of Americans or just making a joke. We were soaked and filthy upon exit and then reversed the route. Elephant travel is not very comfortable. We were sitting on a bench just behind its shoulder blades and felt its every step. The *kwan chung* (the Thai term for mahout) seemed to have the best of it sitting on the elephant's head singing, whistling, and crooning to it the whole way. His ride looked much smoother than ours felt.

From Koh Lanta Yai, fueled with banana pancakes and muesuli with fruit for breakfast, we backtracked off the island and started south again to Pak Meng. I scared a three-foot monitor lizard from the side of the road along the way. The rides on this stage were always hot and didn't have the varied scenery of many of our previous rides. They began feeling more like endurance rides than bike touring. Thank goodness for the SAG van and cold water! The last few kilometers to Pak Meng were along a beautiful beach with great karst formations jutting out of the sea.

The bungalows on Pak Meng beach were nice, but the water along the beach was so murky I decided to swim to the karst directly across the bay. It was a bit further than I thought, about two-miles round trip, but it's always worth it to view a karst close up. The small beach beneath the shear walls had strange sand that I sank deeply into as I walked to a small Buddhist shrine someone had built there. Even here the water was murky, and I saw few fish. By the time I got back to our beach, the tide had gone out so far, and the substrate was so mucky that I floated until my chest was almost touching before I pushed myself up and waded out. This was eleven days in a row I had been able to swim, a real treat in that heat. The rainy season was to begin at the end of the month, and when I asked a local if that cools things down some, he just said, "No."

It was almost a century ride to Pakbara Beach, and, since we got a late start, I took it a bit easier than normal. I rode with Kirby much of the way, and we actually enjoyed cloud cover for awhile and a cool breeze in our faces from one of the thick forests we passed along the way. I stopped at one point to help Stacia move a still tight-eyed baby kitten out of the road and was happy to see Tim and Mr. Rose at several stops along the way. At one stop I discovered chilled sugarcane juice at a roadside stand, a refreshing and energizing drink in the heat. Why I've never seen it in the States is a mystery. Kirby said you could add a touch of carbonization and have a taste sensation, but I liked it just the way it was. As we were passing through town about ten kilometers from our beach hotel, Kirby and I stopped at a 7-Eleven store for a Slushy and a Citrus Gatorade both of which looked and tasted a bit different from what you find in the States, but both were welcome coolers.

We had individual bungalows at Pakbara Beach, our last stop before riding to Hat Yai. After a bit of a rest I walked across the street to the beautiful beach on the Andaman Sea with more of those scenic karsts just a few kilometers out. Unfortunately, the water was not beautiful. In fact, I could barely see my hands while swimming. I swam out a short ways, but the bottom turned to mud, and the water never got very deep. Every so often I would touch something squishy with my fingers. They might have been little jellyfish…or they might not have been. Regardless, it wasn't a pleasant swim. It made me wonder about the local sewage situation.

Our last ride in Thailand was unremarkable. It was still hot so I took it easy, stopping often to drink and finding another sugarcane juice stand. Hat Yai is the largest city in the southern part of Thailand with everything you could want including McDonald's, KFC's, and 7-Eleven stores. Riding into the city was as hectic as any large city riding is, especially when you don't know the language and are following written directions, but we all made it safe and sound. The hotel was another five-star wonder with a pool and all the other amenities, a great way to spend our last two nights in Thailand. My two main foci for Hat Yai were to compose and send out this e-mail and to find one of the former Prime Minister Kukrit Pramoj's novels in English. Finding a cheap Internet proved to be no problem but, although I looked hard for the book, I never did find it.

Before I close out this report, a few more insights and observations are in order. The differences between Thailand and Viet Nam are interesting and illuminating. First, the traffic: I feel like I witnessed the evolution of transportation as I moved from China to Viet Nam to Thailand. There are many fewer bicycles on the roads in Thailand than in Viet Nam, not really that many more than you would see in the States, and I saw no bicyclists traveling the country roads between towns. There were also many fewer motorbikes in Thailand

and proportionately more small cars and trucks. Actually, with the exception of the current American obsession for SUV's and other oversized gas guzzlers, the proportions among the modes of traffic is not much different between the States and Thailand. I saw lots of pickup trucks with beds full of passengers; these, plus the small, open truck-taxis, are the main way common folk get around.

The major roads again were excellent in terms of smoothness and width. On Highway 4 over which we traveled much of the way, we had the luxury of a shoulder more than twice the width of a shoulder on a similar road in the States. However, unlike in Viet Nam, we shared this shoulder with motor-bikes…and they do use the lane. In fact, there are signs everywhere directing them to use it. The secondary roads don't have shoulders with the same width, but they are still sufficient. Of course, when you get off the major roads, you can run into rougher surfaces and once, on our way to the remote beach resort on Koh Lanta Yai, we hit a couple three-kilometer stretches of rough dirt road.

I also got the impression that the drivers are a bit less forgiving to bicyclists. Several times I was beeped back into my bike lane by traffic approaching from the rear. Overall though, drivers and motorbike riders were polite (minus the bounder Stacia ran into, of course). In Thailand, as in Viet Nam and China, young kids and even adults yelled out "hello" as we passed. I'm not sure English is taught as pervasively in Thailand as it is currently in Viet Nam, though, since the pronunciation is not as good, and often the greeting is something other than "hello." However, Thais working in a service profession have better English than those similarly employed in Viet Nam.

I saw fewer people out and about. In particular, the number of school kids along the road was much less than in China or Viet Nam. I did see quite a few school age kids; they just weren't going to or from school. This might be explained by the fact that the Thai New Year holiday is on the thirteenth so maybe there is a two-week school break prior to it similar to our Xmas/New Year school break. Another reason might be the heat. We were riding during the hottest time of the day and often saw people lounging about on porches, in hammocks, etc.—a smart idea. I got chased by just one dog in Thailand. It was almost straight up noon and made me wonder if it were mad a la the phrase, "Mad dogs and Englishmen go out in the noon day sun." A couple of times while riding, I took advantage of the various open-air shelters along the roads at regular intervals to get out of the intense sun. At first I took them for bus stops, but I never saw a bus stopped at one of them, yet I often saw people lounging in them with their motorbikes beside them. Maybe they are there just so people can get out of the sun.

I'm not sure I can provide a general reading on accommodations since we stayed at beach resorts in all but three circumstances and those were five-star hotels. A couple of the beach bungalows were modest and primarily served Thai vacationers. The beds were generally firm, the rooms neat and clean, and the bathrooms more commodious (pun not intended) and of what I've been calling the "flush" type bathroom. That is, the shower is a hose mounted on one wall with a drain in the corner and the whole room is tile, porcelain, or chrome giving the impression that one could just "flush" the entire room to clean it. The rooms had air-conditioning more often than not, and most of the units actually succeeded in overcoming the outside heat. Overall, the rooms were satisfactory. And not a squat style toilet in sight!

E-mail was everywhere and generally faster than in Viet Nam. It was also cheap, one or two baht per minute in most places, with an exchange rate of about B40 equal to US$1. The system I typed this report on was B50 per hour with the second hour free! The phone system is what had me flummoxed. Public phone booths seem to be everywhere you look, but there are six or eight different kinds only three of which that accepted my MCI access number. Every time I stopped to make a phone call I felt like I was playing a form of Russian roulette.

But it was the food that has been the high point for me in Thailand. It's surprising how China, Viet Nam, and Thailand all have about the same basic foodstuffs and yet how differently they prepare their cuisine. Vietnamese food was much more flavorful than the province we biked through in China, and Thailand...well, as young Tim would say, "It's like having a party in your mouth and everyone is invited!" Of course, it's for the curry that many go to Thai restaurants in the States, but the satays in Thailand were delicious as well. The Thai's use of lime juice is wonderful (including iced lime juice as a great drink), and their soups were also great. We had wonderful banana soup two different nights—neither was quite as good as the one Tom's wife made for us in Viet Nam, but they were darn close.

Our last two evening meals in the Hat Yai hotel were probably our best meals yet. That first night my chicken Panang was the best Panang curry I had while in Thailand—beef Panang was my favorite Thai dish for many years. We had real Thai iced tea for the first time on the trip (whenever I had asked about the iced tea on the menu before, it was always Lipton). As some of you know, Thai iced tea is to die for (at least it is if you have a sweet tooth of my proportions). Well, this tea wasn't as sweet as what you generally get stateside, but it was certainly close enough for me to have four glasses. Also, that night we had what I believe is a traditional Muslim dish that was delicious. A ball of dough was spread out on a grill, filled with a chicken concoction (or beef or tuna), and then folded over like an omelet. You could then eat it plain or with a bit of curry or a sweet pepper or cucumber sauce over it. I was in seventh heaven and, of course, overdid it. They had the same Muslim dish at our breakfast buffet our last morning. The unbelievable aspect of the meal that first night is that the tea, the Muslim dish cooked to order, a full salad bar, a full fruit bar, and several desserts were included for B35 (less than a dollar!) if you got a main course, in my case the chicken Panang at B80. So, here we were sitting in the restaurant of a five-star hotel and were stuffing ourselves on outstanding food for less than US$3!!! Heaven to a hungry biker! The next night, by the way, they provided a full Japanese buffet with more sushi and more varied Japanese dishes than I've ever seen before. Absolutely delicious. Stacia was the one in heaven that night as Japanese is her favorite cuisine.

Overall, except for the food, I have been a bit disappointed in Thailand. My expectations were huge from talking to people, including a favorite nephew who has made numerous trips here. I realized fairly early in our stay why this was. We spent all our time in the southern part of the country and missed the more mountainous, wild districts in the north that had sounded so interesting in previous discussions. Very likely the biking and logistics would have been more difficult for a trip in the north, and Tim K. had to make the cut somewhere. I took heart in thinking this would give me good reason to come back and explore some more.

I would much rather continue our ride down the Malay Peninsula and take my chances than return to the States. It is obvious we are in a Muslim area, just sixty kilometers from Malaysia. A friend sent me an e-mail saying the Thai government has received notice that a Thai Muslim faction plans to terrorize westerners on Thai New Year, April 13, which is the day after we leave for the States. I have mixed feelings because the Thai New Year celebration is supposed to be lots of fun with everyone throwing water. I did see a plea by the Thai government for Thai women (not westerners or *farang* as we are known) to respect the occasion by not wearing blouses with spaghetti straps or similar clothing. They don't want the celebration to become a "wet T-shirt contest" which could incite violence in this conservative culture. <As far as I know there were no incidents reported.>

Young Tim was successful in scraping up bike boxes for our trip back to the States. Our routes have us all flying to Bangkok, then to Taipei, Taiwan, and a red eye to either Los Angeles or San Francisco. I have a layover in Los Angeles sleeping in one of Tim K. and Bobbi's guest rooms, but Kirby and Andy have two red-eye flights in the same calendar day. I leave it for you international dateline enthusiasts to figure that one out, but I will give you a hint: we arrive in Los Angeles three hours earlier than we take off in Taipei!

This ends my reminiscences until we rejoin our trip in Prague on April 25. I hope you have been enjoying these rambling thoughts.

Take care and stay healthy,

Ralph

Report #8: A(nother) Tramp Abroad

May 7, 2003

Guten tag from Munich, Germany,

"Travel is fatal to prejudice, bigotry, and narrowmindedness"

—Mark Twain from *A Tramp Abroad*

Well, we're back on the road again after our SARS "vacation," this time in Europe for about six months. We started in the Czech Republic and are making our way west to the French coast.

My brief sojourn home to Albuquerque was relaxing. I rode a half dozen times with the New Mexico Touring Society, went to a couple of movies, completed my 2002 taxes including my first state tax return since 1980, wrote scathing letters to four New Mexican Congress Persons for not stopping this ill-advised and dangerous war, and I ate lots of New Mexican green chile. The flight to Prague was uneventful. I had a seat in the last row of the plane for the long flight over the big pond, but it tilted back and was by a window so I was happy. It was clear I was really leaving the southwest when, on the leg from Minneapolis–St. Paul to Amsterdam, we flew over the southern tip of Lake Superior with waves pushing ice onto its shore wand all the smaller lakes frozen solid. I sure don't miss living in northern climes. The Amsterdam airport is a worldwide hub for travel as I discovered when walking through the terminal where I saw a charity drop-box for South Africans with Nelson Mandela's picture on it.

One of the reasons I was looking forward to this stage of the trip is all the new blood. We have a whole new staff and four new riders. First, the staff: Bobbi, Tim Kneeland's partner, is the leader for this stage of the trip. She is a steady, double-century rider who completed Odyssey 2000 and, as we were to find out, thinks about things from a rider's perspective, a real plus for us. Forrest is a good friend of Bobbi and Tim's who lives in the Los Angeles area and is along as our mechanic. I met him on our initial bike ride in Los Angeles but didn't remember him until I saw him again in Prague. Pierre is a veteran French-Canadian bike tour staffer temporarily out of work because his regular employer doesn't have enough business right now. He will help Tim drive the route and get everything set for us and will then relieve Forrest who will fly home from Munich with Tim. Yes, yes, I know it's all very confusing, but so far it's working fine. I don't know what's up with young Tim, our mechanic for the first three months of the tour. I do know that when he arrived home from Thailand he was running a temperature. He checked in with the doc and was immediately quarantined in the hospital for about eight hours and then again at home for two days before they realized we'd been out of the SARS area for much longer than the incubation period. Anyhow, we all wish him a quick trip back. <The doctors were unable to pinpoint Tim's problems so, unfortunately, he did not join us for the remainder of the trip.>

We also have four new riders joining us for the Prague to Geneva stage. Ron and Sara are a couple from Reno. Ron won this stage in a raffle last fall, and Sara came along for the ride even though she was not previously a bicyclist (despite this, just before sending out this report, she completed a full century ride over nontrivial terrain!). Loic is a French dentist with a wife and three little ones at home that he is away from for the first time. They provided him with a thick packet of letters, to be opened one each day, containing a photograph of his family and a note. He's shared a few of them with me; it's a cute idea, and Loic thoroughly enjoyed them. Amy is a nurse from the San Francisco bay area and a solid rider. Unfortunately, she took a tumble at the tail end of our century ride into Munich two days ago and shattered her elbow, so she's spending the next few days in hospital and will then fly home—what a bummer!!! Finally, Stacia stayed home a few more days to attend her sister's graduation and then joined us when we reached Vienna.

Tim Kneeland and Bobbi met me at the Prague airport and drove me to our hotel. After lugging my baggage to my room and a short power nap, Forrest and I set out to explore the city while waiting for the other riders to arrive. If you come to Europe, make sure Prague is one of your destinations. It is a beautiful city that remained relatively unscathed during World War II and is steeped in history. Many of its streets are cobblestone laid in an attractive fan-shaped pattern (as I've subsequently seen in other cities), and its sidewalks in the older sections are one-inch square granite mosaic. Most of the statues and buildings are covered in a thick coating of soot; nevertheless, the city is "old world" picturesque. After a short walk, we crossed the Vtlana (or Moldau) River to the Mala Strama (or Small Quarter) via the pedestrian Karlov Most (or Charles Bridge) which, with all the street performers and vendors, is a tourist magnet. Here I picked up some koruna, the Czech currency, at about Kčs 30 to the dollar, and we just had time before supper to visit a museum of torture that not only exhibited some sixty implements of torture but also described their use in words and pictures. It's hard to conceive of the brutalities man invents for his fellow man.

At supper I met Ron, Sara and Amy (Loic showed up the next day) and had my first Czech meal: chicken, broccoli, Gorgonzola cheese, an okay salad, and hot raspberries over ice cream for dessert—very different from our meals in Southeast Asia and very good. Then it was to bed. Even the faint beat of techno-pop from a disco in the next building that leaked through my earplugs did not keep me awake that night as I was dog-tired.

The next day we mercifully had a layover in Prague to recover from the long flight. The riders all decided on a four-hour city tour where the young guide, a college student studying languages and music, related much about the city's history and provided a context for the old buildings, wide boulevards, and several bridges across the Moldau which runs through the city. A large astronomical clock dominating one city square was particularly interesting. It provides sun and moon positions as well as the astrological signs for 360 common Czech names which are celebrated on "name day." I also found it interesting to see where Franz Kafka, one of the more tortured authors I've read, was born and lived. I got a better grasp of the term *Kafkaesque* while in Prague. After touring the newer part of the city we crossed the Charles Bridge and took a tram to Prague Castle where we wandered through the courtyards and the large Catholic Church within its walls.

The tour ended at the castle so, after admiring the city view from this dominant aerie, I hiked across town to the National Museum. I browsed its natural history collection for awhile but finally gave it up since few placards were in English. Supper was at a brew pub where I had goulash soup, venison with cranberry sauce, a dumpling, and a sundae for dessert. Unfortunately, it sounds better than it tasted. In addition, after multiple requests for a glass of water, I finally walked back to my room in the next building to get my water bottle as the service for water was much, much slower than for beer or ale.

This region has an interesting history, so I thought a short summary would be in order before I continue on with our tour. The area was colonized (or overrun) by Celtic and then Germanic tribes before it became an actual state. The Czech kingdom was consolidated in AD 995 by King Wenceslas (the "good" king of Xmas carol fame) who created the first dynasty and brought Christianity to the Czech people. He was subsequently canonized and is the patron saint of the Czechs. Charles IV was the greatest king during the second dynasty in the fourteenth century. He constructed the beautiful bridge over the Moldau River which now bears his name. In 1526 the Austrian Hapsburgs took over and ruled as the third dynasty until World War I. An interesting side note is that the Thirty Years' War which lay waste to much of Europe began in Prague when the king had his Catholic councilors thrown from the windows of his castle in 1618.

The Czech Republic came into being for a short time after the Treaty of Versailles, and then Hitler's Germany made a claim and took over the country in 1938. After the Second World War, there was again a short respite before the Soviets, in a grown-up version of Red Rover, claimed the Czech and Slovakian regions (i.e., Czechoslovakia) to be on their side of the Iron Curtain. In 1968 a loosening of the tight communist strictures called "Prague Spring" was squelched when Soviet tanks rolled into the city (a big deal for those of us who are old enough to remember it). Shortly after the Berlin Wall came down, a "Velvet Revolution" ousted the local communists in power; as the name implies, it was a revolution without injury. Democracy finally had its chance under a somewhat reluctant Vaclav Havel as president. Within a short time, the Slovaks decided they wanted their own rule and separated, also peacefully, in what is sometimes referred to as the "Velvet Divorce." Now the Czech Republic consists of just two regions, Bohemia and Moravia.

Our first ride in Europe was very pleasant. We all rode out of Prague together helping each other find the somewhat confusing route, but most of the day I was riding alone on scenic back roads. The Czech countryside was wonderful. It was early spring with flowers just shy of full bloom, the birds proclaiming their lust for life, crows soaring over a freshly plowed field, a pair of deer cropping newly risen grass with a small copse of new-green trees adjacent, and a small village high on a hill, its prominent church steeple pointing toward an azure sky sprinkled with clouds. It could be anywhere in rural Europe or North America, and it made me feel much at home, because during my manic jigsaw puzzle years, I must have worked a dozen landscape puzzles with these same elements. I knew inherently where each piece belonged.

Our route was mostly along river valleys, first the Moldau and then the Slapy, which always makes for enjoyable riding. We did have a couple of good climbs, but I was feeling strong so the kilometers flowed by quickly, and I reached Tabor before I knew it.

Our quaint inn in Tabor was run by someone with a distinct fixation. The hallways, bar, and common areas were filled with paintings of a sexual theme, most with a nude woman or just a breast or two or three. They looked like the results of someone's hobby rather than works bought at a gallery. Supper was also interesting. I tried the pheasant, goose liver, wild rice in a leek and herb sauce, fried Camembert over a green salad with yogurt herb dressing, and hot wood berries over ice cream for dessert. Surprisingly, the things I expected to be delicious, like the pheasant and the Camembert, were just so-so, but the liver and the rest were excellent.

The next day was glorious riding on back roads with lots of fields, ponds, villages, forests, and pastures in a rolling terrain. Surprisingly, Tim had two significant errors in the DRG (i.e., Daily Route Guide) which was ironic since we had praised the accuracy of the DRG's to high heaven just the evening before at supper. Kirby and I wondered if having Pierre with him was actually a distraction since he had done such a great job by himself.

Shortly before crossing into Austria we stopped to examine some old bunkers decaying in the middle of a field. I'm not sure if they were remnants from World War II or from the Cold War, but they didn't look particularly formidable. Just prior to the border I stopped at a service station to get rid of my remaining koruna. The girl at the counter knew what I was doing and helped me find just the right combination of drinks and chocolate caramels to leave me koruna-less as I crossed into euro-land. The border crossing went smoothly, but both the Czech and Austrian guards checked my passport. I suspect it will not be long before this caution becomes a remnant of a former time.

Before supper I rode my bike from our inn up the steep hill to explore the old walled city of Drosendorf since it wasn't on our route the next day. I was surprised to find the wall mostly intact. From what I could tell there are still only a couple of entrances through the wall so the town has just expanded throughout the nearby countryside. However, it appears the town's center of activity is still within those walls.

We had a gorgeous day for our 134-kilometer ride to Vienna the following morning. The day started cool and warmed to 75°F with sun all day long. What more can you ask for? One thirty-kilometer stretch boasted more ring-necked pheasants than I've seen in one place. It was fun watching them trying to hide, but not quite succeeding, in the too short grass, resplendent males, drab females, and a handful of young. I also saw some of the largest rabbits (actually I believe they were technically hares) I've ever seen, on a par with the jackrabbits in the American west. Despite the fact they hadn't yet shed their heavy winter coats, I would guess they carry more meat on them than our jacks. Spring was more advanced here than in Prague. Although the grape vines we passed had nary a green leaf, the crop that looks like grass and the one that looks like mustard (later I found this to be rapeseed) were, respectively, beautifully green and startlingly yellow.

I rode most of the route with Ron, an experienced and strong cyclist. This turned out to be a good thing for both of us. About thirty kilometers before coming into Vienna we hit a bike path to follow the Donau or Danube River. Now of course Tim can't provide all the twists and turns for a bike path on the DRG because he's composing the route guides from his rental car. He must assume that the path will be straightforward. Not so! At least not in this case. Ron and I were the only ones to actually make it to the hostel having followed the prescribed route, but we had to stop several times to scratch our heads or ask directions. The remaining riders resorted to the map on the back of the DRG and the city map Tim provided us to deadreckon their way to the hostel. Besides the bike path taking some counterintuitive turns (e.g., at one three-way fork, the correct path was a 180 degree turn back the way we had come), we also followed DRG instructions to carry our bikes up a wooden staircase where we crossed a bridge to a plaza, then pushed our bikes through the last door in the rightmost building, and rode the escalator down to street level! Ironically, after spending several minutes in deep conversation over whether this was the right wooden staircase, Ron and I looked down from said staircase to see a note from Bobbi written in chalk on the bike path exactly where we had been having our conversation. She had driven the SAG van ahead of the riders to leave us messages at some of the more confusing spots. I felt I was on some sort of treasure hunt rather than a bike tour. We did finally make it unscathed, unbowed, and unbeaten to the Wombats Hostel. Overall it was a fun day. However, some of the other riders didn't think so as they rolled in very late.

We had a layover day in the beautiful city of Vienna. The hostel offered what sounded like a "young person's" walking tour of the city that Kirby and I skipped. It was a good choice as we later heard the young Irish guide was severely hungover, reeking of alcohol, retching behind statues, sleeping on the tour van, and generally obnoxious. About halfway through the four-hour tour, he finally bailed out and returned half the tour fee. Instead, I spent about three and a half hours in the Kunsthistorisches (Museum of Fine Arts) which had many Peter Paul Ruben paintings and a couple of Rembrandts among others. The English language tape deck offered by the museum worked great. I also walked through St. Stephen's Cathedral in the center of town, but I wasn't as impressed with it as with Prague's Cathedral.

I next toured the Academy of Fine Arts with its many fine Rubens and Van Dykes. However, the main reason I hit the Academy is for its original triptych of the *Last Judgment* by Hieronymous Bosch. This is indeed an unusual work and, based on its startling images, I was surprised at its early sixteenth century antiquity. It seems to pander to much more modern tastes. Again the English language taped explanation aided my understanding but, for the Bosch work, the museum also had a setup I've not seen before. A good-sized computer screen, maybe two by three feet, had a segment of the work blown up on it maybe four times the original size. You could then use the mouse to pull up whatever segment of the painting you wanted to see in large format, so you could really get a good look. You could then use the mouse to choose a figure or even a piece of the sky and click on it. Up would pop a short one to two minute silent film depicting a graphic representation of whatever you might have clicked on. Many of the films were very violent or pornographic as you could expect given the subject of the painting; for instance, it depicts the fate of those who have committed the seven deadly sins. I would have liked to play with this awhile but, by the time I finished walking through the rest of the exhibit, which was mostly religious art, the academy was closing. Pretty neat system though. Someone has put a lot of work into the exhibit.

Because many of the museums in Vienna are grouped together, I was able to hurry to the Natural History Museum, one of the top ten museums in the world according to a Vienna brochure, before it closed for the day. Though I didn't have a lot of time, I can vouch they have an exhaustive collection of animals all categorized by family. I was particularly impressed with their huge display of snakes and lizards, each in its own jar of liquid that highlights their shape and color to perfection. The brochure also highlighted their mineral collection as possibly the best in Europe, but I didn't spend much time with it because it was well-nigh supper time.

Upon leaving Vienna the next morning, we rode against a stiff wind and under a lowering sky to the town of Melk where we camped next to the Danube with a huge Bendiktinerstift (Benedictine Abbey) dominating the skyline on a plateau above the city. The ride featured our first distant glimpse of the snowcapped mountains through which we would shortly be riding. After setting up camp, which was our first camp in Europe since the campgrounds don't open until May 1, I walked into town and then up to the recently renovated Abbey. They have done a wonderful job, and I wandered through the courtyards and poked my head into the church before finding a pleasant woodland path back to the park where we were camped. <After the trip I read Umberto Eco's *The Name of the Rose* in which this Abbey plays a small role.>

The next day we rode along the beautiful Danube for about sixty kilometers before cutting cross-country to Steyr. It was a gorgeous day with a perfect temperature, sunny with a light wind. Could it have presaged the very different ride to Weissenbach on the morrow?

My ride into Weissenbach became a saga worth relating. It was one of those days when the good things and the bad things seem to just about even out, so I'll treat it as such:

Good Things & Bad Things

Good: I was in good riding form this day.

Bad: It had rained all night and was raining as we started.

Good: I rode about twenty kilometers before anything untoward happened.

Bad: As I was starting up a steep hill, my chain broke.

Good: I had just passed the van about two hundred yards before, so the walk back was not too bad.

Bad: Forrest pulled out his newly bought (that day) chain tool, but it broke upon first use.

Good: Bobbi had another chain tool she keeps in her camelback (i.e., a water pack you wear on your back).

Bad: Unfortunately, she had mixed up her camelback with Amy's during a rest break moments before, and Amy had left with Bobbi's camelback.

Good: Bobbi jumped into the van, caught up with Amy, and retrieved her camelback.

Good: Within about fifteen minutes and, after much effort, Forrest got the chain back on.

Bad: Unfortunately, he threaded it onto my gear train the wrong way.

Good: He and Ron opted not to take the chain apart again but to pull the pulley off to fix the problem. They were successful.

Bad: After getting things together, the pulley wouldn't go round.

Good: Forrest took the pulley apart, lubed it, put it back on, and it worked. So after one and a half hours, Ron and I were on the road again. The van continued ahead to service the other riders.

Bad: Ten kilometers later, we saw Bobbi riding her bike toward us looking for a gas station. She had turned a corner too fast and blown the side wall of the van's tire on the curb, and she and Forrest couldn't find the jack.

Good: Ron and I stopped at the van and, after a thorough search, found the jack's hiding place.

Bad: The jack was obviously not rated for the weight of the van so, as we jacked up the van, the jack's metal pry-bar holder began twisting off.

Good: Luckily, we were able to get the van high enough to change the tire without breaking the jack. Ron and I were back on the road.

Bad: We were almost at the top of a long, steep hill when the rest of the riders came barreling down toward us. The road ahead was closed due to a car race; only Stacia had scooted through in time.

Good: We found an alternate route to Weissenbach, and it was very pretty with much of it on a great bike path with magnificent scenery. All's well that ends well, just an eighteen-kilometer diversion.

Weissenbach is in a great location with our inn directly across from a beautiful lake. We even got a break from the ubiquitous Wiener schnitzel (not my favorite) at supper. I had a piece of pork roast, a nice dumpling, sauerkraut salad, wild garlic soup, and ice cream with strawberries, all very nice.

We had a short day's ride to Salzburg, planned by Tim to give us the afternoon to explore. The weather was cool enough for mittens at the start but then warmed under an intense sun to perfect riding temperature. The scenery was again magnificent with rolling hills ending in a long downhill run into Salzburg, the perfect ending to any biking day.

Salzburg is a gorgeous town with castles and church spires set against snowcapped mountains. Kirby, Loic, and I took a city bus tour past Mozart's birthplace, Mönchs Hill, where we stopped for a spectacular view of the old city, remnants of the old walls built in response to the Thirty Years' War in the second half of the seventeenth century, the archbishop's horse fountain in the middle of the city, and the Palace of Hellbrunn. From here you can see a house, high on a distant hill, that the archbishop had built in one month on a bet with the king of Austria. Our tour guide told us that the salt mines about fifteen kilometers south of town, owned by the archbishop at the time, gave both the town and the river that runs through it their names. She also pointed out the location of what the Americans called "Eagle's Nest" in World War II, an aerie high in the mountains where Hitler wined and dined important guests. I think this is the setting for that great World War II action movie with Richard Burton and Clint Eastwood called *Where Eagles Dare*. Finally she dropped us off at the foot of the *festungbahn*, or tram, to take us to the eleventh century Festing Hohensalzburg or Fortress of Salzburg.

The three of us took the tram to the fortress where we kicked around awhile enjoying the magnificent views of the surrounding mountains. We were starting to get anxious about riding through the Alps. We then spent some time admiring Salzburg's Cathedral, that masterpiece of baroque architecture called the Dom, and walking along the old market street before heading back to the hostel for supper. That evening I spent time on the hostel's computer doing e-mail before getting hooked into watching *The Sound of Music* which plays on their community television set three times a day.

From Salzburg it was a century (one hundred mile) ride to Munich. It was only my third century ever, and I was surprised at how good I felt during and afterwards. I rode with Kirby for the first fifty-five kilometers and, as he stopped for a snack, Ron came flying by, so I rode the rest of the way with him. He set a pace I could barely keep, but it sure made the day shorter than I expected. We caught up with Loic and Stacia, and all four of us hit Munich in good time. My chain broke again along the way, and Ron was able to pull the bad link out and reconnect the chain in about ten minutes—I was very impressed! My average speed for the ride was just a hair over twenty-five kilometers per hour which, for me, is not too shabby for a bunch of miles. When we arrived at the International Hostel, Kirby's eighty-five-year-old mom and her friend were there waiting for him, and I had the pleasure of entertaining them until Kirby came in. They will be visiting us again in St. Moritz and Geneva in Switzerland. Unfortunately, as the afternoon turned to evening, Bobbi got a call from Andy who was at a hospital with Amy. It seems she had turned to get on the bike path, which in Munich runs down the sidewalk, and had hit the curb at an off angle spilling her onto the sidewalk and breaking her elbow…what a bummer! Good thing Andy was there to help her.

On our layover day in Munich, I took a city tour. There were only five people on the tour, and the other four spoke German, so I was odd man out although the guide did a decent job of translating things for me. I have found that on tours given in multiple languages, there is always a tendency for the guide to favor the largest language group. We did a circuit of the major sites in town: St Peter's Church, the markets, the new and old town halls, etc. We were in time at the new town hall to see the procession of the glockenspiel which occurs three times a day. The first procession in the middle tier of the clock is a jousting contest with all the attendant pageantry. The two knights on horses face off, charge at each other and one knocks the other off his horse. Of course the Bavarian knight always wins—after all, Munich is the capital of Bavaria. After the contest and below it, is the dance of the coopers or barrel makers. The guide told us that when Munich was devastated by the black plague that spread through Europe in the sixteenth century, the people became so frightened that, even after the plague danger was past, they would not come out of their houses. The exception was the coopers who came out and danced while everyone else was in hiding. The king was so impressed that, to honor them, he ordered the coopers to dance every seven years in the plaza before the town hall, and this tradition continues through to today. The last event animated on the clock is the rooster that crows three times above the other two sets of figures.

The tour included a visit to the Alte Pinakothek or Old Fine Arts Museum with paintings from the fourteenth to eighteenth centuries. Our time there was short, but our guide did give us commentary on about twenty paintings including works by da Vinci, Raphael, Titian, Van Dyke, still more Rubens, Rembrandt, and El Greco. I also saw another by Bosch in passing.

This first tour ended just in time for me to catch the train to Dachau with another tour company. This tour was touted as having native English speaking guides; ours was a young Irish lass. In our group were a young couple from

Perth, Australia, a man from India, the lass's Detroit expat boss, and me. The camp is well worth your time if you are in the area. I would suggest concentrating your time in the excellent museum where one could easily spend hours with the informative exhibits all of which are translated into English. The buildings and grounds have been reconstructed for the most part. After the war, the Czechs returned to Germany anyone with any German blood. The Germans needed a place to put these people so they turned the barracks at Dachau into family units. It was only much later, when the survivor organizations protested, that the camp was turned into a memorial.

Although there is still debate over whether Dachau was a concentration/ work camp and not a death camp, it is known that at least 32,000 people died there. While Dachau had gas chambers, there is no proof they were used to gas people; the smaller chambers in the camp were used to decontaminate clothing. When the Americans liberated the camp in 1945, Dachau held more than 30,000 prisoners with another 37,000 in the associated work camps that were part of the Dachau system. An estimated 206,000 people were housed there from 1933 to 1945. Dachau was the first concentration camp the Nazis built. One of the highlights of this tour for me was the conversation among the people in the tour group especially discussions provoked by what we were seeing.

As I edit this report for e-mail, the rest of the riders are heading down the road. Since my flight to North Carolina to attend son Joe's graduation from Duke is not until tomorrow morning, I had considered riding with the others today to the next stop and taking a bus back for my flight tomorrow. However, I have found too many neat things to do in Munich so I have decided to stay here and do them.

So earlier today, I hit the Neue Pinakothek or New Fine Arts Museum, which has works by nineteenth century artists, and again rented the English language tape recorder. Besides a wide range of German period artists, most of which I didn't recognize, they have a smaller collection of better known (to me) artists including paintings by Monet, Manet, Toulouse-Lautrec, Degas, Cezanne, Pissarro, Gauguin, Renoir, and van Gogh and sculptures by Rodin and Picasso. The big draw for me was the original *Vase of Sunflowers* by van Gogh. I wanted to see a painting, with which I was familiar, in the flesh so to speak. A serendipitous treat for me was a large painting called *De arme Poet* (*The Poor Poet*) by Carl Spitzweg which I worked as a jigsaw puzzle years ago; it was a particularly fun puzzle to solve. Seeing the original surprised and delighted!

After visiting the museum, I walked to the subway station to get a schedule since I am to leave very early in the morning for the airport, and then I headed to the town hall area to meet my tour guide for a *Hitler and the Third Reich* tour. The guide really knew his stuff, and I got a good feel for the short history of the Third Reich as we walked to many of the sites where its history was made. I then grabbed a snack and settled down in this massive e-mail café where I am typing this report. There are hundreds of terminals here with no attendants. The entire system is automated with the cost per hour changing constantly depending on how many people are signed onto the terminals. I've never seen anything like it. I have one frustration with the e-mail situation in Europe so far and that is these *$@# international keyboards. They have some of the letters and many of the symbols in different places from when I learned to type in junior high school which is a major pain in the tush, especially when you're paying by the minute or are in a hurry.

To end this report I'll now provide compare-contrast riding in Southeast Asia and what we've experienced in Europe so far. The four world riders are all enjoying the much more diverse scenery of Europe more than the relative sameness we experienced in our Thailand riding. The terrain is rolling hills with a good climb thrown in now and again whereas Thailand was very flat. Of course, it has been much cooler here to the point of needing a light jacket in the morning sometimes. The gals have been riding with long pants and jackets most of the time until just recently. The route is not as straightforward in this part of Europe as it has been in the previous countries we've visited. Most of the last eight riding days our DRG's have run to three pages, and once even to five pages. We have had only a handful of three-pagers before Europe. One reason for this is the increased number of turns on the route since Tim has tried to keep us on back roads to give us the best riding experience; this has been absolutely great by the way. Another reason is the large number of communities we encounter since Tim always notes on the DRG the names of any town we cycle through. On the first day out from Prague, I counted thirty-five DRG entries of the form "ENTER [town name]"! The hamlets, towns, villages, or whatever you call them come along about every two or three kilometers. Some are absolutely adjacent to each other. I don't know what it takes to become a named community here, but it's obviously not much. Many of these communities seem empty of people. After seeing so many people on the streets and roads in China and Viet Nam, it seems disconcerting to ride through a village and not see a single person, but this happens more times than not.

Strangely enough, it has been much harder to find an Internet connection for e-mail than it was in China or Viet Nam. There we found Internet cafés in the most unlikely villages. Here we have been in relatively good-sized communities that cater to tourists but have no e-mail at all (maybe they've just consolidated all the connections into this one mega-e-mail center I'm in now). Also, as expected, the e-mail and phone service are much pricier here than in Southeast Asia. Finally, just so you don't think I've dropped my obsession with toilets, we've found another new type. This one allows your deposit to fall on a raised place in the bowl where there is no water so that you can easily inspect your pile at your leisure. Then your flush brings the water down to sweep the pile off its platform and into the bowl proper to be whisked away. I don't understand the reason for this construction.

Well, I've been at this for over three hours, and I'm getting hungry. Besides, I'm out of stories. By celebrating Joe's graduation I'm missing the climb from here to St. Moritz, but I will rejoin the group there before heading off to Geneva. Tim and Pierre showed up yesterday and told us only one pass is closed that we had planned to cross between here and Geneva. Tim says he's picked a gorgeous alternate route. I'm looking forward to it!

Take care,

Ralph

Report #9: ALP is my Middle Name

May 19, 2003

Greetings from Geneva, Switzerland,

Yes, yes, I know it would've been more appropriate to say in my report title that "ALP is the middle of my name" (as in rALPh), but it just doesn't have the right ring to it.

My sojourn to Joe's graduation is over, and I'm back on the road again. We had fourteen members of our extended family there to see that he wasn't just faking it those four years at Duke. However, his mother and I have convinced ourselves he really did it. Now, it's going to be interesting to see what kind of jobs crop up. Joe told me that fully 75 percent of his class is still looking for employment.

Before picking up the narrative in St. Moritz, I'll backtrack to Munich to fill you in on the details of my travel to and from the States. I got up just after 3 a.m. to catch the subway to the airport. The hostel surprised me by putting together a sack breakfast for me since I would miss the normal one, very thoughtful of them. I thought you'd find interesting the German idea of what constitutes such a breakfast: a carton of milk, three biscuits, butter, cheese, hazelnut-chocolate butter, chocolate pudding, and a liver spread, each, except for the first item, in its own tightly packaged plastic-wrap. I must have been a sad sight sitting alone at a deserted subway station in the middle of the night gnawing on such fare but, hey, beggars can't be choosers…and is airline food really that much better?

The long plane trips over the big pond and back were uneventful. The first trip was Munich to England to Raleigh/Durham and the return was to Dallas/

Ft. Worth (just a bit out of the way!) to Zurich. The tightest security was at London's Gatwick Airport where each passenger had to play twenty questions with a security agent before even reaching the check-in counter. I suspect England is well ahead in the security department since they've been dealing with IRA terrorism for quite some time.

There was not much to see on the flights themselves since most of the time you're over water. However, I did watch an interesting sunrise over a thick cloud layer somewhere over the North Atlantic on the way back to Zurich. My first look at Switzerland was from the air as we banked through the clouds for landing. It was just as I had expected with clean lines of demarcation among the checkerboard fields in various shades of green and brown, neat and orderly. I saw a different side on the train from Zurich to St. Moritz, however, which proved that Swiss youth are as fond of graffiti as any inner-city American tagger. This poor man's art was everywhere there was a smooth surface along the train route. Also, I can confirm the old saw about Swiss trains running on time. At the airport bus terminal, the ticket agent gave me my ticket with two changeovers. I had ten minutes to catch my train and then ten minutes for the first changeover and three minutes for the second! Despite my U.S. bred anxiety about such short layovers, the journey went smooth as silk—everything was spot on time.

Before I continue, I must relate an exciting (to me) incident I experienced during my travels. In one of the airport waiting rooms on my trip back to Zurich, I read a side column article in the middle of a *USA Today* newspaper about a $57 million Cellini sculpture having been stolen in Vienna. Huh, I thought, I was just there. Then on the train from Zurich to St. Moritz, I happened to pick up a German newspaper and opened to a picture of the stolen sculpture and, sure enough, it was one I had admired just a week before! I had taken particular note because the item was a solid gold table ornament that supposedly held salt and pepper, but it is massive and ornate to the extreme with the god of water and the goddess of earth in the nude. (She's fondling one of her nipples...yes, right at the dinner table! My mom and dad would've corrected one of my sisters had they pulled this stunt at the table! They would've been sent to the basement to eat with the pigs! Not an idle threat as I found out during in my smart-alecky postpubescent days, but we won't go there now.) The god and goddess are guarded at the four corners of the base by those blustery four winds and around their bodies are various aquatic and terrestrial creatures respectively. I can't imagine anyone needing a salt and pepper holder so badly they'd steal this monstrosity.

The three-hour train trip from Zurich to St. Moritz was truly awesome. We seemed to be traveling ever upwards following a good-sized river to its source surrounded by green hills and forests. Then, we reached into the steeper hills with snowcapped mountains in the distance and rushing cataracts passing under bridges beneath us or framed against magnificent vistas. Finally, we were in the snowcapped giants. St. Moritz is cradled in a valley surrounded by these giants. Even though exhausted from the overnight plane trip, I was glued to the train windows, first one side then the other as the panorama continuously unfolded.

I was to find out quickly just how small St. Moritz is. After detraining I consulted the town map posted outside the station. After finding our hostel and noting the direction I set off afoot. I hadn't gotten more than a hundred yards when I was hailed by Andy, Ron, and Sara who were having a snack at a small restaurant overlooking the beautiful lake I was circling. I chatted for a few minutes and set off again only to run into Kirby, who was riding his bike to his mother's hotel. Again I set off after saying howdy and met Pierre a few blocks from the hostel. I had run into five members of our group in the mile or so between the train station and our hostel!

Our crew was a bit changed when I arrived. Amy had decided to complete the trip but was now riding in the van and hiking along the route as much as possible. Kirby's mom was in St. Moritz but unfortunately had experienced shortness of breath, and the doctors were holding her in the hospital for further tests. Kirby will stay with her until something is decided, and it looks like he won't be joining us until Luxembourg or sometime after that.

After a short nap, I jumped on my bike to explore the parts of St. Moritz I had not seen during my walk from the train station. As the afternoon waned, the temperature definitely began to drop. With the thick cloud cover, I wondered if we would see new snow in the pass on the morrow. I also seemed to have acquired a bit of a sore throat on my travels, probably in the crowds at the graduation or in the close confines of the planes. Whenever any of the world riders have picked up this kind of crud, it seems to have lingered, so I was not pleased and hoped I could shake it right away. That night we again had the ubiquitous Wiener schnitzel which didn't help my disposition.

My first day of riding upon rejoining the troop was absolutely gorgeous since we were in the highest part of the mountains. Because one of the passes on our planned route was closed, we backtracked over 7,423 foot Julierpass, which the others had crossed to get to St. Moritz two days before. We hit it first thing in the morning which kick-started our tickers. The morning started cold, but I was working up a good sweat on the uphill until about two-thirds of the way to the pass when we hit a good headwind, and the temperature plummeted. On the way down from the pass, I wore my Gortex jacket over my wind jacket with tights covered by my rain pants, and I was still cold, particularly my cheeks, fingers, and toes (though my Woolie Boolies kept my toes from going numb). From that fast descent, we meandered along a back road, my favorite part of the ride. We had two more serious climbs before we ended the day slightly lower and warmer than St. Moritz had been. The heavy cloud cover the night before had indeed been pregnant as manifested by the fresh snow in the pass and on the surrounding massifs. Spring had hit the mountains, and early flowers added welcome splashes of color as we descended from the pass. Overall, we climbed over five thousand feet during the day, and I was pooped by the time I reached the campground in Flims. The hot shower was very welcome.

The next day we crested another pass, this one 6,650 foot Oberalppass. The day was more mild and sunny than the previous day, but we did see a few snowflakes swirling around. I was tired by the time I reached the pass toward the end of the ride. Pierre was there with the SAG van and snacks to stoke the ole engine. I had biked up the pass with Stacia who then decided to stow her bike in the SAG van and run down to the hostel, so I rode to the bottom with Loic…or I should say I followed Loic as he bulleted to the bottom. He and Ron sure like to go fast on the downhills. Upon reaching our hostel in the sleepy hamlet of Hospental, I volunteered to ride in the SAG van back to the pass to pick up Amy who had wanted to hike to the top. When we got there she had about a half mile to go, so I hopped out and walked with her to the top. It gives you yet another perspective to be on foot in these beautiful mountains. You can hear the birds and the running rivulets more clearly, and you see much more when you aren't focused on the road conditions immediately in front of you. It suggests another trip to do some hiking!

Back at the hostel several of us walked to the little church and an old watch tower that are about the only sites of interest in this tiny town. Then we had a bike cleaning session before supper as I wire-brushed some of the grime from my chain and gears. I'm almost certainly the least meticulous in our group when it comes to bike care, and my bike seemed to enjoy the unusual attention. The spaghetti supper with soup, salad, and berries over ice cream was much to my liking as pasta seems to be an energy rich food for my constitution.

The following day I count as the most perfect riding day I have yet experienced. Because Furka Pass was still closed, we rode our bikes about six kilometers to a train station, loaded the bikes, the van, and ourselves, and struck out through a twenty-two-kilometer tunnel that would be the envy of Gimli's kin (Gimli, as some of you will surely remember, is the main dwarf, one of the nine fellows of the ring in the *Lord of the Rings* trilogy). At the other end, we had the choice of taking the road or using a bike path, condition unknown, for the first twenty to thirty kilometers of the ride. Loic and I opted to take the bike path since it's pleasant to have no automotive traffic. Well, the trail was made for mountain bikes with some little bit of well-paved, some poorly paved, some gravel, and mostly dirt surfaces. The route paralleled the young Rhone much of the way with excursions into beautiful forested areas, the trail paved in pine needles, and through green pastures with curious cows clanging their bells. In short, it was gorgeous!

Then, we hit the road. Never in memory do I recall a long ride that both was almost entirely downhill AND had a tailwind, but that was our lot for almost the entire sixty-plus remaining kilometers! To top that off, we had a magnificent view of Furka Pass behind us, if we turned around to look, and, in front of us for about half the route, we had a giant massif framed against the "V" of the Rhone River valley. It seemed to float there in the distance shaded in sepia tones. I don't know if it was some distant pollution causing the incredible color scheme and levitation act, but it looked unreal. Later Loic and Pierre agreed it must have been Mt. Blanc, the highest peak in the Alps, we were seeing. I also consulted a map, and it was certainly in the right place. Needless to say, we both showed up with huge grins on our faces to one of the prettiest campsites yet. And to make things even sweeter, I heard my first European cuckoo calling that afternoon, and it really does sound just like a cuckoo clock.

The campground was a ways from Bramois, the nearest town, so my evening stroll led me down rural dirt roads among fields, orchards, and a vineyard waiting for the full moon to rise. However, the steep cliff immediately to the east of our campsite foiled my efforts yet again as it would be past my bedtime before the moon would clear it.

We continued down the valley the next two days following the Rhone all the way to the western shore of Loc Leman, and then along this beautiful lake to Geneva from which point the Rhone flows out to continue its trip across France to finally spill into the Mediterranean at Marsaille. Though these rides were nice, they couldn't compare to that first day in the valley. However, that next night I did catch a nearly full moon rising in the cleft of the eastern mountains around midnight when I sneaked out of my tent on a relief mission. It was quite beautiful even if I was *half asleep in frog pajamas* (my apology to Tom Robbins who wrote an inventive novel with this evocative title). Loic left us at Loc Leman, and we were sad to see him go. He has been a great addition to our little group.

On our last riding day for this stage into Geneva, I scooted out of camp earlier than the rest in order to have time to visit a couple of museums since they are closed on Monday which is our layover day in Geneva. I did take the time to stop at the Village Medieval in Yvorie for a peek at how an old village might have looked in its day. Of course the shops are all stocked with modern wares, but still it was evocative of the period. As I neared Geneva, I was biking toward that famous skyline, the one you often see in photographs: the beautiful lake with that impressive water fountain shooting high into the sky and the city's skyline in the distance. It is indeed a beautiful city.

I arrived at our hostel before noon, in time to visit the Natural History and Art Museums. The Art Museum had a good collection including a couple Monets and Pissarros, a Renoir, and two sculptures by Rodin, including a casting of *The Thinker*. Actually, the public areas of Geneva itself are filled with many sculptures well worth a look. The Natural History Museum I visited has, purportedly, one of the most complete collections of hummingbirds in the world. Although it was a good museum, I have been spoiled with many good natural history museums and was not as impressed as I might have otherwise been.

Today, our last in Geneva, I spent several hours in the Red Cross and Red Crescent Museum which traces the history of the organizations back to the mid-eighteen hundreds and a book called *A Memory of Solferino*. Henry Durant, a Geneva businessman, witnessed the carnage at the Battle of Solferino on June 24, 1859, during which the French and Piedmontese drove the Austrians out of northern Italy. He was so moved that he wrote his book advocating for societies that would work for the relief of the wounded in such battles. He, along with others, drew up the First Geneva Convention. The Red Crescent was adopted in 1929 by Muslim nations because the symbol of the cross was disturbing to many Muslims since it had often been the conquering symbol used by invading Christian armies. Today the two organizations are partners in relieving human suffering around the world. I enjoyed the museum but was somewhat disappointed there were no stories of specific events in their histories. The reason, of course, is that they must not in any way politicize their organizations, but I suspect they could tell some interesting stories of what they have seen in conflicts around the world during the last century and a half.

I also took the tour of the United Nations building here, the second largest and busiest next to the one in New York City. It is partially housed in the building built for the League of Nations championed by Woodrow Wilson after the First World War. Would not that more recent presidents understand how important and life preserving such a world community organization is!

Amy flew out today, and Ron and Sara will stay a couple more days to celebrate their second anniversary before flying home. The three remaining riders with our two staffers will drive to Luxembourg tomorrow to begin the next stage. Hopefully, Kirby will join us there, but we have no other stage riders until London. Bobbi will stay longer than expected because TK&A doesn't have her staff replacement yet, and young Tim is not ready to return.

Finally, I will hit the food scene in Europe up to this point in the trip. The Czech food was interesting, but the food has gotten progressively less interesting as we've headed east. The Czech dumplings were different, but it was the liver dumpling soup that really caught my attention. It tasted exactly like the liver dumpling soup I first had as a lieutenant in Omaha, Nebraska, many, many years ago—delicious! I tried some nice garlic soup and a pancake soup that was just so-so. I had some overdone pheasant and some very good goose liver and sauerbraten. As noted above, I'm a bit tired of Wiener schnitzel which has never been a favorite. The sauerkraut in all its incarnations has been better than any I've eaten in the States, and I had a few pickled white asparagus one night that were out of this world! Also, the warm berries over ice cream is a nice touch...except they could add several more scoops of the ice cream for my taste. Since we've left the Czech Republic and Austria, nothing has grabbed my taste buds, just the normal spaghetti, lasagna, pizza, etc. We did have what we would call in the States a Mongolian barbecue two nights ago that was tasty...although it included horse meat that was a bit strong for my taste.

That's it for this time. If this seems a bit short, it might be that I'm slowing down...or maybe it's only that I missed six days of riding when I flew back to the States. We'll see if it picks up next time. I'll leave you with a quote I got at the Red Cross/Crescent Museum:

> Zigong (Tzu-kung) asked, "Is there a single word which can be a guide to conduct throughout one's life?" The Master said, "It is per-

haps the word 'shu.' Do not impose on others what you yourself do not desire."

—Confucius (Kong Zi) (551–479 BC)
from *The Analects*, XV.24

By the way, does this quote have a familiar ring (think Golden Rule)?

Take care of yourself and all who belong to you,

Ralph

Report #10: Oui, Monfort is French

June 3, 2003

Bonjour,

The quote for today is from Dostoyevsky; it has been adopted by the Red Cross/Red Crescent Museum as their motto: "Everyone is responsible to everyone for everything."

I last left you in Geneva. The three remaining riders and the two staffers crammed our five bikes, all our gear and ourselves into the van for a long, rainy ride to the Grand Duchy of Luxembourg. It would have been tight with Kirby, who was still in St. Moritz at this point with his mother. Just as Andy and Stacia have apparently learned to sleep anywhere, I have learned to read anywhere without a hint of motion sickness—and that's just what I did for much of the seven-hour trip. Thank goodness *The Tin Drum* is a relatively long book. We drove this segment since Tim had to make some cuts in the Odyssey 2000 itinerary someplace, as we are riding about twenty fewer miles per day than on the first trip, and he tried to pick the nicest riding. Old Luxembourg City is perched upon a high cliff with the newer city sections spread out before it. Our hostel was in the lower part.

On our rainy layover day, while Pierre and Bobbi drove the bike route we would take for the next two days and finalized the Daily Route Guides we would use, I set off on my own travels. Mine took me by train to the small town of Clervaux in the northern part of the country where the *Family of Man* photographs are permanently housed in a castle high on a hill above the town. This collection of photos was commissioned in the early 1950s for a New York City institution (I don't remember which one). Edward Steichen, the collector, made the stipulation that when the show was over, the photos would be kept permanently in Luxembourg. Consequently, they were eventually shipped to Luxembourg, sustained some damage in transit, were repaired, and made a later world tour before settling down in the castle where I got to view them again. I say "again" because we had the collection in a coffee-table book in the Monfort living room for a good long time during my formative years. Unlike the fate of most coffee table books, this one grew ragged from use as I and the rest of the family were drawn repeatedly to the wonderful, heart-wrenching, heart-uplifting, life-affirming, truly human pictures. I was, and then wasn't, surprised at the number of pictures I remembered from my child-hood. I also found some new favorites, probably (hopefully) the result of my increased maturity and fatherhood. I don't know how the book ended up on our table, but I suspect one of my older siblings bought it as a gift for mom and dad (maybe it was Kam since she was living in New York City during this timeframe).

Clervaux was also the site of some tough fighting during the Battle of the Bulge in World War II. In fact, many buildings within the town were destroyed or badly damaged. There is a museum for the Battle of the Bulge in the town, but I was in a hurry to my next venue and didn't take the time to visit it (always save something for next time). That venue was the Museum of History and Art in Luxembourg City. So I caught the next train (great train ride by the way, especially as it goes by the historic part of Luxembourg City perched as it is on its promontory), picked my bike up at the train station and made my way to the museum.

I didn't spend a lot of time there because I wanted to catch a city tour, but I did hit the two floors of fine art. Now, I know my descriptions are not doing justice to the art I've been viewing because I've had no formal art appreciation courses. In fact, in trying to remember where I've picked up the little I do know, all I can come up with are the nuns at St. John's Riedman Memorial Catholic School during the first eight grades (same with my little bit of French, by the way). Anyhow, my taste runs mostly to the Impressionists, and I know precious little about much else. Modern art mostly leaves me cold—I just don't "get it" much of the time. With this disclaimer, I will say they have a nice Rodin sculpture of a standing male nude, one of Picasso's tamer efforts, a Pizarro (or Pissarro as it's more commonly spelled—I'll not defend my iffy spelling, but the artists' names are often spelled differently in different places, very confusing), and even a few Mapplethorpe photographs which surprised me (not the nude photos but the fact that the museum had them). They also had a fair collection of more modern pieces.

I rushed from there (you gotta make use of every minute on your layover days!) to the city tour meeting place. Our tour guide was an older man who seemed a bit miffed about having to give his patter in three languages: English, French, and German (or maybe it was Letzebuergesch, the official language in Luxembourg). I was glad when a young Asian woman showed up who also needed the English translation so I was not alone. The fellow loosened up a bit when I walked and talked with him for awhile after the tour officially ended. I did learn a few things and saw some new sights.

The Grand Duchy of Luxembourg was founded in AD 963 by Count Siegfried who recognized its strategic importance in the center of Europe and also the promontory's defensibility. He became the first Duke. The Duchy has been attacked throughout its history, and the fortress that is Luxembourg City expanded and was rebuilt again and again. From 1443 for almost four centuries, the Duchy was under foreign rule. In the seventeenth century after the great fortress builder, Vauban, rebuilt the fort, Luxembourg became virtually impregnable, earning the moniker, "the Gibraltar of the North." At that time it had three fortified rings with twenty-four forts and sixteen other strong defensive sites surrounding the city. Within the walls, twenty-three kilometers of tunnels were dug where the soldiers could live indefinitely (more on these later). However, after the Congress of London, circa 1867, decreed Luxembourg's neutrality, the fortress and most of its battlements were taken down. What was left became protected under UNESCO as a World Heritage Site in 1994.

Luxembourg City is now a cosmopolitan city with much foreign investment and 984(!) banks and other financial institutions—seems like they are poised to become another Switzerland. In addition, the city houses several of the European Union institutions including the General Secretariat of the European Parliament and the European Court of Justice.

During the tour, we visited yet another Notre Dame Cathedral. I felt as if we were intruding when we walked through it with our guide as it was packed and had been packed all week for an annual pilgrimage. Despite my discomfort, the cathedral was well worth seeing and was ornate to the extreme. I returned to it twice more before I left to have a better look, but that evening after supper it was locked and the next morning it was again filled with pilgrims.

Many of the casements and the Bock promontory ("bock" literally means "cliff") itself offer spectacular views over the two river valleys and the Grund area where the Alzette and Petrusse Rivers intersect. After the tour I was drawn back to the casement area which I found interesting; I wish the information boards had been translated into English. I was just minutes too late to take the underground casement self-guided tour as they require at least forty-five minutes to be able to find your way back out again.

I have to mention the dessert Andy and I shared that evening at supper. After a nice steak meal, we both ordered the chocolate mousse. Instead of small individual bowls, we were served a huge serving bowl that contained at least six large individual servings. Our eyes bulged at the size but, undaunted, we dug in. The mousse was not as rich as I've had before, tasting more like chocolate pudding with egg whites whipped into it. However, we did ourselves proud or proved our gluttony, whichever fits best, and finished the lot.

The next morning it was raining steadily which helped me make a decision; the evening before I had been toying with the idea of delaying my ride to do the casements tour. So while Andy and Stacia made their way out of the city on their way to Belgium, I snuggled up in bed with *The Tin Drum* and read and napped until almost 10 a.m. when the ticket office opened. The casements were worth the delay. You descend spiral stone staircases forty meters below the top of the wall to a network of tunnels that mole their way this way and that, up and down throughout the wall. A cutaway picture of the battlements would resemble a termite mound. Here and there were windows where defenders could look out at the enemy and fire upon them. A few cannons had been set up to show what it might have been like. There are seventeen kilometers of tunnels still extant that could not be destroyed by the Congress of London edict without bringing large parts of the city down with it. Of course, only a fraction of these tunnels are open to the public. During the Second World War, the tunnels were again used to good effect, at times harboring up to 35,000 people.

Well, all good delays must come to an end so I finally mounted my bike and headed the short distance, about sixty kilometers, to Virton, Belgium. The good news is that the rain had let up with just a light mist at the beginning of the ride. However, wet roads are never fun, and the decidedly bike-unfriendly streets of Luxembourg were very disconcerting. I couldn't figure out where I was supposed to ride. The streets are narrow with no shoulders, the sidewalks don't have easy on/off ramps and sometimes just end, and the lane closest to the side of the road is marked for buses which are large and don't seem to like to share (in France the bus lanes are often marked for bicycles too). Suffice to say, I was glad to get out of town and into the beautiful countryside once again. Just after I got to the campground and raised my tent, it began to rain again, so I felt pretty smug at my timing (unfortunately, Andy and Stacia had gotten soaked). That evening I tried my first *quatre fromage* (four cheese) pizza with ham, which became one of my favorites even though it was sometimes a bit rich. I also had a bowl of nutty ice cream with raspberry sauce that was nice.

Tim Kneeland showed up in camp sometime during the night having flown in from the States. The next morning he and Pierre drove off in Tim's rental car to finalize the route all the way to the English Channel. That takes a load off Bobbi and Pierre who had lost their rest day in Luxembourg City checking out the next two days' route. Bobbi had been up much of the previous night typing and printing our route guides, more than a bit frazzling I would think.

We spent just that one night in Belgium before riding into France. The ride was more pleasant than the previous day with the sun peeking out at times, although it was generally overcast. Along the way were placards describing World War II battles that had taken place in this area in 1941. All were translated into five languages, including English, and seemed to be part of a historical tour route. Attigny, the little town in France where we camped, had been the home of Charlemagne when he was ruler of this section of Europe. The restaurant where we supped was separated by only a small *pâtisserie* or pastry shop from an eighth or ninth century arch that was an entrance to one of the great Charlemagne's abodes. It was a good reminder that history is a part of normal life in Europe.

The next day we were not as lucky weather-wise. It rained almost continuously, but not hard, for most of the 130-kilometer ride to Nogent L'Artaud. Of course, we knew before we started that we weren't in a "dry county" since the route winded its way through France's premier champagne grape growing region. The cool forest rides, quaint villages and, beautiful vineyards were all lovely, but it's hard to appreciate the sights when you're wet, the visibility is poor, and you have water droplets on your glasses. It was still rainy when we got to camp so we couldn't even dry out our kits. It was the first time on the trip I've slept in a damp tent—still it wasn't too bad. That evening the small town of Nogent L'Artaud was hosting something like a midwestern county fair in honor of the town's patron saint. So, after supper, we walked through the small collection of rides, food vendors and games of skill before enjoying the fireworks show over the Marne River—a pleasant evening.

Much to our delight, we had sun for our ride into Paris! The overcast sky gradually cleared during the day, and the sun finally broke through for the last half of the ride, then the clouds came in and squeezed out a few drops just before reaching the hotel. The actual riding turned pleasant once my damp riding clothes dried out. When the sun broke through, I caught a glimpse of the morning light van Gogh captures so wonderfully in his paintings of the French countryside. I tried to capture the light and colors in a photograph of a barn with hay—we'll see how it turns out. It was Sunday, and we shared the road with *beaucoup* bicycles—I'm talking a hundred-plus. Most of them were congregated in one fifty-kilometer stretch in groups from three to about thirty riders. They were riding faster than I was, but I did hitch a ride a couple times for short distances. The power of drafting behind a group of riders was palpable and fun.

At one point on the ride, I was cruising a rural road on a slight downhill going maybe thirty kilometers per hour. I had just emerged from a wood when Monsieur Renard leapt from the tall grass at my right, sprinted across the road not fifteen feet in front of me, and then leapt into the tall grass on the other side where it looked like a path had been lightly made. I got a great look at the brute which seemed larger than our foxes at home, almost coyote-size, though much sleeker of course. I felt euphoric!

Speaking of animals, I still haven't seen much animal life in Europe. I've passed a few dead hedgehogs along the roads and occasionally a dead bird. There are lots of live birds, very noisy in their springtime rituals, but they are difficult to spot among all the new leaves. At one stop I spied a titmouse couple streaking back and forth between their hunting grounds and their nest in the knothole of a tree. I had unknowingly leaned my bicycle against the tree about knothole-high, and they had interrupted their parental duties to scold me long and harshly before setting off again on their whirlwind activity. It makes you wonder what they do with all their free time when their young leave the nest.

The ride into Paris was a challenge even though it was Sunday and traffic was lighter than usual. On the eastern outskirts, we followed the Seine River for awhile, a serene diversion before hitting busy city streets. Going through the city center, we discovered the street we were supposed to follow was blocked because of strikes or protests. However, once we negotiated the blockade, it was clear going since we had the street to ourselves. I got to the hotel hours before the support van because Bobbi had gotten caught in the rerouted traffic. While waiting I scouted around for a *pâtisserie* and bought and devoured a three-foot baguette (cost: €0.72) with a can of iced tea. No one can make a baguette like the French! I found evidence in the room that Kirby had made it from St. Moritz as he had left a big smiley face on my bed creatively constructed from the room's coffee-making items.

Because Paris has so much to see and do, we enjoyed two layover days there. On the first day I spent about eight hours in the Louvre. I had seen many of the other sights when I was in Paris on my Corsica trip last fall, but I had saved the Louvre. It did not disappoint. It's a bit of a maze as wind your way from one section to another, made particularly difficult since certain segments of the museum were closed for renovation. Regardless, I thoroughly enjoyed my time there, especially with the excellent audio guide. I concentrated on the paintings and sculpture areas since you can't see everything in a day, and the Louvre was closed on Tuesday, our second layover day. The quality and quantity of works is truly impressive. I saw works by Renoir, Pissarro, Monet, including his winter scenes I had not previously seen, Cezanne, Toulouse-Lautrec, El Greco, Raphael, da Vinci, Botticelli, Delacroix's *Liberty Leading the People*, Giuseppe Arcimboldo's *The Seasons* paintings, which look very modern for the mid-sixteenth century, and David's large painting of the coronation of Napoleon to mention a few. Oh, and Miss Mona still has that famous smirk. I know it sounds like name-dropping, but it's the only way I can give you a feel for the scope of talent displayed here. Surprisingly for such a huge place, I ran into Andy three different times during the day.

The next morning Stacia, Kirby, and I visited the catacombs beneath the streets of Paris where, in the nineteenth century, about six million human skeletons were transplanted from city cemeteries into tunnels that had been originally dug for the limestone blocks used as building materials throughout the city. In fact, there are so many bones stacked for miles in neat piles about four feet tall, that it did not seem the least macabre to me. According to the guide, the bones were stored here to make room in the cemeteries for new occupants. The last time new skeletons were placed in the tunnels was 1892, but now some of them are being shuffled around because of tunnel decay. Our tour group included a family with a ninety-year-old woman who made it up and down the lengthy spiral staircases all on her own. I speculated that the sight of all those bones, a clear indicator of our mortality, might have given her added strength.

After this dark journey, I walked to the Museum d'Orsay. On the way, I stumbled across the statue of Capt Dreyfus, a monument highlighting one of France's less proud moments. In a conspiracy that reached high into the

French military establishment, this Jewish officer was framed for spying and imprisoned. The d'Orsay was closed when I arrived because of a worker strike, so I headed just down the street to the Rodin Museum where I spent the rest of the afternoon. There, I found police all over the street in front of the entrance trying to contain a group of striking teachers. That evening on the news, I learned that the strike, in protest over the government's redistribution of a pension plan, had been extended. I began to wonder if this general strike would disrupt our trip.

The Rodin Museum occupies a grand old house and its grounds that had once belonged to a member of the *nouveau riche* who had died young. The house became a haven for artists to live and work before Rodin acquired it for his own quarters. Again, I made use of the museum's audio commentary, and it was excellent. Although many of Rodin's works caused controversy in his day, he was nevertheless identified as a great sculptor at an early age and enjoyed recognition and fame throughout his life, unlike some of his contemporaries, most notably van Gogh. Many of his most memorable pieces are here: *The Kiss, Monument to Victor Hugo, The Gates of Hell, The Burghers of Calais*, and *The Thinker*, both as a smaller bronze like the one I saw in Geneva and as a large bronze piece that had been displayed publicly in Paris for years. I was previously unaware there had been so many castings of *The Thinker* in a variety of sizes, all directed by Rodin. In fact, I learned much about bronze sculpting I had not known.

The Thinker is also one of the central figures in the *Gates of Hell* piece as are the *Three Fates*. This latter work is interesting because Rodin cast all three figures from the same mold arranging the individual figures at slightly different angles to give the appearance of three distinct figures. He often used replication in his works, a technique for which he was often criticized as it was not common practice at the time.

After leaving the Rodin Museum, I walked along the Seine and again toured through Notre Dame Cathedral to recalibrate my views on churches since I have visited so many by now. I caught a metro back to the hotel, put my feet up for awhile, and then had a nice chicken korma at an Indian restaurant down the street since we were on our own for supper. The next day we would strike out down the Loire Valley to the coast.

I'll close this report here although we've already ridden a couple days out of Paris. But first I'll provide further descriptions of the food and toilet situations, since I'm sure you've been waiting for them with bated breath. The European campgrounds have a few new twists. We've found several toilets with no toilet seats, just the porcelain bowl to sit upon. Also, some facilities are *sans* toilet paper…something you want to know before you are seated. One campground restroom was furnished with just one very large roll of toilet paper in a central area from which you dispensed what you thought you might need to take to your stall—go figure.

As far as food goes, I have not been overwhelmed. I have had many good goat cheese salads (thanks to my Corsican fellow traveler, Tom, for turning me on to these), a good Roquefort steak (ibid., Tom), good bread and ice cream, an interesting locally made sausage, and a chorizo unlike any I've had in New Mexico (more like salami). Otherwise, the food has been just okay but nothing to write home about. So I won't. One item will be interesting to the Monfort and Knecht clans. While in Belgium, our staff prepared breakfast that included store-bought Belgium waffle cookies. They were much like mom's French cookies but not as rich. Also, the bakers had laid one side of each cookie in that waxy store chocolate, so I couldn't really compare tastes, but they looked exactly like the real McCoy.

Two new twists on our meals were introduced by Bobbi on this stage. First, since the restaurants in the small French towns don't open early enough for breakfast on our bike days, Bobbi has been providing a continental breakfast for us. I suspect this is going to be more common throughout Europe and, based on Bobbi's selections to date, I will be a happy camper. Second, when our evening plans have differed within the group, Bobbi has given us the option to find supper on our own within a fixed allowance. This has increased our flexibility and is much appreciated. However, we normally still gather for supper together.

So long and take care,

Ralph

Report #11: I See London, I See France

Howdy from London town,

After we left Paris, we rode down the Loire River valley to the coast for a week before turning north to the English Channel. The area was mostly agricultural with new growth of peas, rapeseed, sorghum, and other crops I couldn't identify, but everything was green, green, green, except for the bright yellow rapeseed of course. We rode through beautiful forests where the canopies formed arches of a cathedral-verdant. We had good weather for the most part, although I spent a couple of hours one day finishing a book under the arch of a church to avoid riding in the rain. We usually had great evening weather with the sun setting just before 10 p.m. Several of these evenings prompted my remembrance of a favorite quote by Thoreau, "This is a delicious evening, when the whole body is one sense, and imbibes delight through every pore."

Our first ride took us past Versailles which I had thoroughly explored on my Corsica trip last fall and so did not stop this time. However, you shouldn't miss it if you ever get to Paris. It was a relief to get out of the city and once again bike rural roads through sleepy villages. That evening, it took Bobbi awhile to find something other than take-out pizza for supper, but her efforts were rewarded. I had chicken with ham in a wonderful sauce, a nice green salad, pasta in a tasty sauce, a healthy portion of Andy's medium-rare duck (anything not well-done is "not cooked" according to Andy), and a taste of his *foie gras* (i.e., goose liver pate, Kirby's favorite French dish). I also had a *boule* (i.e., ball or scoop, a good word to know in France) of three types of sorbet: raspberry, lemon, and strawberry.

On the way back to camp. we were treated to a magnificent sunset. A tangerine sun was setting behind a blue-gray cloud providing a striking contrast. The cloud must have been stratified because it gave the sun a striped appearance. Our campground was in the country and, as night fell, I took a walk through the healthy fields of wheat and rapeseed to a copse of trees and then past a small, dark wood. At one point, the trail dipped into a small dale where it was palpably cooler. I could actually see my breath, not because of the temperature change as much as the moisture in the air. The area was so beautiful I repeated part of the walk the next morning before mounting up.

The ride to Jargeau was a close repeat of the day before. Several of us stopped at the Château de Chamerolles and paid the price of admission. It had been built by Lancelot du Loc but has since been turned into a perfume museum that was somewhat interesting though body scent is not one of my passions. Nevertheless, it was an impressive set of buildings. That evening we camped next to the Loire and, after supper, I took a walk downriver and enjoyed the evening. Again it had been a bit difficult finding a restaurant open as most were closed for the celebration of Christ's ascension forty days after Easter.

We had another gorgeous day for our long ride to Amboise and a layover day. For the first twenty-four kilometers, we were riding atop a levee along the Loire which was very enjoyable. One distraction in the early morning was the profusion of gnats through which we rode in clouds. Since I usually ride in a long-sleeved dress shirt to keep the sun off my arms and neck, I ended up collecting a goodly number of these flying nuisances in my shirt pocket. This looked rather peculiar by the end of the ride as they had accumulated into a black mass at the bottom. I got off easy though as other riders had the gnats stuck all over their exposed skin due to oily sunscreen. This was only the first of several times we had this problem on our journey down the valley.

Although we rode right past one of the most famous châteaux in France, the Chambord Château, I didn't stop since it was still relatively early in the ride and looked full of tourists. Also, it was a bit pricey. The edifice showing beyond its walls was impressive though. Somewhat over halfway to Amboise I stopped at Blois to get a cold drink. I picked up an orange drink and three cans of iced tea. Lipton seems to be the canned tea of choice in Europe, but I was severely disappointed when my first sip proved it to be carbonated. I'll need to check before buying from now on. I rolled on into Amboise and was happy to find that Kirby and I had scored a second story room overlooking the Loire with a great balcony for drying laundry.

On our first evening in Amboise after supper, the three guys (Andy, Kirby, and I) stumbled upon a concert at the fifteenth century church still in use by the local parish. Outside the church an elderly woman played a dulcimer-type instrument accompanied by an accordion while young school children danced what seemed to be a madrigal. Then we entered the church where a group of twenty to twenty-five guitarists of all ages regaled us with a surprisingly beautiful set of music. I would not have thought that many guitars played together would sound so good. Afterwards, we returned to the outside stage where the old folks replaced the school children in dancing. It was all very laid back, a peaceful evening, especially nice since it stayed light so late.

The next day we toured the Château Amboise, but the self-guided tour didn't take us long. These fort-like homes are built on the high ground, and the views of the surrounding countryside never fail to impress. In the afternoon I visited the Château Du Clos Luce where Leonardo da Vinci lived out the last three years of his life. The château was given to him in 1516 by Francois I who was living in the Château Amboise at the time. Francois also gave Leonardo a healthy yearly stipend just for the pleasure of his company. The château, now a museum to da Vinci's works, is located on extremely beautiful, wooded grounds with a small stream meandering through. The museum contains about forty models, most of them full-scale working models, of his many inventions. IBM engineers created the models from his original drawings for a show in the 1990s. I spent most of a beautiful afternoon there.

Our ride to Saumur the next morning started out warm and stayed warm. You didn't notice the heat so much until you stopped creating your own breeze. Also, the gnats took advantage of the overcast skies and lack of wind to venture out without fear of being desiccated in the sun. I had bought a bottle of lemon drink concentrate in Amboise and used it in my water bottles. It tasted great and helped me to stay well-hydrated in this heat. Kirby and I stopped to walk through, purportedly, the most beautiful gardens in France at the Château de Villandry. They were indeed extremely well-groomed, and the designs created by the flower beds and shrubbery were interesting when viewed from above, but on the whole, it was a bit contrived for my taste.

Our quiet campground that evening was on the island in the river (called an "ait" for those crossword fanatics among my readers) across from Saumur proper. Before supper I rode my bike into the town center and then up a steep hill to get a closer look at the Château Saumur sitting imposingly on a hill overlooking the town. On the way back to camp I stumbled upon that rarest of all rare things, a (relatively) cheap French Internet, so I stopped to type in my last report. I had been searching for just such a chimera since Paris. I still had time before supper to swim my normal workout in a full-size indoor pool at the campground, my first swim since Joe's graduation in May.

The ride to Chalonnes-sur-Loire was ten degrees cooler than the day before and overcast. It had sprinkled off and on during the night and repeated that performance throughout the day. The ride was short so I powered straight through with only a broken spoke to slow me down. Bobbi took me to a shop that afternoon to have it replaced. <This was the only broken spoke any of the world riders sustained during the entire trip!>

Supper that night was an adventure. We discovered that it's not so easy to find restaurants open on Monday evenings in the French hinterlands. We searched three separate villages just to find one that was open. The place we finally settled on was called "Buffalo Grill," and I had—no kidding—a piece of American bison, a piece of ostrich, and a piece of beef besides a sampler of five desserts. That night in my tent, I thought I heard a raspy, two-note owl calling in the distance…but it might have just been the ostrich talking.

The next day the weather stayed about the same, and I almost got my tent dry before having to hurriedly pack it up when it began sprinkling. Early in the ride I stopped a few times to eye some herons and other birds through my binoculars and to mail postcards in a small village. Then it began to rain in earnest, so I holed up in yet another Notre Dame church and finished reading *The Tin Drum*. I had begun stashing a book in my bike bag in case I reached camp before the van, and it sure came in handy on this occasion as I didn't feel like getting soaked. Later I found that Kirby had found a coffee shop just down the street for the same purpose. I made it to our campsite at Marcille Robert without further incident or getting any wetter. Tim joined us for supper that night. He had finished the route guides for this stage, and Pierre had already flown home.

It rained most of the night. Once I got up to rid myself of water and saw Kirby and Stacia pulling laundry from their clotheslines. This must have been a dream since the next morning all of it was still there and sodden. Dream walking in the rain. Who da thunk? Anyway, this was one of the times I was thankful I had chosen all quick-drying clothes for the trip, no cotton T-shirts or jeans, as the others were constantly fighting with laundry. The day's ride was pleasant, and we saw Mont St. Michel long before we got there. Andy, Kirby, and I shared a nice little cabin for our two nights here.

I was very impressed with Mont St. Michel as the length of my description below will indicate. Before supper I rode my bike across the causeway to the island abbey. The tide was out so it was surrounded by a sand bank. I walked around it and poked my head inside the lower level where a narrow street was packed with tourists in what used to be a small village. Later that night after supper Andy and I walked to the abbey. The tide had come in which gave the scene a different look from earlier in the day—it felt wilder, more desolate.

The next morning I caught the first English-speaking tour of Mont St. Michel. The abbey was not yet crowded, and our small group included only two couples, one Canadian and one Swiss, besides me. The tour guide was probably my age and an archeologist by either trade or avocation. He will be working on a massive new Neolithic site this summer in hopes of uncovering human remains. Disconcertingly, he started his tour by mentioning that he didn't feel like leading a tour this morning and rhetorically wondered where he would get his inspiration. In a joking response that fell somewhat flat, I told him we would by asking a lot of questions. We were an attentive and inter-ested group, and later he said he didn't understand it, but that he often gives his most detailed tours on days he doesn't feel like touring. Actually, I can understand this since that often happens with my work-outs.

The tour was great, and the guide was the best I've had yet on this trip. He packed a large amount of information in palatable packages during the one and a half hours (supposed to be one hour) we had with him. Some of his pat-ter was either extraneous or, at best, tangential or oddly supplemental to the subject at hand, but all of it was interesting.

According to tradition Aubert, Bishop of Avranches, founded Mont St. Michel as a sanctuary in honor of St. Michel, the Archangel, after having three dreams. Almost immediately it became a destination for pilgrims, even-tually becoming the fourth most visited site after Jerusalem, Rome, and Santi-ago de Compostela in the northwest of Spain. In the tenth century, the Benedictines moved into the abbey while a village grew below it. A pre-Romanesque church was built on the pinnacle of the pyramidal mount and, over the next several centuries, monastery buildings were built beneath and around it. It was an impressive architectural feat for its time as the buildings had to wrap around the pyramidal mount to support the church on its summit. Massive columns and external buttresses were employed. During the Hundred Years' War in the fourteenth century, military fortifications were built around the abbey, strong enough to hold out the English for thirty years. In 1421, the chancel, or that central part of the church containing the altar, collapsed onto the village below causing much destruction and death. The current Gothic chancel was built as a replacement.

After the French Revolution, the religious community at the abbey dissolved, and the structure was turned into a prison for seventy years (further explanation below). In 1803 it was classified as a historical site and underwent a massive restoration to include a neo-Gothic spire with a gilded copper statue of St. Michel to replace the original cupola and cross. Since 1979, the abbey has been listed as a World Heritage Site by UNESCO.

The main monastery building has three large rooms on either side of the chancel, one above the next. On the top level of one side is the cloister where the monks' spiritual needs were met through prayer and meditation (plus a spectacular view of the bay below). Below this is the scriptorium, a work and study room designed to meet their intellectual needs. Two large fireplaces, the only ones I saw in the monks' areas, were present to help the monks keep their hands warm so they could write. Below this room is the larder to meet their physical needs. On the top floor of the other side is the refectory where the monks ate in silence save for the reading aloud of scripture. Below this is the guests' hall with two giant cooking alcoves to entertain royalty and nobility. On the third level down was the eating area for the workers and alms seekers.

The location of Mont St. Michel is perhaps its most striking feature. It is located atop an eighty-meter high rock on a spit of land jutting into a bay of the Atlantic Ocean. Until a raised causeway was built for permanent vehicular traffic, the mount was an island for about half of each day as the greatest tidal bore in Europe flowed in and out at speeds that caught (and still catches) people unawares, often with fatal results. This was especially true of the pilgrims traveling from the northeast who had to cross a seven-kilometer stretch of wet sand at low tide. If fog, quicksand, or bad timing caused them to be late in getting across, the water rushing in could overtake a running man. At the time of my visit the decision had already been made to remove the causeway and replace it with a large bridge to allow the water at high tide to again surround the mount. The causeway, it seems, has changed the dynamic of the tidal bore such that sand had begun collecting, and Mont St. Michel seemed destined to be permanently surrounded by a large beach.

Our guide's information came in tidbits and anecdotes. As a reward for surviving the lengthy description above, I'll share with you what I can gather from my notes. He told us that to be called an abbey there must be at least a dozen members, any fewer members than this is called a priory. To help you remember this I have composed a memory jogger, to wit:

> Twelve monks an abbey makes
> and less than this, a priory.
> If your memory a powder takes,
> it's written in Ralph's diary.

The granite stone to build much of the abbey was brought from offshore islands. To make shipment of such heavy material as cheap and easy as possible, the stones were precut to fit according to a plan. Each stone was precisely cut on location and then fitted together like a puzzle when they arrived at the abbey site. Many of the stones used for flooring have a number or letter chiseled into them. When asked, the guide informed us that the stone cutters were paid by the stone so, to ensure payment, they inscribed each stone they cut with their personal symbol. The artistry of the craftsmen is evident in the finished structure. Perhaps most evocative to me are the abbey's soaring arches that are actually part of the bricks from which they seem to flow.

The abbey is on the border between Normandy and Brittany just north of the Couesnan River which is the dividing line between the two provinces. Both provinces at times have claimed the abbey. There is a saying in Brittany that, "The Couesnan, in its folly, has placed Mont St. Michel in Normandy."

Alan Shepard visited the abbey after his trip to the moon. He asked the abbot if he could present a rosary as a gift to the abbey. He said that when he first landed on the moon, he had placed three rosaries on its surface. Before he left, he gathered them up again and brought them to earth. He traveled to Rome to present one to the Pope, he kept one for himself, and he looked around the world for the most inspiring place to leave the third—he chose the abbey.

You can see part of the abbey in the 1950 version of *The Scarlet Pimpernel* starring David Niven. The beginning and the ending scenes were shot there.

The guide provided us with the etymology of many words. When showing us the huge cooking fireplaces in the guests' hall, he told us that the word "barbecue" comes from the French "from the chin to the rump" (or something like that) in reference to cooking a whole animal on a spit. <I looked this up in an etymological dictionary when I returned and found it actually derives from a Spanish word—you can never really trust a tour guide.>

St. Michel is often shown with a sword in one hand and scales in the other. The sword is to beat back evil or darkness often depicted as a dragon or lizard. The scales are used by the archangel to weigh souls on judgment day sorting out those who will go to heaven from those going to hell. The abbey bookstore displays a large eleventh century frieze depicting St. Michel on judgment day in a grotesque style reminiscent of Hieronymus Bosch. When I asked the sculptor's name, I was told that the artists of that era were basically anonymous.

During the Second World War, the Germans used the bell tower atop the church as a lookout since it dominates the landscape for miles. The bored soldiers scratched their names into the tower. After D-Day when the Americans and English retook the position, their soldiers inscribed their names alongside the German names.

The next tidbit is as best I remember it, but I found it interesting so I'm including it. Our guide said that early Christian monks worshipping St. Michel came from the Orient to Egypt in the third and fourth centuries. There they emulated Christ's forty days and forty nights in the desert by living in stark asceticism; they became known as the Desert Fathers. As the cult expanded, it did not take immediate hold in France but did find fertile ground in Ireland. There Christianity mixed with the paganism of the Druidic cult to form a synthesis religion mixing Christ worship with sun and moon worship. This composite religion is probably the genesis of many of our cultural traditions surrounding Christmas and Easter (e.g., Christmas trees, holly, the Easter bunny, and Easter eggs).

Our guide informed us of a wonderful, ancient site on an island off the western coast of Ireland called Skellig Michel that, in his opinion, rivals Mont St. Michel in historic significance, if not magnificence. The site is composed of a group of low huts and buildings, but the route to the island is treacherous and should not be attempted in winter or bad weather. He referred us to a book called *The Sundancers* to learn more about this fascinating historical period. It's on my list, but I haven't reviewed it yet.

Anyway, eventually the Desert Father cult spread throughout Europe and finally reached France. According to our guide, they chose the Mont St. Michel site because it offered a measure of desert-like isolation when the tidal flow severed ties to the outside world for at least part of each day. He felt it was ironic that an abbey which had moon worship in its past had received a rosary that had been to the moon.

The life of a monk, though harsh by our standards, was still a cut above everyday life for the lower classes of the period. Monks generally came from well-to-do families who traditionally placed the firstborn son at the head of the family business, the second into the army, and the third into the church.

In this way the upper class could control all the power structures. This is the reason that church structures were attacked during the French Revolution and also why the abbey at Mont St. Michel was temporarily disbanded and turned into a prison.

Today, there are five monks and seven nuns to constitute the abbey. They are no longer Benedictine but part of the Monastic Fraternities of Jerusalem which does its work in population centers rather than withdrawing into solitude. While at the abbey I attended Mass for the first time in years. One of the nuns had an ethereal voice that filled the towering chancel and seemed to merge with the diffused light invited by the Gothic architecture. Mom would just love it!

On our second night at Mont St. Michel, we drove to St. Malo to have supper. This extremely well-preserved walled city would have been another great place to spend a day exploring its nooks and crannies. Strangely enough, in the central tourist district, a couple of American Indian street performers in their early twenties dressed in more or less traditional garb played a variety of not so traditional instruments (one was like a long "flutes of Pan"). They were talented and the music was evocative but seemed out of place.

From Mont St. Michel we biked due north across the neck of the Cotentin Peninsula to the Baie de la Seine on the English Channel where we camped on the berm of the shore overlooking the bay—a gorgeous spot. After setting up camp, we drove to the American cemetery at Omaha Beach and were just in time for the lowering of the colors on the anniversary of D-Day. The Prime Minister of Canada had dedicated a new memorial to their servicemen on Juno Beach the same day. The Canadian couple on my Mont St. Michel tour had planned to attend this.

The following day we did our last ride in France for a few months. We passed Omaha, Gold, Juno, and Sword Beaches where D-Day was fought, pausing to read placards and view memorials from time to time. Since it was a short day, I again stopped at Omaha Beach and at a place called Arromanches where a remarkable feat was performed by British engineers. One of the most difficult problems for a successful D-Day invasion was to gain a port that would sustain a full-fledged invasion. The Germans realized that any invasion would fail without a port to offload men and supplies. They therefore fortified all the Normandy ports and gave orders to destroy them before they could be taken by the Allies.

The idea for a transportable port was actually conceived by Winston Churchill himself. Long before it was to be used, and in secrecy, the British built the pieces for such a port. Even before D-Day, portions of the port were towed to the middle of the English Channel and put together so that, immediately after D-Day, construction began at Arromanches. First, seventeen old ships were sunk on the offshore rocks to provide a breakwater for the remaining operation. Next, 115 concrete pontoons were towed across the channel and also sunk. To them seven pier-heads were established with four floating roads leading from them to shore. In addition, 350 barges and amphibious craft called DUKWS were constantly moving between the ships and shore. By June 12, just six days after D-Day, 326,000 men, 54,000 vehicles from jeeps to forty-ton tanks, and 110,000 tons of goods had been offloaded. The allied invasion would have failed if not for this tremendous engineering feat.

We got up early the next morning to catch the channel ferry and had an uneventful, six-hour ride to Portsmouth, England. Once there we set up our tents in an extremely brisk wind causing me to use all of my tent stakes for the first time during the trip. At least the wind dried my tent, wet from the previous night's thunderstorm, in record time.

I had prepared myself for the stomach shock I was likely to find transitioning straight from France to England, so for supper I stuck with the dish the English love and know how to fix—fish and chips. Well, what a disappointment! I sent the first fish back because I could barely cut it with a knife—even the waitress, when she saw how overcooked it was, said, "Ugh, that's gross!" The next piece was marginally better, and I choked it down. At least when I mentioned the problem while paying, they had the good sense to take it off the bill. Regardless, it was not a good introduction to English food.

The next morning the wind was still brisk but not anything like the previous night, and it was slightly behind us. So Stacia and I set out to find our way out of Portsmouth, just a bit complicated. Kirby had taken a bus straight to London to meet his wife who had flown over for a few days, and Andy decided to SAG in the van. The route after leaving town was everything I had hoped an English countryside would be—rolling hills, narrow roads lined with high hedges, little traffic, even a few folks on horseback, lots of forests, and green all around. I even saw some roadkill which means wildlife—I just hope it wasn't Flopsy, Mopsy, or Cotton-tail; maybe it was one of those strange *Watership Down* rabbits.

We rode to a small community on the outskirts of London where the van picked us up and took us to our hotel—staying someplace three nights in a row is a real treat! Winding our way through London in the van made me glad I wasn't biking to our hotel; although, I'm sure Tim would have taken us on side roads had we biked. I would've been game for it, but, by this time, we certainly trust Tim's judgment concerning routes. That evening we met Kirby and his delightful wife Barbara for supper at an English pub before heading out for a night on the town.

I'll spare you the gritty details of my museum visits on the first layover day and will just hit the highlights. Yesterday, I first visited the National Gallery which has a superb collection including van Gogh's *Sunflowers* (not to be confused with his *Sunflowers in Vase* that I saw in Munich). The gallery has a great new audio system that includes commentary on almost every painting in the gallery and also gives a nice summary for each room. However, the three hours I spent there barely covered a quick walk through all the rooms.

From there I strolled down Fleet Street past St. Paul's Cathedral to the Courtauld Institute Gallery at Somerset House. I was not as impressed with this private collection, although it does display some great pieces such as one of Degas' ballerina paintings, Manet's *A Bar at the Folies-Bergere* showing that disaffected barmaid looking straight out of the canvas with all the action of the follies reflected in the mirror behind her, and van Gogh's disturbing *Self-Portrait with Bandaged Ear*.

I crossed the Thames on the Millennium Bridge to the Tate Modern Museum where I quickly strolled through the exhibits as I was running out of time. I soon realized that, to get any benefit from this museum, I would need to devote a healthy chunk of time, in a future visit, to take a guided tour or get the audio guide because most of the pieces left me befuddled.

In those first two nights I attended two plays, *Joseph and the Amazing Technicolor Dreamcoat* and *The Phantom of the Opera*. Both were enjoyable in different ways. We bought "day of" half-price tickets and got lucky with *Joseph* as we were in the second row almost middle! For *Phantom* we had last row seats on the lower gallery and couldn't even see the whole set. I guess you pay your money and take your chances. This was a good experience for me since I've not attended many stage productions. I might be convinced to see more in the future.

I'm going to close this report in the middle of our London visit because I found a good Internet place. However, before I sign off, I want to add a few insights that I did not fit in above. Let me start with food. While in France we ate a lot of pizza which seems to be immensely popular there. One popular pizza is the four-ingredient pizza, but they put a different ingredient on each of four quadrants instead of mixing them together. Boy, was I surprised the first time I got one. Also, when we neared the coast, we had some good mussels and other seafood. In England, so far I've tried the aforementioned over-cooked fish and chips, a nice potpie, a tasty pasta dish, and a better prepared fish and chips. I am a bit apprehensive about what we'll find outside of London though.

As far as biking is concerned, the riding was flat in the Loire Valley but promises to be much hillier in England. As mentioned above I broke a spoke a week ago and had it replaced, but I still have not had a flat on this entire trip! Shortly after having the spoke replaced, I did have a couple of loose spokes, but they were easily tightened.

The campground facilities in France were generally very good (this has much to do with Tim's reconnoitering of course) though several had BYO TP, and one gave you the option of a squat toilet. I don't know to whom they are catering with this one—it looked like the starting blocks for a race as it was just a hole with non-skid porcelain blocks for your feet.

By the time we got to the end of the Loire Valley I was about château-ed out; now that we're in the British Isles, I'm wondering if I'll start getting castle-ated. I guess we'll see. Finally, I'm hoping it'll be easier to find an Internet in England and beyond—France was almost hopeless in this regard, certainly worse than any place we've been yet. Go figure. I'll sign off now. I'm heading to the British Museum and will give you a run down next time.

Take care,

Ralph

Report #12: Irish by Education

June 20, 2003

Howdy from Dublin,

Well, I left you last time on my way to the British Museum. Wow! What a place! I could have spent days there, but I only spent a couple of hours. I wandered around getting my bearings and found the Great Court which is massive, airy, and light—just a great place to be. Then I found the Reading Room which is a high-domed, circular room with bookshelves lining the entire outer wall. Except for its remarkable size, this would be my ideal study. I learned here that the museum actually began as the personal collection of a London doctor named Hans Sloane. He loved collecting things, all sorts of things, from all over the world. His collection continued to grow until it became one of London's attractions for travelers visiting the city. In order that the collection would not be disbursed, he gave the museum to King George II in return for the promise of a stipend for his daughters when he died. In 1753 an Act of Parliament established the museum as the first of its kind: a national museum, freely open to the public with its aim to collect everything. As the collection grew, the building also expanded, and eventually the natural history collection and the book archives were moved to other locations. Even so this museum remains one of the great ones in the world.

One of the endearing stories about Dr. Sloane is that his patients would often make him presents of all sorts of things to add to his large collection. My quote for this missive comes from the letter of one such grateful patient. I include it here primarily for its playful word coinage:

> Since you, Dear Doctor, sav'd my Life
> To bless by Turns or plague my Wife...

118

It is my Wish, it is my Glory
To furnish your Nicknackatory.

After spending time in the Reading Room, I visited an interesting special exhibit called "Memory within Culture." I then wandered through the African Hall before running out of time. I promised myself to come back when I have more time, since I saw only a fraction of the permanent exhibits and would have liked to attend some of the lectures, movies, and other special events on their stacked agenda. Oh, I should say the most surprising thing I found in the museum was a drinking fountain. Even though its chiller was not working, so the water was tepid at best, it is still the first I've seen abroad on this trip since leaving Australia.

From the museum I strolled south getting glimpses of Big Ben and Westminster Abbey along the way. These more touristy places, along with Buckingham Palace, I decided to save for another trip. I got back to the hotel just in time for an early supper as my travel mates were going to a third theater performance (Kirby and his wife to *Chicago*, Andy and Stacia to *Mama Mia*), but I opted, instead, to exlore the environs of our hotel and enjoy the Thoreauesque evening. I first wandered into Hyde Park and found the Peter Pan statue and the monument to John Hanning Speke who (with Richard Burton) discovered Lake Victoria in Africa and the source of the Nile.

This latter monument deserves some copy as I find the story interesting. Speke and Burton were among the many explorers infatuated with the "Dark Continent" and undertook a difficult expedition to find the source of the Nile which was the Holy Grail of its time. They eventually found it after a harrowing trip that almost claimed their lives. Speke later went back to Africa with another fellow and came back claiming he had found a second source. Burton, somewhat miffed and dubious because he knew Speke was something less than meticulous with his facts, called him on it. They were to debate before the Royal Geographical Society. On the day of the debate, word came from Speke's family that he had been killed in a hunting "accident" by his own gun. I suspect that he just could not face his mentor, a man he regarded as his superior, and had committed suicide. The irony is that Speke was correct. He had indeed found the second source of the Nile. For those who would like to know more, pick up Burton's biography, *Sir Captain Richard Francis Burton* or, for those who don't want to spend the time reading a book, there is a good, somewhat fictionalized, account on film called *Mountains of the Moon*. It is very well done.

Still in Hyde Park, I next found a large dead tree that has been carved and decorated with images of dwarves, elves, and other whimsical beings. However popular it might have once been, it isn't exactly the perfect "photo op" anymore as it is surrounded by heavy iron mesh, probably to keep vandals out. Now, as the setting sun shed its last rays on a distant monument turning it a brilliant gold, I hurried the breadth of the park past couples and families picnicking and generally enjoying the perfect evening. The monument was not part of the Royal Geographical Society as I had presumed, but was instead a memorial to honor Prince Albert who was Queen Victoria's royal escort. The Royal Geographical Society building was across the street and, in contrast to Prince Albert's memorial, the society building is unimpressive to the extreme. It is squat and dingy and doesn't at all bespeak of the wondrous events that have been reported therein. Many real and fictional adventures began and/or ended in that building. It does, however, have nice statues of Shackleton and Livingstone along the outside wall.

I continued on toward the hotel past the Science Museum and the Natural History Museum, both closed for the day. At the latter museum there was an outside exhibit of Yaun Arthus-Betrand's photo essay called *The Earth from the Air*. The photos were mounted on placards about four by six feet that were displayed throughout the courtyard with maybe sixty to seventy photographs in all. Arthus-Betrand chose the shots both for the startling images and for the message they convey. The colors were vibrant and striking. Many looked more like surreal paintings than photos of the earth taken from a helicopter. The captions helped explain Arthus-Betrand's message, which is our need to better understand and control the power man has acquired to change the earth's environment. A small gift shop was showing a short film narrated by the photographer explaining his project which is sponsored by UNESCO. If it comes to your town, go see it; you'll like it.

The next morning I met our new rider, Penny, an early fortyish English and literature teacher at a Southern California community college. Although somewhat quiet, she was obviously interested in seeing the settings where many of her literary heroes and heroines lived out their real or imaginary lives. We all loaded into the van so Bobbi could drive us to the Godalming Superstore outside London where we again started biking from the point we had stopped a few days earlier. I had an interesting experience while getting ready for the ride. I was coming out of the store after using their facilities when I passed two elderly ladies, one was helping the other with a cane, both were white-haired and probably in their eighties and nineties. As I passed, the younger one, with all the dignity and conviction a British matron can muster, said to me in a tone that would broach no argument, "You have lovely legs!" In my surprise all I could reply was, "Thank you very much." I should have at least complimented her on the stiffness of her upper lip. It was gratifying, I must say, for once not to be eclipsed by the guys (and some of the gals) in the New Mexico Touring Society of which I am a member.

The ride was much like the one from Portsmouth to Goldaming. The weather was gorgeous, the terrain up and down but with no killer hills, and the landscape was rural-wild with some fields of crops but much forest and high hedgerows. I saw much more roadkill than any place since Tasmania, and it included a dead stoat. I also chased a fat meadow vole down the road a short distance and saw a pair of swans with their cygnets lying alongside the road.

When I got to Winchester, I dawdled awhile before riding to its famous cathedral and casing the joint before deciding to pay the three pounds fifty "suggested donation." Unfortunately, I missed the last tour so I used their brochure to tour myself and to find the graves of Jane Austen and of Izaak Walton, the grandfather of English angling (my dad would have enjoyed this visit). I guess it's a common practice in English churches to have the grave stones set into the floor, but I felt a little uneasy traipsing all over these dead folk. Throughout the cathedral, there were also many coffins with ornate and sometimes grotesque trappings. I caught the tail end of the tour I had just missed and again realized that you really need someone to explain these old buildings because you just can't decipher them and their history by yourself.

Our camp that day was on the outskirts of town at a nice family-owned campground. All of our camp spots were great in England and Wales—very green and well-kept with clean if modest facilities. At this camp, the elderly hosts cooked our supper and breakfast. And what a supper it was! We had roast beef, Yorkshire pudding (about every other thing on an English menu is a "pudding" so I haven't deciphered this one yet) with gravy, peas, carrots, two kinds of potatoes, a cauliflower cheese casserole, and buttered bread. For dessert we had two large bowls of English trifles and a strawberry shortcake topped with meringue. It was all very good but, try as I might, I could not clean up everyone's plates, so they had lots of leftovers. We then chatted until almost midnight with our hosts, their cousin, and his wife. The latter two had lived three years in Australia in the early '70s and had almost moved to Woomera! I had lived in that tiny outback village from 1978–80 when I was in the USAF so we had lots to talk about.

During this evening I had plenty of opportunity to observe an English stereotype. You might have called our hosts the "Bickersons" as they always seemed to be picking at one another. I have also seen this attitude in several waitresses. To us, such behavior borders on rudeness or is at least "cheeky," but I am beginning to realize it is just the way many Brits are. I suspect that's what makes their sitcoms so popular in the States. We find the snide remarks a bit uncomfortable and react by laughing.

From Winchester we rode to Bath through Salisbury and Stonehenge. Kirby and I stopped in Salisbury to tour the cathedral, this time with a guide, and found it interesting. Although the cathedral has been renovated in the past and is now being renovated again with lots of scaffolding all along one side, there are still portions of the thirteenth-century edifice extant. While in the cathedral we saw possibly the oldest working clock in the world. It uses counterweights for its power and an interesting timing system comprised of slots cut into a flywheel at appropriate intervals. It has no face since it was built specifically just to strike the hour. The cathedral also preserves the most legible copy of the original Magna Carta from 1215. Although it is often described as the earliest written statement for the "rights of man," in fact, it is a feudal document providing rights to only about 5 percent of the population. The other 95 percent were serfs and were essentially treated as slaves. Later, just like our own constitution, upon which it was based, the Magna Carta was reinterpreted more broadly (our constitution, if you remember, did not originally mean "all" men are created equal).

Not far down the road I stopped at Stonehenge and took an audio tour. The structure was begun five thousand years ago and was originally made from wood, a small part of which remains. But it is the large, rough, mysteriously located stones providing such a stark image on the wide Salisbury plain that draws the crowds today. Stonehenge means "hanging stone" and the current best guess is that it served as a sort of calendar; the sun comes up through one of the arches at each of the summer and winter solstices and at successive arches each month in-between. Beyond this, everything is pure speculation. While there I took a catnap in the mild sunshine before realizing it was 4 p.m. and I still had over eighty kilometers to ride, so I got on the road and hustled. It turned out to be a 155-kilometer day (almost a century), and I finally got to camp at 8 p.m., by far my latest arrival to date.

The next morning, after a full English breakfast (to be avoided in the future), I walked into town and caught a city walking tour sponsored by the mayor's office and free! Our docent was enthusiastic, loud enough to be heard, and gave one of the best tours yet. She showed us the pump room and bath building, the Royal Crescent designed by John Wood the younger, the Circus designed by John Wood the elder, Queens Square, the old Assembly Rooms building, and generally helped me get oriented in the town.

The three hot springs in the bog upon which current Bath sits were evidently ignored by the Celtic people who lived in the surrounding hills. It wasn't until the Romans invaded about two thousand years ago that they were exploited. The Romans enclosed the springs to create "baths," and used the area as an R & R center for its troops.

When the Roman Empire contracted again, the Saxons from Germany moved into the area, followed sometime later by the Danes and Vikings. It was during this general period that an abbey was founded, and Bath became a religious center. In AD 973 the first English king was crowned there. The Norman Conquest of 1066 again changed the rule of England. Each successive group in the city built on top of what was already there such that Bath today has little that is on ground level. Because it had been both a holy pilgrimage site and a site for the sick and infirm (in fact, one of the three baths was set aside specifically for lepers), Bath was long a tourist destination. The townspeople, wanting to utilize all available above ground space for paying customers, built a layer of underground storage areas that even run beneath the streets. The numerous regimes left quite an architectural variety with probably the eighteenth century Georgian era, represented by the John Wood father and son architects, being the most prominent.

As with most tour guides, this one enjoyed sharing interesting anecdotes. There are evidently several versions of the founding of Bath. One version presents Prince Bladud, eldest son of King Lud, as a youth with promise, intelligence, and good looks. He is sent to Athens for training for eleven years where, unfortunately, he contracts leprosy. When he returns home, he is imprisoned, as was the custom with lepers. But Bladud was a resourceful young man who escapes to lead a free, but solitary life as a swineherd. While tending the swine he notices they like to wallow in the black boggy mud beneath an alder grove and that, upon emerging, having been coaxed out with acorns by Prince Bladud, their cuts and sores are healed. (In the guide's version, the pigs contracted leprosy which was healed by the mud but, as far as I know, armadillos are the only mammal besides man that can get leprosy.) Anyway, the prince gives the mud a try and, sure enough, his leprosy is cured by lying in the bog water. He goes home, is received warmly, and in time becomes a good and just king. He built the baths to show his appreciation.

The postscript to this tale is equally apocryphal. It seems the good king invents a set of wings so he can fly and, with all his subjects watching, dons his wings and leaps with them to his death from one of his towers. Our guide said this Bladud was the father of Shakespeare's Lear.

No tour seems complete without the local etymological stories, and this one was no exception. The springs are hottest where they come from the ground; this area is called the "kitchen." It takes the most heat-resistant souls to go into this area, hence the saying, according to our guide that, "If you can't stand the heat, stay out of the kitchen."

So many people came to the baths for their healing powers that the area's doctors became upset because they were losing business. Many moved to Bath to practice their craft and became known as "aquatic doctors." However, enough of them proved to be charlatans that the term at some point became condensed, through the wonderful process of "vernacularization," to just "quacks."

Of course, the people in those early days did not have indoor plumbing. They used chamber pots or went to the outhouse to "do the necessary" as a quaint English phrase goes. The ladies of the time would say they were "going to the garden to pluck a rose." When indoor plumbing finally became available, most homes did not have any extra room for a commode. Therefore many people built a small wooden structure to the outside of their second story bedrooms to accommodate this new invention. These were called "hanging loos," and there are many still around today looking unseemly appended to the beautiful stone walls.

During the time when the baths were highly fashionable, it was the place to see and be seen, to look for appropriate matches for your children, and to make your consumption (not the disease) conspicuous as it were. To get to and from the baths and your hotel, you would hire a sedan chair carried by runners. These runners found increasingly devious ways to bilk passengers. When their shenanigans finally got out of hand, one of the early town mayors established a set of rules for these runners including a standard tariff. In effect, these runners became the first taxi drivers.

The large, splendid circular set of connected houses called the "Circus" was designed by John Wood the elder showcasing his absorption with ancient Roman styles. However, because Wood was also obsessed with old Celtic legends, he placed large stone acorns at regular intervals along the rooftops of the Circus buildings to honor the story of Bladud coaxing the swine from the bog with acorns. Though the buildings are indeed beautiful, the acorns look a bit out of place.

Much of the city still looks wonderfully old. It is widely considered the most beautiful city in England. While I was there they were filming a new version of *Vanity Fair* starring Reese Witherspoon. In fact, as I was riding into the city that first day, I rode right through one of the sets without knowing what was going on until later.

Bath was the first time we had camped on a layover day. I felt a little uncomfortable leaving everything I owned in a zippered tent while I was in town all day, but the campground was sparsely populated, and we didn't have any incidents. The campground was good-sized and in a great location next to a stream on the outskirts of Bath. Our last night there I caught a glimpse of the full moon rising as I was coming back to my tent after my evening ablutions, so I walked to the upper campground to get a better view. As always, it was quite a sight.

The next day we rode to Cardiff, the capital of Wales. To cross the Severn River that separates England from Wales at that point, we took a transporter bridge, the first I have seen. It is an airborne platform hung by cables to a structure high overhead that spans the Severn River. Perhaps eight cars at a time would pull onto the bridge platform, the gate would shut, and the entire platform would then cross above the river suspended by the cables. The crossing was surprisingly steady. I'm not sure why engineers chose this structure instead of a regular drawbridge unless, this close to the channel, a tidal surge might take down a standard bridge during heavy flooding. Regardless, it was pretty neat. Also, along the way I saw some type of weasel run across the road. It always adds to the ride when there is wildlife about.

At Cardiff we each had our own room (a rare treat!) at the Welsh Institute for Sport which is the national campus for preparing their athletes for events. I had a nice swim followed by a short workout in their weight room. The facilities were okay, but with our obsession for competitive sports in the States, we must have literally thousands of facilities better equipped than this one.

Before setting off the next morning, we were told the local library would let us use its Internet at no cost, so I stopped there on my way out of town. I did indeed get a free hour and then took advantage of their reference section to find answers to questions that had come up along the way. I didn't get on the road until 11 a.m., unusually late for me.

The next couple days were going to be as hot as Wales gets according to one of the guys at the Welsh Institute. According to our sensibilities, the weather was great the whole day. The terrain was all up and down with healthy climbs and fun descents. We also had several rabbit-warren roads where the hedges grow close along a single-track road or a forest closed in on both sides to form a tunnel. These small byways have become some of my favorite riding. On one of the single-track roads I met a couple of vehicles coming from the opposite direction and had to lean into the hedge to let them pass. On another occasion, a farmer pulling a trailer with huge hay bales that brushed the hedges on both sides of the track caused me to turn around and find a wide place so he could pass. I wonder what happens when two such vehicles meet? And poor Bobbi driving that huge van! Again we were grateful that Tim had taken the time to find such wonderful routes…except maybe Bobbi.

Besides these cozy byways, we also got some glorious vistas since we were riding part of the time through the Welsh high country. We often paid for these views of rolling hills that seemed to go on forever with better than 15 percent grades on the uphill. On one of the rides I stopped in a small village to buy an apple-black currant pastry midway between the size of a tart and a pie. I stowed it in my bike carrier and waited until I was on top of the world with grand vistas in every direction before stopping for a snack. It just doesn't get any better than this!

It would be interesting to understand the geology of this place. I stopped at a scenic overlook where a plaque explained that the valley before me was originally formed by a glacier that carved out the characteristic U shape. But the glacier had changed the course of the Twymyn River causing it to now run down the valley thus transforming it from the U shape into the characteristic V-shaped river valley. There was one narrow ridge, steep on both sides, with a big divot in the middle. I couldn't tell what had made the divot, but I'd love to do some hiking in this area to see this feature up close. Speaking of hiking, there are signed walking paths all over the countryside we have been riding through ever since we landed in Britain, but they have been especially plentiful in Wales. We have passed many spots, all along those single-track byways I mentioned above, where small staircases have been positioned so you can easily climb over the hedgerows to cross the roads. Every time I saw one of these crossings my curiosity was piqued—I guess I'll just have to come back to hike. By the way, the name "Twymyn River" reminds me of a remark Kirby made upon arrival in Wales. He opined that the only time a foreigner can correctly pronounce Welsh words is immediately upon leaving the dentist, mouth numbed, after having a tooth filled—I think he might have something there.

Finally, the weather had to change and, for our long day's ride to Bangor, we had rain for about half the day and strong winds for all of it. Luckily, the temperature was surprisingly mild and, except for a few stretches, the wind was at our backs. Once, however, I turned a corner, and the wind almost stopped me dead in my tracks it was so strong. The route was extremely beautiful as we traveled right up the coast of Cardigan Bay and St. George's Channel, the body of water separating southern Ireland from Wales. We had the bay in sight much of the way either from a height that gave splendid views (especially when partially obstructed by one of their old castles) or from close up when we could feel the sea spray from the strong southwest wind. I never like to ride in the rain but, if I must, then this is the way I want to do it.

In a pleasant coincidence, I had just been reading Bill Bryson's *Notes from a Small Island* the morning before we rode to Bangor. In it he was speculating on the singular madness responsible for the hundreds of mobile homes packed bow to stern, row upon row, into a small area of a desolate beach in the north of Wales. Well, on this day's ride we passed several groups of vacationers just as he described. But I must say, having seen similar evidence of this madness in the States, the urge to leave comfortable hearth and home to spend the holidays in different surroundings is extremely strong despite the lack of natural allure evident at the vacation site.

Our last night in Wales, Kirby and I opted to dine in a pub while the others headed to an Italian restaurant. We each had a main course (mine was chicken in a barbecue cheese sauce with chips, peas, and carrots), and then we split a fish and fried mushroom main. To top it off, we walked to the Safeway just down the street from our bed-and-breakfast (B&B) and got a pint each of Snickers and M&M ice cream to share on the B&B stoop. Hey, we were just trying to get back some of those biking calories.

Yesterday, we biked to the fast ferry for the ninety-minute trip to Dublin and then, after disembarking, biked to Dublin University where Kirby, Andy, and I were in a pod of four rooms with a common area, a full kitchen, and two bathrooms...absolute heaven for two nights! This morning I joined a great walking tour of the city, but the Trinity College Ph.D. history student provided so much information that it would be overload if I included it in this report. Also, I'm getting a mite peckish. So, since food is on my mind, I'll hold off on the Irish history lesson until next time and leave you instead with a couple of morsels on food and one more bike related item.

First, the food: we have been eating lots of pub food—fish and chips, chicken and chips, pasta and chips, jacketed (baked) potatoes, pot pie and chips, etc. and chips. I asked my tour guide today if the reason chips are served with, seemingly, all meals in Ireland is that the people are just trying to correct their historical average from the great potato famine (and this goes for Wales and England too). The food has been good but not remarkable...except for the treacle pudding. This heavenly delight is a sponge cake drizzled with treacle and then placed in the center of an ocean of hot custard—a veritable culinary Mont St. Michel! I had almost forgotten how I would heap this hot custard atop almost every dessert that was served at the Woomera chow hall as a junior captain living in Australia. I'm surprised this wonderful dessert hasn't been adopted by America since we seem to glom onto the tasty bits from each country's cuisine. Maybe it's the word "treacle" that puts us off? I've also had good rhubarb and lemon tarts here.

I tried a Snickers (trademarked and everything) "flap jack" for a treat on one of the rides. This snack food is an oat cake with embedded peanuts covered in chocolate. I'm not sure how they get away with calling it a Snickers. Taste-wise, it was just okay, but not as good as the original by far. Speaking of Snickers, Kirby and I agree that they are the ultimate energy bar. They easily beat all the others for taste and seem to provide just as much quick energy. Why the manufacturers of the myriad power bars have not gotten much beyond a well-used athletic shoe insole in the taste department is a mystery to me. They are uniformly bland to awful in my opinion. I still have a good supply of Snickers I brought from the States in April after our SARS sabbatical. I always carry one but generally only eat it when I really need the extra kick and no tarts or other treats are available. The only drawback with a Snickers is the low melting point of the chocolate, but then they do reconstitute nicely.

Okay, a nod to the bike people: I finally had to replace my rear tire in Cardiff after 8,800-plus kilometers as it started showing the red undercoating through the outer rubber. The front tire still looks fine. And, I still haven't had a flat yet. How often do you run through a tire before getting a hole in your inner tube, especially a tube that had a few patches on it to begin with? (Actually, this might not be so amazing outside New Mexico, but for those familiar with goatheads, I know this sounds unbelievable.)

That's enough for this time. By the way, the title of this report refers to the institution from which I received my undergraduate math degree, The University of Notre Dame with its Fighting Irish.

Take care of yourself and those who belong to you,

Ralph

Report #13: Loch, Scot, and Two Smoking Haggis'

July 1, 2003

Greetings from Inverness, Scotland,

Okay, last time I promised (threatened?) you with an abbreviated view of Irish history. Our tour guide (remember, the history Ph.D. student?) met us at Trinity College in downtown Dublin and started her pitch with interesting info about this august institution. Queen Elizabeth founded Trinity College in the sixteenth century specifically as a Protestant college supporting the Anglican Church. Catholics were not allowed to attend. This ban was not revoked until the early twentieth century. However, by then the Catholic Church hierarchy had imposed a restriction of their own requiring any Catholic student wishing to matriculate into Trinity College to first seek the bishop's permission. His permission was almost always denied. This restriction lasted until the 1970s.

Unlike U.S. colleges, Irish colleges at the undergraduate and often at the graduate level are free. The guide said the government tried to impose fees last year, but the protest was so fierce the proposal was dropped. As she showed us the grounds, she pointed out one hallowed building that had been photographed and digitally enhanced for one of the Harry Potter films. This was done without the consent of the college, which then sued...so maybe they'll be able to avoid student fees for a little longer.

As far as Irish history is concerned, I tried to absorb as much as I could and even consulted other sources to put together a good summary. Our guide admitted that their history is very complex. She began in 500 BC when the Celts came from Germany. They brought and developed their own laws, which were kept by their judges, called Druids, a group consisting of both men and women. The laws were practical in that they dealt with people as they are rather than trying to make them adhere to idealized principles. As a result, these laws were popular with the people and existed in some form until the sixteenth century. The guide also emphasized that it was crucial to Ireland's subsequent development that the Roman legions never invaded Ireland. Evidently they got to the west coast of England and Wales and decided it wasn't worth the effort.

In the mid-fifth century, St. Patrick and other monks brought Christianity to Ireland. St. Patrick, as we all know, is credited with driving the snakes out of Ireland. However, there never were any snakes in Ireland, so the experts speculate that the snake of legend stood for the Druidic religion since one of their symbols is the snake. Of course, as I mentioned in my Mont St. Michel summary, the Druidic religion did not disappear but, instead, melded with Christianity to form a hybrid somewhat different from what Rome practiced. For instance, Ireland's Christian churches had female priests and bishops, similar to the Druids. It's no surprise that this caused problems with the Pope later on.

In 795, Vikings began attacking and pillaging the towns of Ireland. Having a strong business bent, they soon established trading posts along the coast including Dublin (literally, "black pool") on the River Liffey. The Vikings assimilated readily since they did not bring their women with them, and soon they began taking sides and fighting for one or another Irish clan leader in the many disputes always taking place. In 1014, Brian Boru was able to join the clans of the south together and rallied them to defeat the invading Vikings once and for all. Unfortunately, he and most of his male offspring were killed in the last battle, and no strong leader emerged to stop the descent back into internecine warfare among the clans.

Finally, one disgruntled clan leader requested England's King Henry II's help to defeat the preeminent Irish clan leader of the time. Henry was only too happy to send his knights on such an errand under the leadership of one called Strongbow. The knights performed their task well, and Strongbow married the clan leader's daughter as a reward. Eventually, he inherited the position of clan leader and became powerful.

This worried Henry who then, under a Papal Bull (the Pope wanted to get rid of Celtic Christianity), invaded Ireland and reestablished the English claim. Henry's influence did not reach beyond Dublin and environs that together became known as "the Pale." Hence the nether regions outside this area were "beyond the Pale," a phrase that stuck in our vernacular.

After this, the history becomes confusing as the distinctions between Catholic and Protestant, Celtic Catholicism and Roman Catholicism, and nationalism (Irish, English, and British) get mixed and matched as different leaders tried to get or maintain power. I'll offer only a few disjointed tidbits to provide a feel for the dynamics.

When Henry VIII wanted his divorce, he was pitted directly against the Pope in Rome. To resolve the dilemma in his favor, he created his own religion. Faced with split loyalties, the Irish decided they could remain loyal to the Pope in religious matters and to their king in secular matters. This did not endear them to their king, causing the Irish still more problems in the years to come.

Queen Elizabeth had to send an army to defeat an uprising in Ulster (in the northern part of Ireland) which, at that time, was the hotbed of Irish nationalism. A later monarch, King James, pushed seditious northerners completely off their land and gave it to English Protestants to end any rebellious intentions the people in Northern Ireland might have had. This, of course, led to the current situation. The Protestants prospered and kept their ties to England strong so that, when the rest of Ireland was clamoring for home rule and eventually independence, they wanted none of it.

Still later, King James II became so unpopular that William of Orange successfully overthrew him (the final battle took place in Ireland), and James fled to France. In one of those bizarre twists in history, the Pope actually backed William, a professed Protestant, in this conflict instead of King James who was soft on Catholics. The Pope did this because of his hatred for the Sun King, King Louis XIV of France, who was supporting King James.

Things got increasingly worse for the Irish, especially the Irish Catholics. In the early eighteenth century, penal laws were put into effect which, among other things, prohibited Catholics from voting, holding office, or even from educating their children. A tax was established based on the number of windows in a building. Known as taxing daylight, it is where we get the term "daylight robbery." To mitigate this tax, many people blocked up any unnecessary windows.

By the end of the eighteenth century, the Irish were ready to rebel and, helped by the French who had just been through their own revolution, they did…but they were crushed. However, the rebellion caused much concern among the English rulers and, in 1801, they forced Ireland into a union with

England, and sectarianism became English policy. In response to these oner-ous laws, Catholic emancipation became a strong movement in Ireland, and by 1829 English parliament felt pressured to pass the Catholic Emancipation Act, which eased the penal code.

In 1845, the Potato Famine ravaged Ireland. It lasted four years causing widespread death through starvation and related diseases. This, coupled with emigration as people fled the famine, reduced the population from 8.5 million to the 4.5 million Ireland has today. The famine was exacerbated by the way it was handled by both the English and Irish in power at the time. One of the results is that Ireland changed from having hundreds of small, one-family potato farms to large consolidated farms of pastureland for sheep and cattle. Prominent Irish landholders would actually buy a passage to America (or wherever) for the peasants, so they could gobble up the peasants' land.

At the beginning of the twentieth century, Irish home rule became the big issue. The Protestants holding power in the north naturally did not want it. The issue was put on the backburner during the First World War while both the Protestants and the Catholics sent their "armies" to Europe to fight for mother England. However, while the war proceeded on its deadly course, one Irish group continued to push the issue and finally rebelled. The rebellion was brutally squelched. On Easter Sunday, 1916, the leaders were captured, and all but two (a man with a U.S. passport and a woman) were summarily shot with-out trial. This brutal act eventually backfired on the English, since it generated much sympathy and support for the rebels and their cause. At the next British general election, the Sinn Fein (literally, "We Ourselves," or "Ourselves Alone") won a majority of the seats in Irish Parliament and immediately decided that their Irish Parliament would not convene in England, as was nor-mally done, but would remain in Ireland. Shortly thereafter, in 1919, the new parliament declared Ireland independent. An Anglo-Irish war broke out with Sinn Fein's Irish Republican Army (IRA) pitted against the British army. In 1921, the Irish Free State was established after lengthy negotiations led by Michael Collins on the Irish side. The treaty also gave the right of choice to six counties in Northern Ireland to stay with England or join the Irish Free State—they decided to stay as part of England. The Free State was later to become the Republic of Ireland we know today.

The turbulence in Irish history did not end there as civil war broke out almost immediately over the terms of the treaty. Irish hard-liners thought the terms carried too many compromises. In 1923, the war ground to a halt and, for the next fifty years, a tenuous peace held during which incremental steps were taken including the establishment of an Irish Republic in 1948 and the secession from the British Commonwealth in 1949. This tenuous peace lasted until 1969 when Catholic rights marchers in Northern Ireland, using the non-violent tactics of the U.S. Civil Rights Movement, were attacked by Protestants. The "Troubles" had begun with a resurgent IRA and an increase in British troops in Northern Ireland. Things continued to heat up as a splinter IRA group broke off from the main body with more radical and violent tactics; this, in turn, spawned a comparable Protestant paramilitary organization.

Finally, in 1994, both sides declared a cease-fire, and negotiations began which eventually resulted in the Good Friday Agreement on April 10, 1998. Since then, the mood has been optimistic that the war is over and peaceful agreement will eventually be reached. The major sticking point at the moment seems to be over the "decommissioning" of the IRA weapon stockpile.

Okay, now that you're all much smarter about Irish history, I'll continue with a few anecdotes from the tour. Our guide said that both the eleventh century Christ Church Cathedral (where Strongbow is buried) and St. Patrick's Cathedral were converted to Protestant Churches during the Reformation. When, years later, Irish bishops asked the Pope if they could have a Catholic cathedral, he replied that they already had two. This clearly points out that, at that time, the Catholic Church did not officially acknowledge the Reformation.

Our guide also mentioned that Ireland has a huge economic gap between the "haves" and "have nots" in the country. In fact, she said it had the largest gap of any westernized nations, second only to the United States (this made me look for some place to hide).

She also mentioned that the Irish don't have anything but good to say of former President Clinton. After all, he gave them St. George. She said that George Mitchell, the American envoy Clinton sent to help mediate the "Troubles," is the only person who has been able to talk to both sides, and they credit him for helping them get to the peace accords.

Okay, enough of a history lesson for now. Dublin University, where we stayed in Dublin, was one of the places housing people who were participating in the Special Olympics. They began showing up in droves the evening before we left as the opening ceremonies, with guest speakers Nelson Mandela and Mohammed Ali (among others), were to take place the next day. It would have been fun to stay for this, but we were told the seats had been sold out long before. These are the first Special Olympics to be held outside the United States, and Ireland is doing it up proud. Evidently, the games are to be held here because it is the "Year of the Disabled Person" in Europe. As we rode through the countryside, we passed town after town each hosting athletes from a particular country and each with a big sign welcoming their guests.

Stacia's older sister, Shana, arrived while we were in Dublin. She will ride with us for awhile. Stacia is ecstatic, and they are having a great time riding together. Even though Shana had never done long miles on a bike before, she is tackling the route like a trooper, even the back to back centuries we hit on her second day of riding (what a dubious welcome for her!). This new edition to our gang put the guys at a numerical disadvantage for the first time on the trip.

The first few days of riding in Ireland did not meet my expectations until we hit the north coast. I had expected lots of single track, rural back roads—actually, the kind of roads we traveled in England and Wales. However, we were doing lots of miles, including back to back centuries into and out of Donegal. I got the impression that Tim wanted us to see certain areas and had to default to more direct, larger roads to get us there. Whatever the reason, I would vote for less miles and more scenic routes (I know they are out there based on what several people have told me about their trips in Ireland).

Riding through one small town on our first ride day, I passed a group of men loitering along the main street. One of them yelled something at me as I passed by. It took me half-a-tick to decipher the accent so I could understand that he was warning me, "Hey, your back wheels are going forward." I just nodded and rode on. This guy was at least sixty and was standing with a group of his pards, and I'm sure they got a big kick out of it. It reminded me of my first "best friend" who used to yell out just the same thing to bicyclists but, if I remember correctly, he quit that joke when we matriculated into junior high school. I smiled at the confirmation that there are all kinds out here in the big world and that we don't have all the "idjits" resident in Small Town, USA.

Another interesting cultural tidbit I observed from that first riding day was a characteristic Irish nod, a subtle tilt of the head, when acknowledging another person along the street. I must have seen the same tilt at least a dozen times in my riding, once from a boy that couldn't have been more than twelve, so it must either be engrained early or is a genetic trait.

We have had a few more mistakes on the DRG's lately, and I suspect it is in direct correlation to how much Tim has on his plate. Not only is he preceding us to check and correct our route guides, but he then must fly back to the States to do the same thing for TK&A's cross the U.S.A. tour his sister is currently running. On his last visit (our first night out of Dublin), he showed up to give Bobbi the next two weeks worth of DRG's at 1 a.m. and then left at 5 a.m. to drive to Dublin for a flight home. I'm sure glad I don't have his job!

On a positive note, we had better weather in Ireland than we had any right to expect. We had nothing worse than light sprinkles the whole time we were there! Tim told us it had rained almost constantly while he was checking our route guides the week before. Also, we have had the chance to be "trailer trash" for a couple of nights as two of our nightly stays were in double-wide trailers. Other than a bit tighter quarters than usual, it was nice to be inside since we never knew when the rain would come.

Unfortunately, on our way out of Donegal, the third day out of Dublin, we sustained our second casualty. Penny took a header going downhill. Bobbi blames the hydraulic brakes on her hybrid bike. Whatever the reason, poor Penny did a face-plant and spent a night in the hospital. She lost a tooth, got her lip chewed up pretty good and has a swollen nose, but she was lucky it was not worse. Penny has a great constitution and an even better disposition and has bounced back strongly. After limping around a few days, she began riding again.

The day of Penny's accident was also a strange day for the other riders. Because Bobbi had to ensure Penny was getting the care she needed in the hospital and then stay with her until she was settled in, she didn't arrive at camp with our gear until just before midnight. Luckily, we were staying in a double-wide trailer in a nearly deserted trailer park that night. The owner was nice enough to let us into the trailer after we told him our situation. Although we didn't have any clothes other than what we had on or in our bike bags, we were able to clean up a bit before walking to the relatively few buildings that constituted this seaside village. Fortune continued smiling on us as the village catered to a vacation crowd so they had a nice hotel restaurant with a magnificent ocean view. It was a more subdued evening than usual as we speculated on how Penny was doing.

After our two century rides, we (gratefully) had a light day, less than fifty kilometers, to Ballintoy with time to explore some of the neat areas along the coast of Northern Ireland. Kirby and I rode much of the day together, and our first stop was at the slowly deteriorating Dunluce Castle on the northern coast. We then met Andy at the next village and took a tour of Bushmill's Distillery, the oldest licensed whisky distillery in the world. Though I'm a teetotaler, I did find the distillery process interesting. The brewers first allow the barley to germinate and then grind it to grist before adding water three different times. They take the first two "waters," add yeast and let the concoction ferment a few days. They then distill it three times and store it in wooden vats of various sizes. These vats have all held other liquors (e.g., sherry, brandy, etc.) in previous lives providing the distinctive taste to the different whiskies. The tour guide hastened to point out that distilleries in America distill only once, so their brew is not as smooth as Bushmill's. Andy and Kirby happily shared my sample shot in an attempt to prove or disprove our host's assertion.

After lunch (yes, for maybe the second or third time on the trip, I actually ate a full lunch, some lovely fish and chips), we rode to the Giant's Causeway, yet another UNESCO World Heritage Site. The rock formations along this spectacular coastline reminded me of a similar site near Mammoth in California called the Devil's Postholes. Geologic forces have caused the rock to be been split vertically into regular geometric shapes that run for the whole length of a cliff—it's a great place for amateur geologists and even a better place for kids of all ages.

That night we stayed in a small town called Ballintoy. With time for a nice ramble along the coast after supper, I visited Carrick-a-Rede (literally, "rock in the road") Island where there is a large gull and fulmar (a large seabird) rookery. The birds sure made a lot of noise. The parents would fly up to alight on the cliff, stuff a fish into the gaping maw of their young and then plunge back down toward the sea for another fish in a continuous parental loop. The small island stands right in the middle of a salmon pathway along the coast, hence the name. The fishermen set their nets along this pathway in the same place every year. After my walk, on the way to a pub where a group of traditional Irish musicians was playing, I watched a spectacular sunset with the brightest, most iridescent red-orange I have seen (especially as viewed through my binoculars). Also, as I was pacing the sun down to this gorgeous set, I passed a paddock full of sheep. Two young sheep (they seemed too big to call lambs) were suckling their mother with their butts near her face, so she could see their tails waggling with delight. While I watched, she walked away, but the young sheep stood still, muzzle to muzzle, for several moments. They were still there when I walked away. I don't know if they were waiting for the milk to settle or what, but it certainly was a cute sight.

From Ballintoy, we rode along the coast to Belfast. We had a bit of a headwind, but the coastal views were great. We crossed one headland that provided a nice, gradual uphill climb blocked from the wind, followed by a great downhill run. The ride into Belfast proper was like most city rides: tense, highly trafficked, and not much fun. My initial impression was that Belfast was dirty, industrialized, and poor, so it came as a bit of a shock when people kept mentioning how much better things are now and how much cleaner the town is than before the Good Friday Peace Accords. I can only imagine what it must have been like then!

I was the first to arrive in Belfast and, having followed the DRG to our accommodations, found myself on a side street near a business district looking up at a series of large brick buildings, none of them having any resemblance to a hotel. Also, none of the buildings had a sign that corresponded to the name of the hotel on our DRG. After asking a few people who were walking by and getting blank stares, I decided to come back later. So I found a store to get a drink and a snack, visited the tourist info center where I discovered there were no city walking tours the next day, and then rode to the local library to check out the e-mail situation. When I later returned to the hotel address, no one had yet arrived, so I lay down in the shade and took a catnap.

I was nearly ready to ride off again when other riders finally arrived and, yes, this was the right place. Our digs for the next two nights was more like an abandoned apartment building than a hotel and somewhat dilapidated. We seemed to have had the whole place to ourselves. On the fourth floor, the guys shared one room and the gals another. On the ground floor, the men had one working shower and one john that still had its seat; I don't know what the situation was for the women. With no elevator, a nightly wander to the john and back brought you fully awake and breathing hard. Tim sure finds some interesting places to stay! However, it was good to be settled for a couple of nights, and it was a super location for exploring the city.

The Black Cab tour of Belfast we took the next day was very good. Norman, our driver, was a good-sized fellow with heavily tattooed arms. He talked us through a little of the recent history before driving us past the shipyards where the Titanic was built and where Hercules and Samson, the two largest cranes in Europe, sit idle. At one time the yards employed thirty thousand people and now employ a hundred and fifty. Norman said he thinks it'll be closed in eighteen months.

He then drove us through both Protestant and Catholic neighborhoods divided by a twenty-foot wall. The murals, especially on the Protestant side, were impressive and ubiquitous as were the Union Jack and thousands of red, white, and blue flags. He stopped at the dividing wall where we added our names and messages to the graffiti that covered it. Norman was matter of fact and straightforward with his answers to our questions which we appreciated. What surprised me most was his constant assertions of how much better things are now—I still feel the city has a long way to go.

The rain finally caught up with us as we were leaving Ireland. It rained all night our last night in Belfast, it rained on the ferry ride to Scotland, and it rained the whole way as we biked to Saltcoats, Scotland, our first night's stay in that country. We were along the coast most of the time, first along the North Channel that separates the two countries at that point and then along the Firth of Clyde. The next two days were progressively nicer with an over-cast day (but no rain) followed by a gorgeous day, as we biked to Fort Williams and our next break. We were riding along lochs much of the time. The lochs, created when the glaciers receded, generally run from the northeast to the southwest in Scotland, so we would head up the east coast of one and then cut cross-country to the bottom of the next and ride along it, gradually making our way north. At Inverary, the in-between day, I visited the Duke and Duchess of Argyll, the "sox" people, at their castle but decided not to take the tour. It's an impressive, new-looking structure. Evidently, they own most of the land thereabouts. I also poked my nose into St. Conan's Kirk, an interesting old church, on my way out of town the next morning.

On my layover day, I hiked up Ben Nevis. The following is my journal entry for that part of the day:

> I let the birds wake me up this morning and rolled out of the sack at 4:42 a.m. I was at the deserted Ben Nevis info center by 5:15 a.m. to begin the ten-mile round trip hike to 4,418 foot Ben Nevis, the tallest spot in Britain. I was impressed with the construction of the path early in my hike: it was a mosaic of large granite stones at least two persons wide. Later, near the top, I found that someone had moved tons of small stone to cover the paths leading to and around the summit.
>
> I tested my hiking legs as I had not done an aggressive hike in eight months and probably longer. I have either been training for this bike ride or on it for the last year and a half. The weather was great as I started. The sun had not come up over the mountain and wouldn't for at least a couple of hours, since I was in the western shadow of the mountain, but it had every promise of being another gorgeous day.
>
> It wasn't until I was about a half mile from the top that I started to hike into cloud and a stiff cold wind. By the time I was on top heading for the old meteorological station, the mist was so thick that I was glad to see the three-foot cairns along the path. I probably could have followed the stone path, but I sure didn't want a misstep or to head off in the wrong direction. Although the tourist path I came up is never very steep, there are some other paths that are sheer.
>
> I explored the old station and poked my head into the emergency shelter on top. The snow pack along the way had convinced me that this was real

mountain hiking despite its altitude. Ben Nevis is not quite fifty-seven degrees north latitude so tundra conditions come much lower in altitude than, say, Colorado, where I've done most of my mountain hiking. After sweating profusely in the lower parts of the climb, I began getting chilled by the cold winds on top so I decided to take a quick photo of Britain's highest memorial and then scoot back down to where it was warmer. Unfortunately, I must have had some moisture in my camera, because it refused to take the picture; the shudder button was frozen. So then I just headed down. After descending below the clouds, it was gorgeous and sunny again.

I mentioned above that we are at almost fifty-seven degrees north latitude. Well, at this latitude and this time of year the sun is setting after 10 p.m., and it stays light for quite awhile after that. The birds start singing sometime before 4 a.m. and, especially when we're camping, can be disconcertingly loud (good use for my earplugs). We will continue north for awhile yet. To give you some perspective, we are just a little south of Juneau, Alaska's latitude.

The rest of that afternoon I rambled around Fort William, picked up a rhubarb pie for a snack, hit the library, and got my hair and beard clipped at the local barbershop. The barber gave me a run down of the history of the run up and down Ben Nevis each September. He's done it a couple of times and has the pictures on his wall to prove it. He said the winners do the ten miles in less than an hour and a half.

That evening TK&A treated us to a dinner show featuring traditional Scottish music and dancing. The troupe included older men on the fiddle and accordion, a young, maybe seventeen-year-old, piper, an even younger dancer, and a mature, lusty-voiced singer. Toward the end of the performance I began wondering how many steps it would take, changing one letter at a time, to go from "quaint" to "shrill." My answer would be, "I don't know, but I know how *long* it takes, less than two hours." Bagpipe music, even when well-played, gets old after awhile. A little bit is nice, but a little bit goes a long way. My chicken in a wine and mushroom sauce, on the other hand, was smooth and tasty.

Sometime later, in the middle of that short summer night, I got up to get rid of some water and heard a snuffling sound just on the other side of the wire fence around our campground. It was light enough to see fairly well, but the grass and weeds were so thick on that side of the fence that I couldn't quite make out what was causing the grass to sway. So I waited patiently for about twenty minutes while whatever it was came incrementally closer to the fence and a clearer area. I almost kicked the fence to see if I could catch a glimpse of whatever it was scurrying away, but I bided my time. Finally, the animal was right next to the fence, and I could see the dark outline and prickly spines of a hedgehog. The snuffling actually sounded a bit like a small pig which is probably how it got its name. Once partially out in the open, it must have sensed me because it almost immediately hurried back into the undergrowth, and I slipped back into my warm bed for a couple more hours sleep, another mystery solved.

Today we rode to Inverness, by one count, the halfway point of our trip: six months gone, six months to go. When we started, the sky looked bruised and ominous, just as it had for most of the time we were in Ft. Williams, but we only had scattered sprinkles. The ride mostly paralleled the eastern shore of Loch Ness. Much of our Scotland riding has been along these lochs, which has been very pleasant. With the water on one side and forests or rolling hills on the other you often feel like you're in a wild place. We had a stiff headwind that slowed me down considerably especially since my legs were sore from all the new muscle activity on Mt. Nevis the previous day.

On the ride, I stopped to take in the memorial to the Commandos and learned some more new stuff. Winston Churchill created the Commandos in the summer of 1940 when England's prospects were most grim during World War II. His thought was to have an elite group raid the European coast and thus regain the initiative in the war, if not militarily, then at least psychologically. The idea took, and the Commandos, with their distinctive green berets, have had a heroic history as an international organization. The Scottish Highlands have been their training ground since 1942.

Once arrived in Inverness, after checking into our wonderful B&B room in a typical Scottish home, I sought out the library and compiled this report, but, before closing, I want to leave you with some more tidbits.

I have had some problems with the language here and have come to the conclusion that, if Hollywood does a *Pygmalion II* or *My Fair Lassie*, I hope they match Professor Higgins with a Scottish lass this time. The Cockney accent is positively lucid compared to the Scottish brogue coming from a Highland lassie. At times I have felt as befuddled with their English as I was in France or Austria. However, it has been fun to just listen. "Jus chu ait, 'enry 'iggins, jus chu ait!"

Speaking of language, I thought you might be interested in the difference between a "loch" and a "firth"—it's actually slim to none in certain circumstances if you take a look at a map of Scotland. According to the dictionary I consulted, a "firth" (also spelled "frith") is an arm of the sea or an estuary of a river while a "loch" is a lake but can also be an arm of the sea, especially when narrow or partially landlocked. So there you have it…now you can finally get some sleep.

This time around, I'm only going to focus on one food, and that is the standard Scottish meal of haggis, neaps, and tatties. To demystify this meal, I'll first explain that neaps are simply turnips and that tatties, as you could probably guess, are mashed potatoes. The haggis is a more complicated dish. The recipe I saw calls for the heart, lights (i.e., lungs), and liver of a sheep, lard, pepper, peppercorns, onions, and cayenne pepper. It's all ground together and comes out as a sort of hash. The traditional cooking method is within the bladder of a sheep's stomach, but one of the chefs I consulted said they could no longer fix it this way because the fear of some disease. Believe it or don't, but the meal is actually very tasty, a little of the taste of liver I would say. Tim Kneeland had set this meal up for us a few nights ago and, to my disbelief, everyone ate most of their shares (okay, I'll admit I cleaned up a couple plates other than my own, but then what's new about that?).

Finally, I will explain this report's title. I grant it is a bit obscure since it is a second order pun. I'm playing off the art-house movie title of several years ago called *Lock, stock, and Two Smoking Barrels* which itself is a play on words from the common phrase, "lock, stock, and barrel." If you don't like that one, I will offer a variety of alternative titles you can edit in if you feel the need. They are "Nessie is the Mother of (Scottish) Invention," "Heart, Lights, and Liver," and "Nessie, We Hardly Knew Ye." So take your pick.

We ride two more days in Scotland to get to Aberdeen and then either catch a twenty-two-hour ferry or fly to Bergen, Norway, to begin our next stage.

Take care of yourself and all your loved and liked ones,

Ralph

Report #14: My Way in Norway

July 16, 2003

Howdy from the land of Vikings, trolls and, of course, the relatives and ancestors of Lake Wobegon, Minnesota,

The last two days riding in Scotland were along the north coast across moors, through pastures, beside rivers, past lovely lakes and dark woods with one nice ride across one of the headlands that got us out of the wind for an hour. Ten kilometers out of Inverness on the way to Huntly, I stopped to tour the Scottish National Trust site for the Battle of Culloden. After seeing the movie *Gallipoli* years ago, I remember thinking it odd and unique that such a total defeat is so honored and remembered by the Aussies and Kiwis, but the history of the Battle of Culloden certainly matches this weird manifestation of national pride (oh, I guess the Texans have the Alamo). I'll provide a little background for the battle because it helps explain the Scottish present.

I had mentioned last time in my Irish history synopsis that William of Orange had ousted King James II. I'll add a bit more explanation here because it is central to this part of Scottish history. King James II of England was also King James VII of Scotland (i.e., king of both realms). He was despotic and disliked, especially by the Protestant nobility. In 1688, his wife had given birth to an heir. This worried the Protestants prompting them to request William of Orange to intervene. When William's forces landed in England, James was forced to flee to France. William and Mary, who was James' daughter, then jointly accepted the English throne. However, James still had many supporters, especially among the Catholics. These supporters were known as Jacobites from the Latin for "James." Supported by France's Louis XIV, James immediately made an attempt to retake the throne, but it failed.

In 1701, when James II died, his thirteen-year-old son was proclaimed James VIII of Scotland and III of England *in absentia*. This James, often called "The Old Pretender," made several attempts, backed by France or Spain, to regain his rightful crown, but each attempt met with failure. This set the stage for "The Rising of 1745." Prince Charles Edward Stuart, King James III's son, or Bonnie Prince Charlie or "The Young Pretender" (take your pick from among his monikers), believed from the age of six that he was destined to reclaim the Stuart throne. While still in his early twenties, he sailed to Britain landing in the Scottish Highlands and, through the force of his personality, won over many of the clan chiefs, who at first advised him to go home. "I am come home, sir," replied the Bonnie Prince.

Beginning with a small force, Prince Charlie began attacking English garrisons in northern Scotland. Moving ever southward, he gathered support and credibility as he came. In a bit more than two months, he was master of Scotland and began heading south to London. By then, the British government had begun massing troops to engage the Jacobites. Acknowledging their superior forces, Prince Charles reluctantly decided to march his army north to return to, and fight upon, the ground they knew best. Although, up to this point, his army had not met defeat, his men were nevertheless discouraged and disgruntled, and many used this opportunity to desert and go back to their homes. As a result, when the two armies finally met at Culloden, the outcome was never in question; Prince Charles' army was crushed. The Duke of Cumberland, second son of George II, was in command of the government's forces. He had a much superior force in number, artillery, discipline, and tactics. In addition, the Prince inexplicably chose a battleground that negated his (primarily) Highland army's main weapon, their ruthless and relentless charge.

The battle lasted less than an hour. The Duke's order to show no mercy meant that of the Prince's nearly five thousand men, thousands were either killed outright or were caught and killed in the following weeks as the Duke's men searched out soldiers or other conspirators. Bonnie Prince Charlie fled for his life and eventually escaped to France by posing as the maid of a Scottish lady, Flora MacDonald, who was later imprisoned in the tower of London. She, perhaps even more than the Prince, is revered by the Scots for her courage.

The Jacobites boasted many non-Highlanders in their ranks, and many Highlanders either stayed loyal to the crown or were neutral in the whole affair. Nevertheless, the English Parliament made sure such a "rising" would not happen again. They banned the wearing of the tartan or any peculiar

Highland garb, confiscated all weapons including the bagpipe (a mixed blessing to music lovers everywhere), and removed many of the powers that the clan chiefs had over their tribes. Colloden was the last battle on British soil, and all the placards and information at the battle site emphasized that this was a *civil* war.

My impressions of Aberdeen were certainly better than Bill Bryson's who had expressed his disdain for the city in the book I just finished, *Notes from a Small Island*. I found Aberdeen interesting and charming. However, we were to forfeit a day off there as we had to drive to Newcastle, England, to catch a twenty-two-hour ferry to Bergen, Norway, on the day that was to be our layover day. Luckily, I got to Aberdeen in time to check my e-mail in the library and then to check out, all too briefly as it turned out, the Marischal College Museum. I found the collection fascinating with a great many oddities from all over the world along with quotes from their contributors. I could have spent much more time there. My quote for this report comes from this collection. It is from Joseph Conrad's *Heart of Darkness*:

> The conquest of the earth, which mostly means the taking it away from those who have a different complexion or slightly flatter noses than ourselves, is not a pretty thing when you look at it too much. What redeems it is an idea only. An idea at the back of it; not a sentimental pretend but an idea; and an unselfish belief in the idea—something you can set up, and bow down before, and offer a sacrifice to.

What a weird way to spend a Fourth of July. We got up early, packed all our gear into the van, drove Penny to her new hotel (she was headed back to England to visit a friend; we'd said good-bye to Shana the night before) and headed to Newcastle. After almost six hours on the road, we still arrived in plenty of time to catch the 6 p.m. ferry to Bergen. The ferry ride across the North Sea was uneventful though we had near gale force winds the entire crossing. Of course, "ferry" is a bit of a misnomer since this thing was huge, like a good-sized cruise ship with casinos, restaurants, play areas, etc. On leaving Newcastle harbor, the waves were striking the breakwater in spectacular fashion shooting the spray high into the air. It reminded me of the scene in the first *Lord of the Rings* movie where the raging river is transformed into a stampede of horses—I could see the horses in these waves. The ferry was so large that the big waves were transformed into a gentle roll that lulled rather than excited. I got a good night's sleep in my berth.

The next morning I supplemented my TK&A food budget to try the breakfast buffet, and it was excellent. I was later to realize it was my first taste of a Scandinavian-style breakfast. Besides cereal and a bit of scrambled eggs, I tried a variety of pickled and creamed fish, several types of cheese including a tasty, brown, sweet goat cheese I'd never eaten before, cold cuts, and some wonderful raspberry jam with freshly cut breads.

While on the ferry, I was again surprised at how nice it feels to be traveling without any of the anxiety normally associated with traveling. Even if Bobbi isn't sure about a place to stay or eat or other arrangements, it means she worries about it, and I don't have to. So I don't. At all.

Before I land you in Bergen, let me provide a short introduction to Norway. Norway is arguably the most expensive country in the world right now. I know that Bobbi is keen to keep the expenses down (and our menu selection on one of our first nights serves as an example: three choices of Tex-Mex fajitas Norwegian-style). Norway's history predates the Vikings of course, but it was their raids on England and beyond, beginning in AD 793 that brought Norway to the world stage. The Vikings unified the country in 872, but their power began waning with their defeat by Alexander III, King of Scots. In 1397, Norway became part of Denmark, an arrangement that lasted for over four hundred years. When Denmark was defeated in the Napoleonic Wars, Norway was ceded to Sweden.

In 1814, tired of forced unions, Norway adopted its own constitution, but the secession from Sweden didn't occur until 1905. It's telling that, when it did happen, it was done peacefully. Norway was able to stay neutral during the First World War, but it was attacked and occupied by the Nazis from 1940– 45. Given its history, you can see why the Norwegians have been reluctant to join the European Union.

Driving in Bergen was a bit of a nightmare. Both driving to our hostel from the port and then later picking up our new riders at their hotel, we had a difficult time. The map we were using did not accurately portray the nuances of their traffic pattern, like one-way streets or forks in the road. I was navigating for Bobbi and felt betrayed by the mapmakers. I didn't envy Bobbi having to both drive and navigate while sagging for us. I also didn't envy her having to give up her Bergen layover day to do the final DRG checkout for our first day's ride in Norway. Tim was flying in to complete the checkout of the route for this stage, but he would be getting here a day late.

Our new stage riders, Carol and Marianne, are a mother and daughter who live near Boston, Massachusetts. They had already been in Norway for several days together with Marianne's twin sister, but the sister has no interest in biking and had left by the time we arrived. Marianne turned twenty-two just a few days after we arrived, the first birthday anniversary she has been separated from her twin sister. The two are a welcome addition to our group. They are not strong riders and began the trip by doing part-day rides to work up to the longer rides on this trip.

On my off day in Bergen, I took a couple of tours. The first was of the historic Bryggen waterfront area that originally belonged to the Hanseatic League or Hanse (which I will explain below). Before the tour, which was to start in the Bryggen Museum, I toured those areas of the museum not included on the tour. One was a special exhibit on the effects of health and disease in the history of Bergen. One of the tidbits from this exhibit was that, at one time, people thought bad smells caused disease. Therefore shoemakers, tanners, and other smelly occupations were moved to the outskirts of towns.

The tour included the permanent exhibit in the Bryggen Museum as well as the reconstructed Hanse area and the Hanseatic League Museum. In 1955, a fire devastated the old buildings in the Hanse area (i.e., the Bryggen). As workers were cleaning up the mess they discovered remnants of the earliest buildings on the site beneath the ruins. These much older buildings were then excavated until 1972 when the Bryggen Museum was built over the eight-hundred-year-old ruins essentially *in situ*—a neat concept because, instead of seeing a mock-up of an archeological site in the museum, you are viewing the actual site! The city then carefully reconstructed many of the old Hanse buildings, and the whole area has become a UNESCO World Heritage Site.

I mentioned the Hanseatic League in a previous report, but I'll treat it further here because of its significant effect on Bergen's history. In the Middle Ages, Germany had no strong central government. Taking advantage of this power vacuum and with the aim of controlling commerce throughout the Baltic and North Seas and beyond, a group of German cities established themselves into the Hanseatic League. The Hanse flourished and, in time, it established four offices outside Germany to control its affairs in remote regions. Bergen was attractive to the Hanse because of its excellent location. In addition, the Black Death had recently devastated the city, its people, and its commercial interests so Bergen could use the business. A deal was struck, and the Hanse established the Bergen Office in 1360.

The Hanse, through negotiation, payment, and/or coercion, acquired the land on the north side of the Bergen harbor. There they built their wooden long houses to serve as office, warehouse, and residence for the full staff they brought from Germany. The compound was surrounded by tall walls, which were locked at night, creating a community unto itself with its own laws and jurisdiction over its own affairs. The men on the Hanse staff served three- to four-year terms in Bergen and could neither be married nor could they consort with Bergen women. After serving their term, the men usually returned to Germany to marry and have families.

Life in the long houses was tough. Fires were allowed only in the kitchen and common areas located at the end of each long house. The rest of the building had no heat and no lights. These restrictions were put in place to prevent fire which was a serious threat in the closely built wooden houses covered by pitch and roofed with peat. Nevertheless, fires ravaged the area several times throughout its history. Because of these fire restrictions, it was extremely cold in the back rooms during the winter. The apprentices slept two to a compartment into which they could just fit lying side by side. The doors to these compartments could be closed, to keep in the warmth, but could not easily be opened from the inside. This arrangement allowed the journeyman to watch over the apprentices while they slept since his compartment was just opposite theirs. The journeyman kept close watch on the apprentices at all times and punished them severely for the least infraction of the rules. A manager rounded out the manning for the Office. The manager had two bedrooms, one in the airy front room in summer and a second in the middle of the building for winter. Our tour led through one of these old long houses, and I can attest that a four-year stint living this way would not have been pleasant.

The main exports in Bergen were dried fish, cod-liver oil, and roe; grain was the primary import. By the way, cod-liver oil was used in lamps during this period; it wasn't until 1870 that it began to be used medicinally. Interestingly, the Hanse sold their produce to different countries or cities based on the quality of product popular in that country or city. For example, they manufactured twenty-three different qualities of dried cod! This reminded me of something Penny had told me about the Harry Potter books. I had been surprised that the H. P. publishers changed the name of the first volume for sale in the States from *H. P. and the Philosopher's Stone* to *H.P. and the Sorcerer's Stone* because they thought that the word "philosopher" in the title would turn American readers off. However, Penny told me that all the H. P. books also get edited to "dummy down" the obscure English terms for the American market. But now I found out this precision marketing strategy was being done by the Hanseatic League centuries ago! They must have been the McDonald's of their time.

As Germany's central government strengthened, the Hanseatic League began losing its influence. However, it was not until 1754, more than 150 years later than any of the other foreign offices, that the Hanse Office in Bergen finally became the "Norwegian Office" under local control.

I took a second tour that same afternoon that concentrated more on the history of the Norwegian part of the city. Our guide took us through a less "touristed" neighborhood to show us older homes and give us a better feel for how people lived. Many of the streets are so narrow and at such odd angles that vehicular traffic is not permitted or even possible. Because wood is plentiful in Norway, it has always been a popular building material. As a result, fire has been a major renovator in Bergen. In response to disasters at different times, wider streets have been added at intervals throughout the city to act as fire breaks. People are required to have fire alarms, extinguishers, and hoses in every house.

The pride the people take in their city is evident everywhere. I noticed this as we cruised into the harbor that first day. The city looks neat as a pin and fairly sparkled in the sunlight we had the two days we were in Bergen. Of course, we were lucky in this respect since Bergen gets 275 rain days a year according to the *Lonely Planet Guide* or 225 rain days according to the city guide, always conscious of putting her city in the best light.

After our layover day in Bergen, we headed out of town, but first I stopped at their famous fish market since it had been closed on our layover day. What a bounteous display of the sea's riches! One display in particular caught my eye. It presented several of the ugliest fish I've ever seen sold for consumption. I'm sure they were some type of anglerfish—those large, lumpish, bottom-dwelling denizens with fleshy appendages dangling just above their huge, wide mouths. When a fishy prey comes to investigate its "lure," the anglerfish suddenly opens its cavernous mouth, and the vacuum created literally sucks the prey in. I wonder how a chef prepares this fish for the table. I hope it's not served whole, with the head on, because it might scare a timid diner away.

From the first day, our riding in western Norway was simply spectacular. We headed north from Bergen and, after four days, were in Norway's westernmost town of Floro. Most of our way was along deep fjords that seemed to go on forever. The roads were sparsely traveled which made for great riding, especially since many are single track (i.e., single lane), and tunnels, some dark and dangerous feeling, are common. Tim routed us around the tunnels when possible.

On that first day, I had an interesting conversation with a young bicyclist who was waiting at one of the ferry stops with me. He had just finished high school with a concentration in computers and now had to spend two years working before he could actually get his diploma. He told me that only three of the twelve people in his class could find jobs in this field. It struck me that son Joe had told me that his 2003 Duke graduating class had just about the same percentage of graduates with jobs. It seems that things are tough for young folks all over.

That night we stayed in the gymnasium of a school near the town of Risnes, rather than camp, which was fortuitous as it began pissing rain just as we arrived. Liv, one of the teachers at the school, was our hostess, as she had been for the much larger Odyssey group in 2000. She fixed us a hearty Norwegian stew with beef, potatoes, and carrots along with flat bread and three large cakes for dessert with plenty of whipped cream (the Europeans seem to love their whipped cream). After supper she invited us to her home. We tried to beg off because it was her birthday, but she insisted. Liv and her threes sons of fourteen, sixteen, and twenty-one entertained us for the evening. She and her twenty-one-year-old did most of the talking since they had the best command of English. Her oldest had just finished his year of compulsory public duty as a mine diver in the Norwegian military. Though he told us he had not spoken much English since 2000 when the Odyssey gang was here before, he had a very good command of the language. Back at the gym I slept soundly lulled by the driving rain on the gym's roof, glad to be inside.

The next day's ride to Dale was challenging with a couple of pretty good climbs. One was up and over a ridge separating fjords with a long downhill to and then along the huge Sognesjøen Fjord to a ferry dock. At one point I had to slow down significantly so as not to spook a small herd of cattle loitering in the middle of the road. Once at the dock, I had a multi-hour wait and so contented myself with a wonderful novel about nineteenth century Scotland (*Sunset Song*, the first book in a trilogy) and spying on a heron rookery in a stand of trees across an arm of the fjord. For someone used to seeing herons in the water fishing, this was an odd site. I'm glad I had my binoculars with me in the bike bag that day.

We camped in the surrounding yard of a B&B that night and were able to use the common room which proved to be much more comfortable than reading in my tent. We met a couple of self-supported riders there, an Australian living in Washington D.C. and a Dutchman living in France. In comparing notes, they described a tunnel they had ridden through in Norway that spirals up through a mountain in a corkscrew fashion! Our group was glad we were bypassing that route.

The next two rides, first to Førde and then to Floro for our layover day, were simply gorgeous with only a little rain early on the first day and then glorious sunshine! The land was rugged and mountainous with many waterfalls and cascading rivers. As with the first few rides, we were adjacent to fjords much of the time and, when we weren't, we were generally crossing a ridge from one to another. Of course, with so many large bodies of water, we took a fair number of ferry rides which was fun. We also had our share of tunnels; one was so dark and long that Kirby and I dismounted and walked the last few hundred feet. Pitch black on a bicycle is a bit unnerving. We were both impressed when Andy told us later he had ridden through the entire tunnel. I began to notice how far north we were. Even at relatively low altitudes (not much above three thousand feet and usually closer to two thousand feet), we began seeing snow in the upper reaches of the surrounding hills.

I had been visiting the Norwegian libraries when possible to check my e-mail even though the librarians were strict, allowing only thirty minutes online at a time. When I got to Floro, I stopped at the public library on the way to our hotel. After typing in a portion of my Bergen report, I logged off and buried myself in a couple of English-language reference books I had found in one of the back aisles. I was evidently so quiet the librarian almost closed the library locking me in, but she heard me shift in my chair just as she was walking out the door. That could have been an interesting situation!

That night I noted in my journal that, since arriving in Norway, my evening repasts had consisted of two pizzas, Chinese, Mexican, and one Norwegian stew. The high prices did indeed limit our selection. Breakfasts have been mostly Norwegian-style, similar to my buffet on the ferry from Scotland described above.

We had a lazy layover day in Floro which itself is a sleepy port town. I cleaned my bike chain and gears, spent more time in the library, and took a hike to the top of the high hill behind our hotel for a sweeping view of Floro and the ocean. Supper was tortellini with ham in a cream sauce served with a salad and completed with a sundae, the best meal so far in Norway.

The next day was a day for rain. It looked like it might clear up when I first looked outside in the morning, but then it looked like it might clear up several times during the day, and it never did. It was pissing rain when I left, and it rained off and on the whole day. We retraced part of our route into Floro to get off the narrow neck of the peninsula on which it sits and then took a different route back to Førde. This one took us over a good-sized hill to bypass a long tunnel on a highway. We climbed right up into a cloud and then maneuvered through a tunnel that had been blocked to cars with large boulders. Bobbi and the support van were waiting for us with snacks and encouragement at the tunnel's near end, but she then had to return down the mountain to the highway tunnel.

I emerged from the tunnel and donned my rain gear to stave off the cold for the long fifteen-hundred-foot downhill run on the other side. Just as I started off again, it began to rain in earnest, and I was sodden long before I reached the bottom. It seemed a very, very long downhill. Førde was only a short stretch further, and I stopped at a library, but it was closed. So it was nothing for it but to wring the water out of my gloves and press ahead to Viksdalen which was our stop for the night. From Førde the ride became more pleasant. Not only did the rain diminish, but the road rose up a beautiful valley with waterfalls wherever you looked. We climbed to a pass and then shot down the other side into another watershed past a large lake. From there our lodging for the night, a small house beside a rushing cataract, was a short coast.

We had supper that evening at a small shop and eatery run by Einar and Alvhild Eldal, a couple in their sixties. Their nephew translated for the couple who had only a rudimentary understanding of English. They served us roast pork, a type of large meatball, boiled potatoes, carrots and peas, a sweet sauerkraut, and fruit cocktail with ice cream for dessert. We passed around the heaping serving bowls once, and the Eldal's refilled them and sent them around again. I was full on this wholesome fare even before dessert was served.

There is a tragic but interesting story about their place. In 1957, all the farm buildings except the horse shed were swept away in a landslide loosened by excessive rain. Einar and his father were the only ones home at the time. Einer was swept down the hill and out onto a block of ice in the river where he rescued himself by grabbing onto tree branches. His father was never found. The farm was rebuilt three hundred meters away.

Einar is a woodcraftsman, and his wife makes various craft items. After dinner they showed us their small shop in the basement. There were some clever woodworking and handsome wool pieces. It was a very pleasant evening. And then to home in the cold, damp night air where the cataract churned and roiled the whole night long—a great way to get to sleep! I ventured out around midnight since it was such a glorious night, and it was still light enough to see without a torch (sorry, I mean "flashlight;" I guess I'm starting to pick up the English vernacular).

Morning broke upon a knockdown gorgeous day! We continued down the valley following our torrent until the river emptied into a big lake. We skirted the lake until the river emerged again, following this new thread for a short way. It was in this valley I first saw the sod-roofed houses and barns that used to be so common here. It looks a bit strange to see grass and weeds, or sometimes even small trees, growing atop a building. Finally, we crossed the river and headed up an adjacent valley past Einar and Alvhild's house. I waved as I rode by.

I continued up the valley, and just before reaching the pass, I saw something moving in the road. When I got to the place, I pulled over and looked down the embankment. What looked back up at me, not three feet away, was a passel of young weasels (or possibly stoats as I later checked a Norwegian animal book). They had a half dozen holes along the embankment and kept popping out to have a look at me, standing upright on their back legs for a good look before diving back into their holes. If you have ever played the "whack-a-mole" game at Chuck E. Cheese Pizza, you can get an idea of how fast they appeared and disappeared. I counted at least five in sight at any one time, but I suspect there were a few more than this. One curious fellow came within about two feet of me and stood up to give me a good once over. I watched them for several minutes until they seemed to have gotten their fill of me and began staying in their holes for longer periods. They were certainly beautiful creatures with bright white chests and bellies set against their brown backs and heads. That might have been more weasels than I've seen in my whole life. They are usually stealthy creatures.

Then, back on the bike, just as I reached the bottom of a serpentine and precipitous descent on the other side of the pass and was slowing to a reasonable speed, I saw a much larger member of the weasel family lope across the road in that characteristic musteline way. I had time to get off my bike and hurry up a rise to watch it disappear into a heavy pine wood. Much too slender for a wolverine, I think it was a marten, the next size down in that family—it was close to three feet long. The Norwegian animal book I later consulted at a library didn't show a fisher which, if I remember correctly, is the next smaller cousin before you get to mink and weasel.

But the day had yet another surprise for, as I crossed Norway's largest fjord on the next ferry, I saw what appeared to be a dolphin breaching for air a couple of times in front of the ferry. I asked one of the crewmen if there were dolphins in the fjord and he said no, that they didn't have dolphins, but they did have a species of small whale there. I can't be sure I didn't lose something in the translation, so this is another thing I need to check on at some point. I have found English dictionaries and occasionally an English encyclopedia in Norwegian libraries, but that is about it as far as reference books go, and I haven't wanted to sacrifice my precious Internet time doing research.

We had a confusing moment as we waited for the last ferry of the day that was to take us within a couple of kilometers of our campsite. The DRG led us to a dock, but there was no ferry sign showing our destination. Bobbi arrived in the van, and she and I checked out a second dock not far away. This too was a no-go and so we returned to the first dock to wait for the appropriate time...but no ferry. So Bobbi drove us in two trips through a cars-only tunnel to yet another dock where we boarded a ferry, only to find it was still the wrong one. In the end, Bobbi had to shuttle us to the campsite in the van—a frustrating experience for all of us.

The campsite was in a magical location, adjacent to the huge fjord and surrounded by mountains. It was a full moon night, and I suspected it would rise late in the narrow valley. I checked at midnight before I turned in and peaked out again around 3:30 a.m., but I never did see it. It made me wonder about the way the sun and moon behave at such a high latitude. I had expected the long days (it never really gets dark) and the way the sun slants toward the horizon as it rises and sets, but I had never really thought about the movement of the moon up here. I suspect I didn't see the moon because we were in a tight valley and the moon never rises high above the horizon—I need to find a local who speaks decent English to check this theory out.

The next morning before riding I took a dip in the world's largest fjord. It was bitingly cold especially around my mask. I had not gone twenty strokes before I slowed way down as my muscles stiffened in protest. I swam a quarter mile and, by then, it was just tolerable. Strangely, it was warmer when I dove down to look at a dead starfish. It must be that the cold fresh water flows into the fjord from the snow-fed rivers over the top of the heavier salt water. I also scared up a few flatfish, like small flounder, and saw a half dozen foot-long eels congregated on the bottom where dead vegetable matter had accumulated. I wonder if the resulting dark patch absorbs the early sun's heat just a fraction more than the surrounding white sand and rock, and the eels were "basking" in the sun's warmth. It was a pretty neat experience, but when I emerged I shivered hard for half an hour making it difficult to navigate my cereal spoon to my mouth.

The next three days we headed east and south to Oslo. The scenery was less dramatic, but we were still riding up river valleys to a pass and then barreling down the other side into another river valley. On one fast downhill, I had to pull up sharply due to sheep in the road. Evidently in the morning the sheep like to lie with their mostly grown lambs right on the road surfaces—maybe it's cooler there as the last couple days into Oslo were real Norwegian scorchers (around 80°F). It's strange to feel overheated and dehydrated while riding this far north. On the last night before biking into Oslo, I decided to cool down in a very fast river that ran beside our camp. I swam against the current for the equivalent of a half mile upstream (when you count the strokes). In reality, I probably only traveled about an eighth of a mile before I turned and mostly floated back while diving down to the bottom next to the river weed. This river was not nearly as cold as the fjord.

Our ride into Oslo was like most rides into big cities—hectic. We had five pages of instructions for the sixty-six kilometers! We have a layover day here before riding to Sweden, and there are a couple of interesting museums I hope to visit. However, I am going to leave that for the next time and will close this report out now.

Take care,

Ralph

ps. I hope this report doesn't sound too disjointed. I wrote it over quite a few days, about a half hour at a time as that is all you can get per day from the strict librarians here.

Report #15: There is Nothing Like a Dane!

July 31, 2003

Howdy,

I will jump right in with my activities since sending out my last report from the Oslo central library. Because there was so much I wanted to see in Oslo and because I still had time before we were to meet for supper, I rode my bike through the city, using their superb bike paths, to the large Frogner Parken which has an area set aside for the bronze and granite sculptures of Gustav Vigeland. According to one tourist brochure, this is the most visited place in Norway, and, I must say, the sculptures are indeed striking. The many sculptures depict nudes of all ages, in a variety of poses, showing the range of human emotions. You could spend much peaceful time pondering the artist's intentions in this wonderful garden setting overlooking the city.

The next day I was the only person on the Oslo city tour which was fine by me. At one hundred Norwegian kroner (NKr) or about fourteen U.S. dollars, I'm also not surprised. The guide was a nice fellow about my age who has lived his life in Oslo and knows it well. He provided me a thumbnail sketch of the city's history which I'll summarize. Oslo was founded in 1048 but was leveled by fire in 1624 and rebuilt as Christiania by King Christian IV of Denmark and Norway (remember from last report that Denmark ruled Norway for a good many years). The city didn't become Oslo again until 1925 just after Christiania's tricentennial.

The guide showed me the impressive, relatively new *radhus*, or city hall, where the Nobel Peace Prize is awarded. The wooden reliefs on the side of the building depicting stories from Norse mythology revealed some grim aspects of these legends. The *radhus* and surrounding area was built upon an old slum but is now an open, wonderful space that has become a favorite of tourists and locals alike.

We walked through the Akershus Festung, a medieval fortress, and into a section of old Christiania that has been preserved and/or renovated. I also stuck my nose into Domkirke (Oslo Cathedral), an ornate and beautiful church. The guide said 90 percent of Norwegians are Lutherans but that other faiths are represented with churches.

I was interested to hear that when Norway was making its break from Sweden at the beginning of the last century, the people voted overwhelmingly for a monarchy over a republic (more on this later). Today the king is well-liked, and the guide feels the Norwegian monarchy as an institution is here to stay (even though people don't approve of the woman the king's son married).

I was able to ask the guide about my whale sighting, and he confirmed that a type of small whale lives in the fjords. He also told me that the whale used in the *Free Willy* movies had been released into the wild but had turned up in one of Norway's fjords where he had to be led out again.

After the tour, I ferried over to the Brydoy peninsula to visit the Viking Ship and *Kon Tiki* Museums. The Viking Ship Museum houses three Viking ships and the artifacts found on them that were excavated between 1867 and 1904. Two of the ships were remarkably well-preserved considering the Viking age was AD 800–1050. The ships had been used as burial crypts for notable personages; one was for a woman and her servant and the other two were for important men. The boats were made of oak with places for thirty oarsmen. What struck me most was the small size of the ships considering the lengthy voyages they undertook. Besides finding their way to the Mediterranean, both along the western coast of Europe and through Eastern Europe's major rivers to the Caspian and Black Seas, these ships are also similar to the craft that first sailed to North America.

The *Kon Tiki* Museum does a good job of depicting the several expeditions of Thor Heyerdahl. It houses the *Kon Tiki* raft from his 1947 voyage where he proved it was possible that people from South America could have sailed to Polynesia and the original *Ra II* raft from his 1970 voyage where he proved it was possible that people from Africa could have sailed to South America. *Ra I* was not there, as it had become sodden, and the ropes had rotted causing the voyage to be abandoned not far from its destination. A replica of the *Tigris* is on display; Heyerdahl burned the original in protest when his voyage was interrupted by war in the Red Sea. The expedition's purpose had been to show that people in Egypt, Sumer, and the Indus Valley could have had contact by sea. The museum also displays one of those eerie *Aku Aku* statues from Easter Island.

Although some of Heyerdahl's theories are still pooh-poohed by many scientists, Heyerdahl himself looked at his discoveries as a string of pearls that would eventually link everything together. However, regardless of what one might think of his theories, Heyerdahl's accomplishments are certainly noteworthy.

From the museums, I found my way to the Norwegian National Gallery which contains works by many Norwegian painters and sculptors and representative works by other artists. Notable, from my perspective, were *The Scream* by Edvard Munch and a van Gogh self-portrait that gives still another glimpse into his insanity. The day had been warm for this latitude, and the museum was darn right hot, so hot that the upper floor of exhibits was closed to patrons. Evidently, Oslo weather seldom presents a need for central air conditioning, so most buildings just don't have it.

I had a bit of time before everything closed and so chose to visit the Film Museum since it stayed open until 7 p.m. This was a small museum with an interested and energetic young docent. The exhibits traced the history of film from its earliest beginnings to more current topics such as censorship. English-language translations were available for many of the static displays, but most of the films were in Norwegian without subtitles. Nevertheless I enjoyed myself.

One of the museum's displays lets you view an animated short from a list of a dozen. I picked one that had been nominated for an Oscar at some time or another. Even though it was in Norwegian I was able to get the gist of it, and I'd like to describe it because it hits the highlights of Norway's recent history. The short's title translates into something like *Grandmother's Shirt Ironing Business*. It began by showing the referendum which resulted in the populace selecting a monarchy over a republic (remember that I said above I'd cover this later). Then, king "candidates" were interviewed and one was selected (note: they eventually selected a suitable Dane!). Unfortunately, the wife of the new king didn't know how to iron shirts so, when he made his first public appearance in a clean, but wrinkled shirt, the people were not impressed.

The scene switches to Grandma's Laundry where she notices the royal monogram on the collar of one of her customer's shirts and surreptitiously follows the person who picks them up. As she suspects, the shirts are delivered to the king. She is very proud and whispers her secret to everyone she meets, even strangers on the street.

Then the Nazi's invade Norway, and the king flees to England. Grandma is incensed that she must now launder the Nazi occupation force's uniforms. She begins a little sabotage by putting itching powder in the shirts or bugs in the shirt pockets and begins scorching the shirts with her iron. She organizes the other launderers to do the same (note: the Norwegians passively resisted the Nazi occupation with this type of sabotage as well as the more normal kind. For instance, the teachers refused to teach Nazism in the schools, even after one of every ten teachers was sent to the Norwegian equivalent of Siberia as punishment.) The cartoon shows the Nazis leaving at the end of the war, shirtless, and the return of the king who presents Grandma with a medal. Very cleverly tongue in cheek.

We picked up a new rider in Oslo, Kim, a young friend of Stacia's. Although pretty strung out after her trip, she gamely tried to ride the next day but ended up having to get some mega-sack time in the SAG van. She did great for several days but became somewhat homesick and bored, so she and Stacia decided to travel to Paris to see the end of the Tour de France when we got to Copenhagen. Kim flew home from Paris and Stacia rejoined us.

I'd like to give an example of the pricing in Scandinavia, and the best way is through one of my favorite foods. After supper in a pub, I ordered a banana split for NKr 45, a bit more than US$6. I was expecting a magnificent confection for that price. What I received was a nice banana, two tiny scoops of vanilla ice cream, a dollop of chocolate syrup, and a gob of that European favorite, whipped cream. Talk about a disappointed pup! I could have easily gotten a gallon of my favorite store-bought ice cream at home for that amount.

I had bike work done in Oslo including the replacement of a gear cable. For the next few days, I had nothing but trouble as the cable stretched (some stretch is expected). On the first day, my chain came off several times. I stopped the first time to put it back on. However, the second time, I was just starting a nice quiet downhill so I bent down and pushed the chain back onto the gear with my hand while pedaling slowly…and then I did it a second time! I'm putting this in because I think the editor of *The Freewheel* (our Albuquerque bike club's monthly newsletter) should put a gold star next to my name in the next edition, or at least a smiley face, for this first time event. I finally got the adjustment I needed, and my gearing is doing better. However, the number of miles is wearing on the bike and eventually, probably sooner rather than later, I'll need a major overhaul.

I didn't have these problems when we had young Tim, the mechanic, on the trip to pamper my bike. He did lots of PM (i.e., preventative maintenance) on our bikes. Unfortunately, he left the trip in Southeast Asia when we came home for the SARS scare and is not likely to come back. In his absence, Kirby's expertise has certainly been a big help to all of us, and Bobbi stays on us to keep our bikes clean and oiled to help prevent problems.

Because of the high costs here, we are camping more often. The campgrounds are nice, and the campers have been extremely polite. Though the campgrounds are generally packed at this time of the year, they are relatively quiet. Even when we camped next to a large group of teenagers who were obviously there for a concert in town, we never heard them at all when they returned early in the morning. This is so different from many of the American campgrounds where I've stayed that I wonder how they manage it...I think it's called old-fashioned manners.

Also at these campgrounds, lots of men and women my age and older walk around in bras and underpants (well, the men aren't wearing the bras of course); it just seems like the thing to do here. This brings me to a remembrance that popped into my head while I was cruising down the road the other day (cruising is the state of mind I get into sometimes when hiking or biking on isolated stretches where your bodily mechanisms are working so smoothly that your mind is free to flights of fancy—for more scholarly insight into this phenomenon try the book *Flow, the Psychology of Optimal Experience* by Mihaly Csikszentmihaly). Anyway, on with the story. Twenty-eight years ago, mom and dad visited me when I was stationed in Australia. After most of the day in the blisteringly hot outback sun touring Ayers Rock (now called *Uluru*), we were ready for a swim. Unfortunately, the folks hadn't packed swimsuits. But that didn't deter the two matronly school teachers from England whom we had befriended. They just stripped to bras and panties and plunged into the only hotel pool in the area at that time. Not to be outdone, John and Bertha Monfort, paragons of their midwest community, were soon cavorting (yes, as big sister Kam is my witness, they actually cavorted) in their skivvies in the pool! They would certainly feel right at home here in Scandinavia with that type behavior.

The unexpectedly hot Scandinavian weather we've been having brings to mind the enormous amount of water I've been drinking to keep hydrated on this trip. In fact, I've been drinking so much I suspect I've passed a significant fraction of the world's cyclic water supply through my system. So, if you think about it, gentle reader, you might be participating much more directly in my exertions on this trip than you ever imagined.

A couple days out of Oslo, I picked up some kind of bug or low grade cold, probably the result of riding most of one day in the rain. I had a slightly sore throat with a raspy cough and my PPS (Phlegm Production System) was on overdrive. This made it inconvenient to bike since I haven't perfected the snot rocket (note: "snot rocket" is a biker term for the technique where you hold one nostril closed with your finger, turn your head in the other direction and "rocket" the snot wad out your nostril; then you reverse the procedure for the other nostril). Instead, I still use the "handkerchief" method much to son Joe's embarrassment. I'm evidently one of the few people he's ever seen using one of these "anachronisms."

While I'm in this "lower" state of mind, I do have another toilet tidbit for you. Several of the bathrooms we have used recently have the toilet, sink, shower combination I previously described where the shower just dumps its water to the floor behind a little curtain (or not, depending on how good the curtain's coverage is). This, of course, leaves the floor wet. Well, of late, there has been a long-handled squeegee to pull the excess water back toward the drain and, in a few instances, the tiled floor is actually heated so that the floor dries quickly (and the warm floor feels wonderful on those nightly trips to the WC).

After five days riding south out of Oslo, we were ready to cross over to Denmark. The ferry took us across the short strategic passage between the two countries in just three and a half hours. The strait connects the North Sea in the west to the Baltic Sea in the east. One look at a map of the area shows why Hitler's generals convinced him to invade Scandinavia. They were afraid the Allies would bottle up Germany's Navy and commercial shipping fleet. For all its narrowness though, we were out of sight of land for some time.

Sharing the ferry with us was a large number of teenage boys whose dress pointed to their belonging to some type of sports teams. I approached one of the coaches to find out where they hailed from and was told they were five teams from different cities in Mexico. I commended him on how well-behaved the young men were and remarked how great it was they were able to travel like this. He was rightfully proud of them.

Denmark is flat...or at least the parts we saw. On our first day, the highest hill we pedaled was the ramp leading onto the ferry. Now, I'm not complaining mind you. It's kind of nice to have a break from all the hills in Norway.

The wind has been from the south, our prevailing direction, so it feels a little like you're going up a continuous hill anyway. The Danes are harvesting this continuously blowing wind across the flat expanse. We have seen many of the ultramodern windmills along the routes we have biked. I wonder if the Danes have gotten them to pay any better than the wind farms in the States—I've heard ours have not done as well as expected.

I took advantage of the beaches at our two camping spots on the east coast of Jutland, which is the main Danish peninsula, to swim in the Kattegut (literally Cat's Throat) Strait. The water was brisk but not nearly as cold as the fjords. Both spots were infested with jellyfish of two varieties. One was a bit smaller than a soccer ball, was yellow, and fed using long tendrils; the other was clear, about the size and shape of a Frisbee (though many were much smaller than this) and fed by pulsing through the water to filter feed. At the first beach there were countless thousands of the latter and maybe a tenth the number of the former. I had to change direction every few strokes to avoid a collision. While the clear ones are not dangerous, you can get a nice sting from the tendrils of the big yellow ones. I might've gotten a couple of mild stings on my legs, but they didn't bother me much. At the second beach, one hundred kilometers further south, both species were present but in far fewer numbers.

We took a ferry from Jutland to Zealand (the island for which New Zealand was named). The rides into and out of Copenhagen, Denmark's capital, have to be the easiest and most pleasant of all the big city riding we've done. First of all, we traveled on nice bike paths almost the whole way into and out of the city. Once in the city, we shared the streets with scores of bicyclists. In fact, Copenhagen has so many bicyclists that most streets have great bike lanes with signals at some intersections specifically for the bicyclists. I was told that biking is the most popular form of transportation in the city, and I can believe it. The traffic is particularly polite to bikers and honors their right of way. For instance, drivers always check before turning right to ensure a biker is not in the bike lane ready to go straight. Not once did I have a driver *not* stop for me. I always waved thanks to them. Copenhagen is certainly the most bike-friendly city I've visited yet.

During my layover day in Copenhagen, I took a city historic tour. It was again a small group, this time consisting of a lady from Norway, another from Scotland, the guide, and me. Although the tour concentrated on the seventeenth century (the guide does other time periods on other days), I did pick up information to fill some of the gaps in the picture of European history I've been piecing together in my head. Because of Copenhagen's location (again, I suggest you check a map out), the Danes were heavily into commerce. In fact, the first mercantile exchange was built here in the seventeenth century with the goal of a positive trade margin. They brought many raw materials back from all over the world and manufactured them into products that could be sold throughout Europe. At the time, the rulers felt that Danish tradesmen were somewhat deficient, and so they encouraged German and Dutch tradesmen to move to Denmark. This encouragement was in the form of tax incentives and lower land prices. This surprised me, and I remarked that this must be one of the first instances of using immigrant labor as "guest workers." However, the guide told us that in the sixteenth century, the same thing happened when Dutch farmers were encouraged to migrate to Denmark because it was felt the Danish farmers weren't productive enough.

Much of the growth in Denmark, and particularly in Copenhagen, was a direct result of King Christian IV (remember him from the Norway report?) who was an energetic and dynamic leader. Unfortunately, he also spent a lot of the government's money and, when he died mid-century, the government was heavily in debt. Then, in 1654, the Black Plague hit Copenhagen hard, and they lost about a third of their 24,000 population. Shortly thereafter, Copenhagen became the center of one of the several wars between Denmark and Sweden. By about 1658, Sweden had overrun the majority of Denmark and began a siege of Copenhagen that was to last almost two years. The Danes sought help from Holland who sent nearly three thousand Dutch soldiers to Copenhagen to help withstand the siege. Although Denmark had to cede much land to Sweden when peace was finally arbitrated, at least the ramparts and canals that had recently been built around Copenhagen kept Sweden from taking over Denmark completely.

The waging of this war was expensive for Denmark, and the nobility, which to date had been extremely powerful (they regularly selected the next king), were much weakened. The government had to borrow money from the population (mostly the richer people of Copenhagen) to rebuild and to pay their Dutch war debts. The situation was rife for things to change. What finally transpired is that the king convinced the richer people to declare absolute monarchy. In return, as payment for their loans to the government, he would provide them with land and money recently taken from the Catholic Church as a result of the Reformation. In this way, the nobility were outflanked, and Fredrick III became the first absolute monarch of Denmark, a slick political move if I ever saw one.

After the tour, I walked to the pier to get a picture of *The Little Mermaid*, the symbol of Copenhagen. I then visited the nearby Denmark Resistance Museum which had a guided tour in English. The museum is comprehensive with an easy to follow chronology of the resistance. The Danes had declared neutrality at the start of the Second World War and were completely unprepared when Germany invaded in April 1940. The Germans did not mess around, pitting thirty-five thousand troops against the thirty-five hundred member Danish military. Needless to say the outcome was foreordained; the Danish government conceded almost before it started. Only sixteen Danes were killed in the two-hour invasion.

The Germans allowed the Danes to keep their own government and police force in a policy called "negotiation," or "accommodation," depending on what text you are reading (plenty of chances for revisionist history here). Many people were saved from execution or deportation to German concentration camps because of this arrangement. However, the Danish resistance began to increasingly cause problems for the Germans and the puppet Danish government until, on August 29, 1943, the Germans rescinded the policy and put a German government in control. Shortly after this, the Germans rounded up all the Danish Jews (during the period of the previous policy, the Jews had lived a normal life in Denmark). However, the Danes got wind of the plan and circumvented it by using fishing and private boats to send seven thousand of the approximately seventy-five hundred Danish Jews to neutral Sweden. Many of the Jews returned after the war and found that their property and possessions were still intact—almost as if they had never left! During the war, King Christian X stood tall, not swaying to Nazi pressure and setting an example for his people. He became a symbol around whom the Danes could gather and feel proud. The Germans could not afford to punish his behavior because of his strong popularity. A final interesting note on all this is that the Germans called Denmark the "Whipped Cream Front" because things were relatively easier there in terms of rationing, war damage, etc., and they sent many troops there for R & R.

One more thing about the Danes, before we move back to Sweden, that endear them to me is the concept of *hygge* which means, roughly translated, "cozy and snug." In fact, *hygge* could be considered a national trait. When I heard this, I began to suspect I must have Danish genes somewhere in my background.

From Copenhagen we rode about forty-five kilometers north to catch a ferry across the strait to Sweden and then started on a generally northeast direction across the southern peninsula to Stockholm, Sweden's capital, taking seven days to do the distance. The first day's ride reminded me of rural Indiana with fields of wheat-like grain turned a rich, van Gogh yellow and the almost misty atmosphere of a humid midwestern day. The puffy cumulus clouds marched across the horizon in all directions. This part of Sweden is generally flat, with rolling hills as you get closer to Stockholm.

The last few days into Stockholm reminded me of northern Minnesota with deep forests, dark lakes, "watch for moose" signs, and lots of clouds. I took advantage of several nice lakes at campgrounds to get in some swimming. I was reminded of the lakes in the Boundary Waters Canoe Area Wilderness where Joe and I canoe every other year with friends. The lakes are dark with a surfeit of tannin from the thick forests surrounding them. You can't see much more than the length of your arm toward the bottom. It always makes me think about the movie *The Creature from the Black Lagoon* (although, when you watch the movie, that lagoon is surprisingly crystal clear). The water is brisk but not numbing like the fjords or the ocean in these parts. At one campsite, I decided to swim out to an island and back. Bobbi said that several folks on Odyssey 2000 swam out but, underestimating the distance, had barely made it back. I pooh-poohed this and said it wasn't more than a quarter mile out. Well, I was wrong; it was closer to a mile one way which really surprised me. I too got more of a workout than I had planned.

At one remote campground, the riders shared a small cabin while Bobbi slept in the van (which is normally where she's been sleeping when we camp). It was here I had my first negative experience with the local populace. About two in the morning, Bobbi heard something and opened the sliding door on the van and stepped out. She thought she saw someone but didn't think anything of it. As I was getting my bike ready the next morning, I could see where someone had cut through the plastic on my bike lock cable and had severed a few of the metal strands—a few more minutes and my bike would have been gone. Thank-you, Bobbi!!!

I also finally got a flat tire...after about 12,371 kilometers or 7,687 miles. That's not the surprising thing though. When I pulled out my two spares which have been stowed in my bike bag all those miles, they both had large holes worn in them. I don't have a clue how that could have happened. I didn't see anything they could have rubbed against. Anyhow, I ended up fixing the flat since it had the smallest hole. Unfortunately, I had to toss one of the new spare inner tubes because the hole was so close to the valve. I haven't tried to patch the other yet, but it might be a goner too.

I haven't seen much wildlife in Scandinavia since leaving western Norway, but I did glimpse a live deer, two large dead badgers, and a variety of plump, dead moles on the side of the road, and I did pick a few mouthfuls of fresh red raspberries while still in Norway. The latter event was more enjoyable. In Sweden, I spotted a couple of cranes that flew just as I pulled my binoculars out. If I were in the States, I'd identify them as sandhill cranes, but I suspect they were more likely Eurasian cranes—I don't think the sandhill cranes travel that far afield, and the two species look very much alike. In Copenhagen, I glimpsed a long-legged fox prowling a residential street behind our hotel. It popped into a thick hedge when spotted.

The food has continued to be unremarkable in Scandinavia. We've been eating lots of pizza (luckily they have my favorite, ham and pineapple, at most places) and pasta with some Mediterranean, Chinese, Thai, and Indian food thrown in for good measure. Only occasionally have I had what might be considered local cuisine (salmon, a piece of pork in a sauce, or meatballs).

One last note before I send this out. The next to last night before rolling into Stockholm, we camped near the Göta Kanal in Söderköping. The canal was dug by hand in the nineteenth century and runs across the south end of the Swedish peninsula. On my walk to the canal, I came upon two ladies trying to discourage a hedgehog from crossing the road. They proved the more persistent, and the hedgehog groped his way into a bush to wait for a quieter moment. Although Söderköping is a small town, the strip along the canal was hopping. Many yachts were tied up there, and the pier was full of food, music, and people eating ice cream. I became one of the latter with a scoop of peanut, one of marshmallow, and one called Turkish pepper which turned out to be red and black licorice and was surprisingly good. I was told that motoring the canal is popular with Americans though I've not heard of it before. From what I could see, though, it would be a great vacation.

Well, our route into Stockholm was fairly easy, but not as slick as Copenhagen. I'll start my next report with my doings on our layover day here tomorrow. Then it's on to Finland for a few days and a train ride to St. Petersburg for two layover days. We will have seven days in a row off from riding—my butt will be very appreciative. Until then...

Take care of yourself and your loved ones,

Ralph

Report #16: To Russia with Rain

August 10, 2003

Howdy,

After e-mailing my last report from Stockholm, I headed down to the old part of town to see the Stockholm Cathedral or Storkirken which contains a famous statue of *St. George and the Dragon*. The heavy wooden statue is certainly interesting with the dragon's ruff comprised of elk antlers. The statue was commissioned to honor Sture the Elder's victory over King Christian's Danish forces when they invaded Sweden in the mid-fifteenth century. The symbology is evident: the dragon is Denmark, and St. George represents Sture the Elder. No matter that Denmark defeated Sweden not fifteen years later.

We were staying in an old school turned into a hostel for the summer and were allowed the use of their laundry facilities and so, to be sure I didn't screw up my day by standing in line for the washer, I arose at 4:30 a.m. to put a load in. Pretty much everything I brought on this trip I can hand wash and air dry in a short time, but it's great to machine wash my towel and sheet once in awhile (I use the sheet to line my sleeping bag; it's easier to clean than a grody bag—works great).

Immediately after breakfast, Bill and I headed downtown for a tour of the old town area or Gamla Stan. Bill and his wife Molly joined us in Stockholm, both are in their late fifties. Bill, who has previously done many bike trips, will ride with us through Portugal and maybe on through South Africa; Molly will keep Bobbi company in the SAG van, but will remain in Athens for further exploration on her own when we begin our bike tour of Greece. They are a great addition to the trip.

Our tour of Gamla Stan was nice but not great. The tour guide pointed out the various architecture patterns used in different periods. Some of the houses had been built on reclaimed land where sand and garbage had been used for fill as the small island was expanded in size. Many of these houses have settled over the years acquiring a distinct tilt. He also walked us through the square where the infamous Stockholm bloodbath of 1520 occurred. The Danes, having defeated Sweden, tried and executed eighty-two people they deemed enemies of the new regime in this square.

After the tour, I visited the Nobel Museum. Though small, this modern museum provides a good history of the Prize and a fascinating glimpse of selective winners throughout the Prize's 102-year history. Small displays, continuous film clips (mostly interviews), and audio selections from speeches and interviews with some of the winners form the core of the exhibits, but computers are available if you want to delve deeper or reference winners who aren't displayed.

Alfred Nobel used his will to create the Prize that bears his name. Unfortunately, his will does not provide much insight into his reasoning for the Prize or his specifications on how it is to be administered. For instance, he directed that the Peace Prize be awarded in Oslo, Norway, while the other prizes are to be awarded in Sweden. Since Sweden and Norway were part of the same union when Nobel wrote his will, it is widely believed he reasoned that Norway's less directive government style was more conducive to the Peace Prize, but the will is silent as to the why Nobel made this specification. I found the short biographical film sketches to be the most illuminating and enjoyable exhibits.

I realized I hadn't previously understood much about Nobel's prizes and found a reading of his will very interesting. I've provided a short segment of it below:

> The whole of my remaining realizable estate shall be dealt with in the following way: the capital, invested in safe securities by my executors, shall constitute a fund, the interest on which shall be annually distributed in the form of prizes to those who, during the preceding year, shall have conferred the greatest benefit on mankind. The said interest shall be divided into five equal parts, which shall be apportioned as follows: one part to the person who shall have made the most important discovery or invention within the field of physics; one part to the person who shall have made the most important chemical discovery or improvement; one part to the person who shall have made the most important discovery within the domain of physiology or medicine; one part to the person who shall have produced in the field of literature the most outstanding work of an idealistic tendency; and

one part to the person who shall have done the most or the best work for fraternity between nations, for the abolition or reduction of standing armies and for the holding and promotion of peace congresses. The prizes for physics and chemistry shall be awarded by the Swedish Academy of Sciences; that for physiology or medical works by the Karolinska Institute in Stockholm; that for literature by the Academy in Stockholm, and that for champions of peace by a committee of five persons to be elected by the Norwegian Storting. It is my express wish that in awarding the prizes no consideration be given to the nationality of the candidates, but that the most worthy shall receive the prize, whether he be Scandinavian or not.

Before I leave Stockholm let me share some other insights. Stockholm is certainly the most openly gay city I've visited. It has surprisingly little traffic even in high use areas which, come to think of it, has also been true of all the Scandinavian cities we've visited. Why? I don't know, but there are lots of bicyclists, pedestrians and good public transport. I haven't seen a single traffic jam the whole time I've been in Scandinavia...what a great thing! Also, more disabled people are out and about, either by themselves or with the aid of other people, than I've seen in any other city.

The eleven-hour ferry to Turku, Finland was uneventful. We navigated through many, many islands, a beautiful voyage for the first few hours. About midway we docked at a large island to let day passengers off and then continued on. As we approached Turku, we again navigated through myriad small islands. I never saw open sea, though Bobbi said she did for a short time. This archipelago forms the boundary between the Baltic Sea to the south and the Gulf of Bothnia which separates Finland from Sweden for much of their lengths.

When I disembarked, the first guy I saw was wearing a T-shirt with "New Mexico" in big letters across the front. I asked him if he was from New Mexico, but he said, "No" in a heavy Finnish accent. I told him *I was*, that I liked his shirt, and shook his hand.

The nineteen-mile ride to the B&B was fast and nice. It was cool in the evening glow with the sun nearly set. We had a memorable supper with delicious pork stew, meatloaf with a stroganoff gravy, vegetable patties, roast and boiled spuds, a good salad with a great dressing, a couple kinds of wonderful breads, and a whipped creamy cake for dessert.

The two-day ride to Finland's capital of Helsinki was pleasant and much like the last few days in Sweden, lots of forests with tundra-like floors, rural countryside and lakes where I kept expecting to see moose grazing. We didn't have a real layover day in Helsinki so we had to catch things as best we could. I missed the walking tours, but when we returned from St. Petersburg, Kirby and I took a bus tour that was very good. The tour's spiel was prerecorded, and you could choose from about ten languages on your audio headphone...including Latin! I'll use the information from this tour to first give you a short summary of Helsinki's history.

Helsinki is a city of 500,000 souls in a country of five million. For about 650 years, Finland belonged to Sweden who ceded the territory to Russia in 1809. At that point, Finland became a Russian Grand Duchy. In 1812, Helsinki became the capital and, in 1863, Tsar Alexander II made Finnish the national language. The popular slogan at the time was "Swedes we are not, Russians we don't wish to be, so let us be Finns." In 1917, the Finns got their chance as Russia became embroiled in the turmoil of revolution. Finland declared their independence and became a western-style democracy. Since then they have joined the European Union and have accepted the Euro as their currency.

A few interesting tidbits from the tour: Finland is a book reading nation and leads the world in lending library books. It is a high-tech country where almost everyone has a cell phone and is connected to the net. The Finns are eighty-five percent Lutheran and one percent Orthodox. They became the first European nation to allow women the vote in 1906. And, smack in the middle of town, Helsinki has a casino that provides all its profits to charity. What do you think of that?

On our first day in Helsinki, after checking into the hostel, I visited the Lutheran Temppelioukio Church hewn from solid granite into a rough semicircle with a low copper dome that allows ambient light to filter into the church. Inside, it is simple to the extreme except for a large organ that someone happened to be playing. It was very peaceful inside—more so than just about any church I've ever entered.

I next visited the Great Church, once called the Church of St. Nicholas, which was built by a Russian Tsar. The name change occurred when Finland became independent. This imposing structure certainly looks more like a church from the outside than the Temppelioukio Church. Inside, however, it has a light, airy feel and is simple, but elegant as many Lutheran churches are. This church had statues of three luminaries of the Reformation: M. Luther (of whom you surely know), M. Agricola (the chief architect of the Reformation in Finland) and F. Mekinchthon (of whom I've never heard).

The next day, before our train left for St. Petersburg, I visited the Ateneum, or art museum, and its extensive collection of Finnish art and smattering of foreign paintings. I was able to immediately pick out the three works of Munch after seeing so many of them in Oslo. Also, there were a couple of paintings by Gauguin, from his island stage, that I liked better than many I've seen on this trip. They had a handful of Rodin sculptures, and again I noted how they stand out from the crowd.

I next wandered to the market area on the city pier. This market did not impress me as the market in Bergen had, but it is obviously berry season here because all kinds were for sale in the market. The last site I was able to visit before catching the train was the Russian Orthodox Church, Uspenski Cathedral. As I expected, it was extremely ornate with icons everywhere, a very imposing church. An unusual feature of Orthodox churches is the lack of pews. During ceremonies, people stand or wander from icon to icon crossing themselves. It looks like there is no order whatsoever, but I'm sure everyone knows what to do. It began pouring rain while I was in the church, so I holed up with a book waiting for a break. When it came, I hurried back to the Ateneum where I had stashed my knapsack in a locker and then rushed to the train station. The knapsack has all I'll need for five days until we reach Athens. The plan is for Tim K. to drive the SAG van with our bikes and gear to Athens while we take a plane.

The six-hour train trip to St. Petersburg was hot and close with six people crammed into each apartment. The steward and stewardess on our car were very stern and checked our passports at least three different times. It all lent an air of foreboding to the journey. The scenery from the train was almost uniformly birch and pine forest. The seemingly endless forest looked cold and forbidding; I could feel the unseen eyes of wolves and other beasties upon me as we streaked past. I was happy to be inside the relatively bright, warm confines of the train. At supper, we saw a beautiful orange sunset. It was the last of the sun I was to see until we crossed back into Finland three days later. The train itself was not spacious. The toilets emptied directly onto the tracks and so were not available when the train stopped which was fairly often. I've had more comfortable journeys.

Upon arriving, we jumped on a metro reached by descending the longest escalator I've ever ridden. Later, I learned that St. Petersburg has the deepest metro in the world. The metro is nicely laid out and relatively easy to navigate; however, knowing only the English translation of your stop doesn't help much. By asking questions and making good guesses about Russia's Cyrillic alphabet, we arrived at the right station and walked to our hotel. The metro was jam packed even though it was nearly 11 p.m. All the riders appeared to be working people, not folks out for an evening on the town—a sea of tired faces. The metro itself is extensive and efficient. I found it easy to use during our three-night stay.

The hotel's lobby presented a pleasant initial impression, however our room was very small, and housekeeping had to roll in another bed to accommodate the three of us (Kirby, Andy, and me). After testing the saggy-springed roll-a-bed, we pulled the mattress to the floor, and shoved the bed, two chairs, and a table out into the hall so we could turn around and spit. Everything was a little dingy and bare bones. You can't drink the tap water, so the hotel provides a large bottled water dispenser in the center of each floor. Ours was empty, and the one on the floor below was almost empty. The tap water is yellowish with a strong smell of iron. Toilet note: both the Finnish hostel and the St. Pete hotel room had what looks like a towel holder, but it was heated, presumably to aid in the drying of towels and laundry; sound reasonable to you?

Breakfast in the hotel both mornings was good, but very busy; even though I arrived just after it opened, I had trouble finding a seat. The buffet was extensive with juice, tasty meatballs in a stroganoff sauce, porridge, cold cereal, cold cuts of all kinds, sliced vegetables such as tomatoes and cucumbers, apricot butter, breads and rolls, bell pepper rings with meat inside and a type of bread pudding that was, both in taste and texture, very nasty. The condensed milk and honey they provided for the cereal was a nice touch.

For our first day in St. Petersburg, Bobbi had hired a woman to guide us. She first took us to Victory Square via the metro. Victory Square is an impressive monument to the citizens' and city's ability to withstand the nine-hundred-day siege (actually it was 872 days) during World War II. Reading in Molly's *Lonely Planet Guide* for St. Pete gave me a better realization of the hardships the citizens suffered. Even before the Germans got there, most of the treasures in the Hermitage, many of the city's factories and two million citizens had been relocated. Over the next almost three years, the people who remained in the city ate their pets, horses, even rats to survive. There is evidence that cannibalism occurred in the latter stages of the siege. At one point thirty thousand people a day were dying of starvation. To put this in context, between five hundred thousand and one million people died in St. Petersburg alone whereas the combined number of dead during World War II for both the British and the Americans was about seven hundred thousand.

It rained most of the day, and those who did not have rain coats got plenty wet. In fact, it rained most of the time we were in Russia and, when it wasn't raining, it was just about to rain or had just stopped. The days and nights were uniformly gray. In many ways, it reminded me of my only trip to New York City. I never saw the sun on that trip either, and it was during an extended garbage workers strike so the feeling was equally dismal. The people weren't any friendlier either.

While waiting for our afternoon city bus tour, I consulted Molly's tour book again and got a bit of info on the city which I'll share with you. The land on which the city lies is at the mouth of the River Neva on the Bay of Finland. Possession of this strategic spot had bounced back and forth between Sweden and Russia until Peter the Great recaptured the land at the beginning of the Great Northern War (1700–21). He built the Peter and Paul Fortress on the River Neva and set about draining the swampland to create a city which he called St. Petersburg after his patron saint. This was a man who seemed to embody Mel Brooks' quote, "It's good to be king!" (from the movie *The History of the World Part I*, I think) because, not only did he force his Swedish prisoners and the local peasants to do the grunt work, he also forced merchants, nobles, and administrators from Moscow to relocate here when he made St. Petersburg his new capital in 1712.

After a brief move of the capital to Moscow when Peter died, and then back again, Russian monarchs for the next hundred years commissioned many great buildings, turning St. Petersburg into one of the grandest cities in Europe. I'll not try to summarize the whole of Russian history from 1800 on, but will provide a thumbnail sketch of key events. The first is Russia's initial defeat by and final victory over Napoleon in the early nineteenth century. Alexander II had pulled his troops back into the Russian countryside allowing Napoleon to capture and burn Moscow. He then led his army after the retreating French army, which had been devastated by the Russian winter, fighting a rear guard action all the way to Paris into which Alexander triumphantly rode. Key events would also include Russian defeats in the Crimea by the Ottoman Empire in mid-century and by Japan at the beginning of the twentieth century.

At this point, revolutionary fervor caught up with Russia. The first revolt was put down in 1905. Then World War I temporarily raised nationalist sentiment (St. Petersburg became Petrograd during this time) and delayed the revolution. But as the war dragged on, it became increasingly unpopular. This, coupled with the people's frustration with the "mad monk" Rasputin's sway over the empress, again fomented revolution and, in 1917, Tsar Nicholas was forced to abdicate. It didn't take long before the provisional government fell to the Bolsheviks. The Bolshevik government almost immediately sued for a separate peace with Germany. This action angered the Allies who consequently supported the anti-Bolshevik forces during the Russian civil war that followed. In 1918, the capital was, yet again, relocated to Moscow as the new government feared outside attacks upon a vulnerable St. Petersburg.

During the Second World War, St. Petersburg, which had been renamed Leningrad in 1924 after Lenin's death, was besieged by the Germans for almost three years (as already mentioned above). Today, since the collapse of the Soviet Union, St. Petersburg has been renamed yet again, back to its original name. The people of St. Petersburg have been struggling, like all of Russia, with the marked changes in their governmental and economic systems. They have a long ways to go in my opinion. Many haven't a clue about what constitutes good customer service, and the infrastructure is, in many cases, dismal (e.g., filthy and non-potable tap water, stinky toilets and plumbing, lack of building ventilation, some of the worst streets in Russia, etc.). A Finnish waiter told me that he travels to Russia often. He views that the older folks still seem to be trapped in the Soviet socialist mentality, but that younger Russians "get it." They are industrious, understand the service industry, and are pleasant to deal with. In any case, St. Petersburg's magnificent museums, treasures, and buildings will continue to draw tourist crowds until things change for the better. Until then, I'm afraid a tourist's Russian "experience" will inevitably include some unpleasant memories. On May 27 of this year, St. Petersburg celebrated its three-hundredth anniversary, and I believe its future is bright.

After the scripted part of the bus tour, we drove up the main road past the Hermitage (an impressive set of buildings) on the River Neva. We viewed the Peter and Paul Fortress, went into St. Nicholas Church (an ornate Russian Orthodox Church) and stopped at a nice souvenir shop. Had we a good way of carting the stuff around, I might have been tempted to buy some gifts here. The guide had scads of facts at her disposal. Unfortunately, most were not particularly interesting (e.g., the length and weight of pillars on monuments, the architect and date for many buildings, etc.). A higher level, broader summary would have been more interesting, but it was okay and still provided value. She had trouble handling several of our questions and seemed perplexed at all the changes in Russia that have happened since the collapse of the Soviet Union. That evening, as if to punctuate our feelings about Russian efficiency, we had perhaps the worst service of the trip; we waited two and a half hours to get our supper served at the hotel restaurant.

The next morning, I headed straight for the Hermitage. When I got there, I passed the group line and then saw another line and headed for it. I asked a hawker if this was the line for individuals, and he said, "Yes." Well, it wasn't. When the Hermitage opened and the line started moving, I realized I was at a special group entrance. So I hurried to yet another entrance and found that now the individual ticket line was very long. Oh well, I had heard that lines are part of the Russian experience, and I always have a book with me to pass the time. Luckily Bill, Molly, and Kirby were far closer to the front. Bill saw me and called me over to stand with them. I felt uncomfortable cutting line, but it turned out that many people were holding places for latecomers. Kirby was talking to a young female judge from Poland. According to her, in Poland you become a judge before becoming a lawyer, the latter being the more lucrative profession. We reached the Hermitage entrance before we could understand how that works.

I spent six hours at the Hermitage wandering its vast halls. The pricing scheme is worth a note here: my cost was the equivalent of US$11. Had I been Russian I would have paid the equivalent of US$0.54. This dual pricing scheme has been a common practice in Russia, but I understand this is starting to change. I rented an audio guide and hit several of the state rooms and the fine art rooms. The buildings that make up the Hermitage are indeed impressive and the objects in them are priceless. It made me wonder then why they don't control the climate in the rooms better, because it was warm everywhere and hot and stuffy in quite a few of the rooms. Also, some of the rooms on the first floor had such poor lighting that you could not see the darker paintings. Luckily, the rooms I found most interesting were better lit.

My particular likes were the building interiors themselves, a large room filled exclusively with Rembrandts (including *The Man in Red*), the twenty-plus Gauguin paintings from his Tahiti period (his earlier works don't do much for me), and two large rooms filled with Picasso works from his pre-cubist, emerging, and cubist periods. The audio tape also pointed out a painting where he seems to have gone beyond strict cubism. I also enjoyed seeing Henri Matisse's *The Dance*. I hadn't realized it was so big. The bright orange dancers set against the vibrant blue and green background really jump out at you on that scale, holding the dreary surroundings at bay for a time. They had a large number of Matisse paintings. They also had works by many of the great artists in smaller numbers (except for Reuben whom I've come to believe was extraordinarily prolific because his paintings seem to be everywhere in large numbers).

It was still raining when I left the Hermitage. I walked down the canal to see and photograph the statue of *Peter the Great* on horseback and then crossed over to the Peter and Paul Fortress. On the way, I passed seven or eight babushkas with colorful dresses and a look of the gypsy about them. All of them were my age or older and probably not a skosh over five foot two. A couple said something to me in passing, but one became insistent, latching onto my raincoat and giving the universal signal that she wanted some coin of the realm. My *no*'s became *nyet*'s, and I finally had to pull away. As I walked away I felt for my camera and the little money I had in my pocket. It wasn't until I got back to the hotel and had taken off my pants that I discovered the gym shorts I had worn under my pants were missing, but if she was that good, I sure don't begrudge her keeping them. (Editor's note: the author sometimes tends to flights of fancy—this qualifies.) Actually, I shouldn't make fun; I found out later that Bill had his wallet lifted on a crowded metro on his way back from the Hermitage which is always a real pain to handle, but especially when overseas.

Before I took a metro back to our hotel, I decided to look for a restaurant near the Hermitage since I could not remember seeing any restaurants close to the hotel. I found a few and went into one to see if anyone spoke English. I was surprised that the waitress spoke good English and even more surprised to find they had a menu with English translations. Jackpot! I settled down to a nice meal of mushroom vegetable soup, an Austrian stroganoff, and a nut ice cream sundae.

While walking around the city, I saw a couple of large domed cages, maybe seven foot tall with diameters of five feet, full of watermelons just sitting on the street. At night, the vendors don't move them, they just lock the door on the cage. One cage had a few melons with large hunks cut out of them, presumably by a thief with a good knife and an appetite for that sweet taste of stolen melon.

On our final morning in St. Petersburg, we got up early and took the metro to the train station. The return ride to Helsinki was uneventful except for the stern conductor asking for our passports and then, several moments later, returning to ask for Bill P. Bill froze, then raised his hand expecting the worst, but the fellow just said "Happy Birthday!"...Bill had turned sixty years old that day! Just about the time we hit the Finnish border, the sky began to clear and, by the time we reached Helsinki again, it was brilliant sunshine.

Our last day and a half in Helsinki was pleasant. We had said good-bye to Carol and Marianne in St. Petersburg as they had to leave a day earlier to attend a wedding in the States. We wished them well and congratulated them again on reaching their goal of one thousand miles on their bikes. They had been very funny about it. On our last ride into Helsinki, when they reached exactly one thousand miles, they put their bikes into the van and SAGed the rest of the way. Yesterday, we caught a late afternoon plane to Athens with a layover in Prague on Czech Airlines. We got into Athens at about 2:30 a.m. I'll start my next report with our adventures in Greece.

Take care of yourself and all those who belong to you,

Ralph

p.s. A quick note about some more food: I tried reindeer meat and had a piece of reindeer sausage pizza while in Finland, and I sampled lingonberries which are like small, slightly less tart versions of cranberries. I had a lingonberry sundae with lingonberry ice cream on an almond shell with whipped cream and a strawberry sauce. The ice cream was just okay, but the combination of tastes was terrific!

Report #17: Greece is the Word

August 17, 2003

Howdy from Roma,

> "Zorba," I said, "you think you're a wonderful Sinbad the Sailor, and you talk big because you've knocked about the world a bit. But you've seen nothing, nothing at all. Not a thing, you poor fool! Nor have I, mind you. The world's much vaster than we think. We travel, crossing whole countries and seas and yet we've never pushed our noses past the doorstep of our own home."
>
> —*Zorba the Greek* by Nikos Kazantzakis

The flight to Athens was uneventful. We were delayed getting out of Helsinki and ended up meeting Tim Kneeland as he arrived from the States to drive our support van from Helsinki to Athens. His long drive will give us another layover day in Athens, but it also means we'll need to make it up later by riding some extra miles. We were all exhausted when we finally landed in Athens around 2:30 a.m. and crashed as soon as we got to the hotel. Although the traffic from the airport was light, as soon as we got on surface streets, we saw some cafés still doing good business—a little surprising considering the time. It gave us some feel for Greece right away.

I'll hit you with the boring historical stuff right off the bat this time and get it over with. Although Greek history is a bit hard to summarize, a little background will set the stage. Greece's classical period began circa 475 BC and lasted about 150 years. It was the time of Socrates, Plato, Aristotle, Sophocles, Euripides, and the Peloponnesian War. The city states of Athens, Sparta, and Thebes were all vying for power. The age ended with their defeat by Philip of

Macedon. A period followed when, under the rule of the Macedonians, the Greek culture, language, and religion were dispersed throughout the territories conquered by Philip's son, Alexander the Great.

Eventually Rome defeated the Macedonians circa 168 BC, and Greece became the cultural center of the Roman Empire. At the end of the fourth century AD, the empire was formally split into the Latin west and the Byzantine east. During this period the Greeks adopted the Orthodox religion. When Constantinople fell to the Crusaders in 1204, Greece again became divided, mostly between the Venetians and the Franks. At the end of the fourteenth century, the Ottoman Turks swept through southeast Europe, and the Greek state essentially became a nonentity. Except for the Ionian Islands, Crete, and a few coastal areas which were captured and held by the Venetians, the Greeks lived under Ottoman rule until the Greek War of Independence in 1822 when they overthrew it.

This was the beginning of the "Great Idea" to bring all Greek peoples under one flag. During this period, the Greeks greatly expanded their territory, but the "Great Idea" ended in disaster when, after World War I, they were defeated while attempting to annex Asia Minor. This began a long period of hard times for the Greek people. They lived under dictators and through a succession of occupations by Italy, Germany, and then Bulgaria during Second World War. From 1946–49, a divisive civil war provided further troubles for the populace. Finally, after suffering through the Cyprus problem in the 1950s (which was never cleanly resolved) and a military dictatorship from 1967–74, Greece emerged as an established democracy and member of the European Union.

Our first day in Athens, Kirby and I just walked around. We tried to get into the Archeological Museum, my number one "must see" venue in Athens, but found it had been closed for a year and would be closed another year for renovation. We found several attractions closed for renovation as the city readies for the 2004 summer Olympics which they will be hosting. Next, we walked across town to a place called the Tourist Police on the far side of the Acropolis. We had assumed it was a cleverly named tourist information center, but it really was an actual police station expressly for tourists. Since it was a beautiful day and we were enjoying the walk, we continued our circuit around the base of the Acropolis heading back to our hotel. On our return we passed a tourist office and set up a tour of the northeast part of the Peloponnesian Peninsula for the next day.

The next morning Bill, Molly, Kirby, and I caught the bus for the tour. We drove over the Corinth Canal which severs the isthmus connecting mainland Greece with the peninsula. The canal, connecting the Aegean and Ionian Seas, was built over a ten year stretch beginning in 1893. The guide said it was six kilometers long, although it looked much shorter than that. From the bridge you can see both seas, and the canal had no locks that I could see.

We stopped at Epidaurus to visit an ancient theater famed for its remarkable acoustics. Several other sites nearby were being excavated. It looks like the archeologists have years of work ahead of them. We next stopped at Nafplio on the Aegean coast to view the old Venetian fortress of Palamidi and the tiny island in the harbor completely covered by a small fortress called Bourtzi. The scenery to this point had been beautiful desert hills set against the blue of the Aegean Sea, but now we headed inland across Argolis, the largest plain on Peloponnese, which was thick with olive, orange, and apricot trees against a backdrop of desert hills. Above these plains are the ruins of Mycene, the city "rich in gold" of the ancient poets. The Lion's Gate entrance to this ruined fortress is the oldest structure in Europe. The view from the top of the ruins across the plain was spectacular. Ancient inhabitants were able to see enemies approaching while still many miles distant. Near there, we visited what had originally been thought to be the tomb of Agamemnon but, when examined by experts, it proved too ancient. The tomb had the unusual shape of a bullet standing on end. Unfortunately, it had been looted before it was officially discovered. Lunch at a roadside eatery was good: a puff pastry appetizer, a Greek salad, bread, a kabob, moussaka (an eggplant lasagna more or less), and melon for dessert. Of course, the bus stopped at the mandatory gift shop on the way back to Athens. The guide's dialogue was standard. I learned that the olive, and more particularly olive oil, is the country's main industry (no surprise). Some of the olive trees we saw were over eight hundred years old we were told. The Greeks also import a lot of crude oil and refine it before selling it abroad.

The next morning, I arose early to tour the Athens ruin circuit. First, I'll give you some general impressions: the antiquity of the ruins is certainly impressive as are many of the ruins themselves. You can see the Acropolis from across the city as it sits on a high hill far above anything else around it. It is the first thing to catch the sun in the morning and holds the last rays in the evening. It is indeed beautiful to look upon, and I found my eyes drawn to it whenever it was in view between buildings. It looks cool and calm above all the bustle and craziness of the city.

On the other hand, there seem to be ruins everyplace you go. I saw fine examples of ancient art, a partial bust or frieze for example, leaning against a fence in an alleyway. These are pieces an American museum would be proud to display. Most sites are still under excavation. I suspect this state of affairs has to do with the lack of money available to deal with the sheer number of ruins in this ancient city.

Greece is hot in the summer and, with the heat wave that has hit Europe this summer, Athens is in its dog days. Literally! There are stray dogs and packs of dogs seemingly wherever you look, especially at the ruin sites. Their favorite activity is to find a cool piece of marble in the shade and nap. The ubiquitous love songs of the cicadas provide a white noise to which anyone can dose off. Because of the heat, you need to drink plenty of water. I was pleasantly surprised and impressed that the Athenians have placed cold water drinking fountains at most of the major tourist destinations. What a switch from our experiences in all the other countries so far on this trip! Most of these fountains even provide a spigot for filling your water bottle.

On the downside, I was negatively impressed with the lack of free information provided to the casual visitor at the Acropolis. There were no brochures, no maps, no good pointers to where things are located, and little information on placards. The other ruin locations are only a bit better. It's as if there's a conspiracy to force you to either hire a tour guide or buy a pricy brochure.

In my wanderings, I visited the Acropolis, that wonderful remnant of Greece's Golden Age. Its Parthenon is the symbol of the city, widely acclaimed for its beauty, and rightly so. Within the Acropolis, I also liked the Erecktheion with its statues of six Carytids, or maidens, used as columns. In 1801, the British Lord Elgin took one of the maidens back to England along with some of the best preserved friezes from the Parthenon and other ruins. The Greeks make no bones about their thoughts on this. I wonder if the treasures will ever be returned to Greece. I next visited the Temple of Olympian Zeus completed in AD 131. A dozen or so massive pillars are all that remain of this seven-hundred-year construction project. I also strolled through both the Ancient Agora (agora is market place) and Roman Agora, with its first century Tower of the Winds, and viewed the Theater of Dionysus from above. Overall, there was much construction and clean up going on. Many of the ruins had scaffolding surrounding them and, as I mentioned above, many sites were closed. All the completion dates are targeted for next summer's Olympics so, if you plan to visit Athens, you might shoot for some time just after the Olympics for the best access to the newly renovated and cleaned sites.

I should mention that Allison, a new stage rider, joined us in Athens. She is an Odyssey 2000 veteran, so she and Bobbi have lots of gossip to catch up on. She is doing this stage because she picked up some kind of creeping crud in 2000 and missed biking this stage. She's early forties probably, loud, opinionated—in other words, she fit right in and we all liked her instantly.

Tim K. returned to Athens after finalizing the first two days' route guides and shuttled us to the outskirts of the city to begin our ride. We didn't protest the van ride because we had had plenty of chances to observe the drivers in Athens who have little respect for pedestrians or bicyclists. Also, the main road out of town has no real shoulder. So we forfeited about six kilometers of riding in a hundred-kilometer day.

After being dropped off, we headed straight for the Corinth Canal. Instead of taking the high, busy bridge, we crossed a small drawbridge off a side street. Well, maybe "drawbridge" is the wrong term because, when I got there, the bridge had been lowered into the canal, and a tug was pulling a large ship over it! I had never seen this type of bridge before. It was interesting to see it being slowly winched up. They keep the gearing covered thickly in heavy grease to prevent salt water corrosion. Tim said that when he was checking the route guide for this stage, two large fish were trapped on the bridge when it was raised, and the operator quickly ran out and snatched one up with a net while the other flopped successfully back into the canal, a nice perk I would think.

Our route around the Peloponnesian Peninsula took us two days down the east coast, two days across the southern tip, and then three days up the west coast where we caught the ferry to Italy. As I mentioned above, this is a desert country. It reminded me of the American southwest but without the bright colors in our cliffs and rocks. Of course, the Aegean Sea to the east and the Ionian Sea to the west dispel any notion of being in New Mexico.

We spent the first two nights of the ride camping near the beach and so I took full advantage of snorkeling in the Aegean. The first spot had me puzzled because the upper ten inches of water were cold, but it was much warmer below. The mystery was cleared up by a couple of guys at the beach bar who told me a large spring empties into the sea at this point. Swimming in it was a bizarre experience with my body immersed in cold water while dipping my arms into warm water at every stroke. Also, some type of optical phenomenon occurred at the interface of the two thermal layers, because the bottom would be blurry one second and crystal clear the next. I did see some schools of small fish and even a few brightly colored reef fish near a rocky outcrop, and once I scared up a five-inch squid on the bottom. The second place was closer to normal with a layer of warm water above with a slightly less warm layer below. Here I took two swims since the water was so nice. On my late afternoon swim, the sun was shooting through the water at an interesting angle making the schools of fish appear as if they were hanging in an abyss. It was way cool! I dove to the bottom and looked back up through the schools to get a whole different perspective. It sure was nice to get wet after the hot rides.

The first night, out I got a chance to see the nearly full moon rise from behind an island in the Aegean. It was the color of a harvest moon and made up for the full moon rise I missed while in Athens the night before. I had gone out for a walk looking for a place I could see the eastern horizon, but, though I must have walked several kilometers, I couldn't find a view in that vertiginous city. Strangely enough, as I walked back to our little hotel, lost in a maze of side streets, I saw Tim K. driving our support van. He was just returning from mapping out the first few days' route, so I rapped on his window, startling him, and then climbed in to help him navigate to our hotel.

Leaving the eastern coast, we crossed a rugged mountain range almost immediately, and then, on the next day, we crossed the range running along the western coast. Both climbs were difficult without being too difficult. Luckily, they both occurred near the beginning of the ride before the sun had a chance to toast things up. We've been getting up for a 6 a.m. breakfast and can start almost as soon as it's light enough to ride safely (except Stacia who claims to like the heat and her sleep, so she gets up later). Of course I'm drinking a lot of water, but I also soak my long-sleeved white shirt with water when it starts getting really hot. It works wonderfully like a swamp cooler type air conditioner.

Along the way there have been many shrines from a foot square to one as big as a child's playhouse. They are too many and at strange places for them to be related to traffic deaths like the shrines we sometimes see in the United States and Mexico. I suspect they re somehow associated with the highly iconic Greek Orthodox religion.

As I was riding over the first mountain, I saw two live foxes and two dead ones. The first live one was leaping up the embankment to get away. My initial impression was of a short-legged, long-torsoed animal. This was confirmed when I saw the second one crossing the road at a leisurely pace, unaware of my presence. It also had a long, white-tipped tail in addition to short legs giving it an odd, but very sleek apearance. These foxes looked a bit strange after seeing the long-legged variety in Scandinavia. Now that I think about it, the French fox I saw seemed about midway between the two in height. Hmmm.

About three quarters of the way up the first mountain, as I paralleled a dry stream bed, I heard singing in what seemed a most desolate place. I rounded the switchback and a monastery appeared with forty or fifty cars parked along the narrow road on both sides for the next couple hundred yards. It looked like people were setting up roadside stalls for some type of festival. This was on August 15, and I thought it was probably the feast of the Assumption, but I was later reading *Zorba the Greek* and found that Zorba calls it the feast day of John the Drinker. However, a footnote in the same book names it the feast of Klydonus and compares it to our Halloween. Crossing the second mountain was equally hot, and it was strange to think that the Odyssey 2000 riders ran into a blizzard on this ride. They crossed the range in April—what a difference a few months make!

The rides up the west coast were more pleasant with fewer climbs and fewer kilometers. I got the chance to snorkel a few times in the Ionian Sea. One site in particular was very good. We had gotten into camp early on a sixty-kilometer day, and I was in the water before noon. Much of the beach close to shore had a rocky substrate upon which spiny urchins, sea grass, and other vegetation grew. Above this were many schools of small fish of several varieties, some of the schools easily had more than a hundred individuals. I swam down the beach about three-quarters of a mile and then headed out to sea. The water stayed only about thirty to fifty feet deep even a quarter mile out, and it was exceptionally clear (later in the day, the water became roiled lessening the visibility considerably). Further out, the bottom was packed sand or silt and looked as barren as a desert. Even so, I found some interesting things such as several black anemones about two inches in diameter. When I would dive down to touch a tentacle, the animal would retract its entire body into a half-inch hole in the sand. I didn't have the patience to see how long it would take for it to reemerge to feed.

I also came upon a three-inch fish hovering next to a collection of empty shells and a round patch on the sea floor of a different consistency. I dove down to it, and the fish dove straight into the dirt! I stuck my fingers into the dirt up to about two inches and felt nothing but sand, but this sand was less dense than the rest of the bottom. Not sure of what I had seen, I found a similar fish a short distance away and dove. This one scurried away but, when I followed, it found a sand hole and dove in! An interesting survival technique, but it makes sense in such a barren scape with no hiding places. I wonder how deep these sand holes go and how the sand stays in suspension?

I saw a few two-inch whelks, one of which had a small flounder laying right beside it (not sure if there was interaction going on between the two, but it was curious proximity on such a barren bottom). I found several small starfish and one sea slug different from any I've seen before. The size, shape, and flexibility reminded me of an overripe banana except it had blunt spines running lengthwise in several rows along its body. Throughout my three swims that day, I saw three different types of filter-feeding jellyfish (none had the long poisonous tendrils). A couple were at least two-feet long with medusae more than a foot in diameter. They had eight leg-like appendages that came to a tube at the bottom, and had "thighs" like cauliflower. Jellyfish are always fun to find because they slowly drift with the current so you can get a close, leisurely look.

We camped the whole time we were on the peninsula and found that the campgrounds in Greece are much noisier than other European sites we've visited. Good thing I've got my trusty earplugs with me. They don't completely block out the noise, but they do make the noise seem further away. I guess the noisy late evenings are to be expected since the Greeks often eat their evening meal at 10 p.m. In fact, we've had problems getting supper before 7 p.m., a late meal for hungry bikers. The campsite at Sparti was quiet because we were surrounded by a large group of mostly English students out on an archeological dig. I suspect they were as beat as we were from their full day in the sun and their evenings spent washing their artifacts. These campgrounds are the first we've seen that prohibited placing toilet paper into the toilets—their sewer systems are apparently unable to handle it. Instead, they provide a small plastic container in which to deposit your waste paper (consider this just another exciting toilet tidbit).

Our last layover day in Greece found us in Olympia, the ancient site of the first Olympics in 776 BC. It is now a smallish hill town of six hundred souls with tourist prices comparable to the other small communities in which we've been camping. Bill and I visited the archeological site shortly after it opened to avoid the midday heat. The ruins are something to see, although I was again disappointed with the lack of posted information. The site was originally established in 10–9 BC as a sanctuary with a temple to Zeus Olympios and other gods. It later grew in importance as a center for athletics and even politics, reaching its peak in 5–4 BC. When the Romans took over the region they "renovated" many of the buildings. As Christianity gained prominence, this

site of pagan worship and festivals increasingly lost favor until, in AD 393, the
Emperor Theodosius forbade further Olympic Games, and in AD 426, the
order was given to destroy the site.

The Olympic Games were revived in 1896 with the first modern games
held in Athens. I visited the small Modern Olympics Museum which exhibits
pictures, stamps, medals, coins, and other memorabilia from 1896 to the
present. Unfortunately, the town's Archeological Museum was closed for renovation in preparation for the Olympics in Athens next summer.

At our Olympia campground, we met a young Belgian couple on holiday
and talked with them for three or four hours over the course of our two-day
stay. They were opinionated, well-spoken, and loved Belgium. We got many
good insights into Europe, the European Union, and their view of the world.
One interesting thing the young man told us was that he had gotten top marks
in his college English classes which he attributed to watching lots of American
television and movies. He said that, in Belgium, as in many other European
countries, the movies and television are not dubbed into the local language,
but are subtitled. Therefore, viewers pick up English almost unconsciously.
Other countries, such as Italy, dub all the foreign movies into Italian (he told
me Stallone sounds like a sissy in Italian). He said, and we later confirmed
when we got to Italy, that we would find few people in the rural south of Italy
that spoke any English at all—a big change from the rest of the European
countries we've visited so far. He also told us his nephew could converse in
fairly good English when he was just six years old and had learned it all from
Play Station! I had never considered this possible explanation before when
confronted with the plethora of English-speaking Europeans, but it sure
makes sense.

Before we leave Greece, I want to talk about food. I've enjoyed a Greek
salad every night I've been in Greece. Their salads have tomatoes (vine ripened
and delicious), cucumbers, onion, black olives, and sometimes green pepper all
topped with a thick slab of wonderful feta cheese and drenched in olive oil
with a little black pepper and maybe other spices. I think I'm developing a
minor addiction. Unlike other places where we didn't eat that much regional
food, all I've had in Greece is Greek food. From spinach pie, wonderful lamb
and veal stews, moussaka, souvlakia (i.e., kabobs either on a plate or in a pita),
to a dessert called kataifi which is like shredded wheat with nuts drenched in a
honey syrup, I've been eating pretty high on the hog here.

Our last day in Greece, we biked ninety-plus kilometers to Patras and
boarded the Superfast II ferry late in the afternoon. The four guys currently on

the trip (Andy, Kirby, Bill, and I) shared a nice room with in-suite conveniences. After a nice evening meal, I wandered the decks ending on the top deck which was also the windiest but, after a hot day and cooling shower, the wind felt like a full-body massage. I watched a fiery sun set behind one of the many Greek isles in the Ionian Sea. Later that night, we passed through the Otranto Strait into the Adriatic Sea as we rounded the heel of Italy's boot on our way to Bari.

There were many young people aboard the ferry, most with backpacks. They took over all the benches, chairs, even tables on all decks and, as night fell, adopted just about every sleeping pose I've ever seen. I arose early the next morning and had to step lightly as they had invaded the hallways of the cabin areas as well as the deck areas both inside and out. It was like the ferry had a huge homeless problem.

We disembarked at Bari and headed south along the coast which gave me a chance for first impressions of Italy. Italian drivers reminded me of Greek drivers: they drive as fast as they can, given the conditions, use their horns for all sorts of communicative purposes, and treat a stop sign as a suggestion. Italy did not seem as hot as Greece had been, but there was just as much trash along the roads. On later rides, I noted that, although there were many orchards and vineyards, most fields lay fallow. I'm not sure if the farmers are between crops, have just harvested, or just did not plant this year.

After setting up camp the first day, I biked into Alberbello to take a look at the local architectural marvel called a *trulli*. The *trullis* are conical stone houses using flat white stones for the roofs with no mortar. On first impression, along the route, I thought they were just old, uninhabited houses but, in Alberbello, a large part of town consists of *trullis* lining the narrow streets. The effect is quite striking.

On the way out of town heading back to camp, I passed the stone entrance of what I took to be a church or temple but, upon further exploration, it proved to be a large necropolis. It was at least a half-mile long, very wide, and was filled with all types of mausoleums from walls, solid with individual drawers, to large stand-alone tombs to small, glassed in rooms with nice drawings etched into the glass. Almost all of the grave sites had freshly cut flowers and nice pictures of the deceased. There were thousands of flowers! I was impressed at the obviously high level of respect for the deceased and would love to have the local cut flower concession.

Our first evening in Italy reminded me of a nirvana summer evening in Albuquerque when a slight drop in temperature occurring at sunset after a scorching day, coupled with low humidity, and a lack of flying insects provide ideal outdoor lounging conditions. After a cool swim in the campground's murky pool and a refreshing shower, I was in a perfect state of comfort.

Our second riding day took us to the Gulf of Taranto on the instep of Italy's boot. On the way, we passed through Matera with its Sassi cliff dwellings. I biked down to the edge of the gorge above which the houses are clustered against the cliffs. It's thought that monks from Eastern Anatolia made refuge here in the eighth century. The dwellings were taken over in the fifteenth century by peasants and evolved into a regular town by the eighteenth century. Coincidentally, Allison's tour book mentions a book called *Christ Stopped at Eboli* which treats Sassi's later history. That book just happens to be one of the two I brought for my Italy reading. Having seen the place, I should better enjoy the book. Also, on this ride I saw what must have been thirty to forty accipiter hawks, or possibly young falcons, which seemed to be hanging together.

When we reached the small resort town of Marina di Genosa, we were overwhelmed by the mass of people who took over the streets forcing the traffic to a snail's pace. I arrived at our campground near the beach just as hoards of brown, bronze, and red bodies were leaving the beach for their prescribed siestas. One thing we discovered quickly in Italy is that, at least in the smaller towns, shops of all types close down from about 1:15 p.m. to 5 p.m., so you better plan your shopping around it. According to Tim, who has been surveying our route the past week, the beach towns are all packed right now, but the inner cities, even Rome, are relatively deserted as the annual European August madness runs its course. Luckily, last weekend was the last hurrah for this season, and things should be getting less crazy again. Since we arrived in Greece, our campsites have been crowded and very loud whenever we've been on the coast, and it seems even worse in Italy. I'll be glad to be away from the crowds. After setting up my tent and rehydrating, I headed to the beach for a much anticipated swim. Here I encountered hundreds of the purple-fringed jellyfish and no others, but they didn't disrupt my swim.

The next two days took us across the peninsula to the west coast. Our first night, we stayed near Senise, a good example of the vertical hill towns in rural Italy. The main streets run parallel across the mountain with very steep walkways, even steeper stairways, and an occasional street connecting them. You don't wander around aimlessly in these towns without wasting a lot of energy. I actually found an Internet café with one terminal on a back alley. It had decent access speed, so I settled in to check my e-mail. I wondered if the brave entrepreneur who owned the shop was making any money in this ancient-feeling hill town, but then I realized I must be using his personal computer that he rents on an infrequent basis to help make ends meet. Nevertheless, it had a good connection, and I was satisfied. Having missed my ride back to our small hotel just outside of town, I took a leisurely evening stroll back for supper and bed.

The next day offered lots of hill climbing as we crossed the range to get to Scalea on the west coast. It was a difficult ride but easily the most beautiful in Italy to that point with the deep river gorges and picturesque hill towns. As a reward, I took a long swim in the Tyrrhenian Sea at our beachside hotel—clear water, a sandy bottom as far out as I could see, and a lone purple-fringed jellyfish accompanied by several small fish (for protection or just scavengers?) hiding amidst its tentacles.

On our layover day in Scalea, we stayed at a Club Med wannabe. It had two large pools, a friendly staff, and a large, beautiful, clean beachfront with blue lounge chairs, each with its own blue umbrella, lined in neat rows—It even used beads instead of money. I had no problems orienting myself during my long swims because after the blue beach chairs, came the next hotel's red beach chairs, then the green- and white-striped beach chairs, and on through orange, yellow, blue-striped, etc. When I turned around, I just swam back to the solid blue mass. One item that rankled a bit was the proscription from using the beach or pools during the siesta hours.

I saw a few more purple-fringed jellyfish on my pre-breakfast, break-day swim, but I also saw a new-to-me species. This one had an inch and a half inch medusa and was about six inches long with another foot or so of poisonous tendrils. I also saw something tumbling along the bottom. It looked like an urchin of some kind or something else that's supposed to be anchored to a rock or reef. It was covered by what looked like the polyps of a communal organism. Maybe it was the sea's equivalent of a tumbleweed at the mercy of the current (I saw no means of propulsion). I'll bet the weird skeletons I saw on the bottom both days are from that organism.

The temperature was scorching along Italy's west coast, so I was constantly searching for cold drinks, especially bottled iced tea. Scalea had a nice Super SPARS, that omnipresent European supermarket, but they didn't sell the large liter-plus sizes cold, and we had no way to refrigerate them in our rooms. So on both days in Scalea, I picked up a large bottle of tea, stashed it under a stack of frozen peas in the freezer bin and then went on to other business coming back to the store a couple of hours later for my cold drink. Hey, whatever works.

On my wanderings through this small village, I saw signs pointing to the hilltop houses in the old part of town, so I climbed up the winding road to the top and then down the narrow, winding stair passages to the bottom. It was like a maze, replete with dead ends, and so circuitous that the only direction I knew for certain was down. I sure wouldn't want to be a "snapper" learning this newspaper route!

On the way back to the hotel, I stopped at a barber shop for a hair and beard cut. Neither the barber nor his young apprentice spoke any English. Luckily, a friend has been cutting my hair since my retirement, so I knew I wanted my beard to be cut to a number one length, the back and sides of my head to a number three length with the top just a little longer (the numbers refer to the settings on an electric hair clipper). This communicated, the barber first washed and dried my hair (the first time I've had that done by a barber) and then commenced to give me a fine haircut. He left the beard to his apprentice who was a little light-handed on the clippers, so I trimmed my beard a bit more when I got back to the room. It was an interesting experience in communication, but then we've run into few English-speaking locals in southern Italy.

The next two days, we rode up the west coast to Paestum, both beautiful rides reminding me of the California coast south of Big Sur. At Paestum, I visited their Greek/Roman ruins and the museum which houses the artifacts collected there for preservation. The ruins themselves are most impressive and, although the Romans took over the town from the Greeks and made some changes in function, it is the Greek architecture that stands out. There are three temples: one to Athena, one to Hera, and one to Poseidon who was the town's namesake and patron when under Greek rule. The museum houses many of the friezes from the temples as well as much ancient statuary. What struck me most, however, were the many paintings from inside the tombs that had been salvaged from the town's necropolis. Their bright colors and excellent condition belie their antiquity. One in particular depicted a naked young man diving from atop a pillar, genitals exposed. It supposedly depicts the edge of the world's knowledge and the transition to a greater body of knowledge through death.

At Paestum, I left the tour to travel to Rome to meet Cheryl who is joining the trip from Rome to Nice. The rest of the group will be in Rome on Monday, so Cheryl and I will get to explore Rome and its environs for a few days before we start riding again. I will end this report here and probably not publish another until after I reach Nice.

However, before I close this out, I want to provide a short history of Italy. I might add to it after my visit to Rome, but it might provide you some context to this and the next report. Although Italy has been unified as a country only since 1870, its history as a land with many claimants reaches far back. From about 700 BC, the mysterious Etruscans claimed central Italy while the Greeks occupied southern Italy. In 509 BC, the people in the city-state of Rome won their independence and set up a republic. Eventually, one by one, they conquered the Etruscan cities and began the transition to an empire. Augustus, Julius Caesar's adopted son, took power in 31 BC and gradually weakened the Roman senate even while the empire expanded.

There was much jockeying for power over the next few centuries and, with an empire so large, it was jointly administered for a time, but in AD 324 Constantine became sole emperor. In AD 330 he dedicated Constantinople (ancient Byzantium, now Istanbul) as the "New Rome" and moved his administration there where the senate became nothing more than a rubber stamp for his autocratic decrees. Constantine, known for his toleration of the Christian sect, actually became the first Christian emperor when he converted on his deathbed. Within two centuries of the move, Germanic armies had overrun the western empire, and a century later, the Lombards divided Italy into three dozen duchies. These duchies, essentially city-states, prospered and bickered. In the mid-fourteenth century, international trade brought the plague which devastated Italy and all of Europe. The Renaissance (1400–1527) brought peace among the city-states, fostered the rise of the merchant class which challenged the feudal lords and the church, and led to a resurgence in thought and art.

In the mid-sixteenth century, the church cracked down hard in response to Martin Luther's mutiny and England's King Henry VIII's proclamation of a new religion separate from Rome. In league with Spain who controlled southern Italy at the time, the church descended into a dark time. By the eighteenth century the madness of the Inquisition had run its course, and a period of new enlightenment occurred. Napoleon overran Italy in the early nineteenth century proclaiming himself king of Italy and plundering Italy's treasures to bolster the Louvre in Paris.

In the middle of the nineteenth century, Italian patriots arose and ran out the Austrians and Bourbons who occupied northern Italy at the time. In time, Italy was united under the rule of King Vittorio Emanuele. In 1921 Benito

Mussolini wrested control for the Fascist Party and later allied Italy with Germany in the Second World War. After the war he was captured and killed by Italian partisans. A year later the monarchy was abolished after just four kings. Italy was a founding member of the European Economic Community in 1957.

Hope you enjoyed this. Take care of yourself and all those who belong to you.

Until next time,

Ralph

Report #18: There's No Place Like Rome

September 25, 2003

Howdy,

As I mentioned last time, I left the bike tour to catch a train from Paestum to Rome to meet Cheryl at the Leonardo da Vinci Airport. We were able to find a room in the small hotel where the Odyssey group would be staying when they arrived on Monday. It is on the second *piano* (or floor) of a building with another hotel on the first *piano* and a third some place else in the building I think. Three little hotels in one moderately sized building! The hotel is not a block from the main train station and meeting point between the two metro lines—location, location, location. Within a nine block square area there must be at least ten Internet cafés, thirty-plus small hotels like this one and over twenty pizzerias/trattorias all serving almost exactly the same things. It's considered a low cost area and shows it as there are young folks with backpacks all over the place.

That first day we took a walking tour of many of the ancient Roman areas. Because our guided tour didn't start until late morning, we decided to walk to the Colosseum, which was the starting point, and see what we could on the way. Our first stop was Santa-Maria Maggiore Church which has the best mosaics in Rome according to the guide book. It was the first such church Cheryl had ever seen, and she was suitably impressed with its grandeur. However, because the church was dark and the mosaics are high on the ceiling, we couldn't fully appreciate them. I should have taken binoculars. Next we toured Palatine Hill where Rome mythically began in 753 BC when Romulus killed

Remus. Many of Rome's emperors and elite, starting with Augustus Caesar, lived there. Of course, now it's just ruins…however, they are impressive ruins.

The Colosseum, or Flavian Amphitheater, is huge. The term, Colosseum is itself just a nickname. It means "the place near the Colossus" referring to the *Colossal*, a statue of Nero as god that, in ancient times, stood nearby. The Colosseum was used for Roman "games" where gladiators fought each other to the death, fought wild animals from all over the known world, and animals fought other animals. At some point the arena was even flooded to stage mock sea battles. Although it has not been proven that Christians were fed to the lions in the Colosseum, it is assumed they were, just as Christian martyrs suffered this fate in other places. Therefore, crosses now adorn some of the archways *in memoriam*. The Colosseum is three stories high with the columns at each level reflecting a different classic design. On the first story, eighty archways allowed the stadium to be emptied of fifty thousand people in ten minutes giving it the nickname of "vomitorium" as the building seemed to vomit people. The arches above each entrance of the two top stories each held a large statue, all of which are now long gone. A retractable roof (guide said linen, book says canvas) covered the seating area, but not the arena. One hundred rope pullers were needed to deploy or pull back the roof. It must have been a truly impressive building in its time, and it still is. Titus inaugurated the games in AD 80 the first of which lasted one hundred days and nights during which five thousand animals were slaughtered. Not to be outdone, Trajan later held games lasting 117 days during which nine thousand gladiators fought to the death.

From the Colosseum, we walked through the ruins of the Roman Forum, the busy hub of ancient Rome, while our guide told us how it came to be so well preserved. After the fall of the Roman Empire, Rome's population gradually declined from 1.5 million to just a few thousand people who lived along the banks of the River Tiber. Over many years, the normal flood cycle of the river covered all but the topmost part of the highest structures of the forum with layers of silt, and the area became pasture land. One tall building had a door, unaccompanied by any steps, abandoned about two stories up one wall. The guide said that, at some point, someone had appropriated the building, or at least that part that was still above ground. Since there was no other way in, they had constructed a door at what was, at that time, ground level. Later, when the area was excavated, the door became stranded in its present location—very odd. It's hard for me to imagine such magnificent structures (to include two triumphant arches) being abandoned and, in some cases, stripped for the material. However, as the guide said in response to my question, the people had been decimated physically and spiritually during those years and were just struggling to survive. These ancient wonders probably had no more impact on their consciousness than Stonehenge had on shepherds in England, interesting curiosities, but hey, you gotta make a living.

We then climbed the steps to Capitoline Hill, the seat of government in ancient Rome. There in the courtyard is a large bronze replica of a statue of Marcus Aurelius on horseback (the original has been restored and is housed in a nearby museum). This is one of the few bronze statues from that era that was not melted down and recycled in the middle ages. The reason for this is that the Christians, even as they systematically destroyed or converted other pagan sites, mistook the statue for an image of the first Christian Emperor Constantine and decided to let it stand.

We then visited the huge, ornate Trevi Fountain, designed by Nicola Salvi, showing Neptune's chariot pulled by sea horses and Tritons (i.e., mermen). Trevi Fountain is the terminus of a thirteen-mile aqueduct called the Virgin Spring. This is one of the many fountains in Rome that provide beautiful, cool places for the citizens to relax while also solving a hydraulics problem. As the water flows downhill from the mountains to the city along Rome's famous aqueducts, it gathers momentum. So the engineers placed fountains where the aqueducts reached their termini to relieve some of the pressure—an idea of genius. The tiny plaza in which Trevi Fountain is located was the most crowded place I'd seen in Rome to that point.

It was a short walk from Trevi to the Pantheon, perhaps the best preserved building from ancient Rome. It is a grand structure under the largest dome in Rome. It is said that Michelangelo so revered this achievement he purposely built St. Peter's Basilica a fractional bit smaller than the Pantheon. The huge dome is open at the top to allow converse between the gods and men so that, as a practical matter, the marble floor beneath has small drainage holes for when it rains. The building survived in such good shape, because it was given to the church which used it as a Christian church after first flushing out the pagan influences.

Our final site on the tour was the Piazza Navona with Bernini's wonder, the *Fountain of Four Rivers*. Bernini selected one river from each of four continents for this masterpiece: the Nile from Africa, the Ganges from Asia, the Danube from Europe, and the Plata from South America. The guide said North America was left out in favor of South America because the latter continent was more Catholic. One of the features of Rome that struck me on this walking tour is the large number of old drinking fountains (one estimate puts the number at twelve hundred) located all around the city. They are left over, or rather stem from, the marvelous aqueduct system of ancient Rome which brought potable water of various qualities from the eastern mountains into Rome distributing it throughout the city. The spigots continuously spill out cool, fresh, potable water. The guide stopped several times for us to fill our water bottles.

On day two in Rome, we took a bus tour to the catacombs. A retired Catholic priest was our tour guide through the San Callisto catacombs, the most extensive in Rome. He told some of the same stories of martyrs that I remember from my parochial school days (e.g., the story of the twelve-year-old boy who carried the Holy Eucharist under his coat to Christian prisoners every morning; one morning he was caught by some boys and stoned to death while clutching the Eucharist tight against his small body). These catacombs were different from the ones I toured in Paris. There were no stacks of human tibiae, fibulae, and humeri and no mountains of skulls. The area we toured was clean of human remains except for two stone crypts with glass covers. All we saw were empty crypts and ancient art work on the walls. The guide said they removed the bones because tourists kept taking them for souvenirs. At one time there were five hundred thousand people, including several popes and about a hundred martyrs, buried in the twenty-plus kilometers of catacombs explored to date.

From the catacombs, we proceeded down a section of the Appian Way which, in ancient times, stretched from Rome to Brindisi, the eastern seaport on Italy's heel (ah, the memories of freshman year Latin that drive evoked). A marvel of its time, the road was almost perfectly straight and wide enough for two carriages to pass. Along the way we stopped at the tomb of Cecilia Metella, the wife of a rich noble, to show the contrast between her huge tomb (it was later used as a fort) and the catacombs. We also stopped to see a portion of the ancient above-ground aqueduct, another striking feat of engineering. However, this engineering wonder also played a key role in the fall of the Roman Empire. A classic siege maneuver is to cut off a city's water supply, so when the barbarian hoards from the north attacked Rome, the aqueducts were easy targets. The citizens of Rome were forced to use the polluted water of the River Tiber which had long been relegated to little more than a sewer.

On day three in Rome, we headed to the Vatican since the last Sunday of the month means free access to the Sistine Chapel and museums. We got there before the museum opened and decided to tour St. Peter's Basilica while we waited. The church is massive, and it seemed particularly big with so few people in it early in the morning. We made the circuit ogling the statuary, paintings, and mosaics. The first thing we encountered was the *Pieta* which has been kept in wonderful shape and simply glows. We had brought a pair of binoculars this time to bring the distant pieces, like the mosaics near the ceiling, a little closer, and they worked fine. Unfortunately, when we finally got in line for the museum, it was three blocks and about an hour long. A cruise ship had just vomited a skillion tourists divided into multiple, numbered groups. If we could have "disappeared" all the boat people with round sticky-patch numbers on them, the line would have shrunk considerably.

Once inside, however, it suddenly seemed less crowded. We had no trouble getting audio tour headphones, and we were off. Again, the audio tour proved its worth with clear, understandable and interesting commentary on many of the facets of the Vatican from its treasures (paintings, frescoes, maps, mosaics, statues, etc) to the selection of a new pope or the renovation of the Sistine Chapel. We spent almost three hours wandering through the various rooms finally finding ourselves in the Sistine Chapel which was packed with people just hanging out. We had seen many guards throughout the tour, but one fellow's *raison d'être* seemed to be shushing people in the Sistine Chapel. He had a Sisyphean task. The silence he would evoke with his shushing and announcement to remain silent would be quickly penetrated as new viewers spilled into the room. The whispers would gradually rise to the level of a hum reminiscent of a huge beehive and so he would be forced to repeat his performance every three to five minutes.

The chapel itself is overwhelming. It seems every square inch is covered in art. The colors are positively vibrant since the restoration a few years ago (see the National Geographic article on the restoration for a "before and after" contrast). This was especially true of Michelangelo's strange *Last Judgment* mural that covers the entire front wall of the chapel. Of course his ceiling frescoes are also magnificent, but they are difficult to view because they are, after all, on the ceiling, and your neck gets tired. I trained the binoculars on them, but the ceiling isn't quite high enough to view a nice swath with them and is too high to see detail without them. It is interesting to note that before this job on the chapel, Michelangelo had not done fresco art (i.e., painting over wet plaster so that when it dries it creates brighter colors). Nevertheless, he became an immediate master of the technique—I don't believe I saw any better than this in all my travels.

After leaving the chapel, we walked through the Vatican's painting gallery which contains many powerful works by Italian masters. Most of the other specialty museums were not open, and the museum was out of floor plans, so I couldn't tell what we were missing. I should mention that on the serpentine path to the Sistine Chapel, you pass through a room filled with wonderful paintings by Raphael and also through a map room that is a cartographer's dream with huge painted maps of each region of Italy—you could easily spend hours in that room alone.

After leaving the Vatican, we made a quick stop on the metro at Piazza Barberini to view Bernini's *Fountain of the Triton* and have lunch before continuing via train to Ostia Antica, ancient Rome's port city. Because centuries ago the River Tiber flooded this abandoned city, covering it with silt, the ruins are exceptionally well preserved. Probably the most striking feature was the detailed black and white mosaics that covered the floors of the bath houses. Unlike the Pompeii ruins, Ostia Antica is not strongly controlled; you can walk right into houses and other buildings except where signs or ropes keep you out. We spent a hot hour or two there wandering among the ruins before catching the train back to Rome for a cool shower, a hot meal, and a soft bed.

On day four in Rome, we slowed down a bit. We walked to the Crypt of the Capuchin Monks where the skeletons and bones of past members of the order were interred in crypts. Five crypts, similar to a series of dioramas you might see in a museum, were on display. They are certainly works of macabre art. Several skeletons, clothed in monks' habits, were posed in lifelike positions, and the bones of countless other monks were arranged in artful ways to create striking scenes. The artist who arranged the diorama for each crypt apparently preferred his own particular medium; for instance, one crypt contains mostly skulls, another has mostly pelvises, and still another of the dioramas is composed of the lower leg and thigh bones. Especially interesting was the use of scapulae to make "winged" skulls. I'll let you draw your own conclusions about what all this might tell you about the ascetic's life.

We also took what we thought would be "just a peek" at the Santa Maria della Concezione Church located directly above the crypts. As we wandered into the church, a man, we took to be the janitor, approached and motioned us to follow him. Confused by our lack of a common language, it took us several moments to realize that he was giving us a personalized tour. Although he spoke no English, I could understand some of his words in context to his pointing. He led us into the back of the church, turning on and off lights as we entered and exited each room. His tour included the sacristy and even the bedroom of the head monk...very weird. We never did figure out who this guy was.

From the monk's crypts, we walked again to Trevi Fountain to just hang out and watch the tourists and the magnificent fountain while sitting in the shade. We then spent an inordinate amount of time and effort looking for the Church of San Pietro in Vincoli (St. Peter in Chains). If they (the mysterious, omnipresent "they") were trying to keep this church from being found by the average tourist, they did a good job because it was misplaced on both city maps we had. We were persistent and not to be deterred and did eventually locate it, only to find it closed for siesta. Sooo, we forged back out into the heat of the midday sun, though neither mad dog nor Englishmen we be, to search out Santa Maria in Cosmedin and the "mouth of truth" (remember the movie *Roman Holiday* with Gregory Peck and Audrey Hepburn?). The mouth is a large, ancient sewer cover in the shape of a face. If you put your hand in its mouth and tell a lie, legend has it your hand will be bitten off—certainly worth a touristy photo and a potential spot on *That's Amazing*. After our photo op, we headed back to San Pietro in Vincoli to view Michelangelo's marble *Moses* which was certainly worth all the trouble. This church, reputedly, also contains the chains that bound St. Peter in Judea and Rome. However, I doubt this disputation has ever been given while the speaker is holding his hand in the "mouth of truth," so what credence can you really give to it?

When we returned to the hotel, all the riders were in; they had been SAGed the last ten kilometers to avoid the dangerous Roman streets. Jeremy, a friend of Stacia had joined the group in Pompeii, but his luggage hadn't, so he had borrowed bike clothes and shared a bike the last few days. Also, Tim Kneeland had returned from Barcelona, Spain, having finalized the DRG's to that point. Barbara, Kirby's wife, had also flown to Rome to visit with Kirby for a few days, so when we went out for supper, we were an extended and lively group. Barbara will fly back to Boston when we leave Rome, and Allison, having completed her stage, will return to Seattle.

This is a good time to add a note on Roman street crowds since Kirby and Barbara had an interesting story to relate at supper. There are beggars around most of the churches and tourist areas in Rome. They are mostly women with small children in tow, but sometimes you'll see an older man or someone with an infirmity. They might not always be what they seem, however. Kirby and Barbara told us they had been approached at San Pietro in Vincoli by several young women with babes in arms, at least one of them very pregnant. One grabbed Kirby's arm and, in an instant, both zippers on his fanny pack, which he wisely had in front of him, were open. He realized what was going on and grabbed his pack. He and Barbara had to literally strike the young women to get away. Shouts for the police did not deter them in the least. We had been warned of this in the tour books but, so far, Cheryl and I have not seen anything like this.

The next morning, however, we got to see our own spectacle. Cheryl came down the stairs of our hotel early in the morning to find a woman squatting to urinate in our downstairs lobby area. A passing man was giving her a tongue lashing in Italian. A few minutes later, after we had gotten into the van picking us up for our Pompeii tour, the same woman reached her hand into the van window and grabbed at the lady guide. The guide pulled away and got the window rolled up. The angry woman spit at and beat the window as we pulled away; our guide was nearly in tears. As far as I could tell, this was completely unprovoked—the woman had serious anger problems.

And so on day five in Rome, Cheryl and I headed out for a full day (7 a.m. to 9 p.m.!) bus tour to Pompeii and Sorrento. The commentary on the bus ride was good. At Pompeii we got a local guide who took us through much of this doomed city. In AD 79, Mt. Vesuvius erupted showering Pompeii, which is out of range for lava flows, with volcanic ash, pumice stone and bits of ejected lava. Although most of the twenty thousand residents fled, some two thousand died, primarily from poisonous gas inhalation. The city was completely buried by the ejecta and abandoned. The city was "lost" for hundreds of years and, even after it was found, nothing was done for 150 years until 1748 when serious excavation began. Digging continues to this day with about a quarter of the town yet to be exhumed. Because of the porous nature of volcanic debris, the buried town has been exposed to oxygen so that almost all organic material has long since rotted away. Despite this, archeologists have been able to reconstruct many objects like wooden beams and even animal and human bodies because, while the material has rotted away, a perfect negative of the object was cast by the surrounding stone. This hollow rock composite of the negative image is filled with clay to then get a positive image. Several of these casts, depicting bodies of animals and men in their death throes, are on display in the town. They can give you a creepy feeling. Many of the stone buildings along with their decorations are still in good shape. Overall, the ruins give one a great idea of how people lived in ancient times.

One of the buildings found in good shape and then further reconstructed is a bath house. You can clearly see the changing room, the central heating room where the first stop would be a hot bath to open up the pores, next the tepidarium with warm water and a massage, and finally the frigidarium or cold water baths. Many of the murals and floor mosaics are intact. The guide pointed out how the ceiling was curved to allow condensed water to run down the walls instead of dripping down on the bathers. Since few people had indoor plumbing, these public baths were primarily for hygienic purposes, but they were also places for social commune and even for business transactions. We also saw the market street with all kinds of shops and poked our heads into a couple of the nicer homes which had central atria open to the elements with a catch basin below where rain water was held for domestic use. One entryway had a mosaic of a large dog with the equivalent inscription to "Beware of the Dog." While we did not get to the brothel (which according to the tour book has some extremely erotic murals and caused one elderly tourist to spew invective at our guide for not including it), we did view the residence of two young, single brothers who were successful merchants. In the vestibule of this house is a large picture of a man with his enormous penis on one side of a balance scale and all sorts of commerce goods on the other. The guide said this symbolized to their visitors the perfect harmony of their business and private lives.

From Pompeii we bussed to Sorrento, a small resort town at the tip of a peninsula near the island of Capri to pick up people from our bus who had gone to Capri for the day. The route high above the sheer cliffs to the Tyrrhenian Sea had magnificent views. At the start, we could see all the small turns along the peninsula and later you could look back at the sweep of the bay where Napoli (or Naples) was framed before Mt. Vesuvius. Also on the tour, we stopped to visit cameo and inlaid wood factories to see how these articles are made and, of course, to have the chance to make purchases (I got my Xmas shopping started!). On the way back from Naples, we ran into two heavy rain storms—the first rain I've seen in Italy and much appreciated. They sure need the rain; everything is bone dry.

On our last full day in Rome, we visited the Capitoline Museum via a slightly different route and found some new ruins (an oxymoron?) to view. We got one audio system which didn't work well with two people, but it did have good commentary. The museum is housed in two palazzos, Nuovo and dei Conservatori, which house many striking sculptures with one floor devoted to paintings and coins. It's probably one of the world's oldest museums getting its start in 1471 when Pope Sixtus IV donated some bronze sculptures to the city. My favorites include the huge severed head and hand of Constantine from what must have been an enormous statue, an Etruscan bronze statue of a she-wolf from the sixth century BC (interestingly, the suckling Romulus and Remus beneath the wolf were added much later in 1509), the original bronze statue of Marcus Aurelius on horseback, and the marble faun (inspiration for Hawthorne's novel). This museum is the best I've seen so far for sculpture. On our walk back to our hotel, we got caught in a thunderstorm and availed ourselves of an avant-garde art gallery that happened to be right there. The exhibit was celebrating the senses and had several unusual participatory displays, a most interesting way to pass the time until the rain stopped.

Finally, we had to leave Rome and begin riding again. The general route for this leg of the trip was north from Rome to San Marino, almost on the Adriatic coast, then west through Florence to Pisa and around the Ligurian coast of Italy to Nice, France. While Bobbi had my bike, she had a bike shop change out the three front gears that Tim had brought over with him. I have become distrustful of random bike shops, because I have almost always ended up with a new problem, but this time I was pleasantly surprised in that I haven't had any serious gearing problems since the replacement. Bobbi shuttled us to the outskirts of Rome to start the ride, but, even so, we ran into pesky traffic for the first twenty kilometers. The weather had turned cooler while we were in Rome, and this was appreciated since we hit some hills as we headed north causing us to generate our own heat.

We stayed in campgrounds most of the first several nights and found most nearly empty of tent campers, unlike the coastal areas which are still drawing crowds. It won't be long before many will be closing for the season. We started running into campgrounds that lock their gates at night, making it challenging sometimes to find a way out for an early morning start. The northern hills offered spectacular scenery as we pedaled from hill town to hill town, many of them with ancient walls.

Our second day out from Rome, we rode to Assisi. We hit some good hills along the way and, remembering the pictures of Assisi perched high on a hill, we expected a good terminal climb into the city. However, that night we stayed in the town just below Assisi which was a nice surprise. Our hotel was run by the Franciscan order and was an overnight for the almost 250 riders on Odyssey 2000, so it's a big place.

After getting settled in, Bobbi drove us into Assisi for sightseeing since we would be riding out the next day. Assisi is a beautiful, old walled town on a hill with lots of history and churches. After grabbing a quick lunch, we stopped to see the Duomo (cathedral) di St. Rufino where St. Francis and St. Clare were baptized (St. Francis was born here in 1182). The church has some bizarre exterior decorations such as a cow and a bull jutting out of the wall in mid-plunge about halfway up the front of the church and, around the main entrance, a series of lizard-like creatures facing each other. Some look like Komodo dragons, and others have very long necks. One of the Komodo dragons looks like it has already eaten the head of another one and is ready to take the second bite. Two of the long-necked ones are biting each others' necks. At another church, the frieze shows two large cat creatures, one on either side of the main entrance, with their claws around another animal that looks like a large hare; the cats' open mouths hover over the ears of the hares. Very strange!

We walked along the narrow streets to a main piazza where a temple to Minerva stands. The large cross above the main door testifies how the pagan temple was "converted" to Christian use. We also took a peek at the church of St. Stefino on our way to the enormous Basilica of St. Francis. The basilica, built in the middle of the thirteenth century, is actually two churches, one built above the other. It houses the tomb of St. Francis which you can view by going down, down, down into a sort of dungeon. I lost count of the number of floors below ground level we walked. The tomb looks positively medieval, which of course it is, and was surrounded by many devotees. Later, we learned we are sharing out hotel with a group of pilgrims some of whom, I suspect, we saw at the tomb. (For a painless introduction to the cult of St. Francis try renting the movie *Brother Sun, Sister Moon*, a late '70s, early '80s movie about St. Francis and St. Clare.)

The views from Assisi over the surrounding countryside are wonderful, and the town itself is worth exploring at some length. Cheryl and I agreed that it is a place in which you could hole up for a few restful days. Construction is obvious around the town as the residents continue to recover from an earthquake in 1997 that, amidst other damage, collapsed part of the basilica's ceiling killing four people. We walked down from Assisi on a beautiful new sidewalk, with what must have been donors' names inscribed in the bricks, and ended up at the Basilica of St. Maria degli Angeli just down the street from our hotel. I particularly wanted to see the statue of St. Francis with the live doves in the bowl he is holding that Andy had told us about earlier. The statue was near the rose garden and the doves were pure white, a nice effect.

The next day, we started on a longish ride to Urbino, the birth place of Raphael, by riding straight up and through Assisi, so we didn't avoid the climb after all, but it's sure better to have a stiff climb first thing in the morning than last thing in the afternoon. Although the town looked dauntingly high from the plain below, it wasn't a bad climb if taken at your own pace. We took a short break just outside the eastern gate, where Bobbi had dropped us off the afternoon before, to admire the view. In the morning light with dawn colors in the "V" of the eastern mountains, it was even more memorable.

Later in the ride, I stopped to pick blackberries I saw growing along the road. Just at that moment, Kirby rode up behind me and whistled softly pointing toward some deer in the meadow ahead and above us. He got out his camera, and I got out my binoculars, both of us moving stealthily. The buck had a magnificent rack of antlers of a type I hadn't seen before. The deer moved to the upper part of the field and struck a magnificent pose with the buck and two fawns, one with normal coloring and one a dark phase all lined up as in a professional tableau. It was at that point, as Kirby snapped a great picture, that I noticed the deer were enclosed by a fence. They were domesticated deer probably being raised for food. This discovery was a bit of a let down, but the scene they presented was a striking one nonetheless. The blackberries were only so-so by the way; it's just been too dry to get juicy berries. A bit later on the same ride, Cheryl and I peered into a small river and saw a plethora of large trout. With the binoculars, we could plainly see their beautiful speckled backs as they moved in and out of a deep pool. We think a sign nearby indicated this was a catch and release location which might explain why there were so many big ones.

The next day, we had a shorter ride to San Marino, but with great views as we were riding up and down a lot of hills. The view of San Marino from a distance was perhaps the most dramatic. The city is perched high atop a mount with one side almost sheer. It looks like something out of *The Lord of the Rings*. The climb was not fantasy though. We gained eleven hundred of elevation in eleven kilometers which only averages out to about a three percent grade; however, given that some of the distance was either flat or downhill, we had relatively sharp grades to climb. Overall though, it was just a slow grind, but the views from the top were worth the climb. Then we zoomed down the other side to our campground.

That evening for supper, Bobbi drove us back up the steep hill to the city. San Marino is a sixty-one-square-kilometer republic of uncertain origin. Citizenship is inherited only through the male line, female domestics under the age of fifty are banned to prevent gold-diggers from preying on the many wealthy, elderly men in the country, and the main street is a series of tourist traps. However, it was fun to wander among the narrow cobblestone streets and to ooh and aah at the truly magnificent views from the precipitous overlooks especially with a striking sunset amongst threatening clouds. Except for the fantastic real estate though, it's hard to take San Marino too seriously.

In the morning, we rode to Caprese Michelangelo, the birth place of...who else but Michelangelo. Cheryl and I paid the price of admission to his birth house and museum and rented a new-to-me type of audio guide. This guide had a magnetic sensor that you touched to an icon on either the guide book for general information or next to a specific picture or sculpture to get information on that specific item. It proved to be a good system. In addition, the museum projected a continuous slide show presentation with head phones in various languages that was very good. Copies of several of Michelangelo's works as well as a garden of modern sculpture dedicated to his memory comprised the bulk of the exhibits. One of the more interesting displays was a series of pictures, commissioned to depict twenty-three scenes from Michelangelo's life, painted by famous Florentine painters from 1613–1620, all with audio explanations. The first scene depicts his pregnant mother falling from her horse (but not aborting the child), and the last shows Michelangelo's ascension into heaven and immortality. I felt as if I were viewing the life of a minor deity much like performing devotions before the Stations of the Cross. Overall it was a great museum for such a small village and was a good introduction to our upcoming visit to Florence.

Upon our return to camp, we found our meal was being prepared by several members of this small community...and it was a feast. For starters, we had bread covered by (1) a spread and a fresh fig slice, (2) a spread with half a cherry tomato, and (3) a pate of chicken liver. Next, we passed around large platters with chicken in wine sauce, thinly sliced grilled chicken, local sausage grilled, a fresh chopped tomato salsa to be eaten with bread, a roasted tomato stuffed with a rice mixture, fresh grapes, pears, plums, and cooked zucchini and cauliflower in a sauce, and all this was followed by great desserts. As our rider table was full, I sat with the locals including our hostess (a transplanted New Hampshire resident) and a Dutchman who had married a local. It was a very enjoyable evening.

The next morning was overcast with fog hanging in the valleys and clouds topping the mountains. We began with a short uphill and downhill followed by a more vigorous uphill and a long, sweeping downhill run gradual enough so that we barely touched our brakes. About two-thirds of the way to Florence, we hit a long steep uphill. At the top it began to mist. The mist turned to a light sprinkle as we headed down a long steep stretch and got heavier as we descended. It was an uncomfortable ride. Even had it not been raining and the road wet, we would have been riding our brakes all the way down. Cheryl remarked she was way out of her comfort zone. We stopped at the bottom to regroup, and Kirby caught up to us. The three of us rode into Florence under steady rain. Just as we began navigating the inner streets of Florence, it began to pour making our journey to the campground a real challenge. When we finally reached camp, we heard that Andy had gone down on one of the treacherous downhill curves in the rain and scraped his arm and hip, but not seriously. He was lucky a car wasn't coming because he had slid into the oncoming lane of traffic.

To our delight we didn't have to put up tents as Bobbi had rented large canvas tents with wooden floors and real beds! It was not long before our tents were festooned with wet riding clothes. Before I continue with our tour of Florence, I'll add a couple of campground notes: (1) It seems to be the fashion in Italian campgrounds to wear large fluffy robes to and from your toilette. It was most noticeable at the beach campgrounds even when it was very hot. (2) Squat toilets are still with us in Italy. Most of the campgrounds have only one or two of the porcelain gods, and the rest are squats. When I go to the john here, I feel a bit like I'm playing Russian roulette with a six-shooter and five bullets—I'm just hoping for an empty chamber.

The storm front moved on during the night and our free day in Florence was glorious. Our first stop was the Museum del Bargello with its many interesting sculptures. My favorite was Giambologna's *Winged Mercury* although Donatello and Michelangelo were well-represented, the former with his bronze *David* and the latter with *Bacchus* done when he was only twenty-two years old. Next we walked to the Uffizi Gallery, but the line was a bit long so we went to see the Duomo or cathedral, an impressive bit of architecture with its green and pink marble. The Gallery dell' Accademia was our next venue and the wait was mercifully short. Regardless, Michelangelo's *David* is worth the wait. Even though scaffolding, used in determining the sculpture's condition, was along one side providing an unsightly contrast, *David* is still magnificent. We had seen two other full-sized replicas, one on a hill near our camp and the other near the Uffizi, but the milky whiteness and power of the original set it apart. Leading up to *David* are the four unfinished "slaves." Originally ordered for Pope Julius II's tomb in 1505, these four nude men continuously struggle to emerge from the uncut marble blocks which "enslave" them. They are disturbing in a way, but your eyes keep coming back to them.

After a quick lunch, we returned to the Uffizi which no longer had a line outside, although we still waited awhile inside. Regardless, the tour groups made for slow going once we got into the gallery itself. This is a much larger collection than either the Bargello or Accademia. We again rented a dual audio system which took us on a tour, room by room, of the whole gallery pointing out specific works—not as user-friendly as the type that allows you to select only those works you want to hear about. Nevertheless, the commentary was very good and clear. The collection is arranged to give you a chronology of (primarily) Italian art. My favorite here was Botticelli's *Birth of Venus* although Raphael, Michelangelo, Rembrandt, Rubens, Titian, and many other masters are significantly represented. By the time we left the Uffizi, the afternoon was almost gone. We just had time to walk across the Ponte Vecchio, the bridge leading to the Pitti Palace, before heading back to camp to rest and sup. While walking back to the campground after supper, we received a great omen, the full moon over the Arno, hopefully presaging a beautiful day of riding on the morrow.

Before leaving Florence, this magnificent city of the arts, I want to offer a short commentary on a little known artist. While touring the great museums of Europe with their untold thousands of ancient and priceless paintings and sculptures, it is easy to forget that these are just the pieces of art that have survived the ravages of time. There were many great artists, about whom we'll never know, who were working in perishable media. For instance there are a few water color paintings that have survived, but most have long since faded to nothing. It was not until oil-based paints and canvas were perfected, so as to hold true colors through time, that we can today appreciate the artists who used them. Similarly, marble and bronze became the media of choice for sculptors striving for immortality. Never has this been so forcefully presented to me as the story of a man called Figatello who, in his time, rivaled the great Michelangelo, even surpassing him among aficionados in the lower classes according to one of our Roman guides. Figatello's medium was the common potato. Potato carving was (and still is in rural Italy) a common art form because of the softness, attainability, and cost of the potato. Many of the great sculptors had been potato carvers as children. Donatello, in particular, won almost yearly prizes at the autumn-fests throughout his school years and reportedly used these monetary prizes to buy his first piece of marble. There are several notable potato carvers in various written art histories, but in these annals Figatello reigns supreme. For him carving was a passion; he devoted the same kind of study to it as did Michelangelo with his study of human anatomy using cadavers. Figatello's particular genius was his understanding of the potato's decomposition process. He would carve a realistic face of a young man and then, to people's amazement, the face would change as the potato dried out over days and weeks so that the face of the young man would age gradually from youth through maturity, reaching its pinnacle in very old age. Others, of course, attempted imitation, but none could affect the process of gradual aging like Figatello. Because the art had such a strong temporal aspect, people would come to view a particular creation again and again over the course of the several months it would take for it to reach a steady state. This was no mean feat for the rural peasants who had to travel many miles over rough roads, but such was Figatello's fame and the draw of his creations.

Figatello's fame reached almost mythical status with the very few carvings he did from life of notable personages who commissioned him to do their busts. Because the carvings reached the subjects' dotage in a fraction of the time the actual person aged, the true resemblance between the creation as it dried to the subject as he aged could not be directly compared. However, many people remembered Figatello's works and, throughout the subjects' lives would make comparisons that, without exception, reinforced the belief that Figatello had accurately predicted the aging process of his subjects. For a short while after Figatello's death, a fanatic monk had tried to use the artist's uncanny prescience to prove that Figatello was actually a minion of Satan, but all his ravings came to naught. Although Figatello's fame continued to grow after his death, it began to wane as his subjects and those who had actually viewed his creations died so that, within several generations, only a few art historians even knew his name. [Editor's note: the author has obviously taken another of his flights of fancy. The above anecdote is of course false. Throughout my research, I found no potato carver called Figatello. However, I did come upon a carver of zucchini squash who reached moderate fame in the middle ages. His name, Alberto Zucchini, is actually the namesake of said squash.]

Unfortunately, while in Florence, Stacia had her backpack stolen at an Internet cáfe and lost her passport, camera, charge cards, etc. Naturally, she was bummed. Bobbi stayed with her the next morning to get a temporary passport at the local embassy, as we began our ride to Pisa on the west coast. It was a great day for riding, cool in the morning, but it warmed up fast. The route out of Florence was a bit of a zoo, but Cheryl said she actually enjoyed it. You tend to get used to the close proximity of large amounts of traffic as you weave in and out and round the roundabouts. We hit morning rush hour traffic which was not too bad until we came to a large roundabout for multiple lanes of traffic. After surveying the situation for awhile (kind of like mapping out your route down a wildly rushing river), we decided that discretion is the better part of valor and used a pedestrian crossing directly through the roundabout rather than risk life and limb going around it. Everyone comments on how biker friendly the drivers are here, but this was one place we decided not to test that particular axiom. It's safe to say that, if Europeans ever get a taste for big cars, trucks, and SUV's, it will make driving here an unmitigated hell. Right now there are two reasons that traffic moves at all here: first of all, most people are on bikes or scooters or in very small cars; secondly, by virtue of having small vehicles, people utilize all the available space on the very narrow roads by passing slower or stopped vehicles in order to keep traffic moving. This "available space" would go to a negative number with the introduction of very many large vehicles. Bobbi has lost years from her life trying to maneuver our huge support van along our bike routes especially in the rural mountain towns.

Once out of town, we had a long stretch beside the beautiful River Arno. The river was perfectly calm and the early morning sun was striking the fall foliage on the opposite shore at an angle to provide us a perfect reflection of this beautiful scene in the Arno. Some of the roads were busy, but they were in decent condition, and we were moving along at a good clip so it didn't bother us too much.

Having arrived in camp, we immediately headed for the Tower of Pisa since we would get no layover day here. Now, the tower is impressive, but even more impressive is the tower with the cathedral and baptistery which are all together on a lovely green plaza. You come upon them through a portal of the old walled city, and the view is striking. The tower itself was a grand mistake from the beginning. It began leaning after only three tiers had been built and continued to lean at about one millimeter a year. Many attempts were made to stabilize the movement, but it was not until 1998 that an attempt was successful. Workers removed soil from the upside of the tower, correcting about forty centimeters of the lean and apparently arresting it.

The walk up the tower is 294 steps between two cylindrical stone walls. You feel the lean immediately and are aware of it all the way up and down, leaning first against the inside wall and then against the outside wall. The steps leading to the top two levels are a tight, narrow corkscrew. Portals at the top three levels allow visitors to walk onto the ramparts for viewing. The day was clear, and we had a grand view. We could see the sun reflecting on the distant Ligurian Sea to the west, which was our goal in two days. A ragged mountain range was to our north, and a rounded range showed to the east and southeast that form one side of the Arno valley we had followed from Florence.

The next day, I rode by myself. Cheryl, Andy, and Bill all left their bikes in Pisa at a bike shop to be worked on; Andy rode Bobbi's bike that day. Both Cheryl and bill brought Bike Fridays and were lucky to find someone who could work on them. (Note: a Bike Friday is a bicycle that folds up into a suitcase, perfect for international travel, but difficult to find parts for.) Our ride the following day to Levanto was beautiful with stunning views of the Ligurian Coast and the small villages perched on hilltops or nestled in sparkling coves. I picked some juicy blackberries and, when we got to camp, we tried fresh figs which a local had foisted on Andy and local grapes Bobbi had been given. This part of Italy must have gotten a bit more rain. After getting settled in camp we took a refreshing dip in the ocean enjoying the idea of a layover day on the morrow.

For our off day, Cheryl and I decided to further explore the Cinque Terre region which we had ridden above the day before. The Cinque Terre are five villages that were, until recently, almost unreachable by car. They are situated along the Ligurian coast just a few kilometers from each other. Vinoculture and olives are their main livelihood and now, of course, tourism. The hills have been terraced over many years to accommodate these crops on the steep slopes. The orange nets used to harvest the olives were still wrapped around the base of the trees, their storage position, for another month, but the grapes were being harvested. We took the local train to Riomaggiore, the furthest village of the five from Levanto, to start our day. The *Lonely Planet Guide* has it right when it says not to blink if you take the train because almost the entire route is through tunnels. The distance to Riomaggiore is short—even with stops at each of the other four towns the trip only took a bit over twenty minutes. At Riomaggiore, we hiked a beautiful, rugged trail along the cliff edge that had been set aside for a botany trail. Someone spent a lot of money and time on this dramatic trail. We then hiked to the next closer town, Manarola, along a short, but beautifully maintained trail called Lover's Lane. After exploring the town, we jumped the train to Corniglia which is the next town, grabbed a pizza for lunch, and then hiked to Vernazza along a much longer and more rugged trail.

By this time, we were ready for a dip in the Ligurian Sea, so we took the train to Monterosso where we had seen a beach. This beach was not as nice as the one we saw in Riomaggiore though, so we used our day pass again and headed back to the better beach. After a pleasant afternoon lazing in the Mediterranean sun, we caught the next train to Levanto having had a lovely and relaxing layover day.

The next day, we were back on the bikes and headed to Genova. The first half of the ride was more of the spectacular mountain coastal riding we had seen coming into Levanto, then it flattened out as we entered the Italian Riviera along which we would ride the next two days. This route took us from beach town to beach town which, although easier on the legs, was not nearly as pretty...unless of course you like seeing lots of nearly naked, overexposed flesh. And of course with the beach towns comes the beach traffic. I'm glad we were not riding here during the high season.

When we got to San Remo the next day, I was surprised to see a campground with no dirt! All the tent pads were on brick or stone. If you needed stakes for your tent, you drove them into the cracks. The grounds were clean with a nice pool, but we decided to use their access to the sea for our dip instead. Unfortunately, because of the rough seas, we had to carefully time our entry into the water when the surge was going out over the big rocks, and similarly, time our return to shore to avoid getting a nasty scrape. In fact, there are lots of rocky beaches here, not what people generally imagine when they hear "Riviera."

Before we leave Italy I'll add a couple of notes. First, we have seen many bike riders in Italy, almost all of whom don the bright colors with which bike racers the world over seem so smitten. Somebody at one of the campgrounds told me that the Italian government has a policy to strongly encourage bike riding, especially among the older crowd. The government gives out free jerseys, shorts, patches, etc. and even pays for injuries incurred while biking! No wonder we saw so many older cyclists on the road. Strangely, the vast majority don't wear helmets, but oh, are they color-coordinated!

The second note deals with food. The food in Italy has been good and plenty, but not outstanding. Almost every evening while in Italy I ate pasta for *primi* (their first course) and a pizza for *secundo*. Pasta, I was told by Igor, the Dutchman I mentioned in the last report, is a filler in Italy (he said we Americans use the potato for this purpose) and is served as a first dish during a standard Italian meal. This course is usually followed by a thin piece of meat and then a salad, cheeses, etc. Our budget for supper is set each night by Bobbi, and I usually try to get my calories for the next day within the budget. If not, we can supplement with our own cash which I sometimes do if a special dessert catches my eye. I ate more pizzas in Italy than I had eaten in the States in the previous two years. Their pizzas are thin-crusted with either one or a small number of ingredients on them. They have something called a four-way pizza that might have ham in one quadrant of the pizza, peppers in a second, mushrooms in a third, and artichokes in a fourth, but seldom do they mix all of them together. They also have a four-cheese pizza, like the *quatre fromage* pizza in the earlier France stage, which I ordered from time to time, but the Italian version often includes chevre or goat cheese as one of the four cheeses. I had duck and pheasant at different times and, of course, there's the gelato (ice cream) which was often very good. Probably the best gelato flavor is lemon—you wonder how they manage to pack so much flavor into such a small container!

Cheryl's last ride was to Nice, France. On the way, we passed through Monaco. As we stopped to consult our route guide in Monaco, we saw two well-preserved, on the backside of middle age, very chichi women each with a fashionably small chichi dog, one a toy poodle, the other a shiatsu, both on leashes. Both women and dogs were dressed and coiffed in the height of fashion. As the women chatted, the dogs, oblivious of *de rigueur* of acceptable behavior in the income bracket of their mistresses, were checking each other out in the manner of dogs everywhere. Though I did not register any reaction from either matron, I did notice the leashes appeared shorter the next time I glanced over. I was somehow comforted by the thought that a perpetually primped, preened, and perfumed pooch is, in the final reckoning, still a pooch.

On Cheryl's last full day the trip, we first walked to St. Nicolas Cathedral so she could experience the grandeur of a Russian Orthodox Church. She was duly impressed, although it was far from the largest or most ornate such church. From there we walked to the Matisse Museum which underwhelmed us both. I enjoyed his vibrant painting of the dancers I had seen in the Hermitage more than all of the works in this museum. For fun, we took a free tour of a confectionary shop on the water and sampled their wares. Cheryl bought some potent ginger candy for her boss which I'm sure she'll enjoy since she has a minor ginger addiction. Later that afternoon, while Cheryl boxed up her Bike Friday, I took a swim on the Azure Coast of Nice. It is aptly named; the water is a startling color of blue. Although the beach is stony, it is kept clean as is the water. The whole beachfront had a highly manicured feel. The water even seemed warmer than other places along the coast. The next morning, Bobbi and I dropped Cheryl off at the Nice airport just a few minutes from our hotel, and I continued down the French Riviera to Spain which I'll cover next time.

Take care,

Ralph

Report #19: 2003,
A Spain Odyssey

Howdy yet again, (Getting tired of these yet? Should be just a few more.)

The alternate title for this report is "The Rain in Spain" due to the wet weather since entering the country.

The route from Nice along the French Riviera was not among my favorites. For the most part, we rode through beach town after beach town where lots of money lives and plays. The beaches are pretty, and the color of the Mediterranean is worthy of better adjectives than I have at my disposal. We had magnificent vistas as we often climbed up and around a headland to get to the next cove. But the traffic, even in this off-season, and the excessive evidence of conspicuous consumption were a bit much for my taste.

My favorite route segments were those where Tim had found rural back roads through the coastal hills. Our route sometimes paralleled good bike paths. We rode them when we could for a nice change from the busy roads. On our second day out from Nice, just after leaving St. Tropez on the coast, we hit one such rural road cutting across a headland. Unfortunately, our DRG had a seven-kilometer error that day. I was getting pretty antsy looking for the next turn, but the road was quiet, had a great surface, and a ripping good shoulder or bike lane. I decided that, if it wasn't the right route, it should be and opted to follow it anyway since it was headed in the right general direction. My instincts were good, and I eventually found the turn. Except for the vague uncertainty, it was a great ride. Of course, I also took advantage of every opportunity our campsites offered to swim in the Mediterranean which was nine of the next ten days after leaving Pisa.

I especially enjoyed our ride to and through Marseille. We had a couple of climbs with gorgeous views. The first one was the hardest, but it occurred early in the day when it was a bit cooler. It was all out in the open, no trees to block the stark vistas as we climbed above a series of box canyons, one of which held a shooting range from which we could hear periodic gunshots. I don't normally think of France as having such rugged terrain. This climb could have been in the American southwest. The last climb presented a spectacular view of Marseille, which I had visited almost exactly one year before on a trip to Corsica with a friend. The descent into the city was fast and got pretty hairy in a couple of places. My bike rims were almost too hot to touch from constant braking; I actually stopped part way down to cool them off a bit. Though the traffic was heavy, the ride through the city was fun for me as our route took us right past the hotel on the port where my friend and I had stayed.

On the longish (139-kilometer) but nearly flat day to La Grand Motte, we passed through a bird sanctuary where I saw a flock of flamingos, gray herons, little egrets, and other water birds. Unfortunately, it rained a good portion of the day under a bruised, greenish sky that made my midwestern tornado antennae tingle. Luckily, the wind was at our backs, and we made great time even in the rain…two flat tires weren't much fun though. I had three more flats in the next two days and decided to retire my rear tire at 6,852 kilometers.

Bobbi garnered our gratitude that afternoon by moving us into a hotel since the campground on our DRG was under water when we arrived, and it continued to rain. This was one distinct advantage we had over the almost 250 riders on Odyssey 2000—TK&A could decide, on the spot, to relocate the few of us for a night. This was also the night that Loic, our French dentist friend from the Alps stage, and his family were supposed to meet us, but he had a dental emergency and had to cancel. Too bad, he could have cheered us up on this rainy day with his friendly insouciance.

The campgrounds on this stage have been increasingly devoid of campers, especially those not on a beach. One night in a particularly out of the way campground, I listened to two owls calling to one another over the course of a couple of hours, with the further one gradually moving toward the closer one until the hooting became an almost purring sound as they proceeded to bill and coo. Later, toward morning, I heard another owl couple from a different species calling to each other. Even knowing the owl myths are false, for example that owls are wise birds, mysterious, harbingers of evil, etc., I still get a thrill when I get the chance to listen in on their conversations and don't, in the least, begrudge them the lost sleep.

That very evening, a front moved through leaving behind a brilliant night sky and a superb autumn day, crisp and clean with a morning sun slant that somehow said winter's on its way. It made for great riding to our layover day in Carcassonne, France. The route was more rural and more enjoyable than the previous several days. Tim had again found some tiny, picturesque roads. One ran along a small canal where I stopped to watch a set of locks in action, letting pleasure craft move up and down the canal, and then past field after field of grapes ripe for the harvest.

Carcassonne consists of an upper walled city called the Cite and a lower, more conventional city. The Cite was almost completely reconstructed in the nineteenth century and so remains largely intact. Therefore, it is impressive to the average tourist with its double wall and many conical towers. Our first night there we had dinner in the walled city. The restaurant served only two dishes: duck comfit or a regional specialty called cassoulet. The latter is a stew of duck, sausage, and white beans cooked and served in a clay pot. We all had the cassoulet and were very happy with it.

Our layover day at Carcasonne was a perfect autumn day, and I spent a pleasant afternoon wandering around the old walled city. I circumnavigated the greens between the two walls catching nice views in all directions. The sky was so blue and the air so clear you could see far and sharp. I didn't take any of the tours or go to the museums but just enjoyed the ambience of the old town. I did visit the Basilica of St. Nazarius and St. Celsus, a part Romanesque and part Gothic church from the twelfth and thirteenth centuries. It houses a "siege stone" from a siege in which Simon de Montfort participated; he is the only Montfort (a variant spelling of my surname) or Monfort I've ever seen in a history book. His tombstone is also there, although his son moved his body to a different location. I'm not exactly clear what a siege stone is, but it appears to commemorate the siege through pictures carved in stone.

Later, I walked down to the modern town to find an Internet café and an eatery for supper. I checked out several restaurants and had almost defaulted to pizza when I found a chichi looking place with white table cloths and fine crystal and a menu for €12.80. A menu here refers to a set of courses you get for one price, and our budget here was €13.00, so it seemed a perfect match. A quick peek inside yielded a substantial buffet spread for starters (i.e., appetizers), and I was hooked. Boy, did I hit the jackpot! The starters included a fish soup with croutons covered with freshly grated Parmesan cheese, a nice pate, several cold meats, and a variety of prepared salads (pea salad, ham salad, etc.). My main meal was a sliced duck breast in rich gravy served with a delicious side of carrots with garlic, fried potatoes with mushrooms and diced ham, and a green vegetable patty. This was presented with a dinner roll and, wonder of wonders, a pitcher of ice water. For dessert I ordered the assorted plate consisting of a crème brûleè, floating clouds (i.e., a meringue in a cream sauce), assorted tarts and cakes, and a couple of cheeses. Had we spent another night here, I have no doubt my description of this feast would have gotten our whole group there.

The next day we began our ascent of the Pyrenees. Up to this point the roads on this southern stage of France had been poor. Italy and even Greece had kept their roads in better condition. But once we hit the route used by the Tour de France (some kind of big bicycle race they have over here), the roads suddenly improved. As we zoomed down one steep hill, Stacia and I stopped to ponder names (including a Lance somebody) and foreign phrases painted brightly on the road. At the bottom of the hill, we arrived at Ax les Thermes for our last night in France. I searched for an Internet café and then soaked my feet in a large thermal pool with a fountain in the main square while waiting for Bobbi and the support van.

That night it began raining and kept it up the next day throughout our relatively short (sixty-five-kilometer) ride to Andorra, an independent principality nestled between France and Spain. On the way, we rode over the highest pass in the Pyrenees at 7,702 feet. The views were awesome, but the light rain made riding a bit uncomfortable and again made me wonder if automatic wipers for eyeglasses is a feasible concept. Bobbi, ever the thoughtful SAG driver, met us at the top with snacks and dry clothes. I changed out of my wet shirt and put on warmer clothes for the long, steep downhill ride also in the rain. Climbing a steep hill in a cold rain doesn't generally chill me because of the heat I'm generating, but rocketing down from a mountain pass is another kettle of fish…it was bone-chilling. This route would certainly be worth further exploration on a clear day. My quote for this report is taken from one of those extraneous thoughts you get about three quarters of the way when riding up a mountain in a cold rain: "Be still my heart, thou hast known still worse than this," which comes from Homer's *Odyssey*.

By the way, we passed into Andorra about a kilometer before the top of the pass; the seemingly endless stream of stop and go traffic heralded the border crossing long before we reached it. Evidently Andorra is a favorite shopping spot for the French. There is something inherently satisfying about passing cars, lots of cars, as you pedal uphill. As we bicycled across the border, the guards were very friendly. Tsk-tsking at our cold, wet state, they gave us welcome packages that we stuffed into our bike bags.

According to the *Lonely Planet Guide*, the nationhood of Andorra is a bit of an historical accident. Charlemagne captured the region from the Muslims in AD 803. His grandson, Charles II, granted the valley to a count. Later it passed to a line of bishops. In the thirteenth century, a system of shared sovereignty was established to resolve a dispute concerning succession. This state of dual sovereignty held until 1993 with the French king or president and the bishop of the Spanish town of La Seu d'Urgell as the two heads of state. This odd situation may have saved Andorra from being enveloped by its larger neighbors. Today, it is a parliamentary co-princedom (whatever that means) with the bishop and president still acting as nominal heads of state.

Since we're heading into Spain, I'll give you a quick history of it too. Peopled first by the Iberians from northern Africa between 8000 and 3000 BC, Spain was later visited by the Celts, Phoenicians, Greeks, Carthaginians, and Romans (I'm not talking about the tourist kind of "visit" here). Under Roman rule until AD 409, Spain was first overrun by Germanic tribes and then again three hundred years later by the Moors coming up from northern Africa. The Christian *Reconquista* began in the eighth century and concluded in 1492 (more on this later when we get to Granada). Spain's golden years began in 1469 with the merging of the kingdoms of Castile and Aragon through the marriage between Ferdinand and Isabella (yes, the same pair who later bankrolled Columbus). Exploration and exploitation of the new world followed making Spain a world power.

This power began waning in 1580 when the British fleet, under the command of Sir Francis Drake, defeated the Spanish Armada. In 1805, Spain's influence took another big hit with the *coup de grâce* of Spanish sea power at the Battle of Trafalgar. The Spanish-American War of 1898 then effectively ended the Spanish Empire.

General Francisco Franco led the Nationalists to victory in the Spanish Civil War (1936–39) and then ruled as dictator for thirty-five years. His successor, King Juan Carlos, moved the country toward a democracy with elections held for the first time in 1977. Spain joined the European Community in 1986, NATO in 1997, and assumed the rotating presidency of the European Union in 2002.

The weather was clearing the morning we left Andorra, and I did not ride in any rain. However, the road was wet most of the way down the big hill, so caution was the morning's buzzword. The thundering stream, which passed beneath our window the previous night, accompanied us for much of the morning, spilling out of the mountains as we followed the contour of the valley relentlessly downward. We had just one uphill of any consequence and then another great downhill into Salsona for our first night in Spain.

Although it rained again during the night, my tent was almost dry by morning. The campsite was closed and locked forcing Kirby and me to lift our bikes over the gate in order to get a head start on our ride to Monistrol de Montserrat (how the campground managers can expect to keep people virtual captives until nine in the morning is a mystery, even if they do keep late hours). The first part of the ride was a pleasant downhill, but then we started climbing up to Montserrat. As we climbed, the scenery became more interesting as the serrated ridges that give the town and the monastery their name came into view. This mountain juts out of the surrounding plains so that, no matter in which direction we pedaled, we were treated to grand vistas of distant hills and vast plains dotted with villages here and there. When I hit the pass, I still had energy to burn and, when I came to the intersection for our hotel, decided to climb the rest of the way to the Benedictine monastery of Montserrat. Founded in the eleventh century, the monastery became a popular pilgrimage destination primarily because of its spectacular location, but it was aided by a wooden carved Madonna and Child to which a string of miraculous occurrences is attributed. *La Moreneta*, or the Black Virgin, is regarded as the patroness of Spain's Catalunya region. The Virgin's darkness comes from the effect of candle smoke on the varnish which covers her hands and face.

Because of the monastery's strategic location, it was attacked, destroyed, and rebuilt a couple of times during its history, so most of the buildings are not particularly ancient. In fact, many modern buildings were in evidence as the place has become a major tourist attraction. I passed at least thirty buses and numerous cars parked along the steep road leading to the monastery…and this was on a Monday during the off-season. As I locked my bike and began poking around, I got the sense of visiting a monastery theme park with all the big plastic information placards, sophisticated parking arrangements, and general bustle. The monastery has three different funicular railways: one to bring people up from the town below, one to save a hike to a natural point of meditation and reflection (and a spectacular view to boot), and one to save a hike to the start of the Stations of the Cross from which a devotee traverses another spectacular section of mountain trail with modern artworks at each station

depicting the appropriate religious scene. There are numerous restaurants, caf-
eterias, and shops where you can buy Montserrat-made wine, Montserrat-
made chocolate, Montserrat-made pastries, Montserrat-made you-name-it, as
well as the normal array of books, pamphlets, postcards, and even stuffed
chamois (Twain's bane in *A Tramp Abroad*). I kept waiting for a big-headed
Dopey in monk's garb to come up and shake my hand.

As luck had it, I got to the monastery just before the 1 p.m. performance of
the boy's choir in the sixteenth century basilica. My pre-trip notes from the
Lonely Planet Guide cautioned to get there early, but I made it into the church
just before the performance. I found an SRO place at the back where, even
with my moderate American height, I was able to look out over a large number of much shorter people to see the boys file in. The place was packed to the
gills with every seat and aisle space taken. Without introduction or preamble,
the boys sang two nice, but unremarkable, longish, appropriately churchy
pieces and then filed out again. Even before the second number was over,
many people, even those within the main part of the church, began moving
toward the back exits as if to say, "Well, I can tick that off my list."

As the boys filed out, I looked around and found myself almost alone in the
vestibule where only a minute or two before there had been a hundred people.
I wormed my way down the aisle to a seat in the main part of the church to let
people escape and then moved closer to the apse to survey the inner basilica at
closer quarters. It was then I realized what the attraction was for the long line
of people I had seen waiting to get into the church via a special door. It was
the E Ticket* ride of this monastic theme park: the shrine of the BVM (for
those not attuned to parochial school acronyms, BVM is Blessed Virgin
Mary). The people in line would very slowly disappear into the bowels of the
church through an ornately carved passageway, maybe a couple every minute
or two. The next time they appeared they were high above the altar where a
large mural of Christ on the cross or similarly large statue would normally
reside. Instead, there was an arched niche containing the shrine of the Black
Virgin lit from above by decorative lanterns. The Virgin, one of the homelier
representations of Mary that I've seen, holding baby Jesus, was surrounded by
garish and shiny bas-reliefs. The penitent would approach from the right,
genuflect or kneel as seemed appropriate (with full realization they were in
view of everyone in the church), and, grasping the orb Mary was holding in
her right hand, would seem to commune with her for a few moments (five to
thirty seconds seemed to be about as long as people dared stay since there were
hundreds behind them waiting their turns). From time to time the solemn

devotion would be disturbed by a flashbulb but, hey, if you're going to spend this kind of time you want something to show for it. Even Disneyland's Space Mountain leaves you with a mild nausea. (* For those old enough to remember, years ago Disneyland had a system where you bought a package of tickets upon entry to the park. Some were A tickets, which were typically kiddy rides like Mr. Toad's Wild Ride, and then they proceeded through B tickets to C, D, and E, which were the most popular and sophisticated...think Matterhorn.)

It had begun to sprinkle just after I got to the monastery, so I had already made my decision to stay and cope with the ride down a wet road later. Well, later came, and I slalomed down the damp road (it was no longer raining) using my brakes as sparingly as I dared. In the village below, we were staying in a quaint hostel, three to a room. The view out our bedroom window was that magnificent serrated mountain.

On the morrow, we set out for Barcelona and a layover day. The route was fast with lots of downhill and flat stretches. The roads got busier early in the ride, and we entered an extensive urban area about halfway. We skirted Barcelona proper to get to our beachside campground for two-to-a-room cabins (good thing too because of the rain). That evening before supper, Bobbi drove us to Parc Gruell where the odd architect Gaudi made his landscape statement. The word "gaudy" derives from his name which should give you some idea of his works. The park displayed many interesting fences, pillars, buildings, and the odd lawn ornament all with his distinctive flair. It was a fun place in which to wander, and many people were enjoying the open space even in the light rain.

On the morrow, the four world riders headed to Gaudi's La Sagrada Familia Temple (i.e., the Temple of the Sacred Family) where I rented an audio tour. The temple is a truly impressive work of art. Construction of Gaudi's masterwork in progress began in 1882. Antoni Gaudi became project director a year later and managed the project until his death in 1926. Before he died, he drew up detailed plans for its completion according to his vision. Eight of the twelve bell towers have been completed as have the extensive facades depicting scenes leading up to the crucifixion and scenes dealing with the nativity on the front and back of the temple respectively. I heard somewhere that the projected completion date is 2030 though work is only about halfway done. The project is funded entirely through alms and private donations.

When finished, the temple will rival any of the ancient cathedrals in size, scope, and complexity. Gaudi used nature as his model; I found the interior columns evocative of a redwood forest. While touring the site, the stone masons and plasterers continue to work since most of the interior is not complete. Scaffolding, dust, and the noise of construction are all part of the show. The visit includes a basement museum depicting the history of the temple and a walk or elevator ride up one of the massive towers. The stairs corkscrew part way up one tower to an external catwalk outside connected to a second tower and then further up to another external catwalk to a third tower. From the catwalks, you can see the intricate artwork of the towers and the decorations on top of the temple and can also enjoy great overviews of the city. It would be worthwhile to return to Barcelona in 2030 to see it upon its completion.

From the temple, I walked to the Picasso Museum which had a nice collection of his works, particularly from his years in Barcelona. The works are arranged chronologically through a series of nineteen rooms and were accompanied by good explanations of each period of work. Picasso began painting when only eleven years old and continued throughout his life. I actually liked his earliest works shown here, including several portraits and miniatures, more than the later work of his "blue" and "pink" periods and on into cubism. It's not that I don't like his surreal works. They do evoke a response, which is what art is supposed to do. It's just that they are full of symbolism I don't understand without doing some research or taking an art appreciation course. The museum seemed to have a better selection of his earlier work than his later work...I suspect that has to do, at least partly, with the exorbitant cost of the latter.

On the way to supper at La Rambla (the main drag), I check out Barcelona's Gothic Cathedral. The cathedral wasn't much to look at from the outside since it was covered in green mesh for renovation, but inside it was something else again. It certainly rivals almost any church I've seen on this trip for decoration. I did a circuit and passed side altar after side altar, each one dedicated to one or more saints, each one cordoned off by a black wrought-iron gate, and each with its own alms box. It was such overkill that I did a second circuit just to count them—there were twenty-eight! The Black Virgin of Montserrat even scored her own niche with a relatively good facsimile of her inside. A side door led into an atrium, which was surrounded by another dozen side altars along with a few niches that were covered as if in renovation. One of the black-gated altar areas was taken up by a gift shop.

Back in the main church, I noted yet another alms box, this one for the maintenance of their organ. I passed a confessional situated adjacent a main aisle and glanced in to see an elderly priest whom, for a brief moment, I thought was an animatronic copy. Amidst all this Gothic splendor and time-less religiosity, a half dozen prominent video screens displayed a continuously scrolling program including, for example, schedules for various special services and tours, a sophisticated graphic on the cathedral's reconstruction, and a warning to turn off your cell phone. The merging of the old and the new can be a bit discombobulating at times.

After a quick supper, I continued on down La Rambla to the huge monu-ment to Christopher Columbus but, by that time, it was too dark to see any but the smaller figures around the bottom. I wonder what the anti-C.-C.-Day folks in the States would say about this showy homage to ole Chris!

The following day, we all jumped into the van for the long and tiring four-teen-hour drive to Gibraltar. We passed through pretty mountains and hills, beautiful beech or birch forests planted in rows (can't think how they might use all this soft wood), seemingly endless terraced hills, what looked like "non-grape" vineyards, and much dry country. As we neared Gibraltar, we also ran into rain with some great cloud formations. We arrived well after dark and Bobbi was frazzled. We found a restaurant still open for supper (no mean feat in this British town) and were glad to hit the sack in a six-bunk hostel.

Gibraltar is one of those weird vestiges of the historical power struggles among nations over strategic pieces of geography. It sits at the mouth of the Mediterranean with the North African coast visible across its narrow strait. It served as the bridgehead for the Moorish invasion of Europe in AD 711 and remained in their hands until 1462. A British and Dutch fleet captured it from Spain in 1704, and it has been a British colony ever since although not with-out considerable disagreement with Spain. Spain and England are currently discussing joint sovereignty. To arrive in Gibraltar by land, you must pass through two customs stations and then cross an active runway that effectively severs the rock from the mainland. To allow sufficient length for large jet air-craft, the runway is built on land that has been reclaimed from the sea at either end. It's a bit like entering the Kingdom of Oz.

On our first of two layover days here, Bobbi left in the van to trace the next couple days' route to produce our DRG's while Bill, Kirby, Stacia, and I took the tram to the top of the Rock. We headed straight for St. Michael's cave, a large cavern with lots of ribbon formations and a few neat stalagmites and stalactites. One large column had fallen, its end polished to show its growth rings just like a tree trunk—pretty cool.

All along the way atop the Rock, we ran into the famous Barbary apes, the only primates in Europe other than man. The apes are relatively tame since they are around people all the time. We toured the tunnels built during the Great Siege, a three-year period when the French and Spanish attacked British Gibraltar while the British were engaged in the American Revolutionary War. The British blasted tunnels so they could bombard their attackers from the northeast side of the Rock. These tunnels were greatly extended during the Second World War. Finally, before walking down off the Rock, we visited a small museum called "City under Siege" that told the story through firsthand accounts and mementos.

Later in the day, I visited the city museum which was just okay. The best part was a fifteen-minute video discussing the Rock's geologic history from Gondwanaland to present. I learned a few interesting tidbits: (1) Evidently the first Neanderthal skull was found on Gibraltar, but it had been filed away for years and surfaced only after another famous skull had been found; otherwise it might have been Gibraltar Man that entered into our common lexicon and not Neanderthal Man. (2) Hercules, during the execution of his tenth labor, shoved Africa and Europe apart using Gibraltar as one of his handholds (i.e., one of the Pillars of Hercules). (3) It is believed that, as the two continents parted, the area known as the Mediterranean Sea, which was then dry land, was flooded by water pouring over a ten-thousand-foot waterfall from the Atlantic. Yeah, I know it sounds improbable, but that's what the program stated.

On our second layover day, we took a day-trip to Tangier, Morocco. From Gibraltar, we walked across the border into Spain and jumped a bus to Algeciras from whence we caught a fast ferry to Tangier. With the two-hour time difference, we didn't arrive until 3 p.m. and only had about four hours before making the return trip. Once in Tangier, we were met at the ferry by a small group of guides, a couple of whom were persistent. One walked us all the way to the tourist office in town for a city map. When we got to the office, it was closed for another hour due to siesta (surprise), and the guy gave us the hard sell for a guided tour. Instead, we headed to the Casbah, their extensive market, seemingly patterned after a rabbit warren, and explored that maze until time for our return ferry.

It was definitely the off-season, and we were almost completely unhassled. It was actually very pleasant. The open-air markets, narrow, winding streets, and filth reminded me of China more than any other place we've been. Some things could definitely be had at reduced prices. We found a nice hole-in-the-wall restaurant to have a late lunch, and it was very good. The best discovery was the mint tea which consisted of a glass half-full of fresh mint leaves over which is poured very hot and very sweet tea. Next we scouted for local sweets, which I was able to get for a song (I chose *White Christmas*). Then it was time for the return trip. We arrived back at the hostel just before midnight, a tiring, but interesting day…and realized none of us took any pictures! Maybe it was because it was overcast and sprinkling the whole time.

The next two days saw us paralleling the coast headed east, sometimes along the coast and sometimes climbing through the hills just inland. I had two flats, both on brand new inner tubes that first day. Both holes occurred at slits that had widened at the weak point until a hole was created, and both were almost in the same place on the tube. I suspect we got into a bad batch of tubes since I can't figure out how a tube gets a slit with no markings on the tire. The second day, we had a stiff head wind the entire time which is like a continuous uphill climb with no chance of coasting down. All in all, not memorable days.

I took swims at both camping locations. The water was much colder than elsewhere along the Mediterranean where I've swum. I suspect it was colder because we were close to the passage to the Atlantic. We were technically on the Costa del Sol in the Alboran Sea—though it sure wasn't a "coast of the sun" for us. At the second place we stayed, the sea was very rough with large waves crashing onto the completely deserted beach. I decided to try a quarter-mile swim. Well, the surf tossed me around pretty good. I actually made it past the brown, roiled section and into the blue-green area for a short while, but then I turned back as commonsense at last prevailed. The swim to shore was ridiculously short as the incoming surge had kept me from going out very far and literally threw me ashore when I headed in. When I finally washed ashore, I couldn't find my shirt, glasses, or shoes. I was worried a large wave had claimed them. After searching up and down the beach for fifteen minutes, I finally found them—a lateral current had carried me more than fifty yards down the beach without my realizing it!

That night, Bobbi decided to put us inside cabins since it looked like we were going to get some weather. Well, she was right; we had a hell of a thunderstorm that dropped a ton of water and put out the lights on the whole coastal side of the city. We all had to pack into the van and drive toward the lit section of town in order to get supper. We were finally treated to some gor-

geous weather the next day on our ride to Granada, enjoying nice climbs in the
Sierra Nevada Mountains to our next layover day.

I had a busy day in Granada. I biked into town to take a city tour and was
the only one to show up, so I had the guide to myself which is always a treat.
My guide began by explaining why January 2, 1492, was the turning point in
Granada's long, two-thousand-plus-year history. This was the date that Gran-
ada, the last Muslim stronghold in Spain, was (peacefully) retaken by the
Christian king. You might remember from above that the Moors entered
Spain through Gibraltar in AD 711. They rapidly spread throughout Spain
and into southern France, ruling until the Christian resurgence in the Middle
Ages. The last Muslim rule was the Nazrid Dynasty (the one that built
Alhambra, of which more later) which was founded by Mohammed Al
Ahmar, who became Sultan Mohammed I in 1238 by agreeing to pay tribute
to the Christian king. Thus Muslims and Christians lived side by side in a
tenuous peace for some time. The ceding of Granada in 1492 was merely the
signing of paper rather than a bloody battle. Nevertheless, for the ruling Spanish king and for the Catholic Church, it was a big deal since it was part of the
consolidation of the five Spanish regions into one kingdom.

The transformation of Granada from a Muslim to a Christian city was
tightly orchestrated. For the first seven years, the Muslims (who were the vast
majority of the people in Granada at the time) had no restrictions on their
religion, culture, dress, foods, customs, etc. After that grace period, however,
Christian rule began tightening the screws on the local population. Arabic
could no longer be spoken, there was a mass conversion to Christianity with
eight thousand baptisms a day, and Muslim dress was no longer allowed. Even
the Turkish baths were closed as potentially seditious meetings places. Any
rebellion against these strictures was harshly put down, though most uprisings
were in the rural areas and not in the city. The typically narrow Arabic streets
were eventually widened, and open spaces were carved out as plazas within the
city. A huge cathedral was erected to dwarf the central mosque which eventually collapsed due to disrepair. In the next phase, Muslims were not allowed to
live in the city and were forced to move to other regions in Spain. Finally, in
1567, Muslims were exiled from Spain, mostly to Morocco. Granada became,
for a time, almost a ghost town with 70 percent of the population expelled.

My guide said that many modern Muslims consider what happened in
Granada the greatest tragedy in Islamic history. She said that Osama bin
Laden, in his speech following 9/11, said something to the effect that what
happened in Andalucia (Granada's province) will not happen to the Palestin-

ians. She said that Granada is thought to be home to one of the planning nuclei for al Qaeda with one of its leaders just recently arrested there. More recently, in June 2003, the first mosque in Spain since the Muslim's sixteenth century exodus was opened in Granada. Funds for its construction came from all over the Muslim world, and Granada has become an instant pilgrimage site.

The tour itself was interesting. She showed me an old merchant's hostel where traveling merchants could retire with their goods in a safe, quiet place when they arrived in Granada. It is the only remaining one of many that would have been in a city the size of Granada. These hostels were built exactly the same way in all major Muslim towns throughout northern Africa, the Middle East and Spain, with a single entrance for security, a large central watering trough surrounded by stables for the livestock and merchants' quarters on the upper floor.

Granada had an extensive silk trade which became so lucrative the Sultan posted guards at each of the four entrances of the market and collected taxes on the trade. This market was one of the many areas that transferred whole cloth to the Christians on January 2, 1492, with the taxes now going to the Christian king of course. The trade eventually disappeared as the Muslims were driven out. The area was reconstructed as a market for tourists, a bit reminiscent of the Casbah in Tangier although not nearly as chaotic or dirty. By the way, the silk being traded at the market was the cocoon of the silk worm and not the finished product.

We also passed Granada's Cathedral, the first Renaissance church in Spain, a well-preserved Turkish bath built on the Roman model with cold, warm and hot rooms, and walked through Albaycin, the old Muslim quarter, where the guide pointed out the different styles of housing. We ended at the River Darro which separates the city from Alhambra and the Jewish quarter. The Darro provides water for the city. The ruling sultan in the eleventh century had a sophisticated hydraulic system constructed that was used continuously until the 1950s. When the modern system was put in, the engineers left the original in place and installed theirs parallel to it. When the Alhambra was built, two-thirds of the Darro's flow was diverted to serve as its water supply.

Water is very important in Islam, both as symbol and in reality. Their paradise is centered around water and nature. Within the city there are water fountains everywhere for both drinking and decoration. The gardens of Alhambra are dominated by the sound and sight of water. In fact, one staircase has stone handrails in which large grooves have been carved so that water flows continuously down them—a neat engineering trick.

The Alhambra was built by the Sultans as a palatine city, or "city of palaces," high on a hill overlooking the city of Granada. It has high walls, a reliable water source and everything else to make it self-sufficient and defensible. It was, of course, also taken over by the Christian rulers in 1492. The Christian King Charles, or Carlos V, felt so much at home there (he had spent his honeymoon at the Alhambra) that he ordered the construction of his own palace on the grounds.

I rented the audio guide for my afternoon and evening at the Alhambra and thoroughly enjoyed my time. The views over the city and to the Sierra Nevadas are magnificent. Of course, the brilliantly clear weather (for a change) added to my enjoyment. The gardens, the fountains, the towers, and palaces are well worth a gander, but my favorite thing about the Alhambra is that it just felt good there. I'm evidently not the first person who has felt its pleasant pull. Washington Irving passed through the area on an extended European tour and ended up staying for quite some time. His book *Tales of the Alhambra* helped put Granada on the western tourist map.

I passed my time waiting for my 6:30 p.m. entrance into the Royal Palace updating my journal and enjoying the gardens of the summer palace. The wait was worth it. The entrance to the palace is unassuming as are the external façades of most Muslim palaces. They save the extravagance for the inside. This one was gorgeous with lots of filigree of wood and marble. The decorations covered the gamut of Arabic art with motifs based on geometric shapes, lettering, and nature, all heavily represented in the ceilings and walls of various rooms. It was actually jarring to enter the several rooms decorated for one of the French kings after passing through so many delicate and restful rooms following an Arabic design.

On my bike ride down the steep road from the Alhambra to camp, the route became one way, and I was diverted down a rough stone road in a completely different direction. It took me awhile to regain my sense of direction and find paved roads to take me back to camp. Riding in the evening gloam in heavy traffic was also a challenge.

Ending with the sublime of the Alhambra without an offset by the droll would be out of place for these missives, so I will report on yet another "bathroom moment." Spain has provided the epitome of absurdity in toilet fixtures. I found a urinal in a public building that deflects your stream such that droplets splash back on your legs and shoes regardless of the angle of said stream...believe me I know, because I tried every conceivable angle and walked away frustrated, bemused, and damp. Was this engineering intentional and, if so, for what purpose?

Well, this is the end of another stage of my year bicycle trip. From here, we ride to Córdoba, Seville, and into Portugal, ending in Lisbon. This will provide grist for my final report from Europe. On October 23, we fly into the spring of Jo'burg, South Africa and a whole new world.

Take care of yourself and those who belong to you,

Ralph

Report #20: Iberian Dreams

October 24, 2003

Bon Dia for my last report from Europe,

We had two excellent days of riding from Granada to our next layover location in Córdoba with sharp, clean, sunshiny autumn days. The first night we stayed at a small pension in a midsized town. I spent quite a bit of time looking for the post office, asking several people who all seemingly understood my quest and pointed out the direction. I felt like I was on a wild goose chase and that the town had a conspiracy to confuse tourists. I never did find it. I did find the tourist bureau door though. I just followed the signs and, with the help of one of the typical town square loafers, I found the building. Once inside, signs pointed me first to one floor up, then a sign pointed me to the next floor which looked a bit shabby, but I was still game. Next a sign directed me down a corridor, and the next one pointed up a narrow staircase that looked as if it hadn't been used in quite awhile. I continued up the stairs which took a sharp left and ended at a door that was obviously locked and probably would not be opening any month soon, so I gave up that quest too.

I actually did find a cheap Internet location though, four terminals in the back of a movie video rental store. I was delighted and decided to come back the next morning to complete my previous report since Córdoba was a short ride. My report took longer than I had expected, and I didn't get out of town until 1:30 p.m., my latest start for the trip. I'm sure the others were already checked into the five-person tent, our Córdoba residence, before I had even left.

On the layover day in Córdoba, I rode my bike into town to get a good map and then spent a couple of hours ogling the mosque-cathedral which is Córdoba's main attraction. It is indeed huge, at one time it was the largest mosque in the world. When the Christians took over Córdoba, instead of pulling down the mosque, they instead built the cathedral inside the mosque! The real claim to fame of this impressive mosque-cathedral, though, is the many revisions and additions it has seen throughout the years so that you can compare the various architectural styles and decorations side by side. The outside is not particularly distinctive, but the inside is mammoth. The basic structure is of Muslim design with beautiful red and white arches down nine wide corridors. The whole building is open and airy. The Christians added many side altars and a large "high" altar for the cathedral in the middle of the mosque. It would be interesting to know the history and understand why the Christians didn't completely rework the Muslim design and motifs toward a Christian slant as they did in most places, but I'm glad they didn't because the effect is unique and satisfying.

The Mihrab, the part of a mosque that indicates the direction of Mecca, and its vestibule are works of art unto themselves. Although a bit busy, the Arabic designs are intricate and beautiful. Within the mosque-cathedral are displays of artifacts found during different restorations and a collection of Christian religious treasures that, if converted to loaves and fishes, would feed a multitude. The juxtaposition of the two religions even shows up in the courtyard where the mosque's minaret has been converted into a bell tower for the cathedral. The inner courtyard has pleasant fountains and a small orange grove both typical in Muslim design for their symbolism. Neither the brochure nor the audio tape I rented explained to my satisfaction how such a mixture of religious sensibilities survived as a place of worship.

Unfortunately, the city's fourteenth century synagogue was not open on my visit, so I wandered around the old part of town for awhile viewing the old city walls, the old Moorish Mills on the River Guadalquivir (literally, "big river" in Arabic) and other old structures before returning to camp to clean the headset and chain on my bike.

The ride to Seville, in the morning, was long and flat except for a small hill in a town that boasted a beautiful castle sitting above it on an even higher hill. It sprinkled three times, but I got really wet only once. The olive trees which had been ubiquitous the last few days gave way to cotton fields with some fruit orchards and even corn fields. I've also been smelling and seeing wild anise along the road the last few days as well as a very large and very dead weasel. I also stopped to examine a small dead owl with a round head and spotted breast; you don't see many roadkill owls.

Seville was easy biking for a big city, but of course we arrived at siesta time on a Sunday. We rode past neat stone bridges along the River Guadalquivir which flows from Córdoba. Kirby and Stacia hurried off to their bull fight as it was getting late when we arrived. We had tapas our first night in Seville, and they were good, but I wouldn't choose them often, a little too much meat for my taste. A tapa is a small portion served on a plate or bowl with a few French fries. We tried a variety of tapas including meat balls, beef hocks (possibly bull hocks which is not bull hocky as you'll see below), tripe, pieces of beef, pork, and spinach with pinion nuts. Then we had a repeat of the last three which were our favorites. Tapas are a traditional Spanish meal served mostly in bars, though there are now small cafés dedicated to them exclusively.

I did not go to the bull fight when we got into Seville, though it was the end of the season and would only occur on that night while we were in town. I just could not justify in my mind paying to watch animals being killed. I realize this is part of the Spanish culture and that I could be accused of being a culture snob, but then aren't we all? It got me thinking about traveling and experiencing other cultures in general. In most ways I've just sipped, and not drunk in, the different cultures I've had a chance to experience. I've tasted some of the food, but, being a teetotaler, I've not tried the beer, wine, and other alcoholic beverages that others on this trip have enjoyed and that are an important part of the dining experience in many of the countries we've visited. I've also not experienced much of the night life, not only because it doesn't appeal to me in normal circumstances, but also because we've been getting up early most mornings and jumping on our bicycles. Maybe it was Bobbi who told me there was a guy on Odyssey 2000 whose goal for the trip was to have sex with a woman from each country he visited...this too I've skipped. I guess my goal hasn't been so much to experience each of the cultures in the countries we've visited, as it has been to observe them and to try to understand them in the context of their history and geography. Even in this I don't know how much will really stick, but it has certainly whetted my appetite to learn more when I return to the good ole U. S. of A.

On our layover in Seville, I opted for a package tour that included a bus ride with a recorded commentary, a tram ride over the same route with a live commentary, and a guided city walk. Neither of the riding commentaries was particularly good. The recorded one was well-spoken English, but the female voice was distorted over the subpar sound system. The woman who presented the live version was not much interested in her job, and had a strong accent I had difficulty translating into meaningful information in a timely manner.

The walking tour was better. Although the tour guide also had an accent I couldn't understand at times, at least he was interested and knowledgeable in the subject matter. The two Brazilians on the tour obviously liked him and had several side conversations, especially concerning the similarities between their two languages, from which I was able to glean a bit.

Seville is the fourth largest city in Spain with seven hundred thousand people. The Christian Reconquesta drove the Muslims out of the city in 1248 (Granada, if you remember, remained Muslim for another 244 years!). The large mosque, a twin to the one in Córdoba, was razed (unlike the one in Córdoba which, as mentioned above, was converted to a Christian cathedral), and a huge cathedral was erected in its place. According to our guide and the Guinness Book of Records, it is the largest Gothic cathedral in the world and the third largest cathedral in the world after St. Peter's in Rome and St. Paul's in London. At this point, the Brazilian couple vehemently argued that a cathedral in Brazil is second largest...they and the guide reached a friendly impasse.

The mosque's minaret is one of the few original structures not torn down by the Christians. When it partially collapsed, they capped the top with a Christian dome and a statue of Christian Victory standing atop. This statue also functions as a weather vane and so the tower got the popular name of Giralda or spinning tower. When I walked to the top of the modified minaret to see the magnificent views of the city, I found that the guide had spoken true. He had told us that you reach the top through a series of thirty-four ramps around the inside of the tower with only a few steps near the top. This feature enabled the muezzin, who must ascend the minaret five times every day to call the people to prayer, to ride a donkey to the top.

After the walking tour, I rented an audio guide and toured the cathedral. It was indeed huge, but did not seem as cavernous as the mosque-cathedral in Córdoba, perhaps it was the architectural style. It certainly was impressive, but I must confess to becoming a bit glutted on Spanish cathedrals by this point. I also took a tour of the bull ring which did nothing to dispel my feelings toward this blood sport. Evidently, one of the bulls killed the night before required six sword thrusts, a bit disgraceful for the matador...but even worse for the bull. Our guide said that no bull leaves the arena alive. If a bull kills a matador, then the next matador in the lineup must kill that bull as well as his own allotment of bulls. The last bull that killed a matador in this arena not only was killed, but its mother was also killed, and her head hangs in the ring's museum. The meat is not wasted but is sold at market and is used by restaurants in the area. I wonder if the meat tastes gamy with all that adrenaline pumping through the bull's system when it's finally killed. By the way, the bulls in Portuguese and Mexican bull fights are no longer killed. In all three countries, the fights are limited to twenty minutes because, after this time, the bulls become too savvy and thus too dangerous.

After Seville, we had four ride days before our next layover in Evora, Portugal. The terrain out of Seville is what I had expected Spain would be like, lots of open rural country with rugged hills and dry-country vegetation. I saw lots of cork oaks, Australian eucalyptus trees that have taken to Spain as readily as to our own west coast, and a variety of small-leafed trees and succulents; in some areas we saw lots of prickly pear cactus. Along the way, we passed a bunch of lean, good-looking pigs chowing down on the oak mast and about forty young, prime-of-life bulls being raised for the ring. Most of the day was overcast with ominous clouds as we got closer to our stop; it was obviously raining off and on somewhere in front of us based on the dampness of the roads. I finally got caught in one moderate shower that dampened my shirt, but it was dry before reaching camp. Because of the humidity, rural smells, both pleasant (somebody must have had a Bit-O-Honey farm somewhere along the route) and unpleasant (a few ripe, dead animals) were very strong. Experiencing the landscape with multiple senses is one good reason to do your touring on a bike.

I reached camp and quickly set up my tent beneath a sky seemingly ready to burst. We got a few drops, but the dark clouds passed by yet again. After my shower, I took a nature walk since we were in a beautiful area with a nice stream, and the birds were active. Bobbi had found a rhinoceros beetle, with its large frontal protuberance, right on the camp road. I spotted a couple of great, new-to-me birds. One of them appeared to be slate gray until it turned toward a momentary shaft of sunlight and revealed a face, chest and forehead of a bright orange-yellow to rival its Crayola namesake. When one of these colorful, new birds pops up in your binoculars, you almost gasp. It's enough to make a birder out of a first time looker, and it's what keeps the veterans coming back. I'm always reminded of mom's first look at the, locally uncommon, purple finch that had come to our Indiana backyard feeder. "It looked like someone dunked its head in raspberry jam," she exclaimed when dad got home. Dad then looked it up in the Peterson bible and found that not only did Peterson agree with mom, but he described it in print exactly as she had. Needless to say, mom spent a lot more time watching the feeder after that.

I don't think I've commented much on the riding conditions in Spain. The roads have been generally good when we've been on major roads. The secondary roads can be rough though. Even in the major towns (i.e., Barcelona, Córdoba, Grenada, and Seville), we hit lots of bumpy old brick or cobblestone streets when we were off the major streets, and there really aren't that many "major" streets. Spanish drivers are considerate, though I don't always trust them in the towns. They actually seem better with bikers than with pedestrians. We haven't seen the hoards of colorful bikers we saw in Italy or France, but we do see serious bikers occasionally, helmetless and brightly colored.

The next morning, I stayed at camp and birded awhile since it was such a bird-rich area. I slipped through a cattle gate and strolled along a quiet, little stream and onto an open cork oak forested hillside. I didn't see many birds, just the same orange-yellow throated bird as the day before, a brown creeper remarkably similar to the one we have in the States, and a chickadee with thin black mask and yellow breast, but I thoroughly enjoyed myself. I didn't leave until almost 11a.m. The night had been cold and clear with heavy dew, although we awoke to cloud cover and fog. Evidently, by starting later, I missed having to ride through a cold, heavy fog with which the others had had to contend.

That night, our last in Spain, I had the best Spanish dish so far, a pork roast in a mushroom and wine sauce. It was delectable! It was served with fries, and I had natillas for dessert (similar, but inferior to the ones at the Los Cuartes New Mexican restaurant in Albuquerque where they are served gratis on Sundays). I pushed away from the table a happy man.

The next morning we had another heavy fog so, since we were undercover and not camping, I stayed in bed and read until the fog let up some. This was a good plan and, just after crossing the Portugal border (only a half kilometer from where we had bunked), I rode out of the fog. Our goal was the walled town of Monsaraz. This old town sits high on a hill with spectacular views of the surrounding countryside. Our little hotel, in a small town at the hill's base, was more like a B&B with lots of old farming tools decorating the halls and living spaces. Our double room was primo with firm, but not hard, beds, a spacious bathroom with full tub and a good shower, and a nice seating area on our own balcony all in a quiet district right on the edge town. However, just over the fence lived a rooster with which we became acquainted the next morning.

The next day we had a short, pleasant ride to Evora. After putting up my tent, I walked into town and was able to join a mid-afternoon walking tour.

The young woman leading the tour had recently graduated from a three-year tourism school in Lisbon and was knowledgeable and well-spoken. There were three English women also on the tour. The following historical items were gleaned from the tour and from what I've read. The histories of Spain and Portugal run parallel to a point. The Iberian Peninsula was overrun and occupied by the Moors as I noted in the Spanish history in my last report. They were ejected from Portugal in 1252. In the fifteenth century, Prince Henry the Navigator led Portugal into a period of world exploration. This golden age ended in 1580 when the eighteen-year-old Portuguese king was killed fighting in Africa leaving no heir. So King Phillip II of Spain, a cousin of the late Portuguese king, also became King Phillip I of Portugal. Portugal regained its sovereignty in 1640.

After an extended period of civil wars and political confusion, the monarchy was abolished on October 5, 1910, and Portugal became a republic. Then, in 1926, a military coup set up Salazar as dictator until his death in 1968. Shortly thereafter on April 25, 1974, the dictatorship was overthrown in a peaceful military coup called the Carnation Revolution because flowers were placed into the end of the guns. The guide said this coup was led by lieutenants and captains of the army disgusted with the wars being fought by Portugal in her African colonies, Mozambique and Angola, both of which were given their independence after the coup. The 1970s and '80s saw much political disruption with stability finally arriving with Portugal's entry into the European Union in 1986.

The tour through the old walled city of Evora, a UNESCO World Heritage Site since 1986, was interesting. Our guide showed us a recently excavated Roman temple at the high point of town. Flanked as it was by the 1536 Inquisition Court on one side and the most expensive hotel in town on the other, it looked out of place. The hotel, which has been converted from an old monastery, has not only the highest rates but also the smallest rooms in town, according to our guide, because the rooms are converted from the monks' old cells; she thought it strange and a bit comical to imagine people paying a premium for an ascetic's cell. She walked us through the town's cathedral and a couple of other churches, all with lovely ceramic tile work. One of the churches has a chapel constructed from the bones of about five thousand clergy from the town. The guide said that, at one time, as many as 50 percent of the town's people were nuns, priests, and monks! One of the churches had a statue of a pregnant BVM which I had not seen before. The guide said that, for a time in Portugal, this was a popular depiction of Mary.

She pointed out red pepper and jacaranda trees that had been brought from Brazil, a onetime Portuguese territory, but said red pepper is not used much by the Portuguese who prefer black or white pepper. She showed us a lovely cork insulator for a cooking pot and told us the cork is collected from the cork oak trees when they are between twenty-five and thirty years old and then every nine years thereafter. She told us the white numbers painted on the tree trunks, which we had noticed the last several days, indicate the last digit of the year the cork was last taken. The trunks turn bright red after the cork is removed which, the Portuguese say, is caused by the tree's embarrassment. The red color fades with time.

The guide mentioned that movies in Portugal are shown in the original language but with Portuguese subtitles. All the English-language movies help the young people learn English. She told us that before the Carnation Revolution, the first foreign language children learned was French, but after the revolution, it is now English. After the tour, I roamed the streets and tried a half dozen roasted chestnuts for the first time in my life—they were interesting, but certainly not among my favorite nuts (some of whom are probably reading this right now). That evening I tried a favorite regional dish of pork fried in olive oil with clams in a wine sauce sprinkled with cilantro. It was very flavorful if a bit overcooked.

The next day was our actual layover day in Evora, but it pissed rain off and on all night long and all the next day. This bad weather, coupled with the fact I had already hit the major areas of interest the previous day, led me to just putter around, getting fairly wet as I wandered through the old town. I finished the evening at a theater watching two throw-away American movies, the only show in town. The next morning when I took down my tent, I counted over fifty granddaddy longlegs between the crown of my tent and my rain fly. I guess they know enough to get in out of the rain.

The next two days we rode through pretty, rural countryside as the terrain became much hillier from what we'd experienced the last week or so. The most memorable event was a huge steak I ate at a small local restaurant near the city campground we occupied alone. It reminded me of the chateaubriand steaks for two that were a favorite "date" meal when I was much younger.

On the second night out from Evora, at Fatima, that famous visitation site of the BVM, we were again inside. I took a hot bath as I was a bit chilled from the ride—I had gotten caught in a rainstorm, just two kilometers from the hotel, on the steep hill leading up to Fatima. However, I was soon out and about. After a pleasant walk, I found the central pilgrimage spot. A modern basilica and a chapel have been erected beside the holm oak under which Mary appeared to the three children for the first time on May 13, 1917. She appeared five more times to the children; the last time, seventy thousand people were present. Two of the three children died within three years after the first sighting, but then Mary again appeared an additional three times to the eldest girl after she was grown and had become a nun. When I arrived, a considerable number of pilgrims and sightseers were milling around, but I suspect it was nothing like the high tourist season. Oddly enough, a family of dogs has taken up residence in the concrete courtyard and were comfortably lying about. I say "family" in the social sense because they didn't seem to be related. Most of them had some type of infirmity and all had the scruffiness of strays. It crossed my mind that maybe they too were pilgrims looking for alms or a cure. Fatima has certainly benefited from all the attention and is now a bustling little town with more shops selling religious art, gewgaws, and such—maybe even holy relics, if they are still in style—than I've ever seen in one place. While searching for an Internet, I even had my own minor miracle of sorts when I stumbled upon a street and a seminary by the name of Monfortinos, the Portuguese version of my surname, I guess. I didn't find the Internet though.

From Fatima, we headed to the coast and a small town called Praia Santa Cruz for our last camp night in Europe. After setting up my tent, I walked to the ocean in Santa Cruz. The coast here is a beautiful sandy beach with clear water and nice rock formations including a large stone arch shaped by wind and water. The town folk have carved steps directly into some of the large rocks to provide access to spectacular views of the sea surging to the shore all around.

I normally don't give myself an out when it comes to exercise, but I had decided on the walk down to the beach that, if the surf was rough or the Atlantic too cold, I would beg off swimming for the day. When I got to the beach there was a cool, stiff breeze blowing in, the surf was rough, and, of course, no one was in the water…actually, there were few people on the beach period. I sat down on a stone ledge back from the water and was absently gazing at the beautiful color of the breakers when an older gentleman of at least seventy years with the air of a college professor sat down beside me and struck up a conversation. I told him I only understood English. He asked me if I was from London. I said, "America." He asked, "New York?" I replied, "New Mexico."

For the next fifteen to twenty minutes, we held a mostly one-sided conversation as he regaled me in his marginal English. He was from Santa Cruz, but now lives in Lisbon and comes back for the sea and the clean air. He carried a thick binder chock-full of handwritten papers. His habit of using the backside of one of his sheets to make drawings and write notes, mostly unintelligible to me, with a black felt-tip pen to illustrate points as he explained things, only emphasized the idea that he was some sort of professor.

From what I could understand, just bits and pieces, seldom a complete thought, he explained the currents off the coast, something about the Russian and Japanese fishing boats, the dangerous waters, and then he talked about Portugal's place in the world, now and throughout history, emphasizing the Portuguese explorers. He mentioned their civil war and how the Spanish fleet was defeated by England. I might have learned a lot had I been able to understand him. When his English failed, he switched to Portuguese and, as I said, his pictures and written notes were of little help.

Finally, he was finished and said goodbye. I watched him walk off down the beach. After a bit I went to the water to dip my toes in to see if it was as cold as it looked, but it didn't feel too cold. I wandered down the beach where I could see steps leading to the top of a large rock jutting out of the water. When I got there, I put my sandals back on and climbed the rocks and steps to the top which commanded a great view. In looking back toward the beach, I was surprised to see my friend, stripped to his boxer shorts, heading to the water. I sat down and watched as he waded in, dove into a swell, and lay there floating on his back in various states of repose for at least as long as it takes me to swim a quarter mile.

He finally clambered out again, and I moved to the next cove over where the large rock blocked the wind. Thus warmed by the sun, I decided to take my dip after all...for how could I not with such a splendid example as I had just witnessed. The water was not that cold and, although the cove had captured a mass of loose seaweed and other ocean debris, the swells here were not as large as those on the main beach. I swam a quarter mile and got out. It was very bracing and, had the water been calmer with less debris, I would have stayed in a bit longer.

As I climbed the stairs from the beach, I saw my friend ahead of me a ways, shirt dampened at the back, trousers sandy, and hair tousled—definitely my kind of guy! I passed him as he stopped to talk to an acquaintance and greeted him with one of my few Portuguese phrases, *"Boa Tarde"* which I hope he understood to mean "Good afternoon."

Our last day's ride to Lisbon was the best ride of this whole stage. We had an absolutely gorgeous day with just a nip in it to keep us from getting too hot on the significant uphills we faced. We were headed more or less down the coast and, for at least part of the time, had ocean views of Portugal's splendid coastline. In many ways, it reminds me of the rugged coastline south of Santa Cruz, California (I wonder if California's Santa Cruz was named for the small town from which we had just come). Although the coast was great, I liked best the climbs through the thick eucalyptus forests which covered the headlands we crossed when the road snaked inland. By the way, the guide in Evora thought they used the eucalyptus to make paper—there sure is a lot of it in Portugal.

While route checking our last European DRG the night before, Bobbi had been unable to find a good bike route into Lisbon's city center, so we met in a small town on the coast at a McDonald's with a vendor roasting chestnuts in front, an incongruous coupling. We bundled our bikes and selves into the van and pressed through the rush hour traffic to our hotel which she had also been unable to find the night before. Our hotel was right in the center of action in Lisbon, which made it convenient for doing all the things we like to do, and for getting ready to make another big jump to a new continent.

On our layover day, I cleaned out my bags and rearranged things to ensure all my bike stuff would also fit into them. Then I spent three-plus hours at an Internet café composing this report. This left not much time before supper. To fill the time, I wandered down to the River Tejo where it forms the southern border of Lisbon before flowing into the Atlantic Ocean and, from there, headed to the old quarter called Alfama. I poked my head into a couple of large churches. What a difference from Spanish churches! Portuguese churches are as plain inside as Spanish churches are ornate. They are positively stark by comparison. It gives them added dignity.

It's always fun wandering around a new city, not sure exactly where you are, and it's especially fun in the old parts of towns with their narrow winding streets. Lisbon adds a new dimension, "up," because there are steep hills all through the city, many of them I found on my walk to and from the old town. It's a wonder that the cars are able to navigate the streets which are even more vertiginous than the ones in San Francisco of which this port city reminds me.

I gave myself plenty of time to get back to the hotel to meet the gang for supper...or so I thought. What looked to be a ten minute walk on my map turned into a trek of over an hour. I kept running into hills where there were no roads, streets that dead-ended without warning, and streets that curved back on themselves pointing me yet again in the wrong direction. Luckily our group seldom gets its act together to leave on time or I would have been eating alone. As it was, I had my best meal yet in Portugal, a couple of chicken filets in an exquisite cream mushroom sauce with both rice and fries. I also had a huge bowl of garlic soup with bread and two fried eggs in it...which is exactly what our English-challenged waiter had said would be in it, we just didn't believe him. I was still tasting the garlic at breakfast.

Well, this is my last report from Europe. This evening we board a flight on Air Portugal to Jo'burg, South Africa.

Until then take care of yourself and those who belong to you,

Ralph

Report #21: Greetings from South Africa

November 10, 2003

Siyabona (Zulu for hello) from South Africa,

Before beginning my African adventure, I'll first fill you in on our last day in Lisbon. After getting a hair and beard clip (again using sign language) and posting my last report, I walked to the Calouste Gulbenkran Museum touted as the best in Portugal by the *Lonely Planet Guide*. The museum managers are definitely enamored with their museum; they have posted a sizable amount of information relating how it all came about, specifically the interplay of architecture and green space. The collection itself is small and fits nicely in this large building. Although small, many of the items are exquisite: tapestries, woven rugs, ceramics from the Moorish occupation, the Orient, and Iberia, furniture, ancient Roman coins, you name it. The museum also offered a small painting collection that included a couple of Rembrandts, a few Rubens, a Van Dyke, several Manets, a couple of Rodin sculptures, and so on. The curators have done an excellent job selecting material for display so items do not appear cramped or cluttered.

When I got back to the hotel, I finished boxing my bike for the plane ride. The box was so big I didn't even have to take the wheels off. Bobbi told me to pack the box with whatever I had available to stabilize it for shipment, so in went my bike bag, my sleeping bag, my air mattress, and a few other things. As a result, I was able to consolidate all my other stuff into just one of my duffels.

We shuttled to the airport in two groups and got there plenty early which was fortuitous as our flight out of Portugal became a saga in and of itself. The

242

first snag came when we reached the ticket counter, and the agent demanded to see our tickets to leave South Africa since that country requires visitors to have a departure ticket. Since TK&A usually waits until shortly before our actual departure in order to get the best ticket price, we didn't have our South Africa departure tickets. Bobbi argued thoroughly but lost and then called Tim in California who, after a lot of long distance haggling, made cheap ticket reservations to Germany from South Africa just so we would have the required tickets. He had his ticket agent e-mail the ticket confirmation to him which he then faxed to the Air Portugal agent.

As you can imagine, this all took time which put us at the end of the ticket line. Then, after we had all our luggage checked and weighed, we got the second shock: we were about 150 kilograms over the weight limit with the bikes, tools, bike stand, etc. and, with a multiplier of thirty-six euros per kilogram, Bobbi was faced with a nearly €5,000 bill after the ticket agent gave her a slight break. This was more than our plane tickets cost! The second bout of haggling continued until essentially takeoff time with the order given to deplane all of our luggage. Finally, the stalemate was broken as higher level supervisors were brought into the fray, and a sum less than half the original bill was agreed upon. Then it was a mad scramble to pay the bill and finish the paperwork. We said a hurried good-bye to Bobbi, who was flying back to the States, and raced to catch our plane.

After this nerve-racking experience, the long flight south was a piece of cake. We had one stop in Maputu, Mozambique, without getting off the plane. However, about three-fourths of the other passengers did deplane, so I ended up with a window seat for the last segment to Johannesburg and got my first glimpse of southern Africa. From what I saw of Maputu, it is a dry, dismal place with few paved roads through a town crisscrossed by red dirt roads. I couldn't figure out what all those deplaning passengers were going to do there.

With no TK&A staff person with us, we were on our own until we got through South African customs. We had one last drama when the bike boxes were pushed out by the airport employees. My bike box came out wet on one end, probably from being set down on the rain-wet tarmac, with both top and bottom ripped open and my stuff spilling out. The only thing missing at first glance was my bike bag but, on inspection, we found it riding around the baggage carousel. I felt very lucky. We pushed the dilapidated box through the exit where we met Mike, our local South African staffer, who drove us to our hotel. Upon arrival, we took our baggage to our rooms, immediately loaded all the bikes back into the van, and drove us to a bike shop to have our bikes checked after the flight. The shop normally closes at 1 p.m. on Saturday, but Mike had gotten the white owner and his two black mechanics to stay open to work on our bikes, since we were to leave the next day. This first view of the new South Africa greatly impressed us. The service we received was absolutely top of the line in every way, and the mutual respect between owner and mechanics was obvious. Even though the local area had gradually evolved from almost all white to almost all black since the end of apartheid, and the locks, gates, alarms, and barbed wire on all the businesses testified to the fact it was a rough place after dark, I felt something must be going right. They finally finished with our bikes around 7 p.m. We were very grateful.

My first meal in South Africa was a nice T-bone with monkey gland sauce…don't know the genesis of the name "monkey gland sauce," but it was a sweet meat sauce of some sort. Stacia had ostrich steak with cherry sauce which was quite good. Actually, despite these two examples, our meals have come closer to typical American fare than anyplace we've traveled so far. I've been eating much more red meat than usual (I had T-bones two or three more times in the next week), at least partly because it is very reasonably priced here, sometimes cheaper in the markets than chicken!

The next morning, we loaded the van again and drove to Dullstroom, a little town known for its trout fishing, from which we would begin our biking in Africa. We stayed in a three-bedroom house with all the amenities of home. We even had the luxury of a washer and dryer which we kept busy throughout the night because the low water-use washer (like several we'd seen before) takes an inordinate amount of time to finish a load. There were also several books, most having to do with trout fishing including a large illustrated book dedicated to nymphs, a favorite trout food. We found a couple of jigsaw puzzles and, while waiting for our washing, actually completed a thousand piece puzzle during the course of the evening.

Our first DRG in South Africa had the fewest directions yet. We turned turn left onto the main road, rode to Lydenburg, and turned left again into our lodging! There aren't many roads in the direction we were headed on this first leg so this was the pattern for that first week…hard to get lost.

That first day of riding was overcast when we awoke and did not get better as we set out. The fog was so thick that, as I climbed the first hill, it condensed on my glasses. I eventually took them off to see the road better. After a steady climb of about twenty kilometers, we reached the top of a plateau and began a nice descent. As we descended the fog began lifting, and I could see more of the surrounding countryside. Unlike the veld (Afrikaans for veldt) we had crossed in the car to Dullstroom, this country was very hilly, and the descent felt like we were riding down a valley. The country was quite dry, although we did spot several small lakes and streams. We passed quite a few signs for inns, B&B's, and such along the way, again testifying to the lure of the elusive trout.

I noted an ostrich farm and stopped a few times to look at other birds, but mostly I just rode on through to Lydenburg. The road was a two-lane highway with a rough bitumen coating, but not as rough as Australia or New Zealand had been. Most of the traffic gave me room, but one large truck honked at me and, when I pulled to the shoulder trying to avoid the chipped rock that littered this particular section, it zoomed by me closer than was necessary as there was no oncoming traffic. So far it appears that drivers are just not used to having bicyclists on the road with them. They are either needlessly cautious or don't think we should be on the road demonstrating their position by getting too close for comfort. We're on the left side of the road again, but this has not caused particular concern for any of us.

The next morning we began a long, slow uphill climb as soon as we left Lydenburg. This persisted, with only a short downhill reprieve several kilometers from Lydenburg, until we hit Longtom Pass at about seven thousand feet. The downhill was appreciated, but the road was rough and had recently been oiled prompting me to be a bit more cautious than usual on the curves. After a series of rolling hills, we arrived at our bushpacker's camp in Hazyview. A couple of times along the way (and a couple of more times since) I caught a whiff of what smelled like roasting chiles—made me a bit homesick for Albuquerque cuisine. We also passed more of the burned fields we'd seen on previous days. From the looks of it, the burning is intentional. Our hostess for the previous night's meal had told us this part of Africa has been laboring under a severe drought for the past three years. You'd never know it from the wonderful lavender jacaranda blossoms that are prominent features of the landscape, especially as you enter the towns, or from the fiery red bougainvillea that began showing up on the latter part of this ride. I've seen plenty of the electric purple variety in the States, Australia, and other places, but I'd never seen the startlingly red ones. Besides these show-offs of the plant world, the ubiquitous Australian gum, or eucalyptus, seems to have become a favorite timber tree in South Africa. I understand it is used primarily for paper.

Our lodging for the night was a sort of hostel arrangement with a comfortable common area complete with seven six-week-old pups and mom. The number of mosquitoes in our room that night made me glad I was taking malaria medicine (though malaria is not much of a problem in this area). The next morning we arose, packed away our bikes and the gear we did not need to take to Kruger Park, and headed into this premier wildlife park for two great layover days.

After registering at the entrance to the park, Mike drove slowly to our enclosure or boma. In Kruger, the people are fenced in from 6 p.m. to 5:30 a.m.—only authorized vehicles are allowed outside the bomas during that time. This rule protects both the animals and the people. In general, while inside the park, you are not allowed to leave your vehicle because, once separated from it, you are considered food by the lions and leopards (shortly after leaving the park, we read newspaper accounts of people killed by leopards). On the way to our boma, we spotted a giraffe with young and several impala. It was a good start to what we hoped would be an animal bonanza. We arrived at the boma and checked into our huts. These round, single-room structures are topped with a thatched local material as are many buildings we've seen. During lunch, under one such roof at the snack bar, we looked up to see a roosting fruit bat staring at us from his upside down perch under the thatch.

Early that evening, we took a three-hour game drive through the park with a ranger in an open touring bus allowing splendid viewing. We spotted four of the "Big Five" game animals: the elephant, Cape buffalo, lion, and white rhinoceros, but not the leopard which is nocturnal and secretive. The elephant and buffalo were at a distance and the rhinos somewhat closer, but the lioness was right there! She was sprawled in one lane of a paved road and didn't budge as we inched forward to about twenty feet. She gave us all the disdain she could manage as she licked herself, crossed her front legs, and yawned a few times before, after a decent interval, she got slowly to her feet and ambled away, but not before squatting for a pee with her back to us. Anyone not able to read her body language would have to be blind.

In addition, we saw several types of antelope: the small steenbok, the waterbok, the sassaby (a mid-sized antelope), and greater kudus, as well as four warthogs, a pair of magnificently colored saddle-billed storks, African fish eagles, an iguana with a bright blue head, upper back, and tail tip, and a gorgeous lilac-breasted roller, a type of bird whose psychedelic color scheme has to be seen to be believed.

The terrain is mostly gently rolling hills with the sparse vegetation you'd expect on an African savanna, dryland brush and low trees. Termite mounds of various sizes and shapes dot the horizon. The sun was warm, and the strong breeze funneled over the windscreen of the vehicle felt good as the evening progressed, overall a very enjoyable evening.

That night we pitched in to make our own evening meal with a nice salad and barbecued steaks and chicken, roasted potatoes, onions and butternut squash. It was a bit messy, as such a meal eaten from paper plates with plastic utensils will be, but the food was good. All evening and all night, we were serenaded by the squeaky-toy chorus of fruit bats, some of which were in the branches of trees just over our heads...so different from the high frequency squeaks of the echolocating bats with which I'm more familiar.

The next morning, the four-hour guided game walk was cancelled (as it was the following day—bummer), so Bill and I opted for a sunrise game drive instead. We saw many of the same animals as the previous evening in different concentrations and locations. We got a great view of a young bull elephant that was pulling up small young bushes and trees as he browsed his way toward us until about twenty feet away. We also got much closer looks at rhino and Cape buffalo. The guide told us that buffalo were generally seen either singly, in small bachelor groups, or in large gregarious groups; we were to see all of these combinations during our stay.

On the tour, we also saw a few duikers, reedboks, and lots of kudus, as well as a male waterbok (we had seen only females and young the afternoon before)...and a rhino toilet alongside the road. This latter was a scraped area where the male rhino comes to crap even if five to ten kilometers away according to our guide (by this I mean he travels the five to ten kilometers back to the toilet, not that he can excrete that far). Supposedly, the female is not allowed to defecate there so she does her thing nearby. Back in camp, I availed myself of the park's unique swimming pool to cool off. The pool is built against an outcrop of solid granite using the granite as part of the bottom. The rocky side gradually gets deeper as though you're entering a lake, but the opposite side is built like a regular pool. It is located in a grassy park with lots of shade trees, a pleasant place where many people lounged to escape the midday heat.

It's odd to just happen upon an animal or bird that captured your imagination as a child, seeming so remote as to be almost imaginary, like a Dr. Seuss character, but that's just what I did with the common hoopoe as I walked back from the pool. When I was about ten years old, my parents gave me a coffee table book called *Birds of the World* to foster my nascent avian interest. It had large, colorful pictures of many of the more exotic birds found in various places around the world. A surprising number stuck in my mind, and their pictures have popped into my head on several occasions when I've finally gotten to see one in life. The African hoopoe was one of these and, although its crest was not extended like the picture in my book, I immediately recognized its long needle-shaped bill and distinctive shape, a "life list" bird for me in a different sense from most birders.

So far Africa has provided more different and easily seen bird species than any place I've ever been. Just about every time I go outside, I see or hear some new-to-me species...not that I'm able to identify many of them...Kirby's pocket guide has distinct limitations, but Mike helps with his local knowledge.

Around 4 p.m. that same day, Mike took us out for a game drive in our support van, and we got to see more elephants, a crocodile just barely visible in a water hole and the same pair of fish eagles we had seen in the morning, but this time they were mating. Afterwards, we all went on the ranger-led night drive, even Mike. Unfortunately, we were on a larger bus than the previous evening making it more difficult to see. Surprisingly, we saw all of the "Big Five" including several good looks at rhinos, a brief glance at an elephant, a briefer glance at a leopard, a close look at a gregarious group of at least a hundred Cape buffaloes and, the treat for the night, two young male lions. When we came upon them, they were sprawled in the middle of the road, looking for all the world like bookends in need of a library. As we approached, they eventually got up and nonchalantly began walking away from us down the road. Our driver pulled alongside where we got about the best view imaginable from about five feet away. The lion would look right at us and seemed to be wondering whether to attack or ignore us. Since I was at the window of the open van, I was particularly interested in the outcome of his musings. We followed (harassed) the pair for at least twenty minutes. I think the driver was trying to keep them around for the other tour buses out that night (the drivers keep in contact with one another by phone). We did see other interesting things, a black-backed jackal and a spotted eagle owl for instance, but the driver seemed focused on the "Big Five."

The next morning, Kirby and I arose early for the 5 a.m. drive again, but the driver evidently didn't, so we did a bit of birding until Mike took us out in our support van a half an hour later when the gate opened for normal traffic. We were very successful. We got great close-ups of Cape buffalo, rhinos, and giraffes. The most fun observation was a swarm of dwarf mongooses living in three old termite mounds that reminded me of apartment buildings. At first one or two would pop their heads out of a hole to see what was going on, but soon they became more adventurous and came out to explore. Soon we could no longer keep count as they ranged in and out and over and around the three mounds. Earlier, we had also seen a troop of banded mongooses moving through the brush.

Later that morning, we checked out of our huts and left the Pretoriuskop enclosure to drive Bill to another gate. Here he was to meet the owner of a private reserve where he was going to spend a couple extra days in the bush. On the way, we passed a water hole with hippos lounging, just backs, heads, and ears visible, and we also ran into several wildebeest or gnus. After dropping Bill off, we drove to Skukuza, the park's main enclosure, for lunch and a look around. We only stayed a short while, but I stuck my head into the small library/museum where displays presented an interesting history of the park and a set of award winning nature photos of the kind that make you wonder how many lifetimes the photographer spent to get just the right shot. Leaving Skukuza, we made a beeline for our bushpacker's hideaway in Hazyview where we'd spend another night before riding out the following day.

I was very impressed with Kruger. The facilities were excellent, clean, and well-maintained with all the amenities you would expect from a first-class operation. The roads within the park were extremely well signed—the best I've seen in any National Park. There might be safety implications to this, of course; it's not a good place to get lost or to run out of gas. The roads themselves were also well maintained, even the dirt roads—no washboards that I noted. This park should be a "must visit" on anyone's itinerary to South Africa.

Leaving Hazyview, several in our group began to experience stomach problems. Stacia was first and worst, eventually going to a doctor in Swaziland a few days later to find she had lost fourteen pounds to her lowest weight in a long time. Andy had similar symptoms though not nearly as severe, and I had a general malaise for almost a week though I didn't develop other problems. We don't have any idea what we might have picked up, but of course this is part of the travel experience (though not especially pleasant when riding a bicycle).

The ride to Barberton was overcast, but hot and hilly. I sweat buckets. The hills in Africa look less steep than they feel which is discouraging, especially when you feel like you've picked up a bug, but we had great downhill runs that, at least partly, made up for the climbs. As on previous days, I saw lots of people walking along the road (many of the women carrying packets on their heads), even quite far from any town, but I've seen few bikes and no recreational bicyclists to this point. People are friendly and, if you greet them with a cheery "hello," you will more often than not get a big smile and a return greeting. Many people wait at small, three-sided taxi stops for the minivans that generally serve to get people longer distances to market, work, or wherever. These taxis are a force to be reckoned with on the road, though we have not had any problems with them yet. Mike told us they are poorly maintained and people are regularly killed on the highways because of this. The government has tried to impose controls, but the taxi drivers group together and block all traffic on the roads to prevent this—so far these strikes have been successful in stopping legislation.

We've had pronunciation problems with some of the South African place names. For instance, when Mike told us the name of our next night's stay, I heard "butt floss" instead of the "p" sound of Badplass, and my pronunciation stuck. Another tricky one is "Hluhluwe" where we stayed a few nights later. This is pronounced "shu shlu wee" in the same cadence as our Native American "Shoshone." You can understand the confusion.

The ride to Badplass was nice and cool, but even so I worked up a sweat on the hills. We climbed to Nelshoogte Pass at just over five thousand feet and had a nice downhill run. The low cloud cover prevented any really long views, but the closer views were quite nice. At one point, I got a good look at a vervet monkey rustling in a tree as I passed. Some of the road had a shoulder and some of it didn't. When there is no shoulder, I get nervous as some cars and trucks pass by very close. The driver of one empty log truck seemed to intentionally get as close to me as he could. I thought about giving him the finger but, because I've never really done this before, he was out of sight by the time I remembered which finger it is you give. Oh well, it's the thought that counts.

In Badplass, we stayed in small two-person huts of a type that seem to be common here. Also, like most of the places we've stayed, it was surrounded by fence and guarded by people or, in this case as I found out, a dog. Late that night, I walked across the street to use the pay phone at a gas station. At the gate to the complex, a big German shepherd on a tether began barking at me and pulling against his rope. I assumed he was there to prevent outside people from coming in and talked to him as I passed by. I tried my call, but got a busy signal, so I walked back to the complex. As I came to the entrance of the camp, the dog barked once, then broke his tether and came on a beeline right at me covering the fifteen yards in a second or two. I went into a semi-crouch and put my arm out so, if he took anything, it would be that. When he reached me he stopped cold like he was a statue, his nose an inch from my arm. I paused to see what he would do next then gave him my hand to sniff while talking to him and then scratched his head. I could feel him relax somewhat, but I wasn't sure if he'd let me pass. After a long moment, a guy came out of the shadows and called to the dog and grabbed his tether. As I walked by to go to my hut, the dog again launched at me. It was a very well-trained guard dog.

For our ride into Swaziland, we were like the walking wounded. Stacia was at the worst of her stomach problems and had not been eating much at all; Andy was beginning to have stomach problems, and Bill was nursing an achy knee and stated his stomach felt like he was about to give birth (unfortunately, this was not the case or he could have made some big bucks). I felt a little achy, like a flu bug was knocking at my door, and I tweaked a muscle in my back lifting my bag into the van making it difficult to take a full breath. Tim Kneeland had arrived at midnight taking the staff baton from Mike who was driving back to his home in Durban for a few days.

The day was again overcast, as we started out, leading to fog later. We had rolling hills with more ups than downs as we headed to the Swazi border; our high was 5,700 feet. I was surprised at the number of people walking along the road even in the remote places. There didn't seem to be any gaps where a modest person might perform his or her toilette, an unfortunate situation for anyone with inconsiderate stomach problems. The scenery provided a diversion, however, with lots of distant views of hills and even the odd cliff face.

There was a good downhill to the border, which we passed through with no problem. My first impression of Swaziland was positive. At the border, a brand new four-lane highway with a great surface and a wide shoulder began. There were as many people walking along the highway as in South Africa, but many initiated the greetings which I, of course, returned. This was different from South Africa where I inevitably initiated any greeting.

The fog was even thicker after the border, and the rolling hills continued for awhile. Then, just when the new road converged to two lanes with not much shoulder and lots of rough patches, we hit a moderately fast downhill run. To make it worse, the mist lowered visibility and condensed on my glasses. I missed any scenery for the next fur to five kilometers until I finally got beneath the cloud layer again. I was surprised at how much greener the hills and valleys were here than in South Africa. I'm not sure if it was an altitude difference, a "side of the mountain" difference, or something else, but the contrast was striking.

As I entered the capital town of Mbabane, the traffic increased although the route did not take us through the town center. A great surprise awaited as the last six-kilometer run was a screamer downhill on a great road. It just kept going and going until I was coasting up to forty miles per hour. The gradient was steep, but the road was nicely banked and curved, and the traffic on it was light, so I was able to just slalom down without brakes for the most part. It was one of the best downhill runs on the trip so far.

I got to our lodge just after the van. We are again in three-to-a-chalet quarters with full kitchens, a television with two movie channels (the official language of Swaziland is English), a long bathtub and nice beds, in short, a dream chalet for tired and cold bicyclists. The first thing I did was draw a hot bath and try to soak my aches away, after which I made a cup of hot tea to help drive out any bug I might have picked up. This seemed to work because I began feeling better from this point.

It was good to be feeling better because the next two days were long and difficult rides. Andy and I rode much of the next day together to Nsoko. The roads were again remarkably good for such a poor country, better overall than what we've seen in South Africa so far. They have mostly smooth surfaces and usually a good shoulder. However, it's clear the drivers here haven't experienced many bikers on the roads. Most are cautious and give you a wide berth, but a bike hasn't registered as an impediment to a fast approaching oncoming car when it's about to pass a slower car. I had a few uncomfortable moments.

We passed through a good-sized town where Andy and I were the only white faces. We got several direct looks since a recreational bicyclist is such an oddity as, evidently, is any white face except in the window of a big bus passing through town. The landscape on this stage reminded me somewhat of New Mexico with its rolling, dry hills. About forty kilometers into the ride we made a sharp turn and ended up with a stiff wind at our backs or side for much of the rest of the day which is always a treat. Boy, did we soar, at times averaging thirty kilometers per hour even up hills!

About forty kilometers later, we stopped at a small roadside grocery in the middle of nowhere for a cold drink and ice to put in our water bottles. We stayed at the shop for well over an hour talking to the three young men there about a variety of subjects. The nineteen-year-old running the shop was doing so for his father who works in South Africa. Kirby rode up and joined the fun about the time the school across the road let out. The kids ogled us like we were from Mars and were captivated by the images of themselves on Kirby's digital camera.

I was happy to reach our tourist game preserve evening location since I had not yet gained all my strength back. Tim had arranged small thatched "beehive" huts for each of us with half-size doors inside a traditional wooden boma—very quaint. However, I found them extremely stuffy and mosquito porous, so I opted to set up my tent in the deserted campground near the lion and crocodile enclosures. The large preserve is open to the living area so animals can move in and out at will (not the lions and crocs of course). An ostrich and a medium-sized antelope with long spiral horns called a Nyala were wandering around the complex when we arrived. During the Odyssey 2000 visit, a three-year-old lion cub had the run of the place and became the darling of the riders and staff. Now grown, the lion no longer runs loose and doesn't sound happy about it; I heard its escalating series of moaning grunts throughout the night.

Quote for this report: "Did I tell you about the time I shot a giraffe in my pajamas? How it got in my pajamas, I'll never know." Paraphrased from Groucho Marx.

I was the only person camping. Sometime shortly after I had fallen asleep, I was awakened by a large animal treading behind my tent accompanied by the explosive exhalation of breath through the nostrils of a worried ungulate. I have often heard deer snort in such a manner when startled. For a time, whatever it was kept just out of my sight which was limited to the mesh doors on either side of my tent. However, after several (very long) minutes, I caught the distinctive profile of an adult giraffe. I saw it a couple more times during the night wandering around the complex. I'm not sure if it was investigating my tent or the trees under which I had camped; I didn't hear it chewing, so I suspect it was the former. I've heard many animals outside my tent in my years of camping but this was the first giraffe! Can you imagine how tall a giraffe looks when you're on your knees looking out of a tent?

Our ride out of Swaziland was the last before a three-day break and was also one of the most tiring of this trip. It was 150 km, almost all of which was into a fairly stiff wind. The day began hot with direct sun and a road that seemed much worse from the day before. The ride to the border was grueling, and I was glad it took awhile to get processed back into South Africa. The next leg was a bit better as the road had improved considerably with a nice, wide shoulder that permitted safe daydreaming. Shortly after crossing the border, the clouds began rolling in and, by about seventy kilometers, it was obvious a storm was brewing behind us. The tailwind actually gave us a bit of a lift for a few kilometers before the storm overtook us. Kirby and I ducked into a service station with lots of services and let the storm blow over. Unfortunately, when we got back on the road, the brief tailwind we had gotten from the approaching storm had reversed, and we had an even stiffer headwind all the way to Hluhluwe. Once in awhile, a large truck would pass giving us a lift from the force of the wind it was pushing; it was the only respite from the wind we were to have. I was actually making better time going uphill because the hill would block the wind somewhat until I hit the crest when I'd have to peddle hard just to continue going forward, even downhill.

We stayed at a place called the Isinkwe Bushpacker's Lodge for two nights. Isinkwe means "bush baby," which is a small sub-primate. We got a chance to see two of these cuties both evenings, as the chef feeds them on a platform attached to a tree next to the camp kitchen. Again we were in small huts with one of the most comfortable beds imaginable. It was a great place to regain strength. While we were here, Tim drove to Durban where he exchanged the van for a rental car and began checking our DRG's to Cape Town. Mike drove the van back to pick us up after our layover day.

On our layover day, we went to a Zulu cultural show. The Zulu were a major force in South Africa in this area, keeping the English at bay for quite some time with their smart, ferocious warrior king. They are still one of the major forces in the area. The program first took us on a tour of a model Zulu village with men and women demonstrating traditional crafts and the art of every day living, for example, pottery, spear and shield making, grinding corn, and beadwork. We were also introduced to the roles of medicine man and spiritual advisor. After all the tour groups had made the circuit, we gathered at a rough stage where the tribe's men and women performed song and dance routines. In this, the native reenactors were as alive and animated as many of them had appeared bored in the demonstrations. At the climax of the show, the rain, that had been threatening all morning, finally came down hard adding an almost frenetic tone to the already vigorous music and dance. There is something in the wild beating of drums that draws you into the excitement of a dance.

Afterwards, we had a nice buffet lunch at the village that I learned later was prepared by a Hungarian chef—so much for traditional Zulu dishes! I suspect this whole operation is white-owned and managed in some type of cooperative with the tribe (the cashier was a middle-aged white women for instance). If true, I wonder how the profits are divided.

I whiled away the rest of the afternoon in a hammock reading, napping, and birding—a true rest day…and much needed. That night we took a short nature hike with one of the lodge staff. We saw some neat spiders, a small scorpion, and a chameleon, that odd lizard with the halting gait. Earlier on the same trail alone, I had gotten buzzed by a good-sized fruit bat. Our guide said the flat-topped thorn trees we've been seeing all along the road the last few days are a type of acacia called Umbrella Thorn trees. He said their shape is partly due to the fact that the giraffes eat the topmost buds causing the tree to maintain its distinctive flat top. I got up early the next morning and walked the same trail again for early morning birding. I saw a large, boxy beetle (the guide later called it a dung beetle—very different from the one with which I'm familar) that makes a tremendous buzzing when it flies reminding me of something out of the *Starship Troopers* movie. I also caught the last part of the meal of a small spider that was eating up its orb web from the night before in order to recycle it later that evening. Unfortunately, I also carried away a significant number of other webs that won't get recycled.

The next day Mike arrived, and we drove to his house in Durban where he, his lovely wife Jenny, and their three-year-old towhead, Sean, were our hosts for two nights along with a young Rhodesian Ridgeback and a fat cat. Mike has a wonderfully located house to the west, or inland, from Durban. The walled property is on a steep hill and has been landscaped to give it a terraced effect. The house itself compliments this situation, providing views on all sides that make the property appear much larger than it actually is. It's quite a compliment that, knowing us as Mike does, he still invited us to stay at his house.

On our first afternoon, we just hung around the house doing laundry and e-mail and reading newspapers and Mike's *Time* magazines (the overseas edition of which is positively skimpy when compared to the one in the States)

On our layover day in Durban, Mike hooked Kirby and me up with a young Zulu man who tours people through the black townships. Thabo is just thirty years old and a better spokesperson for the new South Africa I cannot imagine. He is well-spoken in multiple languages with great English and a realistic optimism that was impressive. If South Africa has many like him, we're going to see it rise above its troubles and take its place on the world stage much sooner than anyone could ever expect. He provided us many insights into the racial situation among the whites, Indians, colored, and various tribes of South Africa. I would not be surprised to someday find his name among the movers and shakers of his country. He is still searching how to make his contribution.

Thabo took us to the house and printing press of Mahatma Gandhi who, you might remember, came to South Africa as a young lawyer and stayed to begin a movement that opened many doors for the Indian population there. I was surprised to see linotypes of the variety used at my family's small town

newspaper, the *Hartford City Newstimes*, before we changed from the hot lead
to the offset printing process many years ago.

We then stopped at the boys' high school where Nelson Mandela cast his
vote in the first truly democratic election in South Africa. This is also the site
where Oliver Tambo, the first president of the African National Council or
ANC, is buried, by all accounts a great man. Thabo said that he was taught
much about European history in school, but almost nothing about South African history. As a result he said, few South Africans know anything about
Tambo or other early black leaders. He is immensely proud of these great men
and takes inspiration from them.

He then drove us to a private girls' high school that was opened in the
1860s by a Congregationalist missionary ostensibly to provide educated wives
to chiefs and other high ranking men, but which has provided upwards of 90
percent (by one account) of the women who are active in great endeavors
throughout South Africa. Just a few years ago, the Congregationalists were
going to shut the school down as their missionary goals had changed and
funds were low, so the "old girls" (i.e., former graduates) took it over and are
keeping it open. Enlisting Nelson Mandela's help, they got a local paper man-
ufacturing company to help refurbish the place and it looks grand indeed. We
were there during an open house and got a chance to meet some of the young
women who attended school there (including Thabo's younger sister) and
then watched a chemistry demonstration given by a few of the students.

Evidently, Mr. Mandela is a force to be reckoned with. Thabo mentioned
several other projects where just the request of Mr. Mandela was enough to
open pocket books. By the way, he also had high praise for Jimmy Carter and
his Habitat for Humanity which, he said, has made significant contributions
in the Durban area. He also praised Bill Clinton who has just started a foundation to provide low cost drugs for AIDS victims and who has helped convince South Africa's president, Mr. Mbeki, to participate.

After the tour, we met Mike and the others for a quick bite at a live jazz
venue (jazz is big here as Thabo made sure we were aware) and then headed
back to Mike's house for more R&R with Sean and the dog. Bill had left for
the airport by this time. He decided, for various personal reasons, to leave the
trip early and fly to Cape Town for a few days and then home. This leaves just
the four world bikers for the ride to Cape Town.

The night before Bill left, Mike and Jenny fixed us a wonderful *braai*
(South African barbecue) meal. We had just sat down to eat on their lovely
veranda when several large (maybe an inch and a half long) termites flew onto

the porch, evidently attracted to the porch light. At first it was just a few, but they just kept coming and coming until the corner under the light was one seething mass of insects. Occasionally one would end up in our food. Once they hit the ground, however, they were apt to stay there and would soon lose their wings. The dog had a field day snapping at and eating a few. The geckos which call Mike's porch wall "home" would skitter down the wall, grab one, run up to the eaves to eat it and then return for another until they were very round. Mike told us this is a yearly event for each termite mound. At the end of the dry season, just after the first rain, each mound disgorges a mass of winged males and females. They swarm out, pair off, mate, and then the female finds an appropriate place to start a new colony.

As the evening wore on, the corner under the light accumulated more and more loose wings, and we could see pairs of termites following each other like little trains (presumably the female was in the lead) looking for new homes. For many other animals, these events are a real feast. Many native clans also eat the termites which Mike (who has eaten his share) said taste like butter and are considered a real delicacy in South Africa. In the morning, the only evidence this invasion took place was the pile of wings and the ants carrying away dead termites.

I know I've been a bit lazy with this report and have not included any historical summaries. I will make it up next time since this one is starting to get too long. From now until Cape Town we ride twenty days with just two break days and pass through some remote areas along the southern coast. I'll let you know how it goes next time.

Until then, take care of yourself and those who belong to you,

Ralph

Report #22: Greetings from South Africa II

Siyabona again from South Africa,

Before I continue with my trip summary, I'll set down a brief history of South Africa and Swaziland that I should have included in the last report. Early hunter-gatherers roamed southern Africa from ancient times. About two thousand years ago, some of these inhabitants acquired sheep from northern peoples and learned about property and territory ownership. Those known as Khoikhoi (or Hottentots) settled in the Cape Peninsula to live side by side a closely related group of Bushmen called the San. At about the same time, a robust group of peoples, the Bantu-speakers, occupied lands in Central Africa and, over the course of hundreds of years, gradually began migrating down the east coast. One of these groups, the Xhosas, then took the lead expanding west across the southern seaboard.

A permanent European presence began in April 1652 when the Dutch established a settlement on the southern tip of Africa to provide food and fresh water for their ships sailing between Europe and the Far East. While originally planned as no more than a refueling stop, this colony gradually grew; slaves from other parts of Africa and beyond were brought in to stem the labor shortage. Trekboers, or "wandering farmers," pushed further inland and outward displacing the Khoikhoi and eventually running into the Xhosa to the east. In 1779, the first of nine frontier wars began.

In the late eighteenth century, the Dutch star was fading and the British took over the Cape. They brought still more immigrants and worked out temporary boundaries with the Xhosa to the east. These agreements did not last long as the white settlers, primarily Boers, desirous of more land and freedom from the constraints of the colony, continued their eastward migration (sounds a bit like the story in America) while many of the British immigrants retreated to urban environs.

At about the same time (around 1820), the British settled in Port Natal (now Durban) on the east coast. Unfortunately, this coincided with the rise to power of a very capable and expansionistic Zulu king, Shaka, who, by introducing the short fighting spear and revolutionary battle tactics, led a successful army from the east coast toward the north and west. Besides setting off the *difaqane*, or "forced migration" of many regional tribes, the Zulus inevitably clashed with the equally expansionistic Brits and Boers. British firepower eventually prevailed over the Zulus in 1879, but only after the whites suffered several disastrous defeats.

Throughout this time, beginning in the 1830s, Dutch-speaking settlers in the Cape area, disenchanted with British control, began a mass migration north called the Great Trek, eventually establishing two independent republics: the Orange Free State and the Transvaal. While the Boers also battled the Zulu, they maintained an uneasy peace with the British which existed until the discovery of diamonds and gold in the Boer republics led to war with Britain in 1881 and again in 1899. The latter war lasted three years and ended with the Treaty of Vereeniging uniting the two Boer Republics with the two British colonies of Cape and Natal into the Union of South Africa on May 31, 1910. Of course, the black population had not participated and had no democratic rights in the new government.

For the next almost forty years, the freedom of movement and participation of blacks in South Africa became increasingly more repressive. In 1948, a radical Afrikaner government won election. Black restrictions and the concept of apartheid (literally, "apartness") were taken to new extremes, eventually leading to the foundation of the homeland system and the banning of the African National Congress (ANC) and other opposition groups. At the same time and in response, black movements such as the ANC were also escalating their tactics, both peaceful and violent.

In March 1960, police in Sharpeville gunned down sixty-nine demonstrators, an event that turned world opinion against the white South African regime and left it isolated. The Soweto riots in June 1976 demonstrated the anarchy that reigned in the black townships and the impotence of the white government to govern. Throughout this period, the South African government tried various methods to regain control, but it wasn't until F. W. de

Klerk was elected in 1989 that real changes were made. De Klerk removed the ban on the ANC and other organizations, allowing Nelson Mandela and others to be released from prison. The next few years generated intense debate and complex discussions but eventually led to a national election in April 1994 in which the ANC gained a clear 62 percent majority, and Nelson Mandela became the first president of a fully democratic South Africa.

Swaziland's history, to a point, is South Africa's history. Although the area of Swaziland has been inhabited for at least 110,000 years, the Swazi people migrated south as part of the great Bantu migration. After fending off the pressures from various other clans, most recently the Zulu, they consolidated their kingdom by 1868. The European presence in South Africa, in one sense, actually helped the Swazis by diverting the Zulu pressures, but it created other problems as missionaries, hunters, traders, and other carpetbaggers had their own designs on the kingdom.

In 1877, the Boers' South African Republic was all set to annex the kingdom when it was itself annexed by the British. From this union of Brits and Boers, the Swazis were ensured independence at the Pretoria Conference of 1881, but it was at a cost of land and the enforced coadministration by the two groups. Twenty years later, after the Anglo-Boer War, Swaziland became a British protectorate. Upset with their loss of sovereignty, the Swazis worked to regain their independence through the sage leadership of King Sobhuza II, who took over in 1921, and his mother acting as regent before the king was old enough to govern. After exhausting the official routes for true independence from Britain, the monarch and his mother encouraged their people to buy back lost lands. Partially as a result of this pacifist strategy, when independence was finally granted in 1968, Swazis already controlled almost two-thirds of the kingdom.

The country's constitution, which had been primarily framed by the British, was the next remnant of colonialism to go when Sobhuza abrogated it in 1973. The new constitution gave all power to the king. Since then, while most Swazis seem content with their government, steady internal and external (e.g., UN) pressures have resulted in the easing of autocratic control and a shift toward democratization.

Okay, with this as a basis, I will continue with my travels. From Durban we headed south down the coast for a couple of short riding days before turning inland to cut cross-country to the south coast. We could not follow the coast all the way around the cape because South Africa's "wild coast" (the southeast coast) does not have a coastal road. The coastal riding south of Durban was hilly and not particularly remarkable; it could have been any one of several places we've been on this trip...except of course for the troops of vervet monkeys crossing the roads.

Our first camp from Durban was down a dirt road about a kilometer at a beachside resort. Because the wind was up (it had been in our faces all day), the surf was rough. Mike said it would be calmer in the morning, so I put off my swim until then (just getting lazy I guess). I made sure all my stuff was secure in my tent as we left for supper, because I saw monkeys raiding the trash at an adjacent site. We had a great opportunity to watch a full moon rise out of the Indian Ocean, but thick cloud cover dashed those hopes. I did see it peeking through a clear place later in the evening though. I have had lousy luck with seeing full moons rising on this trip.

The next morning, I swam a mile in the Indian Ocean before starting our ride. I saw a couple of basketball-sized, translucent jellyfish pulsing along the bottom and a few fish hovering over a pile of rocks, but nothing else. However, before we left the campsite, Stacia pointed out a family of dolphins moving slowly down the coast just offshore.

That evening, we camped on a river maybe a half mile before it emptied into the ocean. Stacia and I took a dip, and I found a half dozen weaver nests on bottom and rescued one to inspect the construction. We've seen lots of the African masked weavers and had one tree full of their pendulous nests in this camp. They prefer a tree hanging out over water as another measure of protection from predators. Their mating rituals are fun to watch. The males build the nests and then wait for the females to arrive. When they do, the males hang upside-down on their nests (the opening is at the bottom to make it more difficult for predators, particularly snakes, to invade) and frantically flutter their wings to attract attention to their handiwork. The season here was still early because, whenever a female came near, all the males went aflutter setting the whole tree in motion.

The amenities in South Africa, both at campgrounds and at inns, have been among the best we've seen. Both of these coastal campgrounds even had bathtubs in their communal ablution facilities!

From here, we turned inland through a much more remote and historically more dangerous region called the Transkei. On Odyssey 2000, more than half the riders got spooked by local stories and, despite Tim's assurances, rented buses to take them to the south coast at East London. Our route guides advised us to ride with another person but, except on the first day when I rode with Kirby for about two-thirds of the way, we didn't even do that. We all got dark looks and comments that did not always sound friendly along this route. Stacia in particular got more than her share, but most people seemed friendly enough. We must have been an odd sight—we did not see a single recreational bike rider along this route until we were on the more developed south coast heading to Cape Town.

The first two days inland were very hilly with climbs above five thousand feet. Both days were mostly overcast with low clouds covering the higher hills. It sprinkled a couple of times, but we had no serious rain. We passed a lot of timberland, mostly pine and eucalyptus, both of which are big industries in this part of the country. We stayed at B&B's both nights, one in a small town and one on a farm. Both were rustic with friendly hosts.

Tim showed up on our second inland night and took the baton from Mike who returned home the next morning. We, on the other hand, rode 175 kilometers or 108.5 miles to Umtata, our longest ride on the trip. Luckily, we had a decent tailwind for much of the way to mitigate the distance somewhat. I felt better at the finish than I had any right to. We had accumulated 8,600 feet of elevation throughout the ride, mostly from rolling hills. The day was clear, and we could often see the road laid out before us for miles as the vegetation was sparse and then, with the wind at our backs, we'd gobble up those miles, pleasant riding conditions indeed.

Nelson Mandela grew up in the Transkei, and Umtata boasts one of the area's three museums in his honor. Tim had arranged for the museum to open an hour early in order that we could visit it before we hit the road the next morning (on Odyssey 2000, the staff opened it in the evening for a hundred riders; I was impressed we got special treatment with just four). The museum has one section following the life of Mandela from childhood through his involvement in the black freedom movement and his subsequent prison term on Robben Island up to his release. His story is told with placards, pictures, and short film clips. The other two sections of the museum display the multitude of gifts and honoraria that people, institutions, and governments from around the world have bestowed on Mandela. He is truly a man of the world. It was an impressive museum.

The only downer in Umtata was an incident the afternoon we arrived. Tim pulled up to a stoplight, and a young man shoved one of the van's back windows open and made off with Tim's sleeping bag. I'm not sure if this impacted Tim much as he slept in the van whenever we camped in South Africa.

The ride to Umtata was long, but the next day's ride to Butterworth, though fifty kilometers shorter, was a real butt-kicker. Because we stopped at the museum, it was nearly 10 a.m. before we started, and hot. Not too many kilometers into the ride the sky clouded up, and we actually got a sprinkle before the sky cleared and the sun bore down again. About sixty kilometers into the ride, the sky darkened again, this time for good—the cooler weather felt great. I ran into a few more sprinkles but got to the B&B while the storm was still brewing and therefore missed the deluge that followed.

But, it was not the sky that made the biggest difference on this ride (though the cloud cover was much appreciated), it was the strong, gusting south wind that was in our faces most of the day. Instead of feeling fifty kilometers shorter than the previous day's ride, it felt considerably longer. Most of the way, the wind had the impact of a continuous uphill climb. We didn't even get relief when climbing a real hill. Often a hill will block a headwind until you reach the crest, but this wind came roaring down the hills so that we fought for every inch forward. I suspect I rode at least an hour at less than eight kilometers per hour, not much faster than a brisk walk and very discouraging on such a long ride. Even more discouraging is pedaling hard to make headway going down a hill—it got to the point where I felt good if I pushed my bike above twenty kilometers per hour on a downhill which is pitiful.

When the wind was coming across the road or at an angle, it could get downright scary. The big trucks would pass, temporarily blocking the wind and providing a momentary tailwind in their wake that would whip my shirt up over my head, and seem to suck you toward them. Then they would be past, and the wind would blow you almost off the road while you were still compensating for the draw of their suction. Stacia said she was pushed off the road a couple times by the wind, and I had a few close calls.

Shortly after the halfway point, I pulled into a service station with an adjacent convenience shop and sat in the shade while sucking down a couple of power drinks. A little later I ate a chocolate bar. From then on, whether it was the sugar, the cloud cover, a slight abatement of the wind, or a combination of the three, I seemed to make better time on both the uphill and downhill runs (there were no level places that I remember). This rejuvenated me to some extent, and I began enjoying the ride more. Regardless though, it was a real endurance test and not my idea of a good time.

While I rehydrated, a couple of young boys came by with their dad. One had his face painted white which, according to Mike, is a sign he has recently gone through a puberty ritual. This reminded me of the women I saw working at road construction sites whose faces were painted red or white which, again according to Mike, is both for sun protection and decoration.

For most of the riding in South Africa, we have seen lots of livestock along and sometimes in the road. The most common are cows and goats, but I've seen sheep, horses, donkeys, and a couple of pigs. Unfortunately, there is inevitably roadkill along the way, but not as much as you might expect given the amount of loose stock. These last two long days through rural South Africa provided the most roadkill I had seen, including a very ripe horse.

The next day's ride to the coastal town of East London was considerably easier. Though we still had the wind in our faces, it did not seem as extreme. Also, for whatever reason, I was feeling strong that day. I'm sure the thought of a layover day helped too. In East London we stayed two nights in a backpacker's hostel, but instead of a bunkroom, we were only two to a room and had in-suite bathrooms. The hostel was just a block from the esplanade along the ocean with beautiful beaches at either end and a long, rocky patch with tidal pools in the middle.

East London is a sleepy little town, which helped make our layover there a true rest day...we all needed it. We had the hostel's full kitchen at our disposal, so Tim made pancakes for breakfast—only the second time in many months we enjoyed pancakes. I took a dip off the rocky shore and saw a school of translucent shrimp and a few fish before the big surf and the rocks made me reconsider, and I headed to shore. Luckily the rocks were not sharp, and I made it to shore without incident, but it reminded me that big surf and rocks are not a happy combination.

The next day to Fish River, we were up and going by 7 a.m. As luck would have it, we had a tailwind almost the whole way, and it was a joy. The day was gorgeous with wispy clouds, and the route was rolling hills for the most part. Very early in the ride, we got a good look at an old shipwreck and, on the way out of town, we rode onto the Mercedes Benz Grand Prix Circuit racetrack, down one straightaway and past the pits. It's strange that a portion of the track is also a major road, for that was indeed the case here. I wonder what they do when there's a race.

Stacia had a bad day as a knife-wielding man came out of the bush and chased her down the road. She was close enough to see from his eyes that he was up to no good. She dodged across the road, and the oncoming traffic slowed him down. Just up the road, a second man also gave chase, but she outdistanced them on her bike. The whole incident really shook her up, as well it might. Tim stopped the police who went back to find the men, but they had no luck. We all ensured Stacia rode within sight of someone else after that until just before Cape Town, when she felt it was safe enough to go off on her own.

After we arrived at our resort hotel, I took a swim in the pool and then hiked down to the beach on a nature trail. I didn't see much, but I did dig out my first ant lion, an interesting creature that digs a conical pit with steep, slippery sides of fine sand and then burrows in at the bottom of the cone awaiting an unwary ant to tumble down. I also ran into a plethora of spider webs. It's always a bit disconcerting to feel a full web across your face with the occupant so close your eyes can't focus on it.

The ride to Alexandria had a moderate headwind, but not nearly as intense as we've seen. We stayed at a nice inn with dogs, a cat, hens, and two peacocks strutting around. Our hosts had a *braai* for us with chicken and *boerewors* (or farmer sausages) over a grill with a green salad, German potato salad, *mielie* (or maize meal) with a tomato-onion sauce, and a nice dessert. Our hosts were a couple who live in Morocco, but who come to South Africa for lengthy periods (she's from South Africa and he's from Germany), and the manager who was Afrikaner, I believe. They were interesting people to chat with around a nice campfire.

The next two rides to Port Elizabeth and Jeffreys Bay were more of the same coastal rolling hills with moderate head and crosswinds. The most significant incident on these two days came on our ride to J-Bay. Just after I saw Tim in the support van, before he drove ahead to set up our night's camping arrangements, the screw that holds my handlebars tight broke making it extremely difficult to steer. Fortunately, I was near a tiny village that had a gas station and so I made my way there. The staff at the station could not fix it, but they were able to direct me to a garage just down the road. The garage was off the main road, and I wouldn't even have noticed it was there behind the foliage had I not been looking for it. The fellow who ran it looked to be of Boer stock (based on what little I know of the Boers) strong, hardy, ready to tackle anything. He and his assistant stopped working on a truck to look at my problem. He was able to back out the broken part of the bolt, file down the stripped end, and then fit it back on. Luckily there was enough left of the bolt to tighten the handlebars down. As they worked on my bike, I began wondering if I would be able to ride the remaining thirty kilometers to camp with loose handlebars. While riding to the garage, I had found that, by applying a bit more pressure to one side of the handlebar, I could lodge it against the neck and make headway on the bike. However, I wasn't sure what would happen when I needed to turn, especially on a downhill slope. I was glad I didn't have to try, and the guy wouldn't even accept payment.

J-Bay became a layover day to make up for the 175-kilometer day in the Transkei. That ride had actually been two ride days according to the original itinerary, but Tim explained that he had to combine the days because he couldn't find suitable accommodations in-between. Once in camp, I put up my tent and headed to the ocean for a swim. Most of the beachfront towns along the southern coast are legendary surf spots with named waves (e.g., Supertubes) that are catchwords among those in the know. Parts of the cult surfer movie *Endless Summer* were filmed here. Needless to say, the surf was pretty rough. Rather than walking down the beach to what I found out later was a nice swim beach, I opted to find a way among the rocks just in front of our campground for a short swim. Coming back in I beached myself on a brain coral skeleton and scraped my arms a bit. Therefore, the next day I took the time to go to a real swim beach and did my laps between the area where the body surfers were and the area where the board surfers were. The water was colder than that along the east coast, but still not as cold as the Atlantic, due to a relatively warm current that graces the southern coast of South Africa until it runs into a cold current coming up from Antarctica around Cape Town.

The next day, we again headed inland, this time to Fish River, and our scheduled layover day. Although our route was more level than most of the past days, the terrain seemed different almost immediately. We began seeing thick forests and mountains. Also, and most importantly, we had a nice tailwind so we were cruising along nicely. Just before our destination, a hostel-like bushpacker's inn, we crossed Storms River Bridge over a chasm that is extremely narrow and very impressive. It is the result of a quick erosion process according to a local.

Tim had arranged a four-person bunkroom as an option to camping. The beds were nice, but the room was a freeway as other people trooped in to use the communal restrooms. Our second night there, I opted to camp and got a better night's sleep. Young women seem to really like this particular bushpacker's inn since several of the young male staff seldom wore their shirts and were all nicely buffed due to the multitude of outside activities in Storms River...I kidded Stacia about having her own Chip-n-Dale staff.

On our layover day in Storms River, Kirby and I took the treetop tour which is a highlight of the area. Since this was their off season, we were the only customers in our time slot which made it even more enjoyable. First the guides fit you into a harness, helmet, and gloves and then drive you to the starting point in the forest. Safety is strongly stressed. For the cable ride from platform to platform, we had three attachments: two to the primary cable and one to a back-up cable. Once we alit upon the treetop platform, we had two attachments to fixed cables. One guide preceded us on the cable, and one guide followed behind us each time we slid from tree to tree. While sitting in the harness, we would slide down the cable to each of the six or seven platforms. Gravity did the work, but we had to supply the brake using our double-gloved right hands. Although it felt a bit odd at first, it was easy to learn. At each platform, Willie, the lead guide, would provide information on the forest and its plant and, to a lesser extent, animal inhabitants. Although the trees are deciduous, the forest is technically an "evergreen" forest because, while the trees do shed their leaves, they do so continuously instead of all at once, so there are always leaves on the trees.

The hard pear and the yellowwood trees are the giants of the forest, but no species seemed to dominate. Willie said this is one of the few indigenous forests left in South Africa; 95 percent of them are gone. In fact, non-native pine forests completely surround this one. The treetop tour has been a going concern for only a couple of years. It evidently took a lot of convincing before the South African forest service would grant permission. Willie told us the engineering for the treetop route was copied from a similar place in Costa Rica and showed us how the platforms and cables are attached to the trees so as not to cause damage. It was certainly a unique tour.

That afternoon we all piled into the van, and Tim drove us the twenty kilometers to Tsitsikamma National Park at Storms River mouth. There we walked first to a suspension bridge over the river's mouth and then to a waterfall right on the coast. And what a magnificent coast it was, one of the most impressive I've seen. The water was in constant, violent motion storming against the rocks along the shore giving us an ever-changing color spectrum from blue to green. It was an invigorating scene.

The walk to the bridge was mostly boardwalk, but the waterfall walk was a bit more strenuous with lots of ups and downs and much rock hopping. As I plunged into one of the thick patches of forests, I came eye to eye with a duiker, a small stocky antelope, only an arms-length away. As I walked past, it merely looked at me and continued browsing. I was sweating profusely when I finally reached the waterfall. It was a good thirty to forty feet high and broad, but didn't spill a lot of water this time of year, enough though to keep full a small, but deep swimming hole at its base. Into this I plunged, after stripping down to my gym shorts, for a refreshing dip. The water was cold without being uncomfortable, and I emerged much refreshed. On the hike back, I spotted a pod of at least thirty dolphins moving down the coast just beyond the rocks. Some of them were emerging completely out of the water as they swam, a beautiful sight. They make swimming in such turbulent surf seem easy.

As I was packing my gear the next morning, I shook an eight-inch black millipede from one of my hiking socks. We've seen lots of these critters throughout our travels in South Africa. That day was another inland day with good climbs and nice mountain views. On one of the rural segments, I saw what I think was a large mongoose cross the road. It was blonder than others I've seen and a bit larger, but it moved and had the general shape of a mongoose. Also, for about fifteen kilometers, I rode with a local biker who told me he had died for forty-five minutes three years ago in his church. They tried the defibrillator three times, but it didn't revive him. Evidently, he came back on his own. They took him to Cape Town and, three weeks later, he was home again as they could find nothing wrong with him—he considers it a miracle. At sixty-two the fellow was very fit (I suspect he was riding slower than his usual pace so he could chat with me) and has ridden in Cape Town's 110-kilometer race eleven or twelve times. He was an impressive fellow and the first recreational rider I had seen in South Africa outside of Durban. When I reached camp, I took a swim in Pleasant Lake, which was a bit murky, but had a nice temperature—not really all that pleasant though. Afterwards I took a nice, but tepid, bath in the communal bathtub just to see what it was like.

The ride to Albertina was more of the same with a passing truckload of ostriches, just their heads visible over the high sides, to make it remarkable. The supper that night is worth commenting on though. We had a fixed menu with several starters (soup, a seafood cocktail, salad), a couple second courses (I had a delicious lightly fried piece of hake, a white fish), several mains (chicken, mutton, ostrich stew, pork chops), and a couple of desserts, all served with homemade bread. But instead of selecting one of each, you could have as many of each as you wanted. It was essentially "all you can eat," but with sit-down style service; a waitress brought our food by course. The crowning touch is that the food was all top quality and well prepared. It was a very satisfying and enjoyable meal for hungry bikers.

The western route we took when we hit the southern coast and headed toward Cape Town has given us a different perspective of South Africa than those of our northern and Transkai rides. The second day after "turning the corner" to head west, I saw my second recreational cyclist in South Africa with bright shirt and the whole bit. Since then, we've seen a few here and there and were even passed by a large pack, out for a Sunday group ride, when we got nearer to Cape Town. At Fish River we met a German couple who were riding around the world unsupported (i.e., they carry all their gear on their bikes)—so far, based on my observation of maybe a dozen long-distance, self-supported riders we have passed during the course of this past year, this particular form of masochism hasn't caught my fancy.

There appears to be more parity in the standard of living here in the south, at least we've not seen the abject poverty and harsh living conditions we did further north…maybe they are just out of sight. However, the people, even those walking along the road, appear much better off. This whole riding segment has a different feel than our first two weeks in South Africa. The roads, on the other hand, are about the same, still rough-surfaced macadam, often with wide shoulders which, like in Texas, are used regularly by slower traffic to allow faster cars to pass even with oncoming traffic. We stayed alert whenever this happened. The traffic signs are still in English, Afrikaner, or both, as are the billboards and other road signs. So far, we haven't discovered many flat stretches in Africa; all the roads we've ridden have been sinusoidal hills of varying amplitude. Starting a week ago, we've begun seeing small trucks, stacked high with household goods, passing by. One of our hosts told us this is the annual migration of workers who have jobs away from home and who are returning for the long summer holiday.

On America's traditional Thanksgiving Day, we started riding to Stanford in a light rain that cleared up shortly after leaving Swellendam where we had camped in a beautiful campground with a spectacular mountain view. About halfway into the ride, Tim flagged Kirby and me down to show us a bird he had hit with the van that had stuck under his windshield wiper. While stopped, an ostrich from a nearby farm came up to the fence and exhibited, what I suspect is, its mating dance seemingly directed at Tim. It lowered itself close to the ground, fluffed up its feathers, and performed what can only be called a hootchy-kootchy dance, undulating from side to side. It was downright lascivious. We didn't know whether to be embarrassed for or envious of Tim and masked our feelings in nervous laughter and guy jokes. At about seventy kilometers, we made a ninety degree turn to head south for the last fifty kilometers, and we turned from one headwind straight into another—how that can happen I just don't know, but it sure was frustrating.

Tim lodged us in an inn for Thanksgiving and planned a special evening meal, but first we took a tour of a small microbrewery in town. The brewer gave us the cook's tour, but it was the origin of the brewery's name, Birkenhead, I found most interesting. It's named after a ship that ran onto rocks just off Danger Point, just south of here, in 1852. The military men aboard stood aside to let the women and children board the lifeboats first. As a result, most of the men perished, but not a single woman or child died. This incident gave us the phrase "women and children first"…according to the brewer. For Thanksgiving supper, I had chicken pate with green figs, a Thai fish curry, and a very sour lemon tart—certainly not roast turkey and fixins, but delicious nonetheless.

From Stanford to Cape Town, we were mostly on the coast with absolutely stunning views all along the way. As we left Stanford, the restaurant owner where we had breakfasted told us to keep our eyes sharp for right whales that calve in the bay at Hermanus on our way to Gordon's Bay. Sure enough, when we reached Hermanus, a right whale lolled in the surf surprisingly close to shore, quite literally a stone's throw from where I was standing on an overlook. We saw it blow a few times and raise its head and tail a couple of times before it slowly swam away and disappeared. Although I kept my eyes open, I did not see another on the ride to Gordon's Bay. The last twenty to thirty kilometers were sweet. The road surface became the smoothest we'd seen in South Africa, the wind was at our backs, and we were rounding the headland into and around Gordon's Bay with spectacular views—it just doesn't get much better than this! Of course, as we rounded the far side of the bay, we inevitably turned back into the wind and had to fight our way the last few kilometers to camp.

Although we were less than a kilometer from a sandy beach, I decided not to swim. First, the wind by that time was howling, then I noticed large drainage pipes leading into the water from town (who knows what that might mean), and the clincher was a line of blue at the waterline which, on closer inspection, proved to be a large number of Portuguese men-of-war (and probably some women-of-war) or close relatives that had been washed ashore.

The ride to Simonstown was a close replica of the day before, beautiful coastal riding with hills and wind. Our last camp in South Africa was on a hill overlooking False Bay which, although technically part of the Atlantic Ocean, is still influenced by the more temperate southeast current and is not quite as cold as the waters just across the Cape. After putting up my tent in pretty stiff winds, I walked down to a small sandy beach and took a dip. The only interesting sight was a bunch of brightly colored urchins hugging the rocks on bottom which is a change from the black urchins I've generally seen. After everyone was in and showered, Tim dropped us off a short way down the coast at a colony of South African Penguins, which are also called jackass penguins because of their braying calls. Here we spent some time watching the penguins which were ashore molting, allowing us a much closer view than we would normally get. The rest of the afternoon we spent shopping. While walking to the shops, we noted a huge column of smoke coming from a point just over the near mountain ridge. While we watched, a helicopter began transporting water from the ocean to the fire. I talked to a shop owner with a heavy German accent who said three years ago bush fires had caused much destruction. Fortunately, this fire appeared to be out by the time we finished supper.

The wind blew hard all night long, rattling our tents, as a series of blasts hit us amongst periods of relative calm. It reminded me of wave sets when you're body surfing. Sometime in the very early morning, I arose responding to the call of nature and was greeted with a magnificent night sky in which the Southern Cross was prominent, and the Milky Way spilled across a section of the sky. It's hard to get back to sleep after a magnificent view like that!

Tim saved the best ride of South Africa for last. Simonstown sits almost due south of Cape Town but is on the east side of the Cape Peninsula, whereas Cape Town is on the west side. We awoke to a crystal clear morning and a strong wind. After a TK&A breakfast, we headed into the wind continuing down the peninsula for five or six kilometers before turning inland to cut across the headland. We had the wind directly behind us as we pedaled up and over the range that runs down the peninsula. From there the route flattened out for a bit (the first flat land I remember seeing in South Africa) with Australian gum trees lining the road, then past an ostrich farm and mostly open country. It was great riding. On this one ride, I saw more bicyclists than all I had seen previously in South Africa. It was obviously a splendid Sunday morning for biking. Heading northwest, we had a great downhill to a spectacular stretch of Atlantic coast with a brilliant aquamarine color where the white sand is reflected up through the water in places not covered with kelp beds. A bit farther up the coast, scuba divers were either suiting up or had freshly emerged from a dive—the water was certainly inviting.

We were forced to reverse course across the central ridge toward the east again because the famed drive over Chapman's Peak was closed for repairs. At the beginning of the climb, I noticed a small animal caught in a large cement rain gutter which paralleled the road for a quarter mile. I couldn't tell what it was. It was a little more than a foot long with thick, silky light brown hair all over and tiny, nocturnal eyes. I thought of a mole, but though it was similarly shaped, it didn't appear to have the digging equipment. It could not climb out of the culvert and certainly could not jump. I laid a wooden fence post in its path and was able to flip it out. It landed on its back and struggled to right itself. I thought I saw two long pointy teeth. I later looked it up at a Cape Town library and discovered it was a common mole rat, an animal I had not seen before. It must have been foraging at night and tumbled into the steep-sided culvert. I wondered how long it had been running up and down the length of the culvert looking for a way out before I came along.

From the top of the climb, we could view the eastern bay as we enjoyed a long coast before again cutting back to the west coast across the Cape's wine producing region. After another healthy uphill along the coast, we earned our first view of Cape Town beneath the fabled Table Mountain which, due to strong winds, was not sporting its tablecloth cloud cover. This was my favorite ride in South Africa. Except for the wind, which was more often in our favor than not, the weather was perfect, and the scenery was nothing short of magnificent. I can't better Francis Drake's chronicler who said of the Cape, "The most stately thing, and the fairest cape we saw in the whole circumference of the earth." Unfortunately, the day was marred when we got to our apartment to find the van's passenger window had been shattered. Tim's laptop computer and camera, that together had all his pictures of this stage of the trip plus all his computerized route guides, financial info, etc., had been stolen while he was checking us in. Bummer!

After doing my laundry, showering, snacking, and updating my journal, I still had time before supper and so I headed to the waterfront, just a few blocks down the street, to pick up some South African rand at an ATM. I found one at a 7-Eleven and immediately had more help than I needed from the people hanging around the store. At one point, a guy actually took my card to show me how to feed it into the machine. He was deft, and I felt, rather than saw, that he had palmed my card. I grabbed his wrist and retrieved the card with my other hand. I suspect he was just waiting for me to input my PIN and then he would have walked away with my card and my PIN. Instead, I walked away to the other ATM in the store which was being used by a woman. She finished and also started "helping" me by pressing buttons, etc. I told her I could handle it, cancelled my transaction before entering my PIN, took my card, and turned to leave. Yet another fellow stepped up and told me I had to finish my transaction or I could lose money. I probably should have found the manager of the store and told him/her that the store had a real problem, but instead I walked down the street to yet another ATM where I could get my cash without people hanging around. At this ATM, I noticed the buttons had to be held down hard before they would register, which is just perfect for someone trying to read your PIN over your shoulder. After Tim's and my incident, I was reminded of a sentence I had read in the "Dangers & Annoyances" section of Tim's *Lonely Planet Guide* for Cape Town, "There is tremendous poverty on the peninsula and informal redistribution of wealth is reasonably common."

On our first layover day in Cape Town, Tim, Stacia, Kirby, and I took the ferry to Robben Island where the political prisoners were held during apartheid. Both guides we had for our tour, one for the bus tour of the island and the walking tour guide, were former inmates of Robben Island who were able to provide a stronger message than might otherwise have been the case. The bus tour guide, along with the information in the ferry terminal, provided a historical perspective of the island pre-apartheid. He told us how it was used as an exile for Khoikhoi chiefs and others who had proved difficult to the early white establishment, and how later, it was used as a place apart from normal society for the insane, lepers, and other misfits. He also showed us World War II era buildings built to be Cape Town's first line of defense if attacked during the war.

The walking tour took us through the courtyard, limestone quarry, and cell block #5 (Mandela's cell), along with other places made infamous in Mandela's autobiography *Long Walk to Freedom* (my next read). The guide gave us insight into how the prison was transformed into a *de facto* "university" where inmates actually earned degrees. I left with renewed hope in the world situation when, in such a short time, a prison can be transformed to a monument to the human spirit as defined not only by tenacity, fixity of purpose, and endurance, but also by forgiveness and reconciliation which were prominent in both of our tour guides' presentations. Our visit was enhanced by a short conversation with the parents of a former political prisoner who had returned to Robben Island for the first time since their son's release. They seemed nearly overwhelmed by the experience.

The wind had come up during the tour, making the ferry ride back to the city much rougher. Sometimes it felt like the hydrofoil would lift off and take flight. Along the way, hundreds of jackass penguins crowded the waters looking for fish; the molting season must be nearly over. After docking and a quick lunch, I returned to the ferry loading area to finish looking at all the Robben

Island information and memorabilia there. Besides examples of the home-made diplomas, letters from inmates and handwritten teaching materials, there was a gallery of drawings by Nelson Mandela. His rudimentary draw-ings, now numbered and signed engravings, are greatly escalating in price and would be a dandy investment. In addition, those purchasing one of the engravings have the privilege of sharing dinner with Nelson Mandala himself!

The next morning, Stacia and I hiked to the top of Table Mountain from the lower tram station. It was a tough, rocky stair-step route up for the first stage, then a mostly level walk around part of the mountain to the Platteklip Gorge, and then another unrelenting climb to the top. There was almost no shade, and the sun beat down with barely a hint of a breeze. We sweat pro-fusely, but the views over the city were spectacular all the way up. I suspect the hike was no more than two or three miles, but my legs are geared for biking right now and not hiking, and I'll admit I was glad to see the plateau top.

After catching our breath, we hiked to the upper tram area to get water and then wandered around the flat top reading the placards and admiring the views from all sides. There can't be many cities with better views then these! It wasn't as clear as the day before since the strong winds, locally known as "the Cape Doctor," had abated somewhat, so there was some haze but, even so, the views in all directions were spectacular. Off in the distance, we saw the begin-nings of a "tablecloth" of clouds on a neighboring plateau.

Table Mountain is what is left after centuries of erosion of the sedimentary rock that once covered the whole area. Once you could walk to Robben Island and beyond (of course it wouldn't have been an island then). The rock of which the mountain is made did not have as much upheaval as the surround-ing rock and so has better resisted the continuous forces of erosion. The mountain is also a great spot to see the fynbos, or fine-leafed bush, a unique vegetation found no where else in the world but in the Cape region. Although geographically limited, the fynbos rivals the rainforests in species diversity. We rode down on a cable car that rotates as it descends, giving views for everyone in all directions, and walked back to the apartment stopping to browse extensively in an open-air market selling all types of African crafts and art.

Later that evening, I packed my bike in a sturdy bike box using my sleeping bag and other gear as packing material and was again able to get my kit down to just one duffle and the bike box. This time, taking Kirby's advice, I bought clothesline rope and tied my box to reinforce the tape. Our flights the next day were in the late afternoon, but instead of sleeping in, we were all up early—nervous energy I guess. Mostly we just piddled around, but I did walk to the beach and take a short, cold swim in the Atlantic just a few blocks down a steep hill from the apartment in which we were staying, and I did a little research in the local library. On our ride to the airport we noted that the tablecloth was forming on Table Mountain, which had been cleared of clouds by the Cape Doctor the last few days...a fitting end to our South African stage.

However, before I sign off, I want to add that this is easily the best birding place on the trip. I didn't want to bore those of you who don't give a hoot (pardon the pun) about birding with a breathless species by species report, but I numbered seventy-two different species sightings with probably another two dozen or more other birds that I saw but couldn't positively identify...and that was just casually birding, no intense stuff. A dedicated birder would be in heaven here.

The big news for most of my readers is that instead of flying to Buenos Aires, Argentina, for our final riding stage, we all flew home. Tim offered us the chance to take a break and spend the holidays at home, and to then return to South America for our final stage in late January or early February. It was a generous offer and, for a variety of reasons, we all took him up on it. The main reason we did is that we were all getting stale and just weren't enjoying the riding as much as we would have liked. So on December 3 at 8:30 p.m. South African time, I began a thirty-hour plane odyssey to Albuquerque via the Cape Verde Islands off the western hump of Africa, Atlanta, and Los Angeles. So don't expect a report at the end of December; I'll forward it in one or two segments in the February timeframe. It'll give those of you who are behind in your reading time to catch up. Hope you enjoy sharing my adventures.

In the meantime, take especially good care of yourself and those who belong to you during the holidays,

Ralph

Epilogue

Howdy from Albuquerque,

This will be my last Odyssey 2003 missive. I was informed a couple of weeks ago by Tim, the tour company owner, that he had to declare bankruptcy on the last day of 2003. I'm not sure of all the details, but I know that the poor rate of the dollar against other currencies, particularly the Euro, coupled with the unusually low number of people signing up for his other trips contributed to his financial problems. He is looking into how we might retrieve a refund for the last stage of the trip. Regardless of the refund, I feel we got real value for our money. With only four world trip riders and a few others here and there on the trip, we received absolutely super service from Tim and his staff. The four world riders often discussed how lucky we were to be on such a trip, and I for one am surprised Tim even sponsored the ride with such low participation. I certainly wish him well on his future endeavors and hope he is able to offer this world trip again some day.

People here in Albuquerque are asking me, "What next?" Well, to stave off a bunch of e-mails asking the same question, I'll say that I've had no problems keeping busy since I retired in July 2001. Since returning to the States, I've taken the two trips: to San Francisco to attend my nephew Kawika's graduation and a mini-Monfort family reunion and to Indiana to spend Xmas with mom and a couple of my sisters. I have lots of busy-work such as reordering my finances and other paper work. I've been trying to get my green chile intake level back on track (I had some form of New Mexico green chile every day for the first two weeks I was home). I've been catching up on movies (four coupons for up to three ninety-nine cent video rentals for the month of January has helped in this regard!). I'm struggling valiantly to catch up on a year's worth of National Geographic magazines, which I've been reading cover to cover for many years. Also, I've been cross-country skiing in-between my days on the bicycle, and I am enjoying having access to a pool and a gym, so I'm keeping in relatively good shape.

I have consolidated my trip reports and printed them, but have not edited them yet. I'm not sure what I will do with all those words yet. I have developed all my film, generated a computer list of all the captions, and eventually will consolidate them and other memorabilia into a number of memory books, since I can't seem to count on my other memory as I get older.

And I've been enjoying reading as a supplement to past adventures and future interests. Cheryl foisted *Brunelleschi's Dome* on me as soon as I got back, and it was fun to read about the designer of the grand dome for the cathedral we saw in Florence and of the times when it was built. I found Mandela's autobiography in the Albuquerque library and enjoyed it immensely. Ditto with a slim book on France's "Dreyfus Affair." I had stumbled upon a monument to Dreyfus in an out-of-the-way square in Paris when there last summer, which reminded me I wanted to understand the whole business better. I blasted through the number one bestseller, *The da Vinci Code*, in a couple of days and enjoyed revisiting the Louvre and the race through Paris. But it reminded me of other areas where I have deficient knowledge, so I have a book on order at the library on the Knights Templar and other subjects. Cheryl and I are reading a book about a young woman who biked unsupported through South America for a year right at the outset of the Second World War. This was to get me ready for the final trip stage to Argentina and Chile and has only served to whet my appetite to get down there in some other way.

In the future? Not sure yet, but I've consolidated my ideas from a variety of old notebooks and will start investigating some of them very soon. International bum, the Peace Corps, using my GI Bill, and some semi-volunteer work with either the National Parks or Forest Service or something similar all hover near the top of the list.

Thank-you for joining me on my world bike adventure. I hope you have enjoyed my reports.

Take care of yourself and those who belong to you,

Ralph

Appendix A

Odyssey 2003 Itinerary

This appendix presents my itinerary for the 2003 Odyssey World Cycling Tour. It gives the place name and date for each sleeping location.

United States

Jan 1-2	Los Angeles, Ca
3-4	night flight to New Zealand with one day lost in air

New Zealand

Jan 5-6	Auckland (on north island)
7	Miranda
8	Mount Maunganui (Tauranga)
9	Rotorua
10-11	Taupo
12	Waioura
13	Fielding
14	Otaki Beach
15-16	Wellington
17	Nelson (on south island)
18	Murchison

New Zealand (cont)

19	Westport
20	Punakaiki
21	Ross
22-23	Franz Josef Glacier
24	Fox glacier
25	Haast
26	Makarora
27	Wanaka
28-30	Queenstown
31-Feb 1	Christchurch

Australia

Feb 2-3	Hobart, Tasmania
4	Bothwell
5	Longford
6	Scottsdale
7-8	St. Helens
9	Bicheno
10	Orford
11	Seven Mile beach
12	Hobart
13-15	Sydney, New South Wales
16-17	Townsville, Queensland
18	Ingham
19	Tully
20	Flying Fish Point (Innisfail)
21	Yungaburra
22-23	Port Douglas
24-25	Cairns

Hong Kong

Feb 26-28 Hong Kong

China

Mar 1	Wuzhou
2	Xindu
3	Zhongshan
4-5	Yangshuo
6-7	Guilin
8-9	Yongsheng
10	Rong'an
11	Liuzhou
12	Heshan
13	Binyang
14	Nanning

Vietnam

Mar 15-16	Hanoi
17	night train to Hue
18-19	Hue
20-21	Hoi An
22-23	Nha Trang
24	Phan Rang
25-26	Da Lat
27	Phan Rang
28	Phan Thiet
29-30	Ho Chi Minh City

Thailand

Mar 31–Apr 2	Phuket
3–4	Ko Phi Phi Don Island
5	Krabi Town
6–7	Ko Lanta Island
8	Pak Meng (Trang)
9	Pakbara Beach
10–11	Hat Yai

United States (home for SARS scare)

Apr 12	Los Angeles
13–23	Albuquerque
24	night flight to Czech Republic

Czech Republic

Apr 25–26	Prague
27	Tábor

Austria

Apr 28	Drosendorf
29–30	Vienna
May 1	Melk
2	Steyr
3	Weissenbach
4	Salzburg

Germany

May 5–7	Műnchen (or Munich)

United States (for son's graduation)

May 8–12	Durham, NC

Switzerland

May 13	St. Moritz
14	Flims
15	Hospental
16	Bramois (Sion)

France

May 17	La Bouveret

Switzerland

May 18-19	Geneva

Luxembourg

May 20-21	Luxembourg City

Belgium

May 22	Virton

France

May 23	Attigny
24	Nogent L'Artaud
25-27	Paris
28	Monnereville
29	Jangeau (Orléans)
30-31	Ambois
Jun 1	Saumur
2	Chalonnes-sur-Loire (Angers)
3	Marcillé Robert
4-5	Le Mont-St. Michel
6	Grandcamp-Maisy
7	Ouistreham

England

Jun 8	Portsmouth
9-11	London
12	Winchester
13-14	Bath

Wales

Jun 15	Cardiff
16	Cilmery (Builth-Wells)
17	Bryncrug
18	Bangor

Ireland

Jun 19-20	Dublin
21	Cavant
22	Portnoo (Donegal)
23	St. Johnston

Northern Ireland

Jun 24	Portrush (Giant's Causeway)
25-26	Belfast

Scotland

Jun 27	Ayr
28	Inverary
29	Fort William
30-Jul 1	Inverness
2	Huntly
3	Aberdeen
4	night ferry to Norway

Norway

Jul 5-6	Bergen
7	Risnes
8	Dale
9	Førde
10-11	Florö
12	Viksdalen
13	Lærdal
14	Gol
15	Høkksund
16-17	Olso
18	Halden

Sweden

Jul 19	Lysekil
20	Göteborg

Denmark

Jul 21	Øster Hurup
	(Hadsund Kommune)
22	Bråby Strand (Ebeltoft)
23-24	Copenhagen

Sweden

Jul 25	Klippan
26	Ljungby
27	Sävsjö
28	Kisa
29	Söderköping
30	Hörningsholm
31-Aug 1	Stockholm

Finland

Aug 2	Piikkio (Turku)
3	Fiskars
4	Helsinki

Russia

Aug 5-7	St. Petersburg

Finland

Aug 8	Helsinki

Greece

Aug 9	flight to Greece (arr. 2 a.m.)
10-12	Athens
13	New Epidavros
14	Tyros
15	Sparti
16	Gialova (Pylos)
17-18	Olympia
19	Gilfa
20	night ferry to Italy

Italy

Aug 21	Alberobello
22	Marina di Genosa
23	Senise
24-25	Scalea
26	Marina di Comereta
27	Paestum
28-Sep 3	Rome*

*   I left the tour and got to Rome 5 days early to meet Cheryl.

Italy (cont)

4	Narni Scalo
5	Assisi
6	Urbino

San Marino

Sep 7	San Marino

Italy

Sep 8	Caprise Michelangelo
9-10	Florence
11	Pisa
12	Ameglia
13-14	Levanto
15	Genova
16	San Remo

Monaco (passed through, no overnight)

France

Sep 17-18	Nice
19	Port Grimaud
20	Sanary-sur-Mer
21	La Couronne (Martiques)
22	La Grande Motte
23	Salléles d'Aude
24-25	Carcassonne
26	Ax les Thermes

Andorra

Sep 27	Andorra

Spain

Sep 28	Salsona
29	Monistrol de Montserrat
30-Oct 1	Barcelona

Gibraltar

Oct 2-4	Gibraltar

Morocco (day trip on Oct 4)

Spain

Oct 5	Torremolinos (Málaga)
6	Playa de Poniente (Motril)
7-8	Granada
9	Baena
10-11	Córdoba
12-13	Seville
14	Aracena
15	Rosal dela Fontera

Portugal

Oct 16	Monsaraz
17-18	Evora
19	Abrantes
20	Fatima
21	Praia Santa Cruz
22-23	Lisbon
24	night flight to South Africa

South Africa

Oct 25	Johannesburg
26	Dullstroom
27	Lydenburg
28	Hazyview
29-30	Kruger National Park
31	Hazyview
Nov 1	Barberton
2	Badplass

Swaziland

Nov 3	Mbabane
4	Nsoko

South Africa

Nov 5-6	Hluhluwe
7-8	Durban
9	Kelso
10	Umtentweni (Port Shepstone)
11	Harding
12	Kokstad
13	Umtata
14	Butterworth
15-16	East London
17	Fish River
18	Alexandria
19	Port Elizabeth
20-21	Jeffreys Bay
22-23	Storms River

South Africa (cont)

24	Sedgefield
25	Albertinia
26	Swellendam
27	Stanford
28	Gordon's Bay
29	Simonstown
30-Dec 2	Cape Town
3	night flight to United States

United States

Dec 4	Albuquerque

APPENDIX B

Inventory

This appendix presents the "list of things to take" that I compiled as I was preparing for the trip. I used it as a checklist to pack my bags and took a copy of it with me in case I lost a bag or had things stolen. Because I returned to Albuquerque in April of 2003 due to the SARS virus scare, I had the chance to juggle items a bit but, surprisingly, the list didn't change much; any changes to the list are shown below as, for example, <2→3>. I've also added explanatory notes in brackets, [ ], to some items.

Bike Clothes

- helmet
- balaclava (a full-head covering)
- wool cap
- bike gloves
- windproof mittens
- waterproof over-mittens [never wore]
- bike shorts (2) [the shorty triathlon variety]
- short-sleeved light-weight under-jerseys (2)
- long-sleeved jerseys (2)
- long-sleeved dress shirts (2) <2→3>[*]
- loose fitting tights
- rain pants
- toe-booties [never wore]
- bike booties [wore only a couple of times]
- bike socks (3 lightweight, 1 heavyweight)
- bike shoes[**]
- rain coat
- wind jacket
- bandanna

    [*] I wore these on most days as a cool way to keep the sun off my arms and neck.

  [**] Originally I wore an old pair of tennis shoes, but these "blew out" so I wrapped one in duct tape until Cheryl could bring me a pair of "real" bike shoes when she joined the trip in August.

Non-bike Clothes

- collared short-sleeved shirts (2)
- long-sleeved fleece shirt
- shorts & belt
- lightweight wind pants <1→2>
- fleece pants
- running shorts (2) <2→4>
- underwear (3) [never wore], <3→1>
- Teva sandals
- light boots
- hiking socks (2 lightweight, 1 heavyweight)
- sun hat
- handkerchiefs (4)
- swimsuit & goggles

Camping, Personal, and Other Items

- tent & ground cloth
- sleeping bag & sleeping pad
- cotton-polyester sheet for liner
- pillow & pillow case
- toilet articles (soap, tooth paste, floss, brush, scissors, tweezers, Q-tips, glasses screwdriver)
- towel, hand towel <1→0>, & washcloth
- medical kit (with ginger chews, diarrhea pills)
- sun block (spf 48, sweat-proof)
- bug repellent [did not use]
- vitamins

- malaria pills
- water purification tablets [did not use]
- toilet paper
- reading glasses
- extra glasses [did not use]
- head lamp [for reading in tent]
- clothes line & clothes pins
- alarm clock
- ear plugs & sleep mask
- journal & 3 pens
- address labels [makes it easy to send postcards]
- books for reading (5 to start with)*
- mask & snorkel
- camera
- film canisters (14 24-exposure, 4 36-exposure) in mesh bag
- small compasses (2) & whistle
- binoculars & cleaning pen
- extra batteries (4 AAA, 4 AA, 1 camera, 1 bike computer)
- knapsack
- duffel bags (1 medium, 1 large) & locks
- zip-lock bags
- large plastic bags for keeping gear dry
- stuff sacks for arranging items in duffles
- bungie cords (1 small, 3 larger)
- duct tape

  * The plan was for Cheryl to send more books when I needed them. However, when I came back in April, I exchanged some, and then Cheryl brought the rest in August.

Bike Stuff

- bike
- bike lock
- bike computer
- bike pump
- bike headlight, taillight, mirror
- bike bag
- water bottles (2)
- fanny pack
- bike tool kit (multi-tool, patches, patch kit, bike levers)
- chain lube & rag
- spare inner tubes (5)

Paper & Plastic Items

- neck carrier for paper/money
- passport
- immunization record
- cash & travelers' checks [did not use checks]
- credit cards (2) & ATM card
- picture IDs (2)
- copies of passport, shot record, trip inventory
- sheet with important personal information
- travel notes [from *Lonely Planet Guides*]
- address list
- 3 blank checks [did not use]
- plane ticket for Joe's graduation
- eyeglass prescription

Appendix C

Book List

I don't like to be without a book and, because I have such a long "to read" list, I generally avoid books that either aren't on that list or would be if I had known about them. Therefore, I spent considerable time selecting books to read during my almost-year on the road. Since I decided right away that I wanted books about the places I would be biking, I obtained most of the books on the two lists below from the recommended reading in the *Lonely Planet Guide* books that I scoured before the trip started. My other criteria were size and weight. So I made an extensive list and then went to a local used book store to see what I could find in the way of old paperback books.

The list below contains the titles and authors of those books I read on the trip. I did not put on the list the few books I read that were unrelated to our travels. The titles are listed by the country they take place in or are about. They are in order based on our itinerary, which is also roughly the order I read them, starting with New Zealand and ending with South Africa. In addition, I've tried to reflect how much they enhanced my understanding of the country and/or the people or just added to my enjoyment of the travel experience. An asterisk is a positive endorsement, two is a better one and three is my top endorsement. I have also added a short explanation of each. Below the line, I have included a double handful of books I read shortly after the trip ended that would've been good reads on the trip.

New Zealand	**	*The Bone People*—Keri Hulme [painful story of "broken" Maoris]
New Zealand	**	*Once Were Warriors*—Alan Duff [painful story of a "broken" Maori family]
Australia	**	*The Recollections of Geoffrey Hamlyn*—Henry Kingsley [historical novel of early Aussie settlers]
Hong Kong	*	*Kowloon Tong*—Paul Theroux [fun story about the Chinese takeover of Hong Kong]
China		*The Woman Warrior*—Maxine Hong Kingston [good stories, but didn't really add to the trip]
Vietnam	**	*Catfish and Mandala*—Andrew X. Phan [true story of boat person's return to Vietnam for a bike trip]
Vietnam	***	*Ho Chi Minh*—Jean Lacouture [bio of Uncle Ho]
Vietnam	*	*The Sorrow of War*—Bao Ninh ["American" War from a Viet Cong's perspective]
Vietnam	***	*In Retrospect*—Robert S. McNamara [describes just how badly the U.S. screwed the pooch in Vietnam with implications for Iraq today]
Malaysia	*	*The Consul's File*—Paul Theroux [entertaining story about consul's life]
Czech Rep.	*	*Love and Garbage*—Ivan Klima [gives some insight into post-Cold War life in Czech Republic]
Europe	*	*A Tramp Abroad*—Mark Twain [fun insights; some are irrelevant, but who can resist Twain?]
Austria	*	*The Third Man*—Graham Greene ["who dunnit" set in Vienna]

Germany	*	*The Tin Drum*—Gunter Grass
		[strange story in post WW II Germany]
France	***	*The Dream of Scipio*—Iain Pears
		[three interconnecting stories about survival during times of change (e.g. Black Death, Vichy France, barbarian invasion of France)]
England		*Pygmalion*—George Bernard Shaw
		[fun, little insight though]
England	**	*Notes from a Small Island*—Bill Bryson
		[travelogue by former resident]
Wales		*Adventures in the Skin Trade*—Dylan Thomas
		[I didn't get much out of this, except the first story]
Scotland	**	*Sunset Song*—Lewis Grassic Gibbon (1st in a trilogy)
		[story set in rural Scotland in WW I timeframe]
Norway	*	*Wayfarers*—Knut Hamsun
		[life of two northern Norwegian wanderers]
Denmark	**	*Miss Smilla's Feeling for Snow*—Peter Hoeg
		[strange mystery, interesting insights into Danes and Greenlanders]
Greece	*	*Zorba The Greek*—Nikos Kazantzakis
		[stark, unrelenting machismo left me cold]
Italy	**	*Christ Stopped at Eboli*—Carlo Levi
		[true story of political outcast marooned in small rural town]
Italy	***	*The Leopard*—Giuseppe di Lampedusa
		[written by a prince about a prince just after Italy's independence]
Spain	*	*The Drifters*—James Michener
		[story of young folks trying to "find themselves"]

| South Africa | * | *The House Gun*—Nadine Gordimer [family drama post African independence] |
| South Africa | *** | *Imaginings of Sand*—Andre Brink [sometimes fanciful story of generations of Boer women through African independence] |

Italy	***	*Brunelleschi's Dome*—Ross King [the story behind Florence's magnificent Duomo]
South Africa	***	*Long Walk to Freedom*—Nelson Mandela [Mandela's autobiography]
France	**	*The DaVinci Code*—Dan Brown [fluff adventure story dealing with fine art]
France	**	*Captain of Innocence*—Norman H. Finkelstein [account of the infamous Dreyfus Affair]
General	*	*The Miraculous Fever Tree*—Fiammetta Rocco [story of quinine]
Italy	*	*The Name of the Rose*—Umberto Eco [mystery in a monastery during the Inquisition]
Vietnam	**	*Song of the Buffalo Boy*—Sherry Garland [story of Amerasian girl in postwar Vietnam trying to find her father]
Spain	**	*The Alhambra*—Washington Irving [Irving's description of his stay in the Alhambra]

APPENDIX D

Trip Statistics

This appendix contains information I thought readers might find interesting. The numbers are based on my eleventh-month 2003 World Cycling Tour experience; my trip mates' numbers would be different since we didn't all ride the same number of days.

• I biked in 32 countries on 4 continents and visited 36 countries[*] touching down at airports in 3 others.

• I biked 20,589 kilometers or about 12,794 miles[**] for an average of 102.8 kilometers/day or 63.9 miles/day.

• Out of 319 days on the trip, I biked on 199 of them and camped on 103 nights.

• I swam 93.25 miles in a variety of pools, lakes, ponds, rivers, fjords, seas, and oceans.

• I had my hair/beard cut 5 times (in Viet Nam, Albuquerque, Scotland, Italy, and Portugal).

- I had the following bike problems/repairs:

  - 1 Mar   replaced chain
  - 8 Mar   replaced rear gear cable
  - 13 May   replaced chain (after previous one broke twice)
  - 2 Jun   replaced broken spoke
  - 16 Jun   replaced rear tire (no flats to this point)
  - 30 Jun   replaced rear brake pads
  - 17 Jul   replaced gear cable (front, I think)
  - 26 Jul   flat on rear tire (first!)
  - 4 Sep   replaced 3 front gears & front and rear brake pads
  - 5 Sep   flat on rear tire
  - 12 Sep   flat on rear tire
  - 19 Sep   flat on rear tire
  - 22 Sep   2 flats on rear tire
  - 23 Sep   flat on rear tire
  - 24 Sep   2 flats on rear tire
  - 25 Sep   replaced rear tire
  - 5 Oct   2 flats on rear tire
  - 25 Oct   replaced gear cable (rear, I think)
  - 5 Nov   flat on rear tire
  - 17 Nov   flat on rear tire
  - 20 Nov   flat on rear tire & broke screw keeping handlebars tight
                          (Note: I never had a flat on the front tire nor replaced it.)

*   Vatican City does not show up on the itinerary in Appendix A; we visited it on our layover in Rome.

**   In most cases my daily mileage was taken from my bike computer's odometer. On the few occasions when the odometer did not work, I used the mileage on our daily route guide adjusted for any side trips or detours I might have made. Our bike computer odometers did not always match the mileage on the DRGs since they derived from the various rental cars Tim K. used over the course of the trip to develop them. Also, I did not include the mileage from bike rides while in Albuquerque for the SARS scare.

About the Author

Ralph Monfort grew up in a small Indiana town with a houseful of books and the National Geographic Magazine to fuel his interest in the world. With a college degree and an Air Force commission, he spent the next twenty-seven years working in space operations with tours in Nebraska, Texas, California, Colorado, New Mexico, and outback Australia. He retired in 2001 and, when not on the road, calls Albuquerque, New Mexico, home. This is his first book.

978-0-595-40754-5
0-595-40754-4

4683489

Made in the USA
Lexington, KY
18 February 2010